Dylan

My dreams came true when I was adopted at ten.
I was the best on the ice. Living the life of what every kid dreams of.
We've best friends since then. Even when she was the annoying little sister following us around.
I would do anything for her.
It is another family vacation; except this time it feels different. Everything feels different.

Alex

All my memories have Dylan in them. From the first time I fell off my bike, to the time I got my heart broken for the first time.
He's always been my protector, but it's time to let the dream of being his go.
One last family trip, one last goodbye.
Except fate steps in and has other plans.
At the end of the day, you only get one forever.

BOOKS BY NATASHA MADISON

The Only One Series
Only One Kiss
Only One Chance
Only One Night
Only One Touch
Only One Regret
Only One Mistake
Only One Love
Only One Forever

Southern Series
Southern Chance
Southern Comfort
Southern Storm
Southern Sunrise
Southern Heart
Southern Heat
Southern Secrets
Southern Sunshine

This Is
This is Crazy
This Is Wild
This Is Love
This Is Forever

Hollywood Royalty
Hollywood Playboy
Hollywood Princess
Hollywood Prince

Something So Series
Something Series
Something So Right
Something So Perfect
Something So Irresistible
Something So Unscripted
Something So BOX SET

Tempt Series
Tempt The Boss
Tempt The Playboy
Tempt The Ex
Tempt The Hookup
Heaven & Hell Series
Hell And Back
Pieces Of Heaven

Love Series
Perfect Love Story
Unexpected Love Story
Broken Love Story

Faux Pas
Mixed Up Love
Until Brandon

SOMETHING SO, THIS IS, AND ONLY ONE FAMILY TREE!

SOMETHING SO SERIES

Something So Right
Parker & Cooper Stone
Matthew Grant (Something So Perfect)
Allison Grant (Something So Irresistible)
Zara Stone (This Is Crazy)
Zoe Stone (This Is Wild)
Justin Stone (This Is Forever)
Something So Perfect
Matthew Grant & Karrie Cooley
Cooper Grant (Only One Regret)
Frances Grant (Only One Love)
Vivienne Grant
Chase Grant
Something So Irresistible
Allison Grant & Max Horton
Michael Horton (Only One Mistake)
Alexandria Horton
Something So Unscripted
Denise Horton & Zack Morrow
Jack Morrow
Joshua Morrow
Elizabeth Morrow

THIS IS SERIES

This Is Crazy
Zara Stone & Evan Richards
Zoey Richards
This Is Wild
Zoe Stone & Viktor Petrov
Matthew Petrov
Zara Petrov
This Is Love
Vivienne Paradis & Mark Dimitris
Karrie Dimitris
Stefano Dimitris
Angelica Dimitris

This Is Forever
Caroline Woods & Justin Stone
Dylan Stone (Formally Woods)
Christopher Stone
Gabriella Stone
Abigail Stone

ONLY ONE SERIES

Only One Kiss
Candace Richards & Ralph Weber
Ariella Weber
Brookes Weber
Only One Chance
Layla Paterson & Miller Adams
Clarke Adams
Onlye One Night
Evelyn & Manning Stevenson
Jaxon Stevenson
Victoria Stevenson
Only One Touch
Becca & Nico Harrison
Phoenix Harrison
Dallas Harrison
Only One Regret
Erika Markinson & Cooper Grant
Emma Grant
Mia Grant
Parker Grant
Matthew Grant
Only One Mistake
Jillian & Michael Horton
Jamieson Horton

Copyright © 2022 Natasha Madison. E-Book and Print Edition All rights reserved. No part of this book may be reproduced or transmitted in any form or by any means, electronic or mechanical, including photocopying, recording, or by any information storage and retrieval system, without permission in writing.

This is a work of fiction. Names, characters, places and incidents are the product of the author's imagination or are used factiously, and any resemblance to any actual persons or living or dead, events or locals are entirely coincidental.

The author acknowledges the trademark status and trademark owners of various products refer-enced in this work of fiction, which have been used without permission. The publication/ Use of these trademarks is not authorized, associated with, or sponsored by the trademark owner.All rights reserved

Cover Design: Jay Aheer

Photo by Wander Photography

Editing done by Jenny Sims Editing4Indies

Proofing Julie Deaton by Deaton Author Services

Proofing by Judy's proofreading

Interior Design by Christina Smith

ONLY ONE
Forever

THE ONLY ONE SERIES

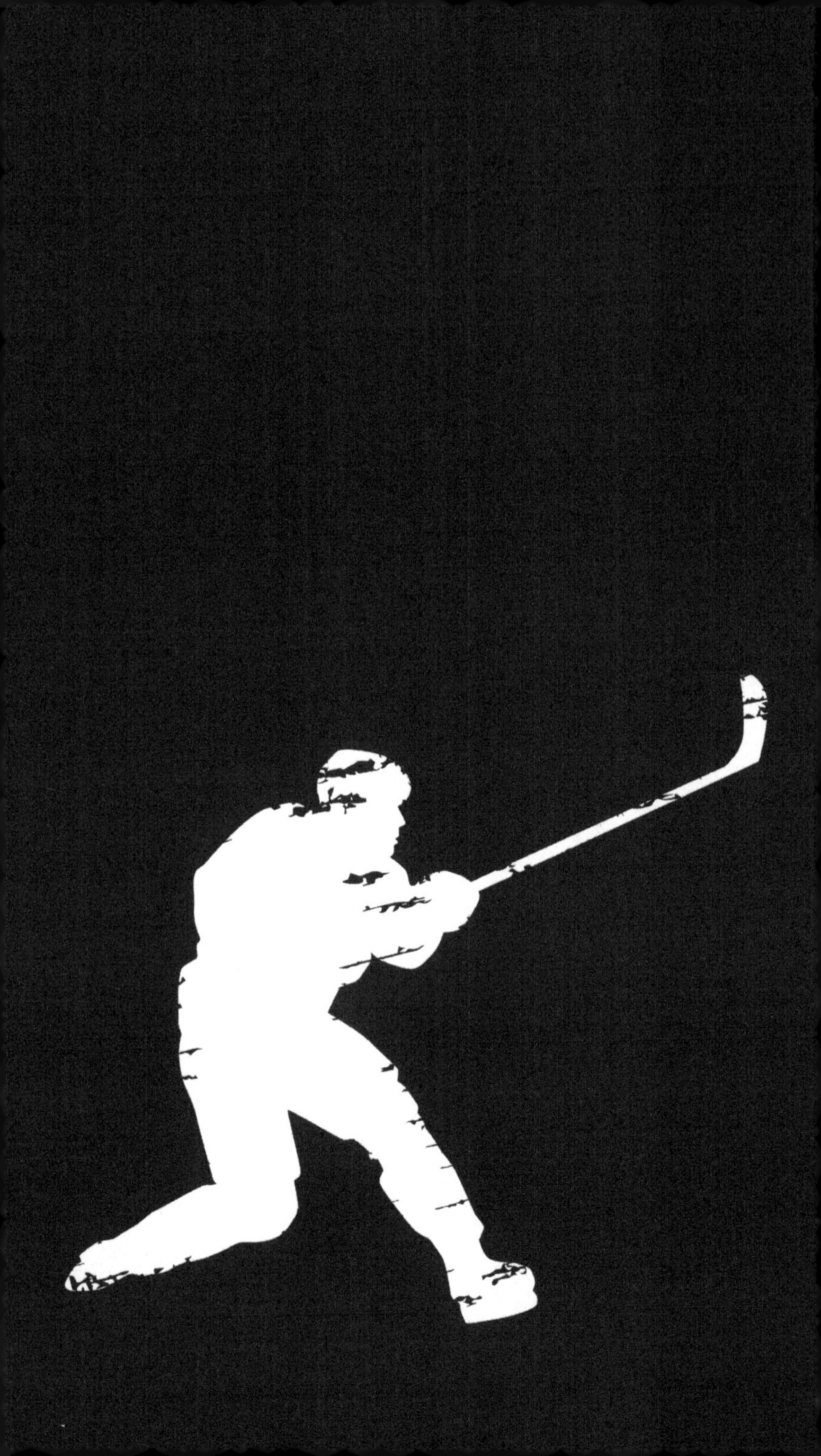

ONE

Dylan

I SIT ON the bench, catching my breath after my last shift on the ice, but my eyes never leave the puck. We're all exhausted—triple overtime with over one hundred minutes on the ice—but our back is to the wall. If we lose this game, we are out of the playoffs. My whole body feels like it's one big ball of nerves. There is so much I want to do on the ice, but I can't do anything. The roar of twenty-two thousand people makes it almost deafening, the white towels flinging into the air as they chant, ole ole ole ole.

The first round in the playoffs is interesting, to say the least. Everyone wants to win the games, but what no one points out is playoff hockey is on a whole other level. You can't just go out there and play like it's just another game because it's not. Everyone is ready to battle to hoist that Stanley Cup over their head. It's every single player's dream.

I can see the play happen in my head before it plays out right in front of my eyes. The trip-up in the neutral zone. The tape-to-tape pass, and then the defenseman is sliding in front of the shot and taking it to the net. It's almost like in slow motion as the puck flies over my goalie. The red light behind the goal illuminates, and all I can do is look down at my skates. The echoing of my heartbeats in my chest as the bench beside me empties, and all I can do is look down the ice at the other team celebrating. "Motherfucker," I say, defeated, and then the feeling of anger fills me. Every fucking year it's the same fucking thing. I also know that there is at least one camera that is pointed at me, waiting for my reaction.

Someone slaps my shoulder, and I throw my legs over the bench to get up and skate on the ice toward the goalie. Putting my helmet to his. "Nothing you can do, buddy. We let you down," I say even though, if truth be told, everyone is to blame with this one. Up by three and the lead gets blown again for the second game in a row. Losing in your building has to be the worst feeling that you can ever have. The boos sound, the brooms being thrown on the ice because we just got swept by the last-place team. The. Last. Place. Team.

I skate to the middle of the ice as we line up to congratulate the other team. I don't even know what is being said because all I can hear in my head is what the announcer is going to say.

Montreal blows another lead to be swept in the playoffs. For yet another year.

I skate to the middle of the ice for the last time this

season and hold up my stick to thank the fans for coming. At the same time, I silently tell them I'm sorry for letting them down. Skating back to the bench, I walk back into our locker room. No one says anything as they sit down and undress. So much is going through my mind on my end, but the only thing that sticks out is disappointment in myself. In my game. In my team. In fucking everything.

"Dylan," the coach says, and my head lifts up to look at him. "You're up for interviews."

I shake my head, knowing the shitstorm that will come my way. I slip out of my gear, grabbing my sport shorts and a T-shirt. "I'm not going out there alone." I look at the coach. "If I do, I'm not going to be diplomatic about anything, and I'll take one question."

I think he can see from my demeanor and my tone that I'm not fucking around, not tonight. He just nods at me. "Leo," he calls my assistant captain, who looks like he was crying. "Get out there with him."

"Why the fuck do we have to give interviews after losing a series?" He stands up, asking exactly what I was thinking. "Like what can we possibly say?" He puts on his shorts and a hoodie, putting the hood up. "Does this say don't fuck with me?" he asks me as we walk toward the press room.

I shake my head, and a soft smile comes out. "Definitely looks thug life." I turn and walk into the press room. The long table has a black tablecloth over it with the backdrop of "Stanley Cup Playoffs" all over it, mocking me.

Ten reporters are sitting there. Some are with notepads

but most with their phone in their hand as they wait for us. I don't make any eye contact as I sit in the chair next to Leo.

The first question is for me. "Dylan," the guy says, and I put one elbow on the table while one holds my chin. "I don't know how to ask this," he says, and I'm already irritated. "What happened? You had full control of the whole game, and you guys lose it in the last minute of the third period."

Wow, I think to myself. I rub my playoff beard and try not to roll my eyes. "Um." I fold my arms in front of me. "Lots went wrong. We were in a good spot, being up three to one. They won the power play every time, and we had trouble with the power kill. It gave them the lifeline they needed, and at the end of the day, the better team won." I shrug. There is nothing else I can say. There is a fuck ton I'm thinking, but nothing I'm going to say out loud, especially not to reporters.

I've been here before. It's been the same story for the past seven fucking years. And every single year, I hope it's different. I hope that whatever fucking monkey is on the team is thrown off.

The next question is for Leo, and he does the same thing as me. Scratching his face, he looks at the reporter. "I don't know what you want me to say," he says. "I don't know. We needed to be better, and we weren't."

"Dylan, the playoffs can be brutal. It seems that every year you come up empty-handed, even though you were the leading scorer of the whole season. Actually, for the past five years the two of you were either one and two.

How frustrating is it?"

"Yeah," I say, and although I want to tell them to fuck off, I can hear my father in my head and also my grandfather. *Whatever you do, never ever let them know they got to you.* I swallow. "Obviously, it's unfortunate. It's something we have to take in and sit down over the next couple of days and discuss what we can do going forward." I look at the reporters and then look over at Leo. "It's one thing to be the top scorer in the league. It's another thing to play in the playoffs. It's the best of seven games, and no matter how many times you ask me or Leo or anyone else on the team, we lost, period. There is no right or wrong way to say it. The other team was better." My tone never goes up or down. "They won. We lost. You can spin the questions, and you can change the words, but that is the only answer we have." I tap my finger on the table. "It's been a long night, guys." I get up, and Leo follows my moves. "I'm sure we don't have the answers to all the questions you have. At the end of the night, we lost. Tomorrow is a new day, and I'm sure there will be more questions." I tuck my chair in. "So let's get some rest, and we can answer all the questions in the next couple of days." I look over at Leo. "Night, boys," I say, and we walk out of the room.

"I don't know why they can't just take us outside and kick us in the balls," Leo says, and I slap his shoulder.

"That would be too easy," I reply and can hear music coming from the small locker room where Edmonton is partying. "It sucks to lose," I observe, walking back to our lockers. "It sucks even more when you lose in your own house." I slap his shoulder and squeeze it. "It is always a pleasure playing with you," I say, and he just nods at me. I'm sure he wants to ask me what I mean, and I have to admit that all I need to do is get out of here before I say something I'll regret. I walk back into the room and can hear the other team celebrating as I grab my wallet, phone, and keys. Leo looks at me and nods as I walk out, not saying anything to anyone.

I get into the car, and it takes me fifteen minutes to get out of the parking lot of the arena and in front of my driveway. The phone in my hand pings every five seconds, but I don't even have the energy to answer anyone. The phone rings in my hand, and I walk up the first two steps. I stop on the third step when I see the brown bag in front of my door with the M logo on it.

My heart speeds up in my chest while I grab the bag and walk into the empty house. Every single light is off, and the silence is almost deafening. I bring the bag up to my bedroom, the phone beeping in my hand yet again.

I look down and see that I have over fifty text messages, no doubt from my family, but the one from Alex is on the top. Alexandra, the spitfire, and also my best friend. I mean, when she's not telling me to fuck off, which lately has been happening more and more.

Alex: Sorry I can't be there with you. But enjoy my Big Mac for me. Just like old times.

I laugh, thinking about how every single time I've lost in the playoffs, she's been there waiting for me. The ping in my chest starts as I think about how she is usually here when I need her. We would come back to my house, but there would be nothing open except McDonald's, so we would order Big Macs and after five bites, then she would tell me how disgusting she felt eating it. I would proceed to finish hers and mine. But she's moving into her new house tomorrow, and I know it's selfish for me to expect her to drop everything for me.

Instead of texting her back, I get in the shower and finish the two Big Macs before I power down my phone. I lie in the middle of my bed, looking up at the ceiling in the dark, and thinking about what the fuck I'm going to do next.

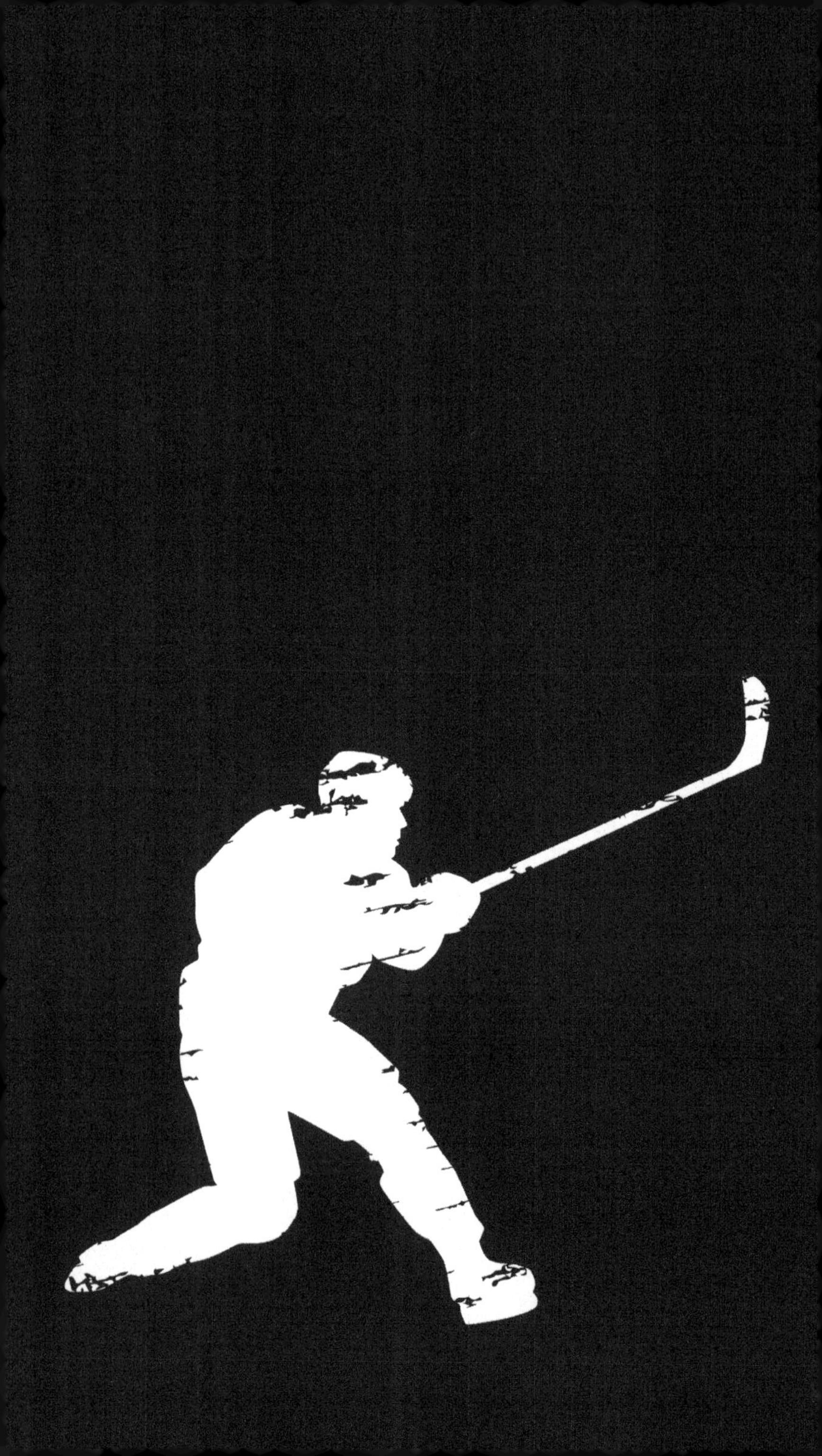

TWO

ALEX

"THIS IS THE last box," my father says, walking into the kitchen with the box in his hand.

"That is for my bedroom." I smile at him. "You can leave it on the counter." I look over my shoulder at him. "I'll take it up later."

"Yeah, right," he huffs out, turning and walking toward the staircase. His big six-foot-four frame heads up the stairs with the box in his hands.

I hear laughing behind me and look over at my cousins, Franny and Vivienne. "What?" I ask them.

"You knew damn straight that he wasn't going to let you carry that box upstairs," Franny points out, shaking her head and washing her hands. The two of them have been over helping me unpack since nine this morning.

"I told him I hired movers." I smirk. "He was the one who puffed out his chest and said he could do all the work." I hold my hands in front of me.

"I come bearing gifts." Erika, my cousin Cooper's wife, walks into the room with three massive pizza boxes in her hands.

"Good," Vivienne says. "I'm starving."

I smile when Franny goes to one of the cupboards and takes out paper plates; she should know where most of the stuff is since I bought the house from her. She didn't want to take my money from me, and then my father called her, and she told him no also. But I refused to take it from her, so I'm renting to own it, and it's the second most grown-up thing I've done in my life. The first being I decided to finally make Dallas my full-time home instead of living out of New York.

I look around the room, not even able to wrap my head around the fact that this is my new home. This should be one of the happiest days of my life, but something is stopping me from having that moment.

"Knock, knock, knock." I look over to the front door and see Julia walk in. Julia is my sister-in-law Jillian's twin.

"What the hell are you wearing?" I ask her as she walks into the room wearing jeans and a white top with high heels.

"What the hell are you wearing?" she huffs out when she gets into the kitchen and sees Franny and Vivi there with me, all of us wearing yoga gear.

"We are clearly underdressed." I laugh, putting my hands on my hips. "Why would you wear that to unpack boxes?"

"Unpack boxes?" she shrieks, looking around at the

brown boxes all over the place. The moving truck got here this morning at seven. "Why didn't you tell me that we were unpacking moving boxes?" She throws her hands in the air.

"What the hell did you think we were doing?" Franny asks her, trying not to laugh.

"I thought we were doing unboxing videos," Julia says, and Vivi can't help but throw her head back and laugh. "You know, like influencers on Instagram."

"Oh my God," I say, putting my hand to my mouth.

"Did we or did we not do unboxing last month?" she asks, and I just shake my head. "You had like the whole glam light blinding me in one eye. I couldn't see for a week."

"That was a merchandise drop." I can't help but laugh now. "It was to help get donations for the Summer Hockey Program." The reason I finally made the leap to Dallas was when I took a job to run the Brad Wilson Hockey School. Wilson and Franny got together, and she mentioned me to him. To be honest, I felt like I had no idea where my life was going. There was nothing I was doing that made me feel like I had a purpose. Until I sat down and had lunch with Wilson. He had an idea, but the two of us together have been unstoppable, and I finally have something that I can call my own. It helped I had some experience from helping with The Max Horton Foundation, which my father started when he was still playing in the NHL. His foundation works hand in hand with sick children making sure that they get the help they need.

In three weeks, we are going to start the first ever Brad Wilson Summer Hockey Program, a program that is very close to my heart. Wilson wanted to do something for the underprivileged kids out there who have the gift but don't have the money to help grow their talent. Little do they know that five kids will be given an all-expense-paid scholarship to one of the best schools in the city with a sports program.

"Who the hell does merchandise drops?" Vivi asks while she opens the box of pizza and grabs a slice.

"The same person who does unboxing?" Julia says. "I don't know. Maybe you got Kendall Jenner's new tequila."

"I would take off your shoes." I point at her heels that I know pinch her feet and make them swell up to the size of elephants. She flips me the bird, slipping off her shoes.

"Where is your wine?" Julia walks to the fridge and opens it. "Oh my God," she says. "All you have is wine."

"It's a fruit," I remind her, and the girls laugh as she takes out five glasses and fills them.

"A toast." Julia smiles. "To finally getting one more person into Dallas." I laugh at her. "Vivi, you're next."

"Bite your tongue," Vivi retorts. "New York has my heart."

"It had mine, too," I say. "But your heart can learn to love two places." I smile at her as she glares at me.

My father comes back down the stairs and sees all of us drinking wine. "Well, that's my cue to go." He walks over to Julia and kisses her cheek and then everyone else's. He gives me a hug, and I wrap my arms around his waist. "Call me later."

"I'll be okay," I say.

"Did you hook up the cameras yet, Uncle Max?" Franny asks, taking a bite of pizza.

My father laughs. "Cameras were vetoed by Auntie Allison," he says, and I look up at him. "I just want you safe."

"The alarm guys just left," I say, and he nods at me.

"Arm it day and night," he tells me, and I don't answer him before he walks out. "And lock the door after me."

"You know it's a gated community," Julia reminds him. "And the crime rate in the area …"

"Is under two percent," my father says, making all of us laugh. "But do an old guy a favor and lock the door after me."

I walk to the front door, locking it after him. It takes me more than four hours to unpack everything around the house, and when Julia leaves, I arm the alarm and walk back into the kitchen to grab the kettle. I pick up my phone and look down to see that Dylan hasn't answered my text from this morning, asking him how he is doing.

The burning in my stomach starts when I think of him all alone in Montreal after last night's loss. I tried to make it work, going to see the game, but with the movers coming, I couldn't change it. I fill up the cup with my ginger lemon tea and head upstairs, the phone ringing in my hand.

Turning it over, I see it's Dylan, and my heart speeds up faster. "You're lucky I feel sorry for you," I say instead of hello, putting the phone to my ear. "Because I almost denied your call."

He chuckles out deeply. "You would never deny my call."

"Um, two weeks ago," I remind him. As I walk into my bedroom, my whole body hurts from lifting boxes and unpacking. "You asked me if I gained weight."

"I did not!" he shouts. "I said that angle is not working."

"Whatever," I say, sitting on the bed and placing my tea on my bedside table. "It took you long enough to get out of the sulking. Did you get my package?"

"I did," he says. I want to FaceTime him, but I probably look like a cat stuck in the rain all day long. "Ate both of them in the dark," he tells me and I fake vomit.

"It's not that bad," he says. "It's the only thing we have here."

I pick up my cup again and blow before taking a sip. "Are you already in bed?" he scoffs. "It's six."

"It's six thirty, and I've been up since four," I reply. "And I spent all day unpacking my shit."

"This is how it starts," he jokes. "One day, you are up partying until four a.m., and the next day, you are going to bed at fucking six."

"I have to shower, and then I'm going to slide my old ass into bed," I say. "How are you doing?" My voice goes soft as I ask him.

"Okay," he huffs, his own voice matching mine. "Fucking sucks. I meet with the press tomorrow. I'm stressed about it." I hear the doorbell ring. "I'll call you back," he says, and he hangs up. I wonder who is at his door.

I put the phone down on the side table and try not to think about it. Even when I step into the shower, I push the thought that maybe he has a girlfriend to the back of my head. If he did, wouldn't he share the news with me? The lump in my throat grows. Maybe he's just passing the time with her. I close my eyes, rushing through the shower and getting into bed.

I shut the lights off and turn on the television. The sudden feeling of a void runs through me, the same feeling I felt all day when I was hanging pictures on the wall. This day was supposed to be a big deal. I was supposed to finally feel at home, at peace, but something was missing, and I couldn't put my finger on it. I kept telling myself it was because it was brand new, and I still needed to get things to make it feel like home. My eyes drift closed, waiting for his call back.

When the alarm sounds softly the next day, I roll over and shut it off. Grabbing my phone, I check to see if he at least texted, and nothing shows. Turning back into the bed, I check my social media. I like a couple of posts, and when the alarm sounds again, I finally get out of bed and walk to the bathroom.

Slipping on my white jeans and a white tank top that molds to my body, I grab a brown belt. My caramel sandal wedges on my feet make my legs look longer than they are. I mean, I'm not short by any means, and five eight for a girl is considered tall. My hand picks up my light-blue jean jacket at the same time my phone beeps, telling me it's time to go.

With my phone in one hand and my purse in the other, I get into my car, stopping to get my coffee on the way to the office. There are no words to explain how excited I am about the summer camp that we are putting on. I made sure that I scheduled all the men in the family to come in and do a day here and there. It didn't really take much for them to say yes. It is summer, and we usually always stay around each other. I have fifty kids signed up for the whole summer, which is going to be five groups of ten and then twenty more kids coming from the sponsorship.

When I pull up to the arena, a sense of pride fills me. It's been over a year we have been working on buying the arena. And when I say we, I mean Wilson and me. When we started the hockey school last year, he thought we could do a couple of clinics for the kids. Well, that blew up, surprising only him since he thought no one would come to it since he was the bad boy on the ice, with a reputation to follow. He had to start renting ice in different arenas, and finally, he just approached the guy and offered him a nice chunk of change for his arena.

The white writing on the door, Brad Wilson Arena, makes me smile as the glass door slides open. As soon as you step in, you are hit with a staircase that brings you upstairs to the sitting area where you can watch all four arenas. Walking past the first staircase, you see my office on the left side, right in front of the players' entrance with a dressing room on both sides.

"Good morning," Wilson says when he walks in right behind me dressed in a tracksuit. It's the tracksuit I had made for the hockey school. The same tracksuits that

Julia helped me unbox a couple of weeks ago. "I brought you coffee." He holds up his hand, and then he looks at the white cup in mine. "Okay, so the question is, why didn't you get me coffee?"

"Well," I say, walking toward my office, "that would be a good question." I smile over my shoulder. "One I don't care to answer right now."

He laughs, following me into my office. "I'm getting them to switch your office," he announces, looking around my small office. "There is no way I need that corner office since I'm never in it."

"But you're the CEO." I joke with him as I grab my files. "The big chief."

"Well, this big chief doesn't need anything big," he says, and I nod my head.

"I feel sorry for Franny." Tilting my head to the side and smirking, he just laughs.

"I didn't mean that. I meant," he starts to say, and it's my turn to laugh. I hold up my thumb and forefinger, showing him how small he could be. "Forget it," he says as we walk to the stairs and head up to one of the conference rooms. This was something that Wilson wanted to add to help the trainers sit down and compare notes.

I push open the door and grab the seat, putting the twenty files in front of me. "Hope you're ready." I sit down. "We have over one hundred and fifty submissions," I relay, and his eyes go big.

"Wait, what?" he asks me, shocked.

"Well, I took it in my hands," I say, smiling. "And I

reached out to the different hockey associations in the city and asked them to have the coaches submit some names for the program." I open the file and hand him the questionnaire I sent to all of them with the criteria they had to meet. "Needless to say, it went over really well."

"You did all this." He grabs the sheet, looking down at it and then his eyes go over to the files that are beside me.

"It's my job. Now let's start at the top."

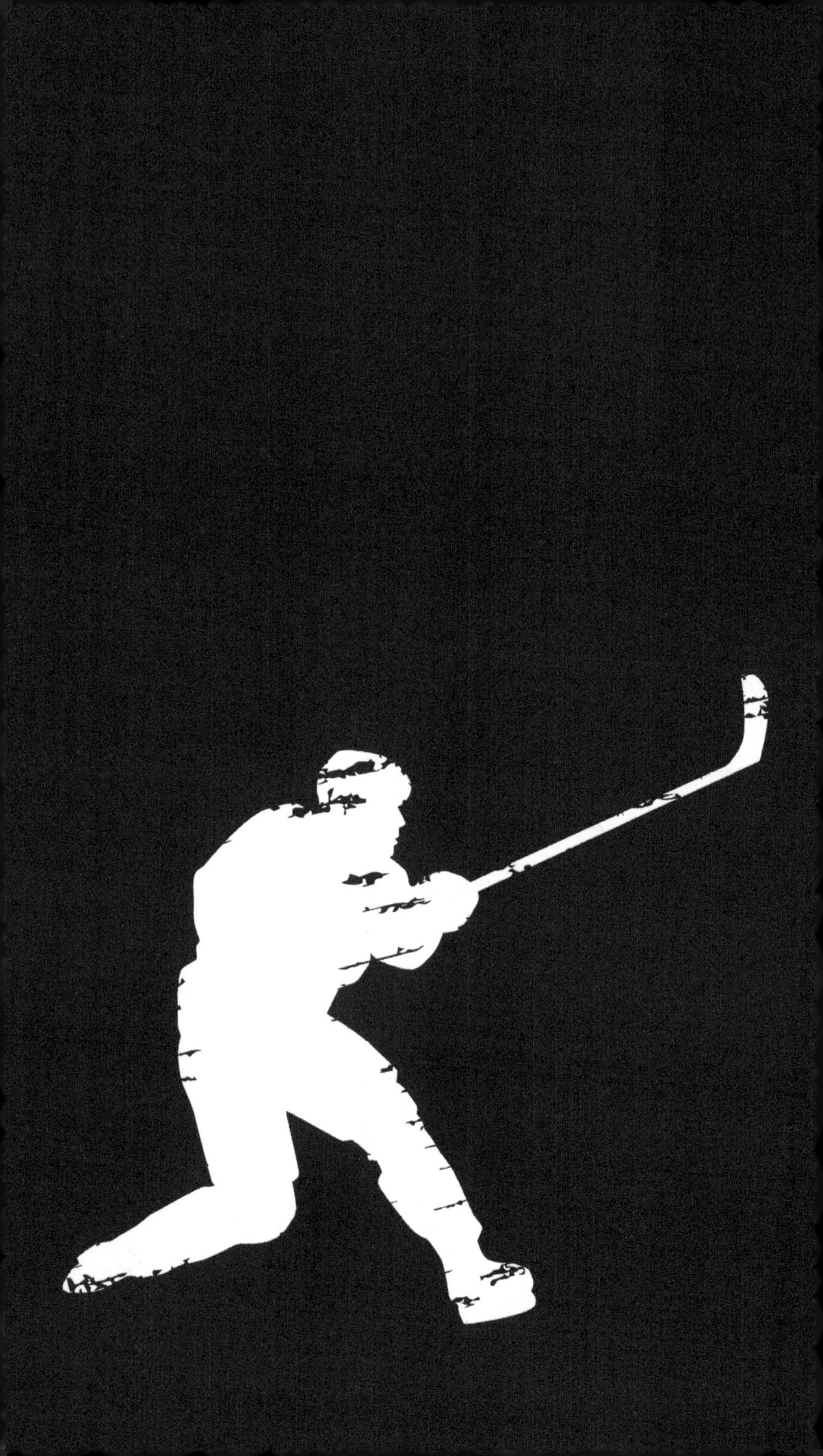

THREE

Dylan

I PARK MY truck and get out, looking over at Leo, who gets here at the same time. He steps out of his own truck wearing the same tracksuit I'm wearing. The only difference is that I'm wearing a baseball hat backward. "Hey." I motion with my chin up at him. He comes over, shaking my hand, and then we pull each other close. It's almost as if we know that one of us is leaving the team, if not both of us. "How are you doing?" I ask as we walk inside the locker room.

"Same old shit," he says, scratching his eyebrow, going to his spot in the dressing room. It's been two days since we were kicked out of the playoffs, and even two days later, it hurts. More this time than any other time.

"Stone," the public relations manager, Gilles, calls my name. "You're up."

I take a deep breath before getting up and following him to the same room I was in two nights ago. I grab a bottle of water and then go to sit down in front of the microphone. "Afternoon," I mumble, folding my hand in front of me, and my other hand comes up to play with the beard I have as I wait for the questions.

"Hi, Dylan." David from *SportsCenter* starts the questions. "Just in listening to your other teammates before you and they are all committed to put this series behind you guys and focus on the goal for next season. Are you on the same page?"

My head screams *no*. "Well, obviously, it's still fresh and very raw," I start as the sadness creeps into me. "Obviously, we have to get over it at some point and move on."

The rest of the questions are the same, just worded differently, and no matter what they are trying to get out of me, I will never say anything. When I get up and walk out of the room, I see David, the GM of the team, with Damien, the coach. "How did it go?" David asks me, and I just shrug.

"It went how it was supposed to go," I reply, looking around to see some of my teammates carrying boxes as they clean up their locker space.

"I heard your father is taking over the coaching job in New York," Damien says, and I just shrug.

"That's what they are saying." I won't ever tell him anything that has to do with my family. Unless my father comes out and announces it, which I know he will next week. "Not sure yet."

"Do you have a couple of minutes to talk to us?" David asks, and I nod as he leads us down the blue carpet toward his office. The office I first stepped into when I was drafted here eight years ago. It was surreal back then. Now it's just frustration.

"We just want to tell you how much we value you in the organization." Damien starts to talk. "You wear that C on your shoulder because there are lots of men on the team who look up to you and follow your lead."

I nod my head. "I'm not going to lie. This time, losing it fucking sucks," I say as I squish the water bottle in my hand. "We were the better team all season long." I shake my head trying to forget, but this time I can't.

"We know," David says. "And we also know we have lots of contracts that are coming to an end and"—he looks down—"I know many of them are moving on."

"Are you telling me what I think you're telling me?" I sit up now.

"We want to make sure that you are on the same page as us," Damien says. "A rebuild is not something that is easy to do."

"A rebuild," I reply, shocked. "We've been rebuilding for the past seven years," I say, my voice going higher a touch. "Like, what the fuck are you talking about?"

"We know that you are upset," David starts, and I throw my head back and laugh.

"Upset?" I repeat, shaking my head. "Upset would be an understatement. We went through four years of rebuilding. Four years of finishing in the last place and not making it to the playoffs, then for the past three years we choke in round one."

"I know this is not what you want to hear," Damien

starts. "And I wish I had better news."

I don't bother saying anything because we are definitely on the same page. I get up, and they thank me for my time, and I walk out toward the locker room. I sit on the bench, looking around the room. The logo is in the middle of the room, and I remember walking in the first time and being in awe. Eighteen and drafted first to one of the teams that had the richest hockey dynasty. Twenty-four Stanley Cup banners hang in this arena. The fans in the city eat, breathe, and live hockey, and I was so fucking pumped to be a part of it.

Leo walks in and sits down in front of his name, the look on his face the same as mine. "That was fucking brutal." He puts his head back. "It would have been better had we not even made the playoffs."

I don't agree with him out loud. "I'm going to head out. See you tomorrow."

He nods at me. "Locker clean-out and more press." He gets up. "Can't wait."

I laugh, walking out of the arena and getting into my car. My first thought is to call Alex, but I know that she's in meetings this morning with Wilson. I can't believe she moved to Dallas. I shake my head, still in shock. I mean, it's not like we lived in the same city before her move, but New York was an hour flight. She would come here all the time and be gone the next morning, but she seems so far away. The burning in the pit of my stomach starts again, and I pick up the phone and call Erika, my agent and also my cousin's wife.

"Hey," she answers after one ring.

"Hi," I respond, making my way home. "Can you talk?"

"Of course," she says, and I hear clicking in the background, so I know she's sitting at her desk.

"What are my options?" I say the four words and immediately hear the clicking stop. "I know my contract is up after this season."

"It is," she confirms, her voice low. "We have an offer on the table from Montreal. We spoke about it."

"I know," I say, parking my car. "But what do you think?"

"Dylan." She says my name. "Where are you right now?"

"In my car," I tell her.

"Okay, so you can talk freely?" she asks, and I laugh.

"Well, yeah."

"Good," she huffs out, and her voice goes tight. "I'm going to need you to start doing that and not playing a guessing game with me."

I can't help but laugh because I can picture her face and the way her teeth are probably clenched together. "Okay, what if I leave Montreal?" I ask and close my eyes. "I don't know if it's just the emotions of losing or what it is, but I want to know what my options are."

She laughs. "You're kidding, right?" she says, and I just sit here shocked. "You will have every single team coming in with an offer. The question you should be asking yourself is where do you want to go?"

"I have no idea," I answer honestly.

"Why don't you think about it, and then we can make

a game plan? I don't want you making a big decision like this because you're pissed off."

"I'm past pissed off, Erika," I huff out. "They are talking about rebuilding the team."

"Damn," she says. "Okay, go think about it, and we can talk more tomorrow. No one is going to come in with contracts during playoffs, but if they know you aren't signing with Montreal again, they might start calling in."

"Okay. Let's touch base tomorrow," I say and hang up, opening the text to Alex

Me: Call me when you have a minute.

The phone rings as soon as I press send and get out of the car. "What's wrong?" she says as soon as I answer.

"Why does something have to be wrong?" I ask as I walk up the steps to the house and open the front door.

"Because you never say call me when you have a minute," she huffs out. "Usually, it's like 'can you get off your lazy ass and call me?'" I laugh when I hear Big Mac run through the house to get to me, her tail hitting the wall as she sees me—the golden Lab that I adopted when I came out here because I was lonely.

"Hey there, little lady." I rub her neck and walk to the back door letting her out. "I never call you lazy." I walk over to the couch and sit down.

"So what's wrong?" she asks again, and I put my head back on the sofa.

"I don't know," I answer her honestly. "There is so much going on in my head." I wish she was here with me. "I don't know if I'm going to sign with Montreal. I asked Erika about my options."

"That's a big step." Her voice is soft. "You love it there."

"I know." I rub my hands over my face. "But I just feel stuck."

"Well, where is your notebook?" she asks, and I look over at the side table, seeing the notebook. It was something I started when I was thirteen when I had to make a decision on the school I wanted to go to.

"Here," I say, grabbing it.

"Well, you know what you need to do. Start making your list. Why don't you come out here? Maybe getting out of the city will be good, and you can have a fresh look at things."

"I mean, I have nothing stopping me," I tell her. "I have to bring Mac with me."

"Oh, my baby." She claps her hands excitedly. "I'll go and get her a bed and everything."

"Okay." I sit up, finally feeling a little bit of weight lifted off me. "I'm going to go in tomorrow and pack up my locker and then get on a plane to you." I smile for the first time in a week.

"Sounds good," she says. "Now I have to go back to my meeting with Wilson."

"Thank you, for always knowing what to say."

"It's a gift. I tell you." She laughs at her own joke and disconnects with me. I sit here for a minute, the smile still on my face. Whatever happens, it'll be okay. I turn on my computer and book the plane and make sure I have everything packed by the time I walk out of the house the following morning. I will have to come back and get Mac, but other than that, everything is set.

WHEN I WALK into the arena with my bag in my hand, my heart tightens in my chest, thinking this might be the last time I walk in here as a member of the team. Leo is the only one here. "You cleaning out your locker?" I ask. We share a look but don't say the words, and he just nods his head.

"Yeah, might as well get it over with," he says, and I nod at him as I start to put the things in my bag. "It feels different." I just look over at him, nodding.

Usually, we always clean it out at the end of the season, but this time, I make sure not to leave anything behind. Zipping up the bag, I look over at Leo. "Whatever happens," I say. "It was a pleasure being your brother." I hold out my hand, and he pulls me to him.

"Want to come hang with me?" he asks when he lets me go. "A couple of friends of mine are in town, and I know a couple of single girls will be there."

I smile at him. "Nah, I'm going to go visit Alex," I say, slapping his arm. "Thanks for the invite."

"See you around, Dylan," he says, and I sit on the bench for just a minute longer. A tear comes to my eye as the sadness sets in. I wanted to achieve so much here. I wanted to hoist the Cup over my head here. I wanted to do it for the team and for the city. I wanted to do it for my family and me.

I get up, taking one look around before finally walking

out, knowing in my heart this really is the last time I'll be here as a player for the team.

Pulling away from the arena, I watch the building in my rearview mirror until it disappears. Parking my truck in the garage, I walk into the house and change out of my tracksuit and put on jeans and a white T-shirt with my sneakers.

My four suitcases are at the front door with Mac's leash on it. My phone rings, telling me that my private driver is here. I open the door and start carrying out my bags. He comes over to load them in the Lincoln he is driving. "Let's go see your favorite person, Mac." I grab the leash, and she just looks at me. "You want to go see Alex?" I ask, and she looks outside to see if she is there, and her tail starts wagging back and forth.

The plane is waiting for me when we get there, and I step out with Mac, who walks beside me. I wait for her to climb up the steps before walking in. "Welcome aboard, Mr. Stone," the flight attendant greets, and I just nod at her. "We will be taking off as soon as your bags are loaded."

"Thank you." Walking past the table with four chairs and straight to the couch, I sit down, and Mac sits at my feet. The door closes, and I look out the window as we make our way down the runway.

I take my phone out and text Alex.

Me: On my way.

The bubble comes up with the three dots, and then the text comes through.

Alex: But is my girl with you?

I laugh. Looking down at my feet at Mac sleeping, I take a picture and send it to her.

Me: You know she's my dog, right?

Alex sends me a picture of her in her car with the whole back seat filled with dog stuff.

Alex: Why don't I keep her here?

I shake my head and put my phone away as I look out the window. The thoughts of the past two weeks rush back to me. All the games, all the times we thought we would win only to lose in the last minute of play. It was fucking depressing. I grab my phone and go on Instagram, scrolling through my private account. Watching little clips from the game, I see myself on the bench, my head just hanging, and it guts me yet again.

The wheels touch down, and I stand and so does Mac. "You ready, girl?" I ask, and she gets up and smells the air. "Alex is here," I say and walk to the door as soon as it's opened. "Thank you." I duck my head out of the plane and look out to see her standing there by her car.

"There she is." I hear her voice, and Mac goes nuts. She runs down two steps and jumps the rest of the way, pulling me with her. I can't help the smile that fills my face when I see her.

She doesn't even pay attention to me. She squats down, and Mac runs straight to her. "Oh, my girl." She hugs her around her neck. "I missed you so much," she says, and then she finally looks up at me, her blue eyes shining in the sun. "Hi." She gets up and comes over to me, hugging me. I wrap my arms around her as she lays her head on my chest.

"You look good, Alex," I compliment when she lets go of me, and I look at her up and down. She's wearing blue jeans that are all torn in the front with a white T-shirt that falls off her shoulder. The strap of her pink bra shows against her tanned skin. "Dallas agrees with you."

She throws her head back and laughs. "What does that mean?" She smiles, and I wrap my arm around her shoulder as I walk to her car.

"Your skin is glowing. Sun-kissed," I say, thinking of the word.

"It's called self-tanning lotion. It comes out brown, and you apply it like cream. If you want, we can give your pasty white skin a try."

"I'm not pasty," I defend, and all the feeling of unsettledness is suddenly gone just by being with her. "I just have been in Canada for a long time."

"Is that your excuse?" she asks, folding her arms, and all I can do is hug her. She must sense that I need the extra hug and wraps her arms around my waist. "It's going to be okay." She looks up at me at the same time Mac barks at me.

"Yeah, yeah. You are all over me when she isn't here," I mumble when we get her into the car.

"Did you leave any clothes in Montreal?" She looks at me as the four suitcases are brought and left by the car.

"I just didn't know what to pack." I shrug. "I left my suits there. And my parka." I wink at her and hold out my hand for the keys. "You can sit in the back with Mac so you can let me drive."

I sit in the car, and the whole time, I watch her talking

to Mac from the rearview mirror. We stop to eat and finally get back to her house when the sun is going down. When we get inside, she gives me the house tour, and I stop once we get into the living room and I see the picture of us on her mantel. I walk over to it, picking it up. "This was when I broke Gramps's record," I say, looking at it. The smile on both our faces as we look at the camera. "I still remember this whole day." I look down at the picture of the two of us. "You were the first one on the ice to get to me."

"You threw up four times before heading over for the game," she reminds me, and she is the only one who knows that since she was there with me. Michael doesn't even know that little detail. In front of everyone, I acted cool, calm, and collected, but in front of Alex, I let my nerves show. I knew she would calm me down. "It was something else." She walks over to the couch and sits down, curling her feet under her. Mac gets on the couch next to her and sits down, ignoring me.

"Get off the couch." I motion with my hand, and she literally ignores me as she looks at Alex. "Mac."

"It's okay," Alex says. "She just missed me."

"Well, it's been what, a month," I remind her, sitting on the couch in front of her. "I think that is the longest we've ever gone without seeing each other."

"Really?" she asks, and I nod. "So how was today?"

"It was strange," I admit to her. "It's like I knew in my heart that I wasn't going back."

"Did you tell anyone?" she asks me as she rubs Mac.

"Leo was the only one there when I got in." I rub my

hands over my face. "I think he's leaving also."

"That's going to be a sad day if both of you leave," she says, and she isn't wrong.

"I just …" I shake my head. It's so fucking crazy that this morning I woke up with dread on my shoulders. I couldn't even breathe, and suddenly, it's like everything is washed away. "I don't know what's the right or wrong thing to do."

"Dylan, you know you are allowed to make mistakes, right? It's okay for you to fuck up."

"I just, I feel like a traitor if I walk away from the team," I admit.

"What about the fact that they promised you the world and never cashed in on it?" She sits up, her voice going loud. "Everything that you did for the organization. Every single time they said that it would be different, and it wasn't." She shakes her head. "You need to think of yourself for once. What does Dylan want?" she asks, and all I can do is sit here and think about the question, wondering if I can put into words what I really want. "If you can picture yourself in five years?" she asks. "Where do you see yourself?"

I shrug my shoulders. "Never really thought about it," I tell her. "I guess I'll still be playing hockey. Married for sure." My stomach sinks for a second, making me stop talking to look up at her. She sits there, not saying anything, her eyes blinking really fast. She does that when she is fighting off tears. "I definitely want to have kids. That is for sure."

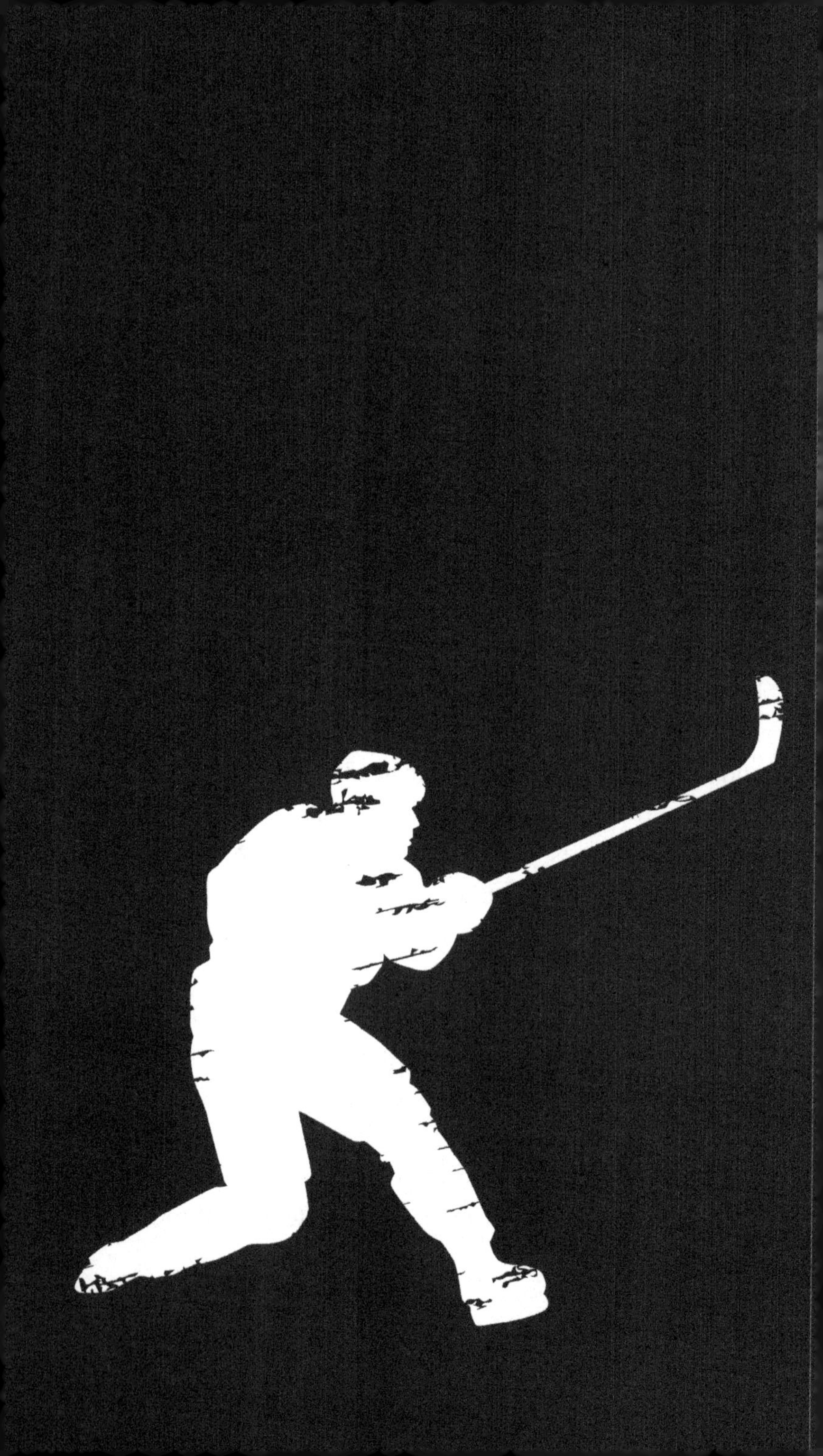

FOUR

ALEX

WHEN I ASKED him the question, I didn't know what I was expecting, if I'm being honest. I was trying to get him to talk things out and calm him down. It's not like it's the first time we've done this with each other. Even when I was thinking about taking the job with Wilson. I wasn't sure I would be good enough for it or have the experience he needed to make it successful, so Dylan sat with me, and we talked things out. It was not supposed to be a loaded question, but the minute he said the words, my heart that was beating normally suddenly shattered in my chest. "I guess I'll still be playing hockey. Married for sure." The burning in my stomach rises to my throat as my nose starts to tingle, and my eyes start to burn with the tears that want to come. I blink them away rapidly the whole time, trying to breathe, but the tightness in my chest makes it so hard. And if I thought hearing those words gutted me, I was wrong. "I definitely want to have kids. That is for sure." I felt like someone cut me off at the knees while kicking me in the chest. The pain was something that I have never felt in my whole life.

"It's late." I force the words out. "I'm going to bed." I push up from the couch and hope like fuck I don't fall down when I take the first step. I ignore his eyes, and if I could, I would run to my room. Instead, I look down at Mac. "Night, girl," I say, walking and never turning back. I can feel his eyes staring at me. "Sleep tight." I try to make the tremble of my voice not show. I try to ignore the pull to turn and take one more look at him, but I can't because the tears are already rolling down my face.

I walk up the steps, and my stomach is in knots as I roll my lips, trying not to sob. My vision is blurry from the tears building up, ready to fall over. With every single step, my legs get heavier and heavier, and when I walk into my room, I close the door. It's the first time I've ever done that. Usually, I leave the door open, and he comes in and chills with me while we watch television. But not tonight. Not now. I walk past my bed and into the walk-in closet that leads to the bathroom.

I turn on the shower at the same time that a sob escapes me. Hoping he doesn't hear me, hoping that the shower drowns out the sound. He's going to marry someone. I close my eyes as reality hits me. This time I have to hold on to the shower door because my legs do give out. My knees hit the floor, and then I turn to sit with my back against the wall facing the shower.

I sit on the cold tile floor, next to the tub, watching the shower fill with steam. My body feels like it's been run over front and back. My eyes focus on the drops of water on the glass door, watching one turn into over a hundred. "He'll never look at you like that," I whisper out the words, rubbing the tear off my cheek. "So stupid," I tell myself, peeling myself off the floor. How the fuck could I ever tell him that I am in love with him? I try to laugh at the ridiculousness of it, but all that comes out is another sob. I can't even picture how I would be able to tell him. How it would change everything, not just for me, but also for him. For the family. "God." I put my head back and close my eyes. How the fuck would I be able to tell my family that I was in love with him? What the fuck would people even say? We grew up together. He's my family. Granted, he's not blood-related to me, but we grew up together. Side by side from when he was adopted at eight years old, and I was five.

Every single memory I have is with him beside me. Learning how to ski and almost breaking my face, he was there. Family vacation of us sneaking off to drink on the beach and then laughing until we had tears running down our faces. When I was going to prom, and my date flaked on me at the last minute, he put on a suit and took me to prom.

Every single memory has a story with him in it. Every single milestone is with him beside me. He knows everything about me, except this. Except for the fact I am in love with him.

I undress and step into the shower, the hot water hitting me feels like pellets of ice. My body trembles, and I have to sit down. I put my head forward on my knees as the hot water tries to heat my body that has turned to ice inside. How could I be so stupid? It's the only thing going through my head. To fall in love with him, I mean, in all honesty, I didn't even know it until it hit me like a car hitting a brick wall.

It was during Michael's wedding that it suddenly dawned on me. When we walked back down the aisle, his arm around my shoulder as I held Jamieson in my arms. I looked over at him, and it just came to me. That I was head over heels in love with him, so I did what I thought was the only thing to do. I stopped calling him every day, I stopped texting him fifty times a day, and instead, I threw myself into the dating pool of New York. I was on all the apps—Tinder, Bumble, Elite Singles, Zoosk. You name it, I signed up for it, but every single date I went on only showed me that I was in love with Dylan.

After the dating apps failed or, better yet, crashed and burned, I did the blind dates; I went on any date that my friends fixed me up with. I would go on double dates; I went through it for three fucking years. Three years I went through this phase, three years of being the life of the party when deep down inside, I was the most miserable, unhappy person in the room. I faked it until I finally gave in and stopped fucking dating and just let the universe take control of it. But instead of delivering me my Mr. Right, it pushed Dylan into my face once again. Showing me that the man I loved was right in front of my face this whole time. So I did the only thing I could. I decided to put more distance between us, and I moved to Dallas.

I turn my head on my knees, and the warm water is running cold now. Getting up, I turn off the water and grab the thick white plush towel and wrap one around my hair and another around my body. Walking to my closet, I slip on my pair of pj shorts with a T-shirt. Then going back into the bathroom to brush out my hair, I look at my reflection in the mirror. My eyes are puffy and bloodshot, and the tip of my nose is red. There is no mistake that I was crying, and I don't even have an excuse if he came knocking on my door and asked me.

I braid my hair on one side and shut off the lights before going to bed. Walking to the wall-to-wall windows in front of my bed, I look out at the stars blinking in the sky. "Help me," I ask the universe. "Forget about him. Make me fall out of love with him." I fold my arms over my chest and turn back to my bed.

When I moved in, the bedroom was the only room where I moved everything out and moved all my stuff in. My bed is custom-made and is a soft tan color. The box bedframe feels like velvet when you touch it. The side tables are both a beige color with a crystal lamp on it and a vase of fresh flowers. A picture of Jamieson and me is on one nightstand and a picture of me with Bianca and Bailey is on the other. On top of my bed are three frames. Live. Laugh. Love. I pull the thick cover off the bed and slide into the bed. Not even bothering taking off the six throw pillows I have. Instead, I just lay my head down on the pillow and look out the window. My head is turning and turning around as I try to change the fact that I can't love him.

I close my eyes, and the minute I do, I hear sniffing coming from the bottom of my bedroom door. I smile as I hear it again. I get out of my bed and walk over to the door and open it. Mac sticks her head in, and I see that all the lights are off in the house. "What's the matter?" I ask, squatting down in front of her. "Are you scared?" She nudges my hand with her head. "Okay, let's go to bed," I say, walking back to the bed, and she gets up on the bed with me. I throw the cover back on top of me, and she turns in a circle before sitting beside me and putting her chin on my hip.

I hear footsteps, and I close my eyes as I hear him come into the room, pretending to be asleep. He walks in softly and whispers for Mac. "Mac, come on," he says, and Mac just stays at my side. "Leave her alone," he whispers and comes closer to the bed. I hold my breath as he stands there. "Let her sleep." Mac doesn't move. The only thing she does is wag her tail up and down on the bed. He waits to see if I'm going to open my eyes, but I don't. The tear rolls from my eye to the pillowcase. Luckily, the lights are off, and he can't see my face closely. That and the fact the covers are up to my chin. I try not to make any movement as he stands there. After a minute, he turns and walks out of the room.

The sound of his feet walking away from the room has me finally breathing normally.

I wait until I know he's in his bed before I open my eyes, and Mac looks over at me. "Tomorrow," I whisper to her, rubbing the top of her head. "Tomorrow, I start to unlove him."

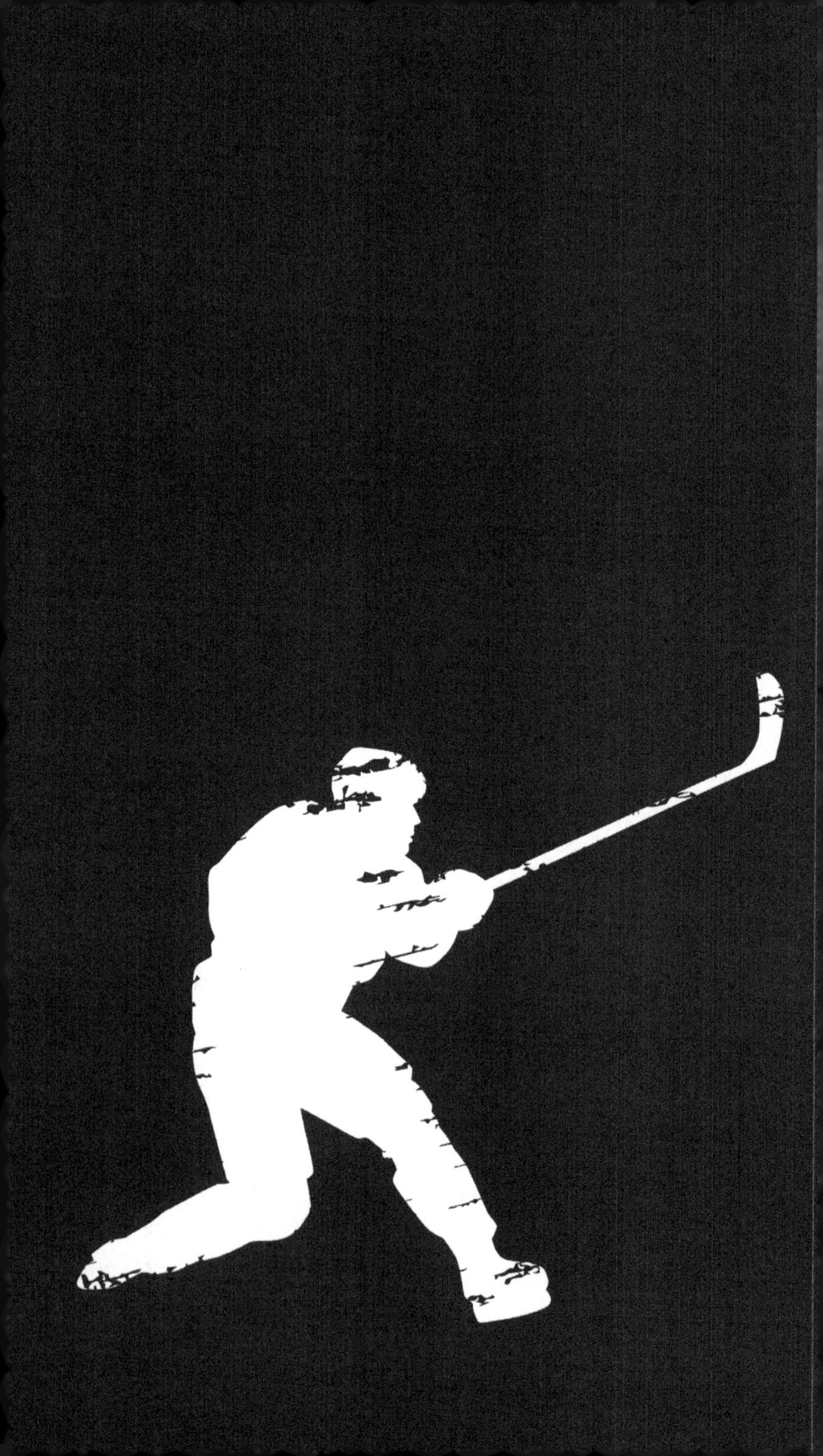

FIVE

DYLAN

ALEX: CALL ME when you get up.

It's the first message on the phone when I open my eyes. "Alex!" I yell, and then I hear the sound of Mac and her nails coming up the stairs. She comes into the room slowly with her head down. "Is she gone?" I ask her, and she gets on the bed and just sits down, looking at the door.

"You are all full of love when she isn't there," I say to Mac, turning and dialing Alex.

"Hey," she answers right away. "You're up."

"Not really. I turned over, and the sun blasted in my face. I forgot to close the curtains last night." I look over to the window, seeing the shades pushed to the side. The blue sky is shining bright.

"I left my car," she says. "Wilson gave me a lift this morning."

"You didn't have to do that. I could have called and

got a car," I say, throwing the cover off me and standing up.

"I've already got a car. I picked it up with Wilson," she says. "I'm off to work. See you later," she says and disconnects, and I just look down at the phone. What the fuck was that? Where was her humor and her jokes? Her telling me that I'm a lazy ass.

I look down at the phone and see the screen saver of the two of us. The same picture that she has downstairs of us when I broke the record. "What is up with her, Mac?" I ask the dog, who just lays her head down and watches the door. Last night was weird, and I stayed up all night thinking about when it turned weird. Even when I walked up to the spare bedroom and saw her door closed, I knew something was up. She never ever closed her door.

I walk downstairs to make myself a coffee when the phone rings in my hand and see it's Erika. "Hello."

"Hey," she huffs out, and I can hear her heels clicking, so I know she's walking somewhere. "I'm outside." I look at the door.

"Of where?" I ask, and she laughs as the doorbell rings.

"Jesus," I say, running back upstairs. "I'm not dressed."

"What the hell, Dylan?" she says as I hear the lock at the front door open. "Why are you walking around the house naked?"

"I wasn't naked!" I shriek as Mac walks past me and toward the door. "I'm in my boxers."

"Well, get dressed and come downstairs. I brought breakfast," she announces.

I slip on my shorts and a T-shirt and head downstairs. Mac is sitting beside her, wagging her tail. "Hey," I say, walking to her and hugging her. Erika is the agent to most of my family members, except Cooper. She was his agent, and then they fell in love, and he fired her. "Where is your husband?" I ask, sitting on the stool next to her.

"Why the hell would he come to a business meeting?" She shakes her head, grabbing the brown bag and taking a container out and handing it to me, and then taking one out for her.

"A business meeting?" I gasp, opening the container and seeing eggs, bacon, sausage, and two pancakes. "I just got here."

She pushes away from the counter and walks over to the drawer, grabbing utensils, but I'm too busy grabbing a pancake and putting an egg on it with sausage and bacon and wrapping it like a wrap. "You are a savage." She points at me with a fork. "And because of that stupid concoction you have in front of you, my kids refuse to eat pancakes any other way." I laugh, thinking about Christmas when I did it in front of them, and they gasped out loud as if I told them Santa was coming back.

"You're welcome." I dunk my pancake in syrup and eat it. "Hmm, salty and savory."

She gets back on the stool and grabs her own container that is some sort of fruit bowl with oatmeal. "That looks gross." I point at the oatmeal.

"It's not that bad," she says. "If I want to drink wine,

I have to eat like this."

"Or you can eat like you want and drink what you want," I suggest. "Cooper doesn't care what you look like."

"Anyway," she continues. "I was checking things out. Seeing the options and whatnot."

"And?" I look at her as I drop a piece of bacon for Mac.

"Bottom line, I think New York or Pittsburgh are your best bets. New York because well, it's obvious, and your father is going to be the coach." She looks down, and I know she is waiting for me to ask her.

"What aren't you saying?" I ask.

"New York is on a rebuild. You know this. They lost their goalie, who retired, even with the number one pick last year. The kid didn't do anything. They have injury over injury, and their cap space isn't that much."

"Okay." I take a deep inhale. "And Pittsburgh?"

She laughs. "You get to play with the best on the ice. Word on the street is he's going to be retiring, so getting you in there will leave the team at the elite level."

"It's going to be so bad if I go to either of those teams," I say, closing my eyes.

"It could be worse. You could go to Toronto or Boston," she tells me, and I make a grimace with my face.

"I would never," I tell her. "I'd rather rebuild with Montreal."

"Nico called me," she says, and I want to laugh because if anyone reached out, it would be Nico. He doesn't let his GM do the legwork. Nope, not Nico. Dallas is his baby, and he's showed it over and over. "Heard you were in town and wants to sit down with you."

I nod. "Set it up," I say, and even Erika is shocked. "There is nothing wrong with me sitting down with him."

"The press is going to spin it," she reminds me.

"Michael and Cooper play on the team," I tell her. "I could be visiting." She just tilts her head. "It's fine."

"He's expecting you at one," she tells me, and I stare at her with my mouth open. "I've been doing this a while. And well, I know you, and I knew you would meet him. Just like I know that you will want to meet with other teams." I nod my head, not sure I want to meet other teams. Maybe Alex moving to Dallas was another sign I should be here. Half my family lives here now.

She finishes her oatmeal and gets up. "Good to have you here." She smiles now. "Also, just so you know, your father called me." She tries to hide her smirk. "He wanted it on the record that he would like to talk to you."

I throw my head back and laugh. "He doesn't want special treatment."

"Well, he's not going to get any special treatment." She folds her arms over her chest. "Especially after last Christmas."

I clap my hands, laughing. "It was the shirt."

"He asked me if I was pregnant!" she yells, and all I can do is hold my stomach.

"You hip-checked him to get at the food." I point at her, and she glares.

"I was starving." She throws her hands up to the sky.

"Matthew took an hour to decide how the fuck to cut a turkey." She shakes her head. "Anyway, don't be late," she says, grabbing her bag. "He's going to be at the rink. Nico said he'll pretend to be surprised you're there."

I nod at her and take my phone to call Alex. It rings twice and then goes to voice mail. At the same time, a text comes in from her.

Alex: In a meeting. I'll call you later.

Me: Going to visit Michael at the rink. I'll be back later.

I clean up the kitchen and make sure that Mac has water before walking out the door and heading over to the arena. I park my car in the visitors' parking lot, getting out and spotting Michael right away.

"Look who it is," he greets, getting out of the car, and the heat from outside fills the garage.

"Fuck." I look around. "It's hot as balls outside." I grab him around his neck when he gets close enough. "You look tired." I slap his shoulder, happy to see him.

"The twins are teething," Michael says. "And if one of them cries, the other cries." He closes his eyes. "Even with the earplugs, I can hear them."

"How's my godson?" I ask him as we walk into the arena. "I haven't seen him since January. I've only FaceTimed him."

"He came home from daycare the other day, and he told his teacher she wasn't the boss of him," he tells me, and I roll my lips because I kept telling him that, every time I was on FaceTime with him.

"I mean, he's not wrong. She isn't the boss of him,"

I say as he opens the door, and I come face-to-face with Cooper, who claps his hands when he sees me.

"There he is." He hugs me, and fuck, does it feel good to be here. "The grouch who told the media to fuck off."

"I did not tell them to fuck off," I reply, slapping his back, and he lets me go. "They ask you the stupid questions," I say, looking around to make sure there is no press, which I should have done beforehand.

"Don't worry," Michael starts. "Nico blocks the press from coming in after our final interviews. We came to clean out our lockers last week, but we wanted to hit the ice a bit, so a couple of us have come just to skate around."

"Well, if I knew, I would have brought my stuff," I say. "You know, get people really talking." I laugh at them and then look down to see Nico coming our way with a smile on his face.

"There he is," Nico says when he gets closer. "Glad you could visit. Mind if I borrow him for a bit?" he asks Michael and Cooper, who just smile and walk away.

"Let's go to my office," he suggests, and I walk with him down the same hallway that I used to walk down when we would come and play here. The same hallway I had to hold Cooper back from attacking Wilson when it came out that he was dating Franny.

"How are you enjoying Dallas?" he asks when we walk into his office. He waits for me to enter before closing the door.

"It was one hundred and four when I got in the car."

"You get used to it." He smirks. "Just like the cold."

It's my turn to smirk. "Let's sit on the couch." He points at his seating area, and I walk over, and I'm surprised that I'm not more nervous.

"So ..." I sit on the couch, looking over at Nico, who sits down. "You wanted to meet with me?"

"I did." He sits with his elbows on his knees and his hands crossed in front of him. "Word on the street is that you might be looking to expand ..." He tries to think of the words. "Your horizons."

"Look, it's no secret that this last round fucking sucked," I say. "I also will not talk shit about my team." I take a deep breath. "They will always have a place in my heart."

"Time to make the heart bigger." He smiles at me. "What do you want?"

"I want what every single person who laces up their skates wants," I say. "I want to win the Cup."

He laughs. "I can't guarantee you that," he says. "It would be stupid for anyone to guarantee you that, but what I can guarantee you is that no one wants to hoist that Cup as much as me." He looks into my eyes. "It would be the biggest *fuck you* to everyone who said I wouldn't be able to do it because I was too young. I knew nothing. Our team is solid." He's not wrong. "And no one is leaving. I have everyone locked in for another year, and I think you are the missing piece, Dylan," he says. "Come to Dallas."

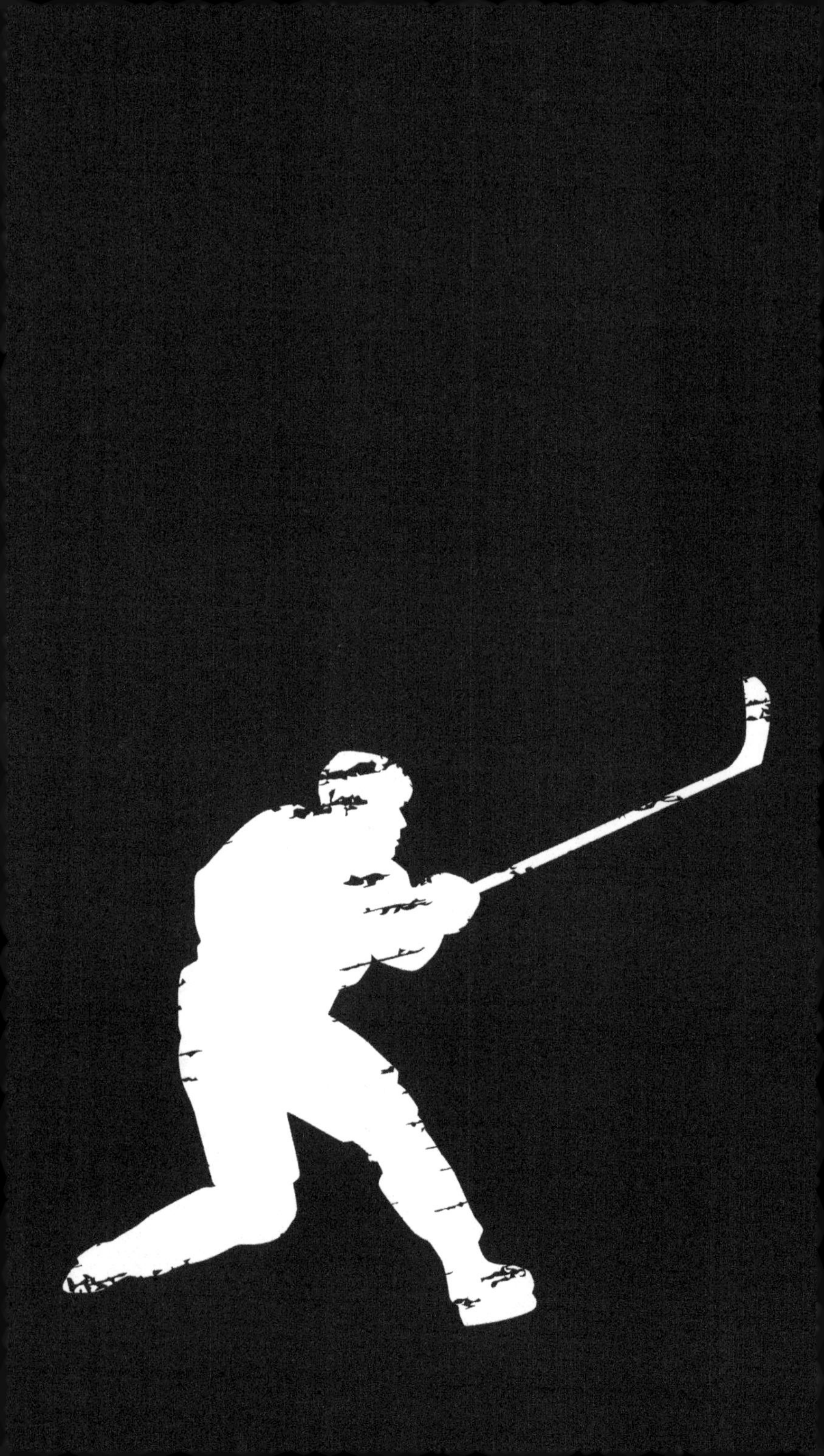

SIX

ALEX

"THANK YOU SO much, Jamie." I hold out my hand to shake his. "The kids are going to love all the new gear." He works for Hauer, the leading hockey equipment company in the country, and has graciously donated all new gear to the twenty kids who won the scholarship for the summer.

"It was great working with you, Alex." He smiles at me. "You should let me take you out for a drink to celebrate." I look at his perfectly styled black hair with his brown eyes. I think about it for point one second before I let him down.

"Thank you, but I don't like to mix business with pleasure," I answer him honestly. "Can you imagine? We go out, and obviously, I'm fabulous." He laughs at that, nodding his head. "And for whatever reason, things don't work out? It'll be awkward for both of us."

"You have a point there," he says. "But if I ever leave

this job, you can bet your ass I'm going to keep your number."

I throw my head back and laugh. "Fair enough." I smile at him as he walks away. "Why can't you just fall for someone else?" I mumble to myself as my phone rings in my pocket. I take it out and see it's Julia. "Hey, ho." I can hear her chuckle. I met Julia when Michael had a one-night stand with her sister, and they created the most amazing little boy I've ever met. We instantly clicked, and she is really my best friend, that is after Dylan. Dylan, who I've thought about all day long. Dylan, who all I do when I close my eyes is hear him say he sees himself married with children. Dylan, who I love with every fiber of my being. Dylan, who I have to get over. Dylan, who I have to slowly fall out of love with.

"Hey, ho, yourself." Her voice is less than chipper.

"What happened?" My voice goes soft as I walk back to my office.

"Are you free for lunch?" she asks, and I look at my watch.

"It's three o'clock," I say, walking into my office and sitting in my chair.

"I just had to pry a seven-year-old girl off her dead mother's body," she says, and my heart stops in my chest. I don't know how Julia does it every single day. She works for Child Protective Services, and I can just imagine the stories she has.

"I can leave in five minutes. Where do you want to go?" I ask, turning off my computer and grabbing my purse. "Or do you want to come here?"

"As much as I love chicken fingers and French fries." She laughs. "I need some whiskey and wings."

"Fine, let's meet at Louie's." I suggest the bar we always go to.

"Deal." She hangs up, and I turn around to head out. The heat hits me right away, and I groan. I love hot, but this hot is almost too much.

When I pull up to the restaurant, I find parking around the corner, and the sound of my heels click on the pavement as I make my way inside. I pull open the glass door and look around. I'm surprised so many people are already here, but the televisions playing in the corners have the baseball game on. The hostess stand sits empty with the "please let us seat you" sign.

"Alex." I hear Julia call me and look over to find her sitting at a table against the window. Turning, I make my way to her, and she stands. "You just strutted over here like you are on a catwalk." I laugh and shake my head. "I wish I could pull off your style." This morning when I got up, I almost dreaded that he would hear me and come ask if I wanted coffee. I was up way before my alarm, turning it off not to make noise, and when I peeked into his room, he was on his stomach with his head facing away from the door. I quietly shut the door so as not to wake him. I grabbed the first thing in my closet, which was the light gray high-waisted pants I am wearing that tie around the waist. The black bodysuit molds to my chest and comes up to my neck with small spaghetti straps holding it up. My shoulders and arms are bare. I laugh at her and sit in the chair in front of her. "Instead,

I look like a poor Ellen DeGeneres."

"Shut up." I laugh at her.

"Those shoes alone are a kill." I roll my eyes.

"Shoes are my jam," I say, looking down at the black heels I'm wearing. They have a strap around the toes and they crisscross to tie around my ankle. If I'm honest, I dressed up way more than I needed to today, and I'm trying to tell myself that it was to make me feel better. "So how bad was today?"

She looks down and then looks back up with tears in her eyes. "Brutal." She stops talking when the waitress brings over two glasses of whiskey and puts one down in front of me.

I just smile. "I'll have a glass of wine, please." I slide the second glass over to Julia, who takes her glass and brings it to her lips.

"I don't think I will ever get over that little girl's blood-curdling screams." She looks down at her glass, spinning it in her hands. "Anyway, tell me something new." She shakes her head. "Take my mind off it, please."

"Well, we selected twenty kids to get in the program." I smile happily.

"You have no idea what that will do for some of these kids," she says. "They are usually handed the short end of the stick and"—she takes a sip of her drink—"some end up a product of their environment because they know nothing else."

"I don't know how you do your job," I say. "After going through the files and reading their backstories, I wanted to give it to each and every single kid."

She takes another drink. "Just remember you can't save everyone." She laughs bitterly. "No matter how much I remind myself of that every single time I get a file. The younger they are, the easier it is, but sometimes, you get a fourteen-year-old who has been through more than I can even put into words and looks at me like I'm just another person coming into their life." She takes a sip. "The woman who died today." She looks at me. "She was in the system herself and got pregnant at fourteen." She rubs her face. "It makes me so thankful for what I have."

"We are very privileged."

"Okay, this is a little bit depressing," she says. "Let's talk about our family vacation." She laughs. "Can I just say how crazy it is that I consider myself family?"

I laugh at her. "You are family," I insist. "My father thinks you're his daughter. Sometimes, he counts you before me." She just smiles. "And we leave in two weeks to go to Hawaii." I put up my hands.

"I can't wait." The light returns to her eyes. "Two weeks of sun, sand, and activities."

"I want to do the sunset cruise, and then I want to do the paddleboarding, and then maybe I'm going to try surfing," I say excitedly.

"So you are going on an Instagram vacation." She laughs, and I roll my eyes.

"It's Hawaii. I just looked up the hotel." I use finger quotes. "It's insane! I'm not going to admit it to Matthew, but he did good."

"I caved, and I'm going to stay with Michael and

Jillian. To help with the kids."

I open my mouth, shocked. "We were supposed to be roommates."

"You can room with Vivi." I shake my head.

"No, she promised Emma and Mia." I put my head back and groan.

"It'll be good. You can share with Dylan." I look down and try not to show anything as my head starts to spin.

"He's already here." I try to sound chipper about it, but instead, my heart starts pounding so hard in my chest I can only hear that in my ears.

"When did he get here?"

"Yesterday." I try to change the subject as the tears start to sting my eyes. The burden of having no one to talk to starts to eat at my stomach. "I have to tell you something," I say, my voice going soft. The waitress brings over my glass of wine. I smile at her and blink away the tears, but one falls, and I wipe it away.

Julia reaches her hand across the table and puts her hand on mine. "What is it?" she asks, her own eyes filling with tears.

"Oh my God," I say, swallowing the lump in my throat and taking a sip of wine. "I don't know if I can say it out loud." I try to smile, but the tears continue to fall. "Because if I say it, it's like out there in the universe."

"Oh my God." Julia puts her hand to her mouth, and her own tears come. "Whatever it is, it's going to be fine."

I'm terrified to finally admit this to anyone, but I'm going to get over it. "I'm in love with Dylan," I admit softly. I watch her eyes to see if she looks at me with disgust or shock. What I'm not expecting is for her to throw her head back and laugh.

"Oh, good God." She takes her hand off mine, putting it on her chest. "Jesus, thank fuck." She grabs her glass and downs the rest of the whiskey. "I thought you were going to tell me you were dying or you had cancer."

I look at her, surprised. "Aren't you shocked? Maybe you didn't hear me. I'm in love with Dylan." She just stares at me. "Like Dylan Dylan."

She looks at me as if I'm stupid. "No shit." I just stare at her. "I sort of had an idea at the beginning, but then I thought maybe it was in my head. Then seeing you guys together more and more, I kind of figured out that you both had feelings for each other." My head spins even more when she said both. "What are you going to do about it?"

"Probably nothing." I shake my head. "What can I do?"

"Well, you could tell him how you feel." She looks at me, and the nerves of my stomach start to rise.

"I can't do that to him." I swallow down. "I can't burden him with this. Can you imagine what he might think of me?"

"But what if he feels the same way?"

I chuckle. "No, there is no way." I take a sip of my wine. "This is definitely just my problem."

"Alex." She calls my name. "You are in love with your best friend." She tries to calm me down.

"I'm pretty sure me telling my family that I'm in love

with Dylan will definitely not go over well." I laugh at myself. "Jesus, I can't believe I finally said it out loud." I put my hand to my chest. "How crazy does that sound?"

"Or maybe everyone else knows and is just waiting for you guys to realize it." All I can do is shake my head. "If I caught it and I don't even know you guys, I can just imagine that they suspect it."

"If I say anything, two things can happen. One, Dylan looks at me differently, and it changes everything between us." I take a long gulp of wine. "That would kill me." I take a long inhale. "Or it could ruin the whole family."

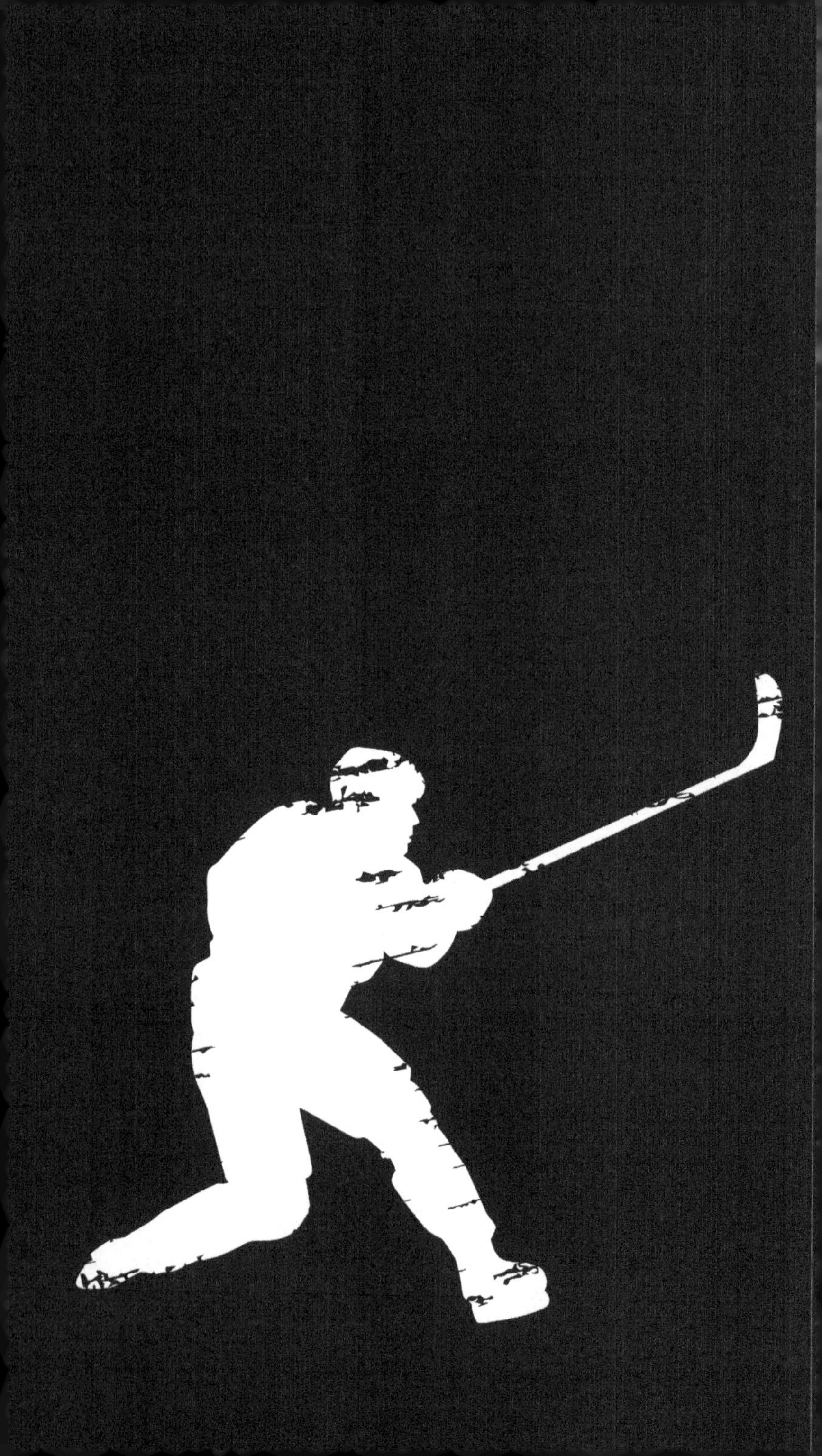

SEVEN

DYLAN

"THANK YOU." I stop in front of Nico as we walk out of the workout facility. "For taking the time to sit with me and go over things." After our meeting in his office, he wanted to show me around, but it wasn't all that different from Montreal. We stopped to watch how practice was going, too, and it looked like everyone was on the same page. Which was different from Montreal.

Nico slaps my shoulder with a grin. "Wherever you go, they will be lucky to have you."

"Thank you." I smirk at him, looking around to see who is lingering. The locker room is empty, so I know the guys are still on the ice. "You've given me a lot to think about."

"Good." He puts his hands in his pockets. "Means my job here is done. Stick around and talk to the guys. Maybe they can convince you." He pulls out his ringing phone and looks down at it. "I have to take this, but my door is always open."

I laugh at him as he walks away from me, and I take a deep breath. I think about sticking around but then see that it's almost five o'clock. Instead, I walk out and get into the car, my head going around and around with all different thoughts.

I start the car and pull out of the garage, calling my father, who answers after one ring. "Well, if it isn't my missing child," he says, and I laugh, I was eight years old when I was chosen to train with his summer hockey school, and I met him. Hockey was the only thing in my life I could have controlled back then. Our life was not easy, and my mother tried to shield me from most of it, but you see things you never want to see. Things to this day I can't forget. He fell in love with my mother and vice versa. He took care of everything, and my life changed even more. When I was ten, he asked my mother to marry him, and we both took his last name, and he officially adopted me.

"I am not missing," I reply, making my way toward Alex's place. "I'm in Dallas with Alex."

"Should have known," my father says. "Guess she couldn't come to you."

"No, she's preparing for the summer hockey school." I come to a red light. "Plus, I needed to clear my head."

"What's going on?"

I look around, thinking about what to say but not even sure where to start. "Erika tells me you want a meeting on the record."

He chuckles. "Is that why you are quiet? I know you

have a lot to say."

"I just—"

"Dylan," he interrupts me. "I'm going to be your father first every single time." I smile. "Except if you come and play for me and I tell you to do something." I can't help but laugh. "You can talk to me about anything. You know this."

I never doubt that he has my best interests at heart. I never have to doubt that he loves me. "I met with Nico." It's his turn to laugh.

"That's not a surprise," he says, and it shocks me. "I'd be surprised if you didn't meet with him. How did it go?"

"It went great. He asked me about what I was looking for, and of course, he didn't bullshit me and tell me he would deliver the world on a platter. But he did say he would fight with us."

"He's a solid guy. His team is solid also." He breathes out heavily. "Fuck, I'm not going to like playing him next year if you join the team." His voice goes soft. "Can you imagine you playing on the same line as Cooper and Michael?" I can't help but smile. The best times I have are during the summer when we get back from vacation and we all train together. We get on the ice, and it's just magical. "Fuck, no one is going to be able to stop you."

"It'll be easy for everyone with one jersey," I joke. "Instead of everyone having a different jersey."

"What about you?" he asks. "Forget about what everyone is telling you or what the press is saying. Forget about the outside noise." His voice goes soft. "What does your heart tell you to do?" he asks the loaded question.

"I have no idea. I always thought I would retire in Montreal, so I never ever imagined being in this position. But something changed along the way, and I don't know how to describe it," I confess as my head laughs at me. "I have this itch to settle." The words come out before I can stop them.

"Were you not settled in Montreal?" He asks the same question I've asked myself since I started feeling out of sorts.

"I was, but something was missing." I tap the steering wheel with my finger, pulling over when I see a flower shop. "I don't know what to do, Dad."

"It's a big, big decision," he tells me. "And it isn't one that you should make lightly."

"I'm afraid to take the step, and then my game suffers for it," I admit.

He laughs at me. "Dylan, you are in the prime of your career. Top scorer in the whole league every year and that's with not that great of a team behind you."

I sit here listening to what my father says. "Don't rush into anything. Sit down with as many people as you think you need to sit down with." He clears his throat. "Especially the new coach in New York." I laugh at his subtle push. "But no matter where you go, it'll be a challenge." I think about what he is saying. "But if anyone is up for that challenge, it's you."

"Thanks, Dad," I say softly. "I needed this."

"I'm going to let you go so I can call Erika again and demand a sit-down," he says, and I laugh.

"I'll see you in four days." I get out of the car. "We

can talk in Hawaii."

"Fuck no." He shakes his head. "That's my vacation. I'm not doing anything on that except spending time with my family."

I laugh, walking into the flower shop. "Fine." I look around. "We'll see."

"Love you," he says as always, right before he hangs up.

"Love you, too. Say hi to Mom." I disconnect the call with him as the lady behind the counter asks if she can help me.

I grab a bouquet of peonies, and she wraps them up for me in brown paper. I walk out of the shop and send Alex a text.

Me: Headed home. I'll start dinner.

It's only after I send the text do I sit here and look down at it. *Headed home.* The flutters start in my stomach as I think about when I first started to get the feeling something was missing. It's only after I start playing the months over in my head that I realize it came right after Alex told me she was moving to Dallas.

I start driving toward the house, my head reeling over the fact that before she moved to Dallas, I was okay. Before she took that leap and finally made her decision to start planting her roots, I was fine. Everything was fine before, or was it?

Pulling up to the house, I grab the flowers and walk inside, the cold air hitting me right away. "Hello!" I shout out just in case she is home, but she isn't. I hear Mac running from upstairs and look that she came out of her room. "Did you make a mess in there?" I ask, and she comes to me as I bend and hug her neck. "Let's get you outside." I open the back door, and she steps outside.

Turning around, I search for a vase to put some water in and then place the pink peonies in the middle of her island. I take my phone out and see that she hasn't even answered me back, which is weird. Mac scratches at the back door, and I walk over and let her back in, bending to fill up her water bowl with fresh water.

Walking over to the fridge, I see that it's fully stocked. Putting some veggies in the oven to roast, I grab the piece of salmon she has and slice some lemons to put on it. After seasoning the salmon with salt and pepper, I put it in the oven. It's almost five thirty, so she should be home soon. I walk over to the living room and turn on the television as I wait for her.

My eyes roam around the room, seeing how she has already settled in. Her touches are everywhere, just like she did at my house in Montreal. It's the soft touches with a blanket here and there. Pictures left in a frame on the counter. It's the tray with all the remotes in it instead of just thrown on the couch. I smile as I get up, going to the oven and seeing that it's past six.

I'm about to grab my phone and call her when I hear the front door. I grab the salmon out of the oven and look over my shoulder when I hear the click of her shoes coming closer to the kitchen.

I can hear her talking to Mac. "Look at you, my pretty girl. Did you have a good time today?" I smile as I hear her heels moving toward me again.

The minute I see her walk into the room, my heart starts to speed up, and the smile fills my face. She looks so beautiful. "Hi," she says, walking in and going to the fridge. "It's so hot out." Grabbing a water bottle, she opens it and drinks it.

"It's a scorcher," I tell her. "I hope you are hungry. I made salmon."

"Oh." She looks at me, and her eyes go big. "I ate already."

"You ate already?" I ask, confused. "It's six."

"Yeah, I had a late lunch." She avoids my eyes, and I just look at her.

"Did you have a date?" My stomach starts to clench and my heart speeds up as I wait for her to answer. *What in the actual fuck* is the only thing I can think. That, along with the thought of her on a date, and I have this sudden anger that goes through me, this blinding rage, and all I can do is look at her as she walks around the counter without answering my question. Why isn't she answering my question? "Oh my God, you were on a date." I try to get my voice to come out calm, surprising even myself when I don't shout out the words.

I watch her sit on the stool in front of me. The whole time, my hands clenching into fists, and I have to take a second to think about what I'm going to say if she actually tells me she was on a date. I also have to take a second to think about why the fuck it bothers me so much.

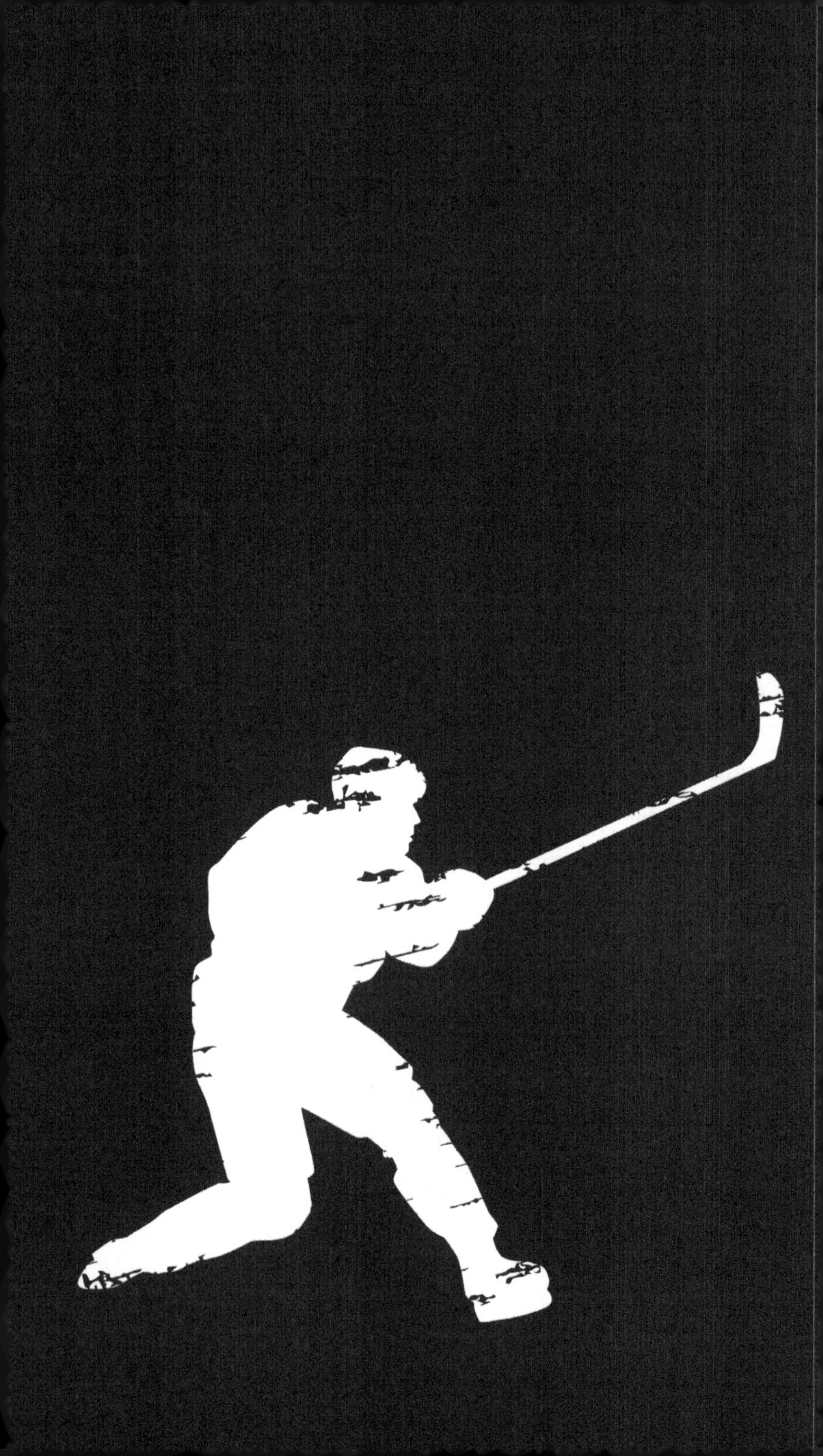

EIGHT

Alex

"Oh my god, you were on a date." His voice is high-pitched, and I ignore the question altogether. I look up at him, and everything in me stops, the tightness in my chest starts again. After I had lunch with Julia, I decided it would be good to stay out as long as I could. I hit up the mall and shopped and bought things I don't even know if I'm going to wear. To be honest, I went all-out sexy, as if I was going on a mating vacation instead of a family vacation. I try to talk, but my mouth is so dry I can't even swallow. "You were on a date." He puts his hands on his hips, and I'm about to answer him when his phone rings. He looks over at the couch, and I watch him walk toward the phone, and my heart speeds up.

"Saved by the bell, my girl," I say to Mac, who sits beside me, wagging her tail. "Did you eat?" I ask, and look over at Dylan when he laughs at the top of his lungs.

"Okay, fine," he says to whoever is on the line. "We

can go but early. There is no way I want to be out in this heat."

I walk over to get Mac some food and then turn back to look at Dylan, who is still on the phone, his eyes bright and his smile big. His free arm reaching behind his neck is making his arm flex. I watch him longer than I should. Turning my eyes away from him, getting Mac food, I put food in her bowl, and walk over to the stairs, taking off my heels finally. When I walk back into the kitchen, he puts the phone on the counter. "Everything okay?" I ask him, watching his every single move. I'm waiting for the feeling of looking at him and not feeling anything. When I walked in the room today, I expected to just laugh loud at the stupidity of falling for him, but instead all I could do was watch him watching me.

"Uncle Matthew wants to take me golfing," he says as he walks to the kitchen and makes himself a plate.

"Um, why?" I ask, walking over to the door and letting Mac out.

"He heard through the grapevine that I went to talk to Nico today," he replies, and my eyes go big.

"I'm sorry, what?" I ask him, not sure I understood him. My hands start to tremble as I walk over to the other side of the counter, not sure I can sit next to him. "You met with Nico?" I inquire, and he cuts a piece of his salmon and takes a bite.

"Yeah," he says. "Erika was here this morning, so I went to meet with Nico."

I swallow, trying to come up with the words to tell him not to do that. I don't know if I can handle us living in the same city when I'm trying to get over him. "Are you really thinking about moving here?" I thought having him here for a visit would have been hard, so I can't even imagine having him living here full-time. My head spins around and around as I think about the excuses to give him as to why he shouldn't move here.

"I have a couple of choices," he tells me and I hate myself for not being there for him. It's not his fault I feel this way. I push down my head screaming at me to run away and instead go to sit next to him.

"What are your choices?" I ask, holding the water bottle in my hand in front of me. My eyes are on the label instead of turning to watch him eat. My hands are moving so nervously that all I can do is turn the bottle around and around on the counter.

"New York and Pittsburgh," he says, and I look over at him now.

"New York?" I ask, shocked. I get why Uncle Matthew wants to take him golfing. Even though he's not the GM of the team anymore, he still has a seat on the board and is very involved. "You'll be playing for your father."

He nods his head. "Um, forgive me for saying this, but the last time you did that, it did not go well." He laughs.

"I was fourteen, and everyone was fawning all over him." He glares at me. "I didn't like it."

"Oh, we know." I laugh and push his shoulder with mine, something we've always done when we were teasing each other. "I believe you told one guy he liked your dad better than his because his was bald."

"He did have a bald head." He tries to justify how he behaved. "And was also looking at my mother every time she walked by." He takes a bite of his veggies. "Pervert."

I can't help my full-on belly laugh. This, this right here, being with him and laughing and talking is how it's supposed to be. I'm not supposed to want to be in his arms. I'm not supposed to wonder what it would be like to kiss him. All of these thoughts should not be entering my mind. But when he looks at me and smiles, all I think about doing is leaning in and kissing him. He would probably never talk to me again and look at me with disgust each time. "Do you know where you want to go?" I look at him. "I'm sure you can pick any team you want. Especially with your stats and numbers." There is no denying that Dylan is good at hockey. He's the best I've ever seen on the ice. Every year, his numbers reflect it, always making him the one to beat.

He nods. "That is what Erika said. I don't want to go to a team that is in a rebuild because if that is the case, I could just stay in Montreal." He sounds like he has so much on his mind, and I know he needs me to be there for him. I'm just not sure I'll be left standing at the end of this.

"Which team are you leaning more to?" I ask nervously, holding my breath the whole time.

Please say New York, I silently beg, *or Pittsburgh*. Basically, anywhere but here. "I haven't really decided. I want to sit down and look at all my options before I commit. It's a big fucking deal." I just watch him. "Being drafted is easy. You just get to go to the team that picked you, but sitting down and thinking about a team you want to go to is a whole different ball game. I've never had to make this decision, so I'm doubting everything I know. Which I shouldn't."

"It's going to be a big step," I say. "All you know is Montreal, and you're starting over again. It's like the first day of middle school. You were the cool kid on campus in elementary school, and then all of a sudden, you're back at the bottom, and you have to work your way up." I shrug. "You know what to expect with your teammates. You know what to expect with the organization. Starting over is …" I try to think of what I can say to make things a touch easier on him.

"It's scary for sure." He finishes the thought for me. Putting his fork down in the middle of his dish, he walks over to the sink to rinse his plate and put it in the dishwasher. "But I think it's time." He turns to look at me. "If I don't do it, then I'll just think about the what-ifs, and that will kill me." He was never good at not having a plan. "I'm going to have a lot to think about on this vacation."

"So no surfing and sailing for you?" I ask, knowing he was most looking forward to that.

"Oh, definitely surfing and sailing. Just more talks with the OGs for their opinions." He shrugs. "I want to hear what they have to say. Some of them have been in my shoes before."

"Well, you know one thing for sure," I say, and he rolls his eyes. "I'm sure they have all the advice to give."

"Great," he says sarcastically. "All I need to hear for

two weeks is *back in my time …*" I can't help but laugh because they all say this. "Like they grew up in the war with one shoe."

"What about *when I was your age.*" I remind him of the other thing they tell us.

"Ugh, don't remind me." He shakes his head and then rubs his face. "You remember the first time we stayed on the beach all night long?" He looks at me, and I smile.

"How could I forget? All I heard all night long was Michael dry heaving." I close my eyes. "I told you idiots not to finish the whole bottle of tequila." He can't help but laugh.

"We used to always bitch about the vacation," he says. "And now it's the one thing I look forward to the most."

"Well, Julia told me today she's staying with Michael and Jillian." I get up and walk to the door to let Mac in. "I'm going to end up staying with my parents."

"Nah," he says. "You can stay with me. I'm going solo. My suite has two bedrooms."

My mouth gets dry when he says that. "Um …" I try to think of ways to tell him no. "Have you packed?"

"I have to unpack the bags I brought down, but all my summer clothes are in one of them, so I'm going to unpack and pack what I'll need tomorrow," he says, and I yawn.

"I'm going to go up and start." I tap my finger on the counter nervously, "I'm exhausted."

I push the chair back in, afraid to look at him. "Your date wear you out?" he asks, and something about his tone gives me shivers.

I put on my best poker face, then look at him. "Something like that." I smirk. "I also need a shower." I turn and walk toward the stairs, grabbing the bags I put down there when I walked in and my shoes.

"See you tomorrow," I say over my shoulder, and I can feel him staring at me. Walking into my room for the second night, I close my door behind me. Hoping that with the door closed, my heart won't yearn for him, except this isn't how it works. In fact, it's almost the complete opposite because all I want to do is go back downstairs to him. "Forget it," I mumble to myself, trying to somehow convince my brain that it's a bad idea. "It'll never happen." The words come out, hurting me more than I ever thought they would.

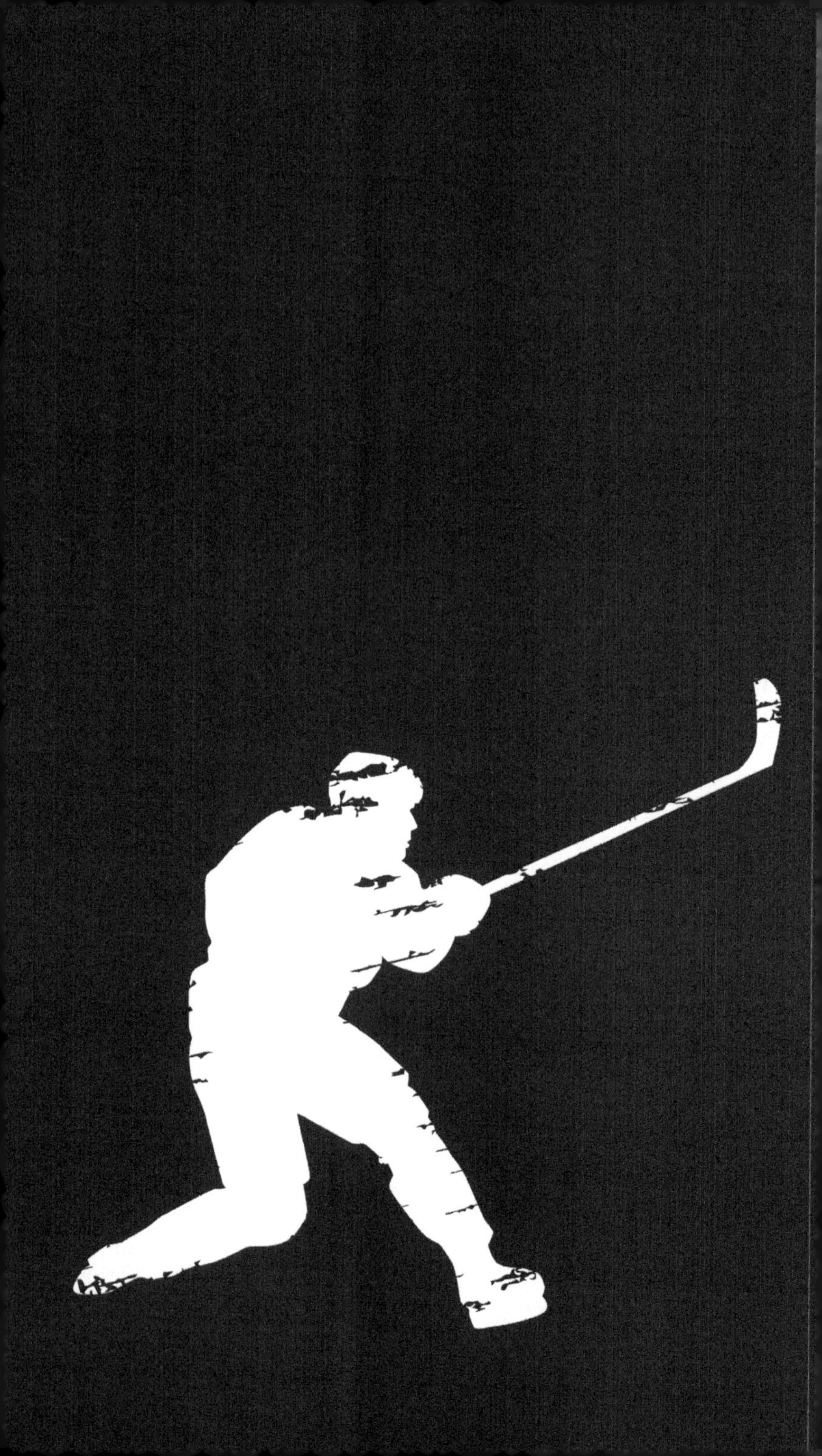

NINE

DYLAN

"WHAT'S UP YOUR ass?" my uncle Matthew asks me when he drives us back to the clubhouse. I look over at him. "You've been pissy since I picked you up this morning." He picked me up at seven this morning. My alarm went off at six thirty, and when I walked out of my room, I was expecting her door to be open, but it was closed, which pissed me off so much more than I thought it would. And started my whole mood for the day. My golf game was shit—not that it was good to begin with—but it was worse than it's ever been. I literally just wanted to get this over with. I tried to get into it and enjoy it, but every single time I put the tee down, I thought about her being out on a date. Last night after she left me in the kitchen, I watched her walk up the stairs, never turning back. My eyes fixated on her ass, and I turned around so fucking quickly, afraid she would catch me checking her out. But instead, she shut the door. It was as if she was shutting me out, and I fucking hated it. I tossed and turned all night, thinking about her dating and wondering why the fuck she didn't tell me.

I shrug. "I'm just tired, I guess." I swallow and avoid his eyes in case he can tell that I'm lying through my teeth. Pulling the baseball cap lower down to block my eyes.

I'm thankful he has a business call on the way back to the house, and he doesn't press me. I get out of the SUV, grabbing my golf clubs that Michael kept at his house, and walk back into the house. The cold air hits me right away. Mac meets me at the front door as I walk into the garage and put my clubs down.

Walking back into the house, I take my phone out and call Alex. It's just so natural to call her all the time. I'm expecting her not to answer for some reason, so when she does, it throws me off. "Um, hello?" she says after I don't answer her the first time.

"It's me," I say, my stomach filled with nerves.

"I know." She laughs. "What can I do for you?"

"I'm wondering if you are coming home for dinner." Walking to the kitchen and grabbing a water bottle. "Or do you have another date?"

"Nope, all free tonight," she says, again avoiding talking about her date. "I have a fuck ton of things to do before we leave," she says, and I hear guys talking in the background. "I have to go. I'm headed to a meeting."

"With your boyfriend?" The words come out of my mouth, and I close my eyes as soon as they do.

"You are so fixated on this boyfriend." She laughs

out. "Don't you have other things to do?"

"Why the secrecy?" I ask, and I can hear the voices in the background getting louder.

"Okay, got to go. I'm getting looks from my boss," she says and hangs up. I look down at the phone, staring at the picture on my screen saver.

"Does she have a boyfriend, Mac?" I turn to look at the dog, who just sits there looking up at me. "Did she tell you anything?" She just tilts her head to the side, probably telling me that I'm an idiot.

I pull up Michael's name on my phone and send him a text.

Me: Hypothetically speaking.

I press send and see the bubble come up with three dots, and then the phone buzzes in my hand.

Michael: Okay.

Me: If some girl told you she was out on a date, how would you feel?

Michael: Considering I'm married, is this woman my wife?

I groan when he answers, so I just dial his number, and he answers after two rings. "Hello," he whispers. "One sec, I'm putting Bianca down." I hear rustling from the covers, and then he comes back. "Okay, why the fuck is my wife going on a date?" he demands, aggravated and cranky.

"Why would it be your wife?" I answer him. "It's not your wife." Getting just a touch frustrated because the way he answered with his crankiness is how I feel, and I don't know what to do with it.

"Well, then, why would I even care?" I close my eyes, pinching the bridge of my nose. "Why don't you just cut to the chase?"

There is no way to cut to the chase. "Okay, let's say a friend of yours." I start talking. "Before you met Jillian and you lived happily ever after, yada yada yada." He starts to laugh. "One of your friends who is a girl tells you she was on a date."

"Okay," he says, paying close attention.

"She tells you she was on a date." My leg starts to bounce up and down. "Is it normal to be pissed?"

"No." He doesn't even take a minute to think about it.

"But what if she's a good friend?" I ask him, my finger tapping the counter at the same time my leg goes up and down. "And you are worried about her."

"Do you want to date this good friend of yours?" he asks me, and my whole body stops shaking, and I want to scoff at him.

"No," I say, knowing full well that I can never go there.

"Then it's not normal," he says, and I roll my eyes.

"Fine, that's all," I say. "I'll call you later." Hanging up the phone, I let my head hang. The phone buzzes from the counter, and I see it's Michael.

Michael: Are you sure you don't want to date her?
My fingers answer right away.
Me: Yes.

I press send before I delete it and write maybe or no, I'm not sure. I get up, walking upstairs, and stop when I walk past her room. Her bed is made, and I know something is up with her. She never ever makes the bed. Like ever. Her excuse is always I'm going to sleep here tonight, so why clean it to mess it up.

I need a nap, I think to myself, walking back into the room and seeing my bed still a mess. I throw myself on top of the covers and look out the window. I grab my phone, and I call the only person I know who won't try to analyze me.

"Hello?" my mother says after one ring.

"Hey, Mom," I say, smiling. "What's going on?"

"Nothing much. Packing up to leave," she huffs out. "Your sisters are modeling their new swimsuits, and I think the vein in your father's head is going to pop." I laugh, imagining what they are doing now. "What's up with you?"

"I don't know," I say, and then I hear her stop moving. "I'm just … there is a lot going through my head, and I'm not sure what to do."

I can hear her moving, and the sound of the door closing lets me know she stepped out of the room to give me her full attention. My mother has not had an easy life. To be honest, her life was shit before Justin came into the picture. "What do you mean?"

"I don't know," I admit, and she just listens to me. "I just … my head is messing with me." I close my eyes, and all I can do is see Alex smiling at me.

"Well, from what your father told me, you have very big life changes coming," she says softly. "And I know it's scary for you."

"I'm not scared," I tell her. "I just don't want to make

a decision I can't undo," I confide, not sure if I'm talking about Alex or my career. Or maybe it's both. "I want to make sure that what I'm doing is the right thing to do."

"It's okay to make a mistake," she says. "Heaven knows I've made enough mistakes to last a lifetime. But if I hadn't made those mistakes, I wouldn't be where I am today. I wouldn't have you or your brother and sisters."

"Yeah," I say softly. "I'm just not used to being so in limbo."

"I have faith that you will make the right decision," she reassures me, and I sit up, my stomach turning when I think about how she would react if I told her exactly how I was feeling these days. How would she look at me if I told her I was crushing on Alex? How would she look at me if I told her I couldn't stop thinking about her? How would she look at me if I told her that last night I dreamed of kissing her? Fuck, how would anyone look at me? How would Alex look at me? She would probably never talk to me again. "Whatever it is, you know that you have us behind you."

"Yeah," I reply, the pain in my chest coming on, and I have to rub it to relieve the pressure. "Thanks, Mom."

"I don't know why," she says, "but something tells me that you have something else on your mind."

I laugh. "It'll work itself out. It always does."

"It does. We'll see you in two days," she replies, and I hang up the phone with her and turn to grab my notebook out of my bag.

I make columns for New York, Pittsburgh, and Dallas. I sit up, tap the pen on the lined paper, and look out the window, not sure if I want to put what I'm thinking down on paper. Instead, all I can do is think in my head. I'm the best on the ice. My game is only going to get better.

"So why the fuck aren't you happy?" I ask myself the loaded question. "Why the fuck are you so pissed off? Why are you so pissed she was out with someone?" I swallow down the lump forming in my throat and fight back the burning sensation in my stomach. It feels as if my stomach is eating itself. My hands get clammy when the answer comes to me, shocking me. "You can't ever go there," I tell myself. "For everyone's sake."

I close the notebook without writing anything else in it. I slam it shut just like I do the thoughts that are coming into my head. I lock it away behind my mind. When I hear the front door open and slam, I get up and walk downstairs and see her crouched in front of Mac. She looks up at me. Her hair is tied on top of her head in a bun and her blue eyes are shining bright. The smile on her face makes me stop moving. My whole body stops, and a shiver goes up my spine. "Hi," she says with Mac licking her face. "I see someone missed me." She hugs her around the neck, and I want to tell her that she's not the only one who missed her, but instead, all I can do is stand here on the stairs and look at her. "Did you eat?" she asks, standing up and I see that she's wearing a pair of white jeans that mold to her and a blush-pink silk tank top tucked in the front.

My head screams at me to get the fuck out of here, but my mouth moves before I can do anything about it. "No," I answer, walking down the stairs and standing next to her. My arm goes around her shoulder like it's done many times before, except this time it feels different. "What do you feel like eating?" Knowing that every single time we go through this, it's a good forty minutes before we actually decide. I sit on the couch while she sits beside me and turns on the television. I open the app and start naming restaurants. "Pizza."

"No." She shakes her head. "There aren't any good places around here."

"Burgers?" I ask, scrolling down.

"I would kill for a diner burger right now," she groans, putting her head back.

"Then let's go." I get up, and she just looks up at me. "We can go and eat and be back faster than if we order and it takes over an hour."

"Fine," she huffs out. I hold out my hand for her, and she slips her hand in mine, sending jolts up my arm. She looks down at our intertwined hands, but neither of us says anything.

She gets on her phone the minute we get in the car, and it gives my head time to go through everything, which isn't a good idea right now.

Going through the motions of everything, it feels like it always does, but inside, inside something tells me that it won't be.

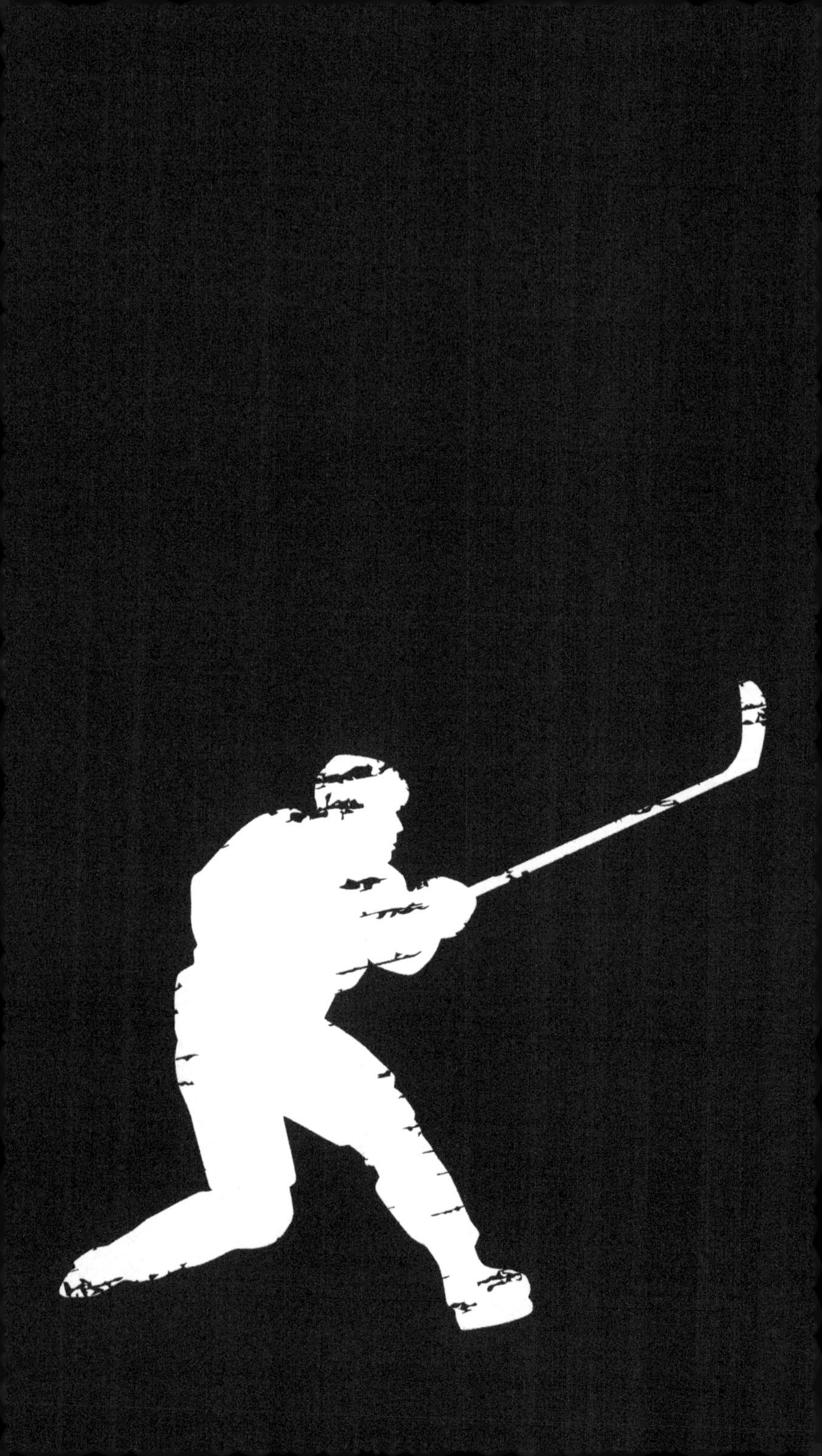

TEN

Alex

THE ALARM STARTS to ring, and I slip my hand out of the bed. I feel the bed move and look over to see Mac lying on her side, wagging her tail. "Morning," I mumble to her, closing my eyes again and sinking into the bed.

"Good morning," Dylan says, and I open my eyes and look at the bedroom door. He stands there with two cups of coffee in his hand. Last night when I got home, he looked like he had the weight of the world on his shoulders. He looked so defeated that I pushed everything to the back of my mind and acted just like old times. I mean, just like old times, except I got to bed and wondered what it would be like to go to bed with him. Naked. "I made you coffee."

"I see that." He walks over to my side of the bed, handing me one of the coffee cups. He walks around the side of the bed and sits on the empty side, on top of the

"So what are we doing today?" He sits with his back to the headboard and takes a sip of his coffee. Mac doesn't move as she lies between us, as our barrier.

"What do you mean?" I ask him, laughing. "I have work." I turn to look at the clock, seeing it's just after seven thirty.

"Play hooky with me." He looks over at me, and I take a sip of the coffee, sitting up. Making sure the duvet doesn't slip down and he sees my boobs.

"I'm not playing hooky with you." I shake my head.

"Come on, you've been acting weird since I got here," he says, and I look over at him. He sits there in his gym shorts and no shirt. His abs are on point and his arms flex when he lifts the cup to his mouth. His hair looks like he's been running his hands through it. It also looks like someone was pulling his hair while he slammed into her. I swallow and look away from him, afraid that he'll see in my head.

"I have not been weird. I've been busy." I don't dare look back over at him. "I have all this work to do before the camp starts. We get back home the day before camp."

"I know that you have everything already done and scheduled." He laughs, and I can't help look over at him because everything is done at this point, and I'm checking and rechecking and calling everyone to recheck.

"There is still stuff that I need to do," I say, huffing out and taking a sip of my coffee.

"Is there?" he asks. I side-eye him with a glare, and he laughs. "Good, so it's settled. We are going to go out today and do something fun." He gets up, and my eyes go straight to the elastic of his shorts that hang low. My eyes lift right away like I've been caught with my hand in the cookie jar, except the cookie jar is his shorts, and my hand is going to grip his dick and not a cookie. "Be ready in an hour."

"An hour?" I repeat, looking at the clock. "You want to go somewhere at eight thirty?"

"Yeah, we can have breakfast before," he confirms. "I'm going to go make plans." He smiles so big there is no way I can say no to him. When have I ever said fucking no to him? Never, that is when.

"You think you could do me a solid." I look at Mac as she wags her tail stretching. "And bite my foot off?" She barks at me. "Fine, whatever." I throw the covers off me and get out of bed. I put the coffee cup on the side table when he comes back into the room, and I shriek, turning, and he yells.

"Oh my God!" he yelps, and then I turn to see him standing, hiding his eyes but then looking. "Jesus, what the fuck? I thought you were naked."

I put my hand on my tits to cover them. "I am naked," I retort, and his eyes roam up and down. Okay, fine, I'm not naked, but I suddenly feel naked when I'm around him.

"No, you aren't. You're wearing your pjs." He points at me, and I'm pretty sure that I've worn this in front of him a dozen times, but ever since I looked at him differently, things have changed. "You scared the shit out of me." He laughs. "Let's go, Mac, and get you something to eat." He turns and walks out of the room, and Mac follows him.

I grab my phone and rush into the bathroom, locking the door behind me. I lean against the closed door and pull up Julia's name and call her. She answers after three rings. "Hello," she mumbles.

"Are you sleeping?" I ask her, shocked. "It's like seven thirty." Pushing away, I go to start the shower.

"Why the hell are you calling someone, or better yet, anyone before eight?" she asks me grumpily, and I hear her covers rustle in the background.

"I need a huge favor," I say, my voice going low as I look at the door, wondering if he is in the room eavesdropping.

"Why are you whispering?" she asks me.

"Because I don't want Dylan to hear me," I reply, and she laughs. "Anyway, I need you to do me a favor and call me in about twenty minutes and tell me that you are in the hospital."

"What?" she shrieks. "Are you insane?" I roll my eyes. "Don't answer that. I know the answer to that one."

"Dylan wants to go out today," I share, looking toward the door. "And I'm trying to get out of it."

She laughs. "And you want me to tell you I'm in the hospital?" Her laughter gets louder. "You know that he talks to Jillian and Michael, right?" I groan.

"Well, then call and tell me that you need me." I look up at the ceiling. "Like a support phone call or something like that." I clench my teeth.

"Like a support dog?" she asks me, still laughing.

"Julia," I hiss, closing my eyes. "You're smart. Think

of something." My voice goes low. "You have to think of something. I can't go out with him."

"Why not?" she asks, and I can hear a cupboard slamming on her side, so I know she's out of bed and making coffee. "It would be the perfect time to tell him how you feel."

"Oh, yeah, perfect time. Hey, can you pass the salt, and by the way, I'm in love with you. Are you going to finish your fries?" I put my hand to my stomach, feeling the burning as soon as I say the words out loud again. "I think I'm going to throw up."

"Alex," she says softly. "This is Dylan. It's you and Dylan."

"What the hell does that mean?" I shriek.

"It means that he knows you, and you know him." I roll my eyes.

"I doubt he knows I checked out his dick this morning."

She laughs. "That's my girl," she says. "You can either bite the bullet and tell him how you feel or wake him up sucking his dick."

"Okay, well, thank you for your advice," I say sarcastically. "You've been really helpful."

"There is no right or wrong answer, Alex." Her voice stays soft. "When it's going to be the right time to tell him, you'll know. But running away from it isn't going to make it go away."

"Yes, it will," I tell her. "I can ignore it until it's gone."

She laughs. "Let me know how that works out for you. Text me later."

I hang up the phone and step into the shower, trying to come up with excuses as to why I can't go with him. When I get out of the shower, I call Wilson, who answers right away. "Hi, it's me."

"Good morning," he huffs out. "What's up?"

"Dylan wants me to play hooky," I say. "Unless you think I should go into work and make sure that …"

I don't even finish the sentence. "You deserve a day off. Have fun," he says, and I want to stomp my foot.

"Call me if you need me." I hang up the phone, looking at myself in the mirror. "It'll be fine," I tell my reflection. "It's just another day." I fix my hair, turning to slip on my panties and a bra, then stepping into the walk-in closet to grab my favorite pair of jean shorts. They are frayed at the front but hug my hips perfectly and are loose around my legs. I grab a white tank top that comes just above my waistline, showing some skin. Turning to look at myself in the mirror, I grab my white sneakers and sit on the floor, putting them on.

When I have my shoes on, I walk downstairs and see Mac lying on her bed. "You sure you don't want to bite my leg?" She just looks at me.

"Okay," Dylan says, coming down the stairs, and I look over at him. He's wearing shorts and a black T-shirt. A baseball hat is on his head, and you can see his blue eyes. "Ready?" he asks, and I have to swallow down the nerves that have risen from my stomach to my throat.

I nod my head and look back over at Mac. "Last chance," I whisper to her, and she just lays her head down. "How long are we going to be out?" I ask him.

"No idea," he answers, grabbing the keys on the counter. "She'll be fine." He looks over at Mac.

After breakfast, we get back in the car. "So where are we off to?" I ask, and he looks over at me, smiling.

"It's a surprise," he says excitedly, and I can't help but smile at him.

When we get to the place, he looks over at me. "The aquarium." I clap my hands. "I love these things."

"I know," he replies, getting out of the car and meeting me on my side.

He puts his hand around my shoulder. "And the best is I got us a private tour." I look at him, shocked.

"What?" I ask, looking around and seeing it empty.

"We have the place for two hours with a private tour." I don't have time to say anything because the door opens, and the man comes out.

"Welcome, Mr. Stone," he says, holding the door open for us. Dylan puts his hand at the base of my back, the heat from his hand seeping into me. I can't help the smile that fills my face as we walk through the aquarium. When we stop at the shark tank, the guide goes on and on about all the different sharks as I look up, seeing them swim over us.

"We should go swimming with sharks," I announce. Looking around, I go to the side of the tank and put my hand there.

"I swim with sharks every time I lace up my skates," he jokes, and I just shake my head.

"I'm going to look into swimming with sharks when we get to Hawaii." I look over at him as he looks at the sharks swimming on top of us.

"I'm going to pass," he says, and I laugh at him. "Did you not see that movie?"

"It's a movie," I joke with him, pushing his shoulder.

"Movie or not, the sharks actually eat you," he says.

"They don't eat you," I say. "They bite the limb, but then let it go. They don't like the taste of humans."

"Good to know." He shakes his head. "Also, how the fuck do you know that?"

"I watch Shark Week," I joke with him as we walk out of the shark room to the upper ground.

"Right over here," the guide says, "is stingray bay." He smiles as he leads us over to them. "If you want, you can lean in and touch them."

"Um, I'm good," I state, standing at the edge of the glass window looking down into the water. It reaches my thigh, and it's only a couple of feet deep.

"You will swim with sharks," Dylan says from beside me, "but you won't touch a stingray?"

"Those can kill you. Did you not read about the Crocodile Hunter?" He just shakes his head and laughs. He walks up beside me and sticks his hand in the water as a stingray swims by him, and he rubs the top of it. He laughs, looking at me.

"Come on, you can do it," he encourages, and I look down and try to put my hand in but I snatch it back as soon as I see a stingray come close to me.

"I can't do it," I say, holding my wrist with my hand.

"Sure you can," he says and steps behind me, placing his hands on my hips. My whole body shivers under his touch. His thumb is on my bare skin, and my whole body breaks out with goose bumps. I'm suddenly petrified that he'll see and know. He'll know what I feel for him.

"It's cold." I turn my eyes from him, afraid my secret will be out.

"You can do it," he urges, grabbing my hand with his, leaving his other hand on my hip. His fingers go through mine. "Let's do it together," he says, and I can't even focus on anything because my heart is beating so fucking fast in my chest, I'm afraid he is going to hear it. My mouth is so dry, and it's a good thing he is holding my hand because it's trembling like a leaf. "Don't be scared, Alex," he says softly in my ear. "I won't let anything happen to you."

With his hand on mine, he guides us to the water. The coldness of the water makes me pull back a bit, but his chest to my back fills me with heat. The flutter in my stomach starts as I look at our hands in the water. The stingray swims by us, just missing the tips of our fingers, but another one comes over now. My hand is entwined with his as the stingray swims right under my palm. I laugh as another comes. This time, he lets go of my hand a bit. "See," he says, his face right near my face. I turn so close to him, and all I can do is smile and look into his eyes. "Told you I would protect you," he says softly, not moving from beside me, and if I move just a touch into him, my lips could be on his. If I thought my heart was beating hard before, it's nothing like it is now. My whole body is on fire, and my head is screaming at me to lean in and kiss him. Everything in me is screaming, but it's the guilt that comes crashing into me like a bucket of ice water thrown on you.

I quickly blink away the tears and turn back, shaking his hand off mine by taking mine out of the water. "You okay?" he asks me as I step out of his touch and toward the side, where I grab a bunch of paper towels.

"Yeah." I push away everything that I'm feeling, looking up at him. His eyes look into mine as the guilt of loving him hits me, knowing I'm never going to be able to tell him. "That was cool," I say, turning to hand him the towels I wiped my hand on. "Thank you for helping me face my fear." The smile on my face is so forced it hurts my cheeks. "What's next, the lion's den?"

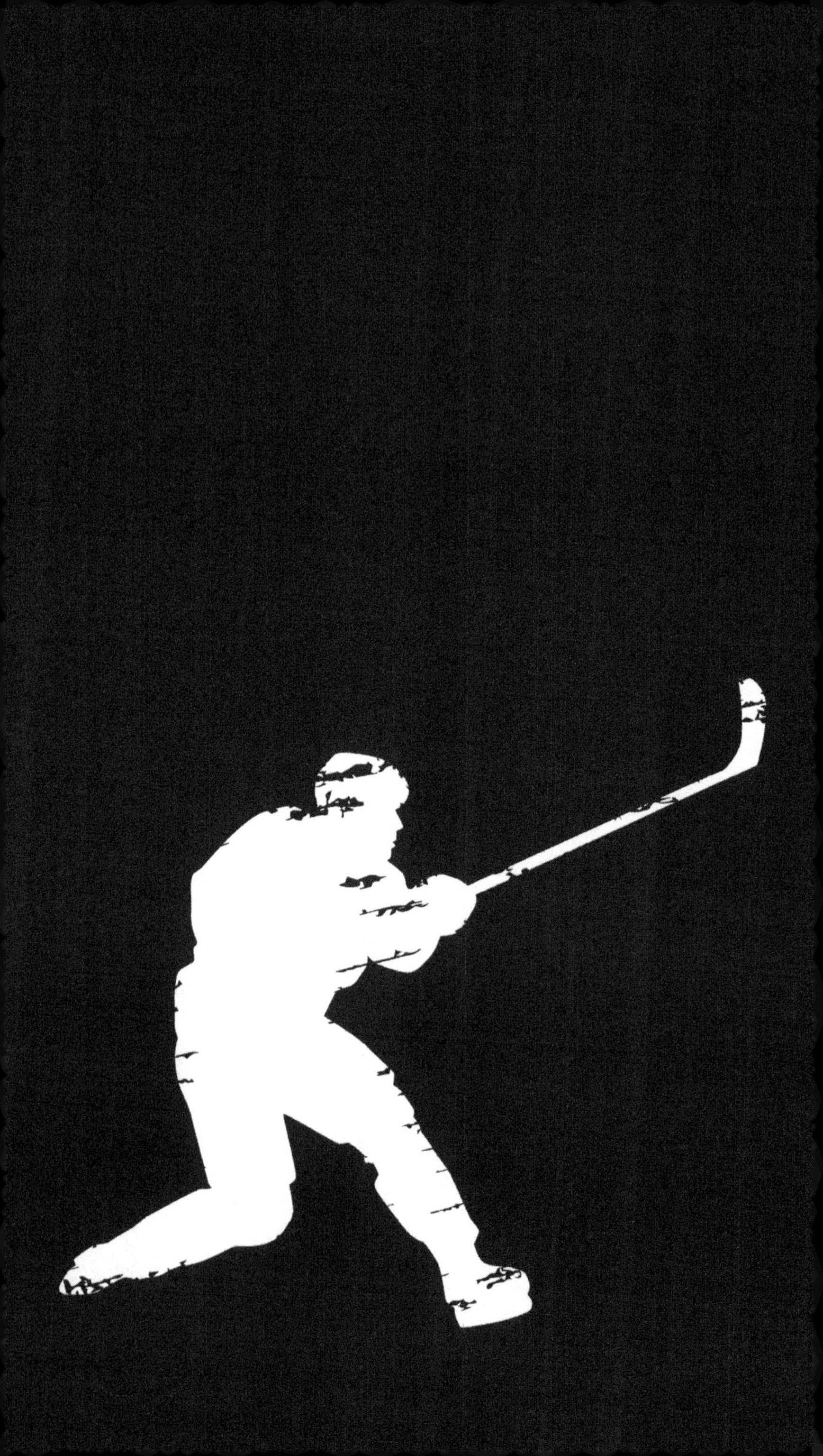

ELEVEN

Dylan

"Dylan!" I hear her yelling my name from downstairs when the doorbell rings. "She's here."

I grab my suitcase and head out of the room, stopping when I see three suitcases in front of Alex's door. I grab one and walk down the steps as she stands there holding Mac's leash. "Here is the leash." She hands it to the woman, and Mac just sits by Alex's side. "She likes lots of love and kisses," Alex says, getting down in front of Mac. "We will be back in two weeks, and I'm going to bring you so many surprises."

"What are you going to bring her back from Hawaii?" I look down at Alex, and my chest contracts. Yesterday, when we were at the aquarium, I was so close to kissing her, and then she jumped away from me, probably with disgust.

"I already bought her stuff, but I'm going to give it to her when I come back." She stands up, and I see her wearing a white short-sleeved one-piece cotton dress. "Stop being bitchy." She turns back and hands the girl the leash. "You can send me the login and password, and we will check in as soon as we land."

Mac looks back at us, walking to the van and getting in. Alex stands there waving her hand at her. "She's going to be fine. She has a better time there than she has with us."

"Speak for yourself," she huffs out. "I'm a fucking fireball to be around." She crosses her arms, pushing her tits up, and I have to turn around before I moan. "The car is going to be here in ten minutes."

She walks up the stairs, and I see her trying to bring her suitcase down. I run up the stairs two at a time. "Would you move out of the way before you break your head, and then I get my ass kicked by your father and my father for not doing it for you?"

She looks at me, and I look back at her as she glares. "You're so fucking crabby," she huffs out and walks back down the steps, her flip-flops making a racket as she gets down. "You need to eat a piece of bread or something." She walks to the kitchen.

"Bread is not going to help me with this," I mumble to myself and bring the bags down. I don't even know what is going to help me with all these feelings. The only thing I do know is that I need to get over these crazy feelings I have for her. Feelings that came out of the blue, or did they? "Why the hell do you have three bags for two weeks?" I shout toward the kitchen, and she comes back with a hat on her head and her carry-on bag in one hand.

"Dylan." She says my name, and I have this sudden urge to ask her to moan my name. I close my eyes, trying to get the sound out of my head. "This is not the first vacation we are going on. You ask me this every single year."

"And every single year, you wear only half the shit you bring," I point out, and she rolls her eyes, walking to the door when her phone beeps. "I bet you one hundred dollars you won't wear half the stuff."

"Now I'm going to wear everything twice just to spite you." She puts on her sunglasses. "I'm going to change three times a day."

I shake my head, knowing that even if I argue with her, she's going to win because I always let her win. Why? Because the last time I won a fight with her, she tormented me for six months. She would leave doll heads all around the house for me to find, and she knows how I hate them. Grabbing my glasses, I put them on as I walk out, rolling out the suitcases for the driver to load in the car.

It takes us five minutes to get into the car. She sits on her side, and all I can smell is her perfume. I put my head back, closing my eyes, and when the car stops, I open my eyes and can see the commotion already. The big charter plane is parked, and there are fifteen porters running with luggage carts and trying to load up the bags. "Here we go," I say, opening the door, and I look around. The black truck pulls up next to us, and when the back door opens, I can't help the smile that fills my face. "Dad." I walk to him, and he takes me in his arms. Almost like when I was younger, except I'm taller than him, and I wrap my arms around his neck.

"Hey," he says, slapping my arm and then letting me go so he can squeeze my neck. "You look like shit," he says.

"Oh, look, it smiles," Alex chides, coming next to me and pushing me to the side. "He's been a grouch since he got up this morning." She smiles at my father and reaches up to kiss his cheek. "Thankfully, I don't have to sit with him on the plane." She turns and walks over to my mother, who she hugs and laughs with, kissing her on her cheek. My brother, Christopher, comes out of the back seat with his earbuds on.

"Hey, squirt," I say to him, hugging him and kissing his head.

"I'm going to be seventeen," he reminds me, pushing my shoulder. He goes over and bends to kiss Alex, who looks over at me, shocked at how tall he got.

"Do you remember what you did at seventeen?" my father says to me, and I shake my head and laugh because it was probably stupid, and I must have paid dearly for it.

Michael gets there next and comes out of the truck with Jamieson, who claps his hands when he sees me. I'm about to grab him when Alex scoops him up, and he just smiles at her. Julia comes out with Bianca, while Jillian gets out and hands Bailey to Michael.

Another truck gets there, and the back door opens, and I stand here shocked. Chase gets out, but he's not the Chase we saw last year. This one has been hitting the gym and not the hairdresser. "Who the fuck invited

Thor?" Michael shouts. Chase throws his head back and laughs, his man bun on the top of his head and the beard trimmed. "Where is your hammer?"

"I don't know where he keeps his hammer," Julia says from beside us now. "But I volunteer as tribune."

Alex rolls her lips. "It's tribute," she says, trying not to laugh.

"He can call me whatever he wants to call me," Julia gushes, and Michael pretends to vomit.

"If I wake up and hear sex noises and it's Chase," he says, and she just shakes her head.

"I know how to keep quiet," she reassures him, kissing Bianca's head. "Is Auntie going to get her rocks off?"

"Why have you never invited him over?" She looks over at Julia.

"He's been doing Doctors Without Borders," Alex says. "Apparently, it's right next to a gym."

"Nah," Michael butts in. "His ex-girlfriend said he was too skinny and wasn't attracted to him."

"Oh my God," Julia says. "He got sexy to tell her to fuck off." She puts her hands to her chest. "I think I'm in love."

"Let's get on the plane," Jillian suggests, pulling Julia with her.

I look around and see everyone slowly arriving. Hugs and kisses are passed around, and I stand next to Alex and Michael. "Why does it feel like we aren't the cool ones anymore?" Michael asks, and I just look at him.

"Dude, you fell asleep yesterday at six fifteen." I laugh, and Alex just smiles.

"I think it's time to pass the torch," she says. "Time for the other generation to get drunk on the beach." I put my arm around her shoulder.

"And vomit by the house," Michael adds, putting his hand by his mouth.

"Do you remember, one year …" I start laughing as I think about it. "I ended up in your house, and you ended up in mine. I got up and threw up in your father's shoes."

"Oh my God," Alex says. "And he put his foot in there. I thought he was going to throw up everywhere." The three of us can't stop laughing.

"Those were good fucking times," I say. "But sadly …" I look at the young kids all excited about going on vacation. "We are the old ones."

"Speak for yourself," Alex retorts, walking away from us. "I'm younger than you two by two years." She walks to the steel steps pushed against the plane.

"I'll remind you of that when you fall asleep on the beach!" Michael yells after her, and she just flips him the bird.

"Why does she always get to have the last word?" Michael asks me.

"Because we let her," I say, watching her walk up and then smile at Uncle Matthew as she kisses his cheek.

"Let's get on the plane before they leave us here," Michael says, and I smile at him as we walk in.

We walk onto the plane, and the seats are practically all taken. I walk down the aisle, my eyes automatically searching for Alex, and the seat next to her is empty. "Why are you sitting here?" she asks me as I sit next to her. "Why don't you keep walking?"

I laugh. "You would be lost without me," I tease, and she rolls her eyes looking outside.

"But would I?" she asks, and for one second, I forget that there are so many people around us.

"Well, I know that I would be lost without you," I admit to her, and she just looks at me. Her eyes searching mine, not sure what to say, and I want to kick myself for saying too much.

"Mimosa?" the attendant asks us, and I grab a glass for Alex and another one for me.

"Thank you," she says to me, and the plane starts moving. "How long is this flight again?"

"Eight hours," I answer as one of the babies starts crying. "Let the good time roll." I hold up my glass to her.

She clicks her glass to mine, smiling, making me just stare at her. "To an unforgettable vacation."

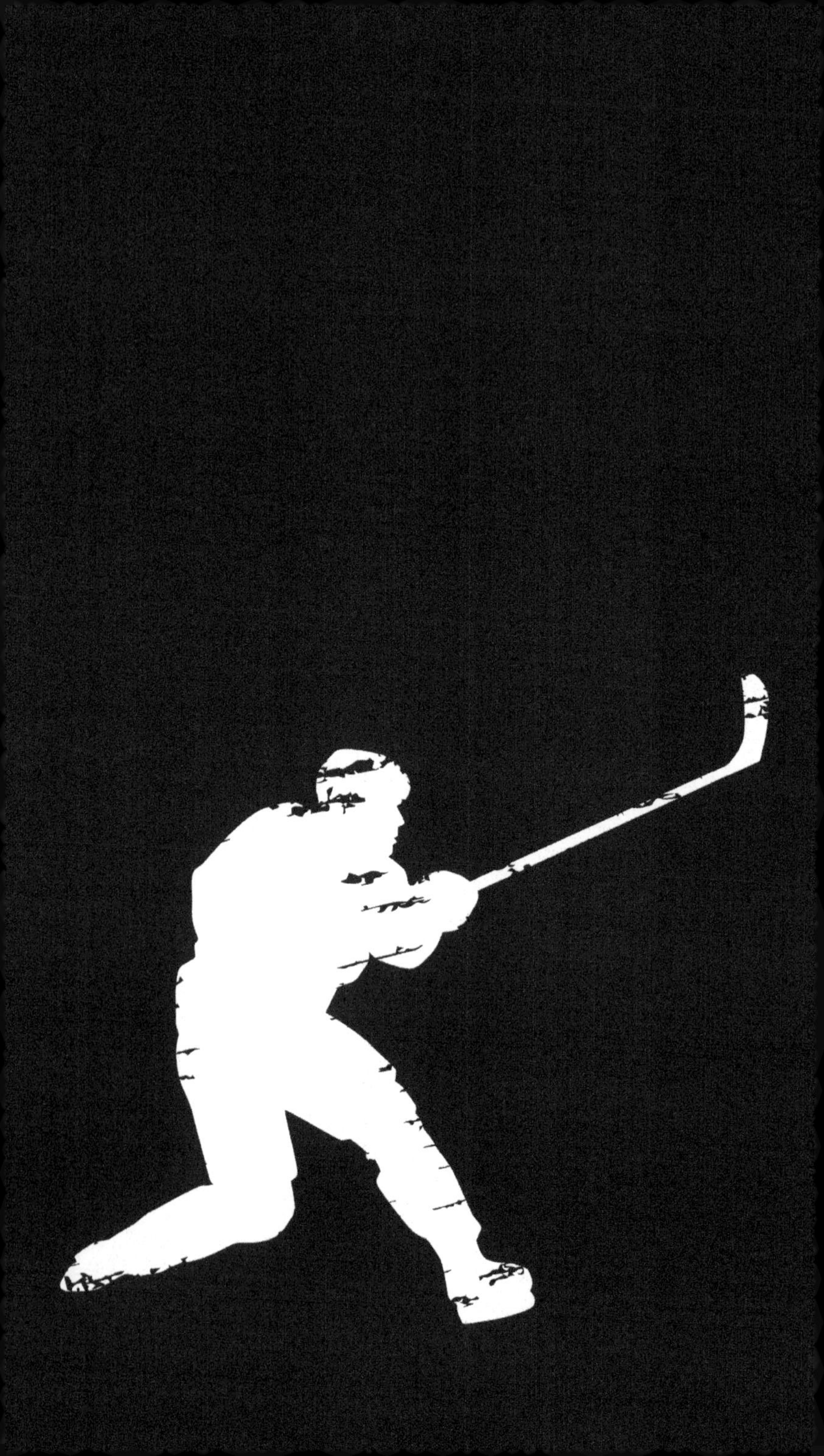

TWELVE

Dylan

THE PLANE RIDE is one of the longest of my life. Everyone is walking around, switching places as we catch up with each other. Even though the plane is huge and there are always people walking, my eyes always seem to find her. "You look like you have the weight of the world on your shoulders," my father says from beside me, and my eyes fly to his. With everyone around, I have to make sure that no one catches me. I look at him for a second to see if he caught me watching her again for the tenth time in five minutes.

"Just trying to figure everything out," I reply, grabbing my bottle of water and drinking it. The captain comes on to tell us that we are landing in twenty minutes. To say it's pandemonium is an understatement. People are rushing to get back to their seats, and when I get back to mine, I buckle my seat belt, then I look over and see that her eyes are shining. "You're drunk."

"I am not drunk," she defends and follows that with a giggle. "Leave me alone. I'm on vacation."

I look out the window and hear Julia from behind. "So do you have a hammer?" Chase's laughter fills the plane as soon as the wheels touch down. The whole plane erupts in applause, and I'm not sure if it's because we landed, or the fact we can get the fuck off the plane.

Standing, I grab Alex's and my bags as she puts the hat on her head. She gets up and then sits down again, laughing, and I groan. "It's fine. My leg was asleep."

"Sure," I say, waiting for her to walk in front of me before getting off the plane. She holds Emma's hand, looking down at her, smiling. The sun shines high in the sky as six people hold up the letters to spell Hawaii. Another group of people dance on the side, two people stand at the bottom of the stairs with leis.

"Are you ready to play in the sand?" she asks Emma, who just nods her head as we creep down the stairs at a snail's pace.

"No one would believe me," Julia says from behind me. "If I said yeah, I took a private charter, and the whole island came out to greet me." I can't help but laugh because she is not wrong. "And with a tour bus, no less."

"Two tour buses," Jillian corrects her, pointing at another bus coming onto the tarmac.

"One must be just for the luggage," Cooper says in back of Julia. "I told you that you overpacked." He looks at Erika.

"Remember one year when someone asked Vivi for hand cream, and she handed them her KY?" Erika says, making us all laugh.

"That was me," Franny confirms.

"I don't know why you're laughing. You never gave it back to me," Vivi scolds, standing behind her as we slowly walk down the steps.

Alex takes off her hat and bends her head forward when the woman places the lei around her neck. "Look, I got lei'd." She turns back to us, thinking it's the funniest thing she said.

"I got lei'd too," Emma announces, making Cooper groan.

"I wonder if I can get double lei'd," Julia says.

"I want to be double lei'd," Emma echoes, and everyone except Cooper laughs at that.

"Can you move along?" Cooper prods.

"Yeah," Julia says. "Let other people get lei'd."

I don't even know how long it takes us to load the bus, but when we finally get to the resort, all of us are ready to see other people. There are more people waiting for us all with clipboards and a slew of golf carts.

The massive open hotel lobby behind him is filled with cream-colored marble with a front desk. I don't pay attention to the guy as he explains the private resort we are at. They hand each of us a map of the resort, and I look down. "We will meet in thirty minutes for our first meal."

There are twenty-five private villas scattered around the pool and the beachfront. The center of the resort has the lobby as well as the place where the main dining area is. When they call Alex's and my name, I look up, heading to the golf cart with the guy. We walk into the villa, the cold air hitting us right away. "Go choose the room you want," I tell Alex, who just stares out the floor-to-ceiling window with a view of the dark blue waters. The living room is in the middle and with one bedroom on each side, with their own private bathrooms.

Dinner is a mess with the kids cranky from the time difference, and when I collapse into bed, I don't even care that it's only seven o'clock local time.

We spend the first four days out half by the pool and the other half by the beach. Alex spends less and less time with me, and I have to wonder if she is doing it because she felt me wanting to kiss her or she's just disgusted by me. It's not to say we don't talk, but it's not the same. She is out of the villa before I wake up, and at night after dinner, she sits with Vivi and Julia most of the night. My head is all over the place as I try to make the decision on what to do.

I sit down with my grandfather on the fifth day, and all he does is listen to me. Finally, after I pour my whole heart out to him, he looks at me. "You are going to regret the decision no matter what you decide." If anyone knows what hockey is about, it's him. He holds most of the records out there, and I say most of them because I've beaten a couple of them. "You will forever have Montreal in your heart and always look back to that time. If you go to another team and you kill it, you'll regret not doing it in Montreal. If you go to a team and you suck, and the team sucks, you are going to regret leaving."

"That doesn't help me," I say, laughing.

"Time for you to do what you want to do," he says. Leaning back in the chair, he looks out at the ocean water where Chase is standing on one of those paddleboard things. "Where does your heart want you to go?" I look over at Alex, who is getting up and walking to the ocean water now, as she laughs about something that Chase is telling her.

Chase comes out of the water, pushing his hair back. "Hey, Fabio," my uncle Matthew calls him. "Did you put on sunscreen?"

Chase just laughs at him. "Nah." He stands there with his hands on his hips. "I sprayed myself down with oil, so I glisten." We can't help but laugh. He comes up to the lounge bed where I'm lying, trying to stay out of the heat. "Are we hitting the bar tonight?"

"Yes, please," Vivi says, lifting her head from the other lounge bed beside me. "There is a local bar five minutes over."

"How do you know?" Franny says as she laughs beside Wilson, who makes sure his arm is over her, so you know she's taken.

"We went out last night," Vivi says, and I look over at her. "Julia, Chase, and I hit it up."

"Great," Alex says. "Let's do that tonight."

We walk back into the villa after dinner as she walks to her bedroom. "We leave in ten minutes," I say, and she ignores me and comes out two minutes later, changed out of shorts and a top. This time, she is wearing a long black skirt that goes to the floor, but when she walks, her legs come out of the two slits in the front. Her legs are long and tanned from all the time in the sun. The black tube top leaves her shoulders and arms bare and falling just a bit above the skirt, showing her toned stomach. My mouth hangs to the floor, and I don't have a chance to say anything when the front door is opened, and Chase comes in wearing white pants and a pink shirt.

"Forget Thor," I say. "You look like Aquaman." I get up and look down at my shorts and T-shirt, not even caring what I look like. It's not like I'm going to the bar to get anyone. My head isn't even focused on anyone but Alex.

We walk out and take a couple of golf carts over to the bar. "Oh, it's a tiki bar," Alex says, getting out of the cart, her long legs making my cock semi-hard. I really need to get the fuck out of here. This was not a good idea. This is getting so out of control.

Walking into the bar, I look around in the dim lighting. The hostess smiles at us as we walk in, and we all decide we want to be by the bar. Tables are all around this little dance floor. The bar is at the back with ten empty stools in front of it. Most of the tables are taken as people laugh and eat. A little stage in the corner has a guy singing on it. Franny, Vivi, Julia, Jillian, and Alex all hit the bar first with Wilson, Chase, Michael, and myself behind them.

"My name is Scarlett. I'll be your waitress," she says, standing next to me, and I look at her confused as she bats her eyes at me. "If you need anything, let me know." She walks away, and I look over at Chase, who slaps my shoulder.

"She wants your dick," Chase says, and I look at

Michael and Wilson, who just smirk and walk over to the bar. Both of them are sitting on the stools on the outside of the girls to box them in.

I hear Alex laughing and look over to see the bartender talking to her. His black shirt molds to his body, and he winks at her. My stomach forms knots as I walk over and pull out the stool in the middle of the girls. "What are we having?" I say, looking at the bartender.

"What is your specialty?" Alex asks him.

"I'll have a beer," I say to him, and he nods at me and goes to grab me a cold one. I have to get out of the way when the girls descend on the bartender to discuss shots. I move to the side of the bar, leaning on it next to Michael, who is still sitting down. Chase comes over and sits on the stool on the other side of me.

"Would you like something to eat?" Scarlett comes up to me, leaning a little too close to me.

"I'm good," I say, and she walks away.

"I'm good also," Chase says to the spot where Scarlett just left, making me laugh. Michael laughs, taking a pull from his own beer in his hand. "You shit on me about my looks and shit, but what about Tom Cruise over there?" He motions to the bartender, making us both laugh.

The bartender comes back with some drinks for the girls and then smiles at Alex a bit longer than he should be. My blood boils, and I'm so fucking irritated by this whole fucking place.

"How are we doing?" Scarlett says, and I don't even look at her. Instead, I'm looking at Alex, who takes a sip of the drink, and her eyes open, meaning she loves it.

She takes another drink of it, and Julia moves over so I'm next to Alex now. "What do you have?" I ask. She holds out the drink for me, and I shake my head. "Try it."

"It's probably too fruity," I reply, and she just smiles at me as she takes another sip of it.

"It's so good," she says, taking another sip. "Your loss."

The bartender comes back over to us. "Can I get you something else?"

"We have our drinks," I say. "We'll let you know." He nods at us and walks to Wilson, who sits with Franny. "Why is he always in front of us? There are other people here."

"He's doing his job," Vivi states. "Let him do it." I roll my eyes now.

I put my beer down on the bar and look around to see if I see the bathrooms. I walk over to the right side, seeing a door for the kitchen as it swings open, and someone comes out. I walk to the other side, going down the dim hallway, the walls look like they're made of straw. Four big colored lantern balls hang down, giving just a touch of lights as I see three doors.

"Can I help you?" I hear Scarlett from behind me.

"Just looking for the bathroom." I turn to look at her, and she's standing in front of me, just a touch too close.

"It's right over there." She steps in even closer, her chest almost touching as she leans even more into me to point at the door over my shoulder. My hand goes to her hip to make sure she doesn't get any closer to me, and I don't have a chance to say anything else because I look over her shoulder and see Alex just looking at us.

Her eyes take in the waitress stuck to me and then to my hand on her hip. "Excuse me," she mumbles, walking past me.

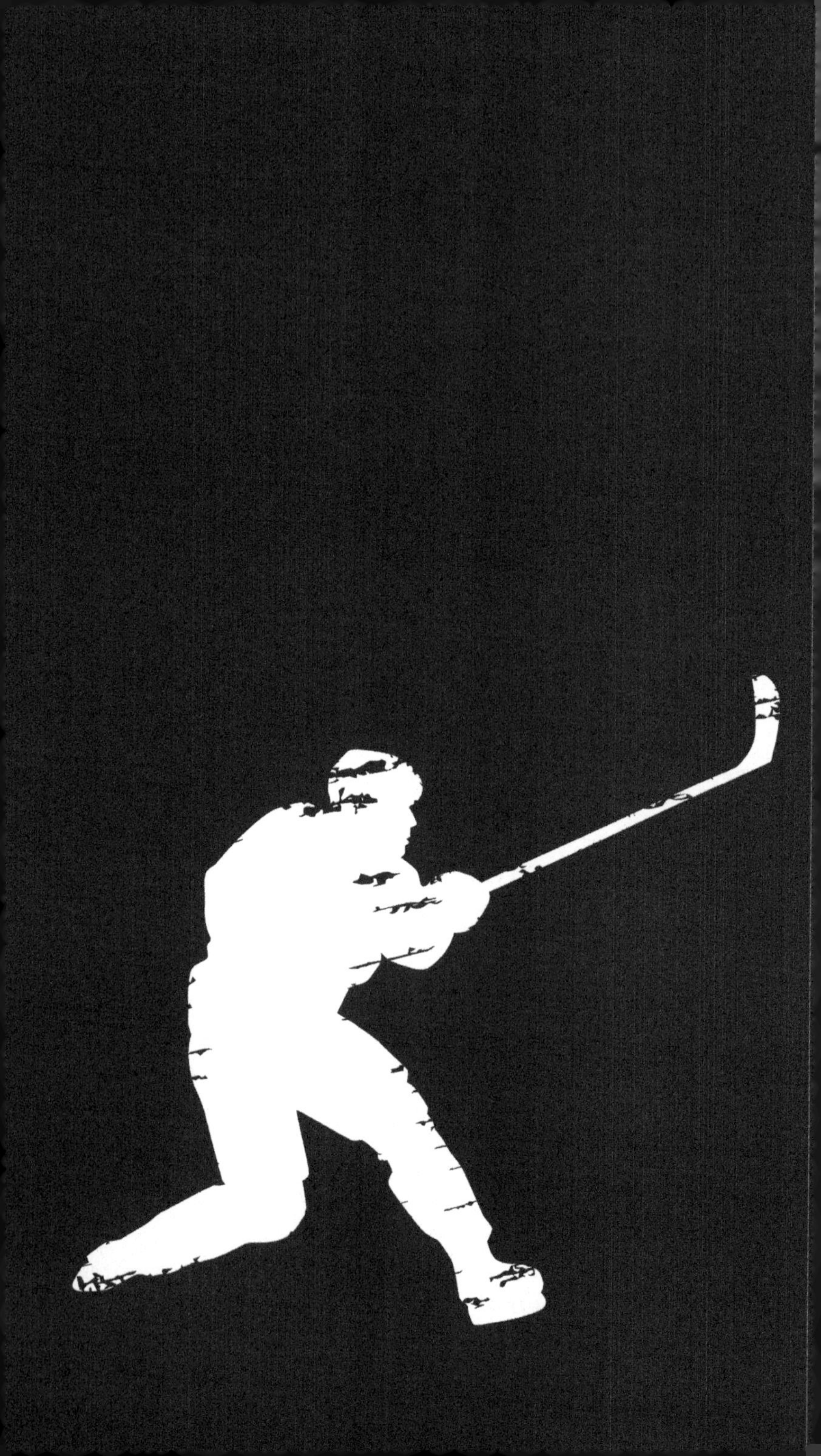

THIRTEEN

Alex

"Excuse me," I say, trying to make sure my voice doesn't tremble when I walk past them to the bathroom. When I pushed away from the bar to ask where the bathroom was, my whole body was hot with the alcohol flowing through it, but then I came face-to-face with Dylan and the waitress, and it's as if ice was poured into my veins.

I walk into the bathroom and go to the sink, turning on the cold water. Placing my hand under the water and then dabbing my cheeks to fight off the stinging of the tears. For the past four days, I've been fighting with myself to get closer to him. Fighting with myself every single fucking night not to ask him to sit with me and watch the water. Fighting with myself every single night not to ask him to take a walk with me. Missing him so much, but not trusting myself. I close my eyes and take a huge deep inhale before walking back out of there, and I don't know why I'm expecting to see them having sex against the wall. I stop moving when I see Dylan there standing with his back against the wall. "Hey," I say, trying to sound all peppy and cheerful, pushing the hurt down into my stomach. "What are you doing?"

"I was waiting for you," he says, standing up and coming over to me. "Listen, what you saw."

"Oh, don't worry about that." I swallow down the lump in my throat. "I'm going to stay with Julia tonight." I smile as the tears sting at my eyes. "So you can use the villa." I wink at him, pushing away the tears and walking away from him. I step back into the room, seeing the dance floor starting to be used. "What are we drinking?" I ask when I lean on the bar, and the bartender looks at me and smiles. *Why can't I like this guy?*

"Can you do a cum in my panties drink?" Julia asks, looking at the bartender, and Chase suddenly chokes on his drink. Michael groans as Jillian just slowly laughs.

"I definitely can make that," he replies, winking at me and turning to walk away.

"You are not drinking that," Wilson says to Franny, who just laughs.

"Don't worry, dear, the only one who makes me come in my panties is you." She wraps her hand around his neck.

"Dude," Chase says. "That's my sister." He shakes his head in disgust while we all laugh. I look over and see Dylan coming back to the bar.

"I'm going to take your sister," Wilson says, getting up. "And make sure that her panties are in good order."

He grabs Franny's hand.

"I'm not wearing panties," she announces. "Let's go have sex on the beach."

"It's not as fun as you think it is," Chase warns, and Julia just looks over at him. "You get sand in places."

"What did I miss?" Dylan asks, his eyes going to me but I turn away and look back at the dance floor.

"Not much," Michael says to Dylan. "Julia is getting cum in her panties, and Franny and Wilson are going to bang on the beach. Just normal everyday stuff that families do on vacation."

I can't help but laugh, and so does everyone else. The bartender comes back with the shots, and I don't even know what it is, but I take it. "That was good," I say, putting the shot glass down and licking the whipped cream off my finger.

"Well, since you did that shot," Chase says. "You have to go with wet pussy shot."

My mouth opens at the same time Julia puts her hand to her heart. "Be still my heart."

"I think you mean be still your vagina." I push her shoulder.

"So who is getting a wet pussy?" the bartender says, and Julia and I raise our hands.

"I'll have a couple, and then how about sex on the beach?" I wink at him.

"Name the time and place." He winks back at me, and my tongue is suddenly stuck in my mouth.

"Yeah, I'd like to see you try," Dylan says, leaning onto the bar as the bartender walks away from us to go make the shots.

"So, how do you know what a wet pussy is?" Julia tries to flirt with Chase, and he just shakes his head.

"I'd know a wet pussy anywhere." He brings the bottle of beer to his mouth as the two of them perform some mating ritual staring into each other's eyes.

"Your eyeballs are going to be tired tomorrow," I tell the both of them and they look back at me. "From eye-fucking each other." I clap my hands together at the joke when the bartender comes back with a tray of shots.

"Okay, I have some wet pussies," he says. "Some buttery nipples." He puts down a shot glass with whip cream and cherries on top. "Some killer pussy shots." He puts four shots with lemon slices in them. "Dick sucker shots." He looks at me, and all I can do is look at him with big eyes, the drink looks blue. "And my favorite," he states, putting down four of the last shots that are half red and half green. "Lick my pussy shot."

"Okay." Michael stands. "You can go," he tells the bartender. "We've got all the drinks we need right now."

"You are no fun," Julia says and hands one of the shots to Jillian. I don't know how we finish all the shots and then order a couple more, but when the songs start to come on, the four of us head to the dance floor.

We dance right near the guys, and I see the waitress come back over, and she walks to Dylan and hands him a white paper. He listens to whatever it is she is saying, and then when she leaves, he tosses the paper on the bar. Michael says something to him, and his face grimaces.

"We need more shots," I say, walking back to the bar.

The bartender walks over.

"Can I have a couple of shots?" I say, laughing. "Umm, is there a shot that is called sit on my face?"

"Oh, I want to sit on your face," Julia says, but she's looking straight at Chase, who just smirks at her. There is no beating around the bush with Julia. She has made Chase very aware that she wants him.

"Can I sit on your face?" Jillian asks Michael, and Dylan just laughs, closing his eyes.

"Baby," Michael says. "It's time to go."

"Are you going to let me sit on your face?" she asks him as Dylan stands up and so does Chase.

"Time to call it," Chase decides, and I whine.

"No," I say. "I didn't even get his name." I point at the bartender.

"It's Tom," Dylan says, coming to me. "Let's go."

"Oh, please." I roll my eyes at him, and the room spins just a touch. I mean, maybe more than a touch. "Where is your girlfriend?" I ask him, and I hate that it bothers me. I'm supposed to want him to be happy. I'm supposed to be happy for him, but instead, the thought of him with her makes all the drinks I've drunk want to come up.

We walk out of the tiki bar, and all I can do is giggle, stopping at the hostess stand where the girl is standing. "Can you tell Tom that I'm staying in a villa?"

"Okay," Dylan says, pulling me away from her.

"Let's walk back on the beach," Julia suggests. "We can sneak up on Franny and Wilson."

"Or we could not," Vivi rejects, stopping to laugh. "That works for me. I'll take the cart back."

"I could drive?" I say, running to one of the carts. My head is spinning but all I can do is laugh. Someone grabs me from around my waist, and I feel his hard chest to my back. I know right away it's him from his smell.

"I'll drive," Dylan says, and I'm lifted off my feet as he walks to one of the carts.

Julia gets in the cart beside me. "Chase, should I sit on you to give you enough room?"

"Oh, I can sit on you, too," Jillian says to Michael as she tries to crawl into the front seat and I clap my hands.

"Hold on," Dylan says, getting into the cart with me, and he leans over me. My cheeks feel like they are on fire as he takes my hand and holds it out to the side. "Hold on to this," he adds with his hand on mine. He turns his head, and he looks at me. My hand wants to come up, going to the back of his head while I bend and kiss him. "You okay?" he asks. "Are you going to throw up?"

"No," I reply. "I'll be fine."

He nods at me, then sits up and drives us back to the villa. "Can you walk?" he asks me, and all I can do is laugh.

"I don't know about walking, but I can strut my stuff like I'm on a catwalk," I state, pulling myself up and hitting my head on the top of the golf cart. "Ouch," I say, and the burning starts at the top of my head.

"Oh, God," Dylan says, coming to my side. "Come here." He puts his hand around my waist and holds me.

He lifts me up in his arms, and I yelp, putting my arm around his shoulder.

"Don't make me fall."

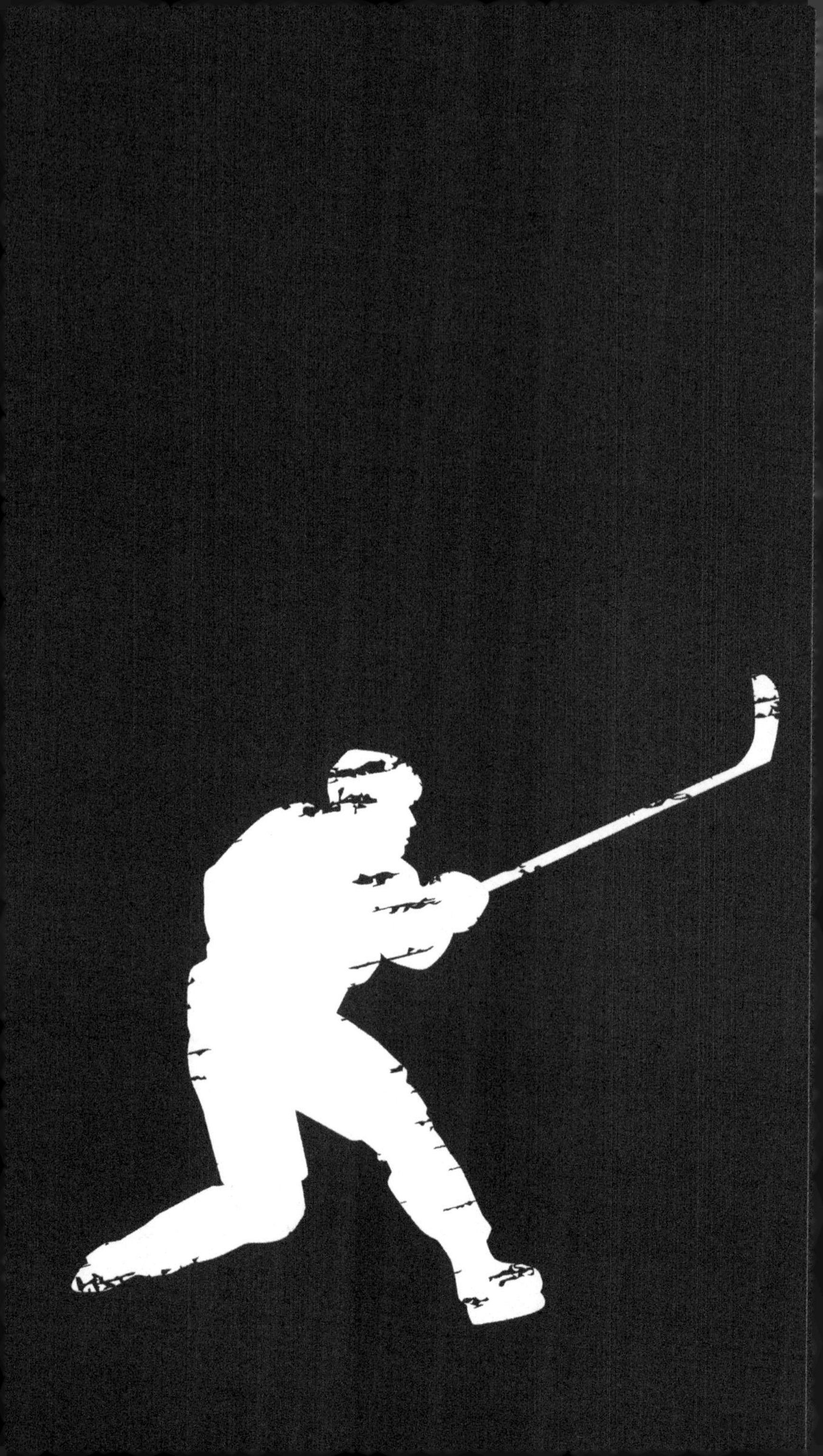

FOURTEEN

DYLAN

I LIFT HER in my arms as she yelps, and then it's followed with a giggle. She puts one hand around my shoulders. "Don't make me fall."

I look down into her eyes as my hand brings her closer to me, her head falling on my shoulder. "I'll never let you fall, Alex," I assure her, looking into her eyes. "You can always count on me."

"You're the bestest," she says, slapping my chest with her hand. "Of the bestest." She holds out her hands to the sides. "In the wholest of the world." She throws her head back.

"If you keep yelling like that," I say as I start to make my way to the villa. "You are going to wake up your parents, and then they are going to know you're drunk."

"I'm not drunk!" she shrieks. "I'm tipsy."

"Yeah," I mumble as I carry her up to the door and open it. "You had so many shots."

"I had wet pussy shots," she says. "The cum in my panties was good also." My cock stirs in my pants.

"Why don't we not talk?" I mumble as I walk into the villa. The soft light from the living room glows as I walk to her side of the house.

"Water." She points at the fridge off the living room. "Need water to hydrate." She puts her head on my shoulder and buries her face in my neck, and if I thought I was going through hell before, it's nothing compared to now. This is what torture is, having the woman you have been dreaming of in your arms, but not able to do a fucking thing about it.

"I'll drop you in the bed," I tell her, trying to keep my head from self-combusting. "And then go get water."

"No." Her head pops out from my neck, her face filled with fear. "Don't leave me." I look at her as her eyes look into mine. "Are you going back to the blonde? I don't like her. She only wants your dick."

"I'm not going anywhere," I confirm, swallowing as I turn to walk back into the kitchen, I turn to the side grabbing the fridge handle with the same hand that holds her legs. I grab two water bottles and then the dress she is wearing falls off her leg and all I see is a bare leg. I close my eyes and count to ten, but nothing can calm down the way my body just woke up.

"Are we stuck?" Alex asks as she looks around. "Why aren't we moving?" I laugh at her. "My head is moving." She puts her head back and closes her eyes. "You know what we should do?" she asks, her eyes going big. "We should dance."

"We should not dance." I roll my lips trying not to laugh at her. "What we should do is …"

She puts her finger on my lips. "Don't say it." She sings the words. "If you put it out into the universe." She looks around and then whispers, "They'll know." I can't help but laugh at her. "If you don't say it, no one is going to know."

"Let's get you to bed," I say, walking over to her side of the room. Walking into her room, I see that her bags are still packed, which is weird since she loves to unpack as soon as she gets here. One suitcase has a pile of clothes in it like a bomb went off. The light on the side table is on but on low, just giving the room a glow. The windows are open so you can hear the sound of the water crashing onto the rocks.

"You want to know a secret?" she says in a whisper, but because she's drunk, it comes out louder than a whisper. "Julia wants to have sex with Chase." She laughs as she puts her finger to her lips. "Shhh, don't tell anyone."

"I don't think that is a secret at all," I say, and she laughs.

"Franny is having sex." She slaps the bed. "On the beach."

"Okay," I say, not wanting to think about sex, especially with her in my arms, after thinking about her all night naked.

I lay her on the bed and slip my hands from under her. "I'll get you some ibuprofen," I say as she lies there with her head on her pillow and her eyes closed. Her hair is spread out on the pillow like a fan. She's so fucking beautiful she takes my breath away.

"Are you stuck again?" She opens one eye and sees me staring at her. "You should get checked." She laughs. "Maybe your knees are stiff." All she can do is throw her head back and laugh hysterically. Shaking my head, I turn and walk into the bathroom, seeing all her products on the counter. She is obsessed with making sure she has everything she will need. Before every trip, she goes to the pharmacy and goes aisle by aisle, buying stuff she will need just in case.

"Dylan." She calls my name, and I walk back into her room. "I thought you left."

"Here, take these," I say, handing her two pills, and she takes them from me. I grab one of the water bottles as she takes a gulp, swallowing them.

"Thank you." She smiles at me, putting her head back and scrunching up her nose.

"Good night," I say to her, but my feet don't move.

"Why are you leaving?" she asks, sitting up and then falling back down on the pillows. "I'm pretty enough." She looks at me, and my tongue is stuck in my mouth or at least that is what it feels like. "I've got a nice enough body." She looks down at her body. "I'm all that and a bag of Doritos." She falls back onto her pillow. I'm about to tell her that she is more than pretty enough when she looks at me. "Stay with me," she says softly. "Like old times."

She moves over in the bed to give me space to lie down, and my head is telling me to run in the other direction. It's telling me that this is the most horrible idea I've ever thought about. It's telling me that nothing good will come from this moment right here. "Only for a little bit," I agree, getting on the bed and turning off the light. "I'll stay here until you fall asleep," I say, and she laughs.

"I'm falling, and I'm afraid I'll never be able to get up," she mumbles, and I just watch her as she turns to face me. "Dylan," she says, and her eyes close. "I," she starts to say as I watch her. "This is nice," she says, coming closer to me and putting her head on my shoulder. I don't move. My body is on fire, and I'm afraid if she comes any closer, she's going to find my cock rock hard, and then it'll be something I don't want to explain. My heart hammers in my chest as she puts her arm over my stomach. I wrap my arm around her shoulder and then place my other hand on her arm. "Tomorrow," she murmurs softly. "Everything is going to be better."

I look down at her and hear the softness of her breaths. Everything I thought I knew comes crashing to me like the waves against the rocks. All the feelings I've been having for her are not normal. I don't love her like I am supposed to. I don't love her like I do Vivi or Franny. Maybe I never fucking did. I keep thinking about all of the times we were together. All the times she told me she was going on dates and me not being okay with it. I would get super cranky or when I went on a date with someone and all I kept thinking about was how much fun I would have had had Alex been with me.

The realization just comes at me like a freight train. My chest tightens so tight I have to focus just to breathe properly. She could have gone home with the bartender tonight had I not been there. I can't even think about it. I can't even begin to imagine it. I slip out from under her touch, moving slowly as not to wake her. The energy in me is starting to make my whole body shake.

Not only am I in love with her but there is also nothing that I can do. All I can do is sit in the chair in the corner, my legs not steady enough to walk to my bedroom. I can't even talk to anyone about this. The burning starts to form in my stomach because no one would even understand. I keep trying to play how a conversation would go in my head, but even starting it, I know that it would not go over well. With anyone. My legs start to move up and down. There has to be a way.

I sit here in the room all night long as the sun slowly starts to rise, and even after six hours of sitting in the dark room, I know I will never ever be able to love her like I want to. I know if I say anything to her, I risk never being able to be next to her again. I risk never getting to see her smile again. I risk never getting to hear her laughter anymore. I risk living the rest of my life without her in it. And it's a risk I'm not willing to take. I'd rather love her from afar in secret than not at all. It's a sacrifice I'm going to have to make, and I know that I'll never get over her.

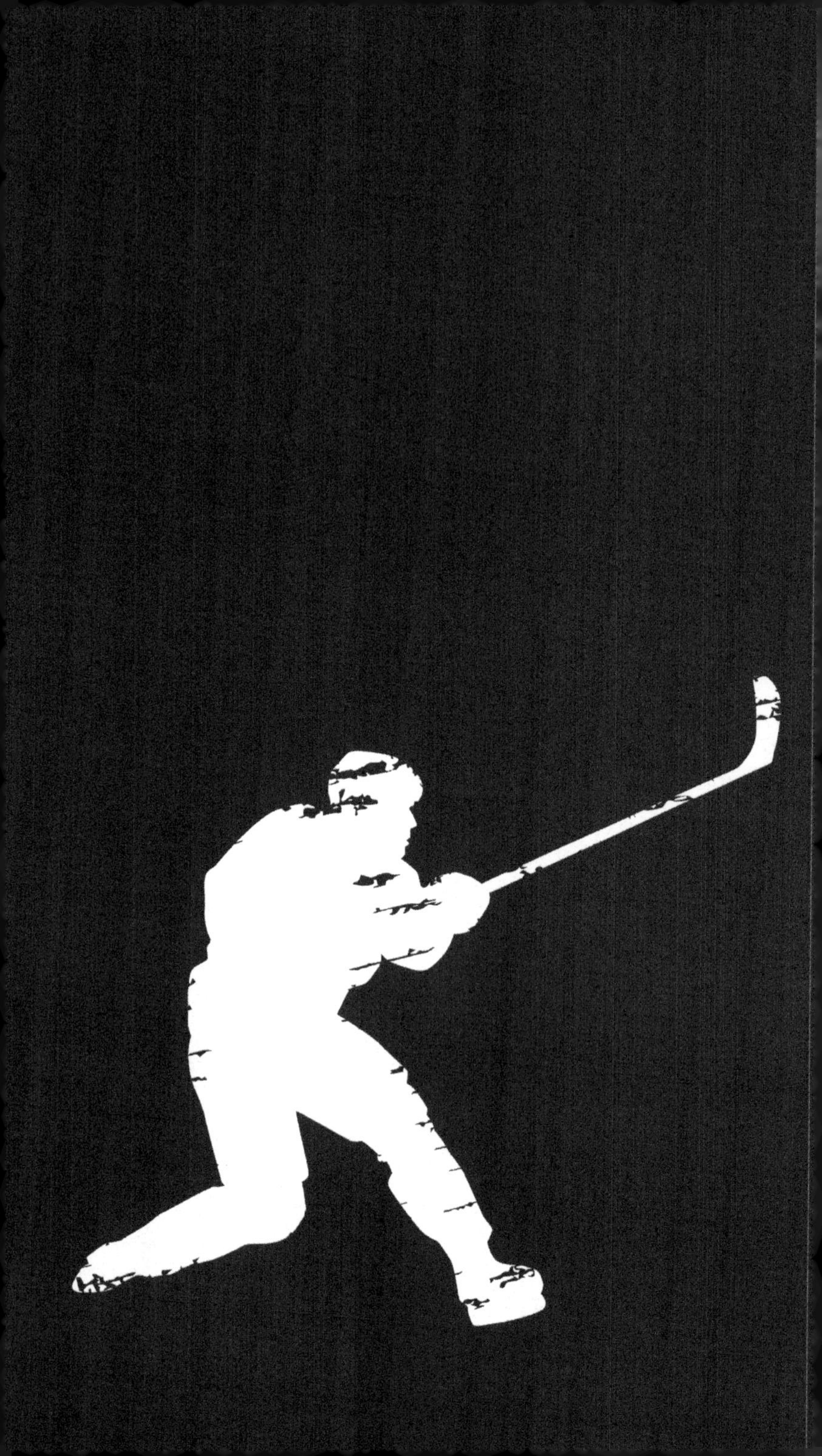

FIFTEEN

ALEX

"WHAT IS THAT noise?" I ask of the sound that I keep hearing over and over again. "Is that whistles?" I open my eyes. The hair in front of my face tries to block out the sun, but it shines straight into one eye, making me groan. "No," I moan, and my mouth feels like I swallowed a whole fist of sand. I turn my head to the other side when I hear the noise again. I want to get up but I'm lying facedown in the middle of my bed. "What is that?"

I open one eye again and see the clock on the bedside table showing me it's nine fourteen. My eyes go to the water bottle right next to the clock, and I reach out my hand to grab it, but I'm in the middle of my bed. The energy to get the bottle is more than I can give right now. The throbbing in my head starts. I try to swallow, but my tongue feels even bigger. "Ugh," I moan, trying to pull myself to the side of the bed. I move not even an inch when I try to reach for the bottle only to come up at the same spot. "Why didn't I study how to make things move with my mind?" I mumble when the whistling starts again.

"Good morning." I hear Dylan's voice, and I blow out to try to move the hair from my face, but nothing happens. I hear him chuckle and move my hand up to push the hair away from my face. Opening my eyes, I see him standing there in gym shorts and nothing else. His hair is wet from the shower he probably just took because I can smell his soap from here. He leans against the doorjamb. "How are we feeling this morning?"

I'm about to answer him when the whistling starts again. "Do you hear that?" I try to turn to the other side, but the sun feels like a spotlight shining straight onto my face. I turn my head and lie back down on the pillow. "Is it just me who hears that?"

"Do you mean the whistling?" he asks, coming into the room and going to the window where he shuts it, and the whistling stops. "Uncle Matthew gave it to all the kids to prevent them from being kidnapped. It's called the stranger danger whistle."

"How many strangers are on our private beach?" I ask as I hear him close the shades.

"Zero," he says, and I open my eyes looking over my shoulder at him. He walks to the side of the bed, and I hear the sound of pills. "But they just like blowing the whistle for fun."

"You need to go out there," I say. "And take them all away."

He laughs, and when I watch him come back, he

hands me two pills and then sits on the side of the bed, handing me the water bottle I tried to combat crawl to. "Take these. You'll feel better."

I turn to sit up on the bed, my head pounding even harder. I put the pills in my mouth and the water feels so good when it finally hits my tongue. I finish the whole bottle and then lie back down on the bed. "I'm assuming you're going back to bed."

I roll to the other side of the bed, grabbing the cover. "I'd appreciate if you stop judging me." I close my eyes. "It's a judge-free zone."

I ignore the need to open my eyes and look at him again. "I'll be in the living room." I feel the bed move when he gets up.

"I don't need a babysitter," I state, annoyed that I like the fact he's going to be staying back with me and then annoyed he's staying back with me.

He doesn't say anything and sleep comes right away, and when I open my eyes again, I see it's just past three. I think about staying in bed all day long when my bladder starts to burn, and I have to get up. I swing my legs over the bed, and when I get up, I have to close my eyes and breathe through my nose as I make my way to the bathroom.

When I look at myself in the mirror, all I can do is groan. My tube top is spun around and the seam is in the middle of my chest. I tie up my hair and turn on the water to wash my face and rinse out my mouth. When I walk into the bedroom, I grab a pair of jean shorts and a black bikini top. Throwing a white oversized shirt over it, I slip my feet into my slides. I grab my sunglasses, knowing that the sun is not going to be my friend today. Walking out of my room, I come to a halt when I see Dylan lying on the couch with his eyes closed. One of his hands is over his head and another is on his stomach as he sleeps. I try to tiptoe out of the room and not wake him, but he hears me.

"What time is it?" he asks. I look over, and he stretches and my eyes go to the middle of his shorts. I'm thankful that I put on my sunglasses.

"I'm going to head out and grab something to eat," I say. "You sleep."

"Nah." He gets up and walks over to me, and he still has sleep in his eyes. "I'm starving."

He grabs a T-shirt from the counter, and we walk out into the hot air. We get in the golf cart and arrive at the eating area.

I hear the whistles again. "Those fucking things," I hear from the side of me and look over to see Julia and Jillian walking. Both of them pretty much look like I do.

"Oh, look, it's the Three Stooges," Michael says, parking the golf cart next to ours.

I flip him off, getting out of the cart, and then walk to a table and sit down. The waitress comes over right away. "Can I have a plate of bacon and sausage? Some hash browns and scrambled eggs."

"Make that for two," Julia says, sitting down as she nods at us.

"Can I get a cheeseburger with bacon?" Jillian says.

"I'll have one of those also and some chicken tenders,"

I say, and everyone just looks at me. "I'm going to do a buffet."

"I'll eat the rest of the food they don't," Dylan says, and she looks at Michael, who also orders a burger. She walks away from us.

"How about we get some cum in our panties?" Michael says, rolling his lips. "Or some wet pussies?" I groan at the same time as Julia, and I lay my head back on the chair.

"How about we try no sex for a month?" Jillian retorts, making him laugh. "That's what I thought."

"How much did we drink?" I ask them, trying to remember last night, and it starts to get fuzzy after the fourth shot.

"Well, these two." Michael points at Julia and Jillian. "Decided it would be a good idea to do tequila once we got back to the house."

"Yuck," Jillian says. "Also, you didn't care when I did that dance for you."

"Dance for me?" he says, shocked. "You fell asleep in my lap."

The whole table laughs, and when the waitress comes back with the food, I eat even less than I thought I was going to eat. My stomach is rising and falling each time I take a bite, but I push through and eat as much as I can.

"I'm going to go and see the kids," Jillian says.

"Just follow the whistles," I direct. Getting into the golf cart, we make our way over to the beach. The kids are all running around, and when Cooper and Erika see us walking, they laugh.

"Usually, it's him with the glasses," Cooper says, pointing at Dylan. The whistles start again, and it feels as if my ears are going to bleed.

"I'm going to go for a walk," I say, looking at Emma and Mia chasing each other with the whistle in their mouth. Slipping off my slides, I start to walk.

"I'll come with," Dylan says, and I want to tell him that I don't want him to come with me. I want to tell him to stay there and let me clear my head. But instead, I just nod as we walk side by side down the beach. "This has been nice," he says, and my eyes just look down as his fingers graze mine. When my stomach flutters, I blame the alcohol instead of something else. The warm water washes over our feet when I look into the water.

We get to the end of the beach, and I look down to see the waves hitting the rocks. "Want to go sit on the rocks?" he asks, and when I nod, he holds out his hand to me. I slip my hand into his, and the whole time my heart is hammering in my chest. He climbs up on the rocks before me as he leads us to the middle. I turn to sit down, and he walks over to look at the water. "Look, a starfish," he says, and I get up, walking to him. The waves hit the rocks, splashing us.

"Oh, it's so pretty," I say, looking down into the water seeing it on the floor before another wave comes and crashes.

"Let me go get it." Taking off his shirt, he hands it to me. "Hold this," he says and I grab his shirt. I watch him walk to the edge of the rocks and slowly slip into the water. The water reaches his waist as he turns around when the wave comes in, hitting his back. He reaches down into the water, picking the starfish up and holding it up so I can see it. "Hold it." He holds it over his head for me when another wave comes and hits his back.

He gets up on the rocks, bringing it to me, and I hold it in my hand. The little spikes pinch my hands. "It's so pretty." I hand it back to him. "Go put it back where it was," I say, and he gets back into the water. I watch him. "Put it back at the same place, so he knows where he is."

He nods at me and bends to put him back in the water. He comes back out and we sit on the rocks as we watch the sun set. Neither of us says anything as each of us are lost in our thoughts. I don't know what he's thinking about but I catch glances over at him and each time my stomach flips and then my heart contracts in my chest. Finally, he gets up and holds out his hand to me. "We should get back for dinner," he says softly, and I put my hand in his as he helps me climb down the rocks. I don't know when it happens or how it happens, but when I look over at him, all I can do is watch him, and when I do this, I realize how unhealthy this is for me. How my longing for him from afar is doing nothing but making me want him even more.

I look down at my feet the rest of the walk back to the villa, the beach deserted now. All I can do is feel these things I can never do anything about. It makes the back of my neck heat and my stomach rises to my throat when I finally do say something. "I can't do this anymore." I stop walking, and I should have waited until I was at least closer to our villa before I said anything, but the words just came out before I could stop them. The waves in the distance slowly roll onto shore. It's so peaceful yet painful. I look up at him, pushing my glasses on top of my head.

He just looks at me confused. "What do you mean, what can't you do?"

"This being best friends with you." I point at myself and then at him. "Being there for you all the time." I look around to make sure that no one else is around. I don't think I could handle that. "Always around, I just can't do this anymore." I blink away the tears starting to come, but in the darkness, I let them fall. My hand comes up, and I wipe the tear away from my cheek.

"What the hell are you talking about?" His eyes roam my face as worry fills his own face. No doubt he has no fucking idea what I'm talking about because how could he.

Here in the middle of the beach where we started a normal walk, I tell him what I'm pretty sure everyone already knows. Everyone but him. "I'm in love with you," I say right before the lump starts to rise up to my throat, but I push through. "Every single part of my soul is in love with you, right down to my bones. I'm in love with you." I finally let out the words. I avoid his eyes, not ready for what I'm going to see in them. When the lump in my throat grows bigger and bigger, I know I'm about to crumble, but I won't do it in front of him. "And it's time I stop loving you with the hope that you feel for me what I feel for you." My heart feels like it's shattering in my chest. "So …" I wipe the tear away when I see

Michael walking out of his villa and headed toward us. Without knowing it, he is my saving grace. "I'm walking away. You should choose New York," I say and take one look at him before running up toward Michael and leaving my heart in the middle of the beach.

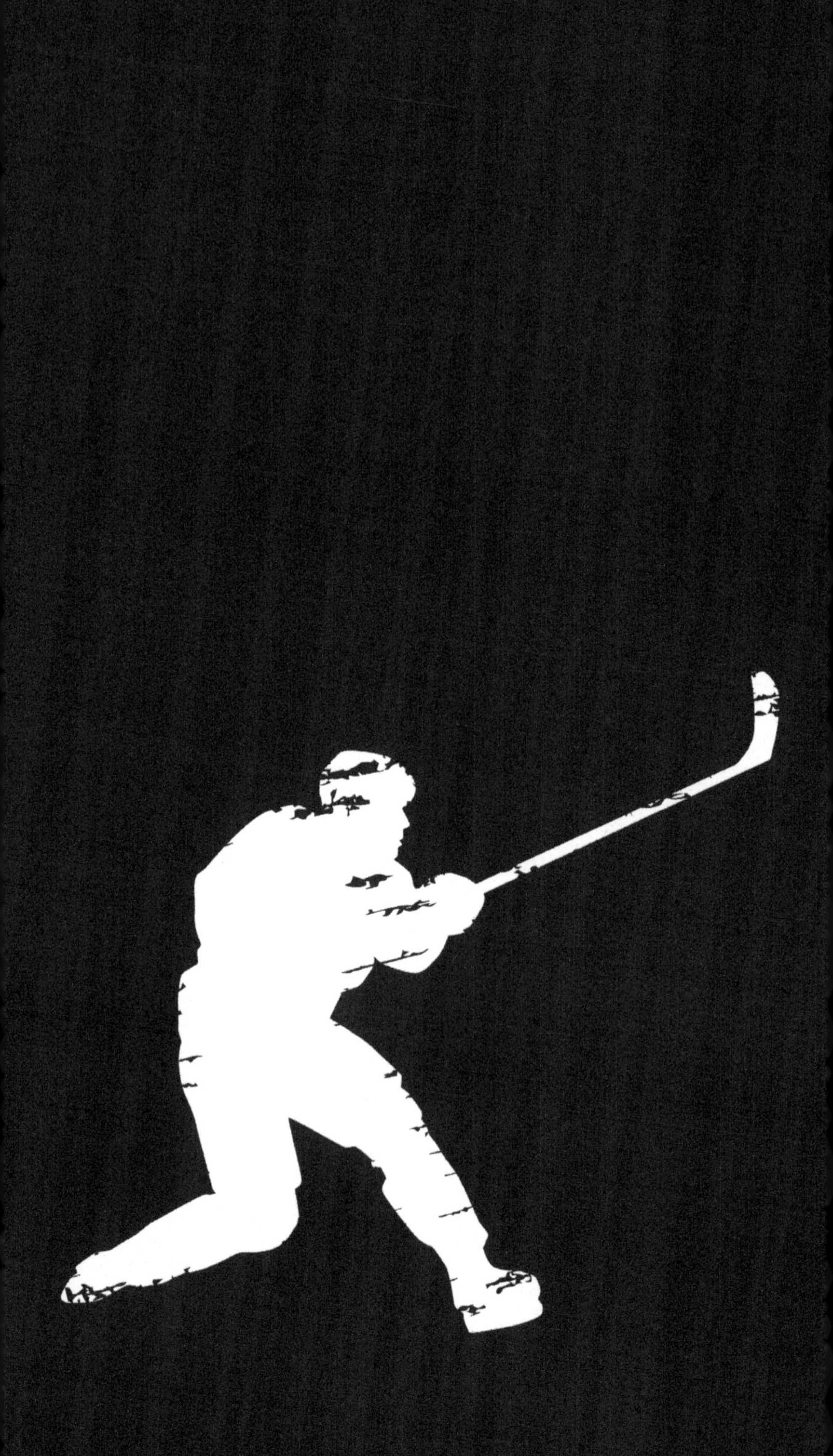

SIXTEEN

Dylan

I TURN TO chase after her but see Michael walking toward us. "You going to be sick?" he asks her, and she just rushes past him into Michael's villa, slamming the door right behind her. My head is spinning around and around. "Guess she's out for dinner," he says, and I look at him and then look back at the door she just shut.

I run my hands over my face and through my hair, holding on to my neck. My heart is beating so fast in my chest I don't know if I can even talk right now. "What the fuck are you doing?" he asks me when he gets closer to me, and I turn to sit on the beach because my legs give out on me.

"I'm …" I look into the dark of the night at the water. I don't even know what to say to him. I try to think of anything to say. "Thinking about what I'm going to do." My stomach burns as I sit here not able to go after her. And if I'm honest, she would have pushed me away if I went after her. She would not listen to me, and she would spin it to me, just saying that I loved her back to just say it. No, I know her enough to know she needs to settle down before I tell her anything.

Michael sits next to me, and I wish I could tell him I want to be alone. I wish I could be like *get the fuck out of here*, or better yet, I wish I could tell him I'm in love with his sister. But how do I even say the words? Also, before I tell him, I need to tell her. We need to talk about this.

Chase comes out and walks toward us. "Don't go in there." He points at Michael's villa. "They said to get the fuck out and not to disturb them for the rest of the night."

My stomach burns so much looking over my shoulder. "I'm going to go and make sure Alex is okay."

"She's fine," Chase says, sitting on the other side of me. "She said to tell you that she's fine."

I don't know what Michael and Chase talk about nor do I know how long I sit out here. Finally, I get up and dust my pants off. "I'm going to get dinner in my room," I say to them. "I'll see you both tomorrow." I walk away from them toward my villa. My eyes go to Michael's villa as I walk by and I try to see the light coming out from the living room and the shades are closed.

Walking into the cold villa, I see the light in her room is off and the door open. I walk to the doorway, hoping by some miracle she is lying in bed, but all I can see is the empty bed in the darkness.

I walk back over to the couch and sit down, running my hands over my face. Her words replay over and over in my head. She's in love with me. The minute she admitted she was in love with me, I couldn't believe what was happening. I was shocked and then I waited to make sure I heard her right. My heart was beating so fast in my chest as it soared and all I wanted to do was claim her mouth and stop her from talking. I leave the light off all night long, knowing it might make her not come here if she thinks I'm up. The whole night all I can do is replay the whole thing over and over again in my head. How she looked so sad telling me how she felt, how she shed those tears, and the pain I felt in me to watch them fall, not being able to wipe them away for her. Knowing she was crying because of me, gutted me.

I put my head back on the couch as I wait for her, but when I open them up again, I see the light coming in from outside as the sun is shining high in the sky. Rubbing my face, I check the clock on the desk and see it's past 9:00 a.m. I get up and walk over to her bedroom, and my body turns cold as ice when I see that her luggage is gone. I turn and rush out of the villa, going straight to Michael's. I knock on the door once and then walk in.

"Hello," I say, frantically looking around, and Julia comes out of her bedroom. Her eyes spot me as she glares at me. Okay, so she knows. "Where is she?" I ask, looking around for any sign of her. "Alex!" I yell and push my way past Julia into her bedroom, seeing the bed not made but her luggage isn't there. "Where is she?" I walk back out, and she just stands there folding her arms over her chest. "I'm not playing, Julia, where the fuck is she?" I say as calmly as I can, but it comes out harsh with my teeth clenched together. My whole body feels like it's going to explode.

"She left," she says, and I look at her, not sure I heard her right.

"Is she with her parents?" I ask and take a step toward the door and stop when Julia says the next sentence.

"She got on a plane last night," she replies. I slowly turn and look at her, my heart sinking to my feet, making it so heavy I can't move from this spot. "She made up an excuse that there was an emergency with the rink."

"She left alone?" I ask, shocked that she would do this.

"She refused to draw any attention to her," Julia says. "Michael didn't even know until this morning. He thought she was in bed sleeping."

I pull my phone out of my pocket and call her number, not surprised it goes straight to voice mail. "I told her it was a bad idea."

"You think?" I say, and she just glares at me. "You let her leave in the middle of the fucking night alone."

"Hey," she snaps at me. "I'm not the one who fucked up here. Why didn't you come after her?"

"Because she wouldn't have listened to me!" I shout back at her. "I was waiting for her to calm down."

"Well, she was pretty calm when she left," Julia says. "Calm or numb."

I shake my head. "Did she land yet?" Julia just shakes her head. "Can you tell me when she gets home all right?"

"I will," she says, and I put the phone back into my pocket as I turn and walk out of the villa. I walk down the path going to the only place I know that I can be me. I knock on the door, my heart is beating so hard in my chest I feel like I can't even breathe. I put my hands on my knees as I try to calm down. The door swings open, and he stands there, his face going from a smile to white as he takes me in.

"Dylan?" my father says. "What happened?"

I shake my head; not sure I can talk when he comes to me and walks me into the house. "Let's get you some water." He puts his arm around my shoulder as he walks me into the villa. He sets me on the couch and rushes over to the fridge, grabbing a water bottle. He comes over to me, and I sit here with my head in my hands. "Here," he says, handing me the water bottle and sitting in front of me on the coffee table.

My hand shakes as I reach out and grab the bottle, bringing it to my lips. The cold liquid hits my tongue as I look at my father. The worry is written all over his face, and he gives me a chance to find my bearings. He leans forward, putting his hand on my shoulder squeezing it. "Thank you." My voice comes out in almost a whisper as I look at the water bottle in my hand.

"What happened?" he asks, and I shake my head.

"I don't even know where to start," I say honestly, my voice cracking as my heart feels like it's going to come out of my chest. "I don't know what to say." I look at him with tears in my eyes. "I don't know."

"Hey," he says now, his own tears forming in his eyes. This man who saved me from my private hell and took me into his life and loved me like I was his own. I took it all, and I'm going to ruin it by admitting this to him. But I can't live like this anymore, especially now that I know she loves me.

"I'm so sorry," I start by saying, the tears just pouring out of me.

"Dylan, whatever it is," he assures me, squeezing my shoulder. "We will get through it."

"I really fucking hope so," I say, wiping my eyes. "Because what I'm about to tell you could change everything."

"You're my son," he says, choking on the words. "Nothing, and I mean nothing, will change that, ever."

I take a deep breath in and look at him, straight in his eyes when I say the next words. "I'm in love with Alex." My father just looks at me, his eyes blinking—once, twice, three times. I wait for him to say something, and all he does is look at me.

"I'm sorry?" is all he says as he watches me, blinking.

"I'm in love with Alex," I say it again, and this time when I say it, my chest is less heavy. The pain is less constricting than the last time.

"Alex?" he asks, sitting up as he looks at me, and all I can do is nod my head. "Like Alex Alex?"

"Dad," I say, and I get up because I can't sit still anymore. "Alex Alex."

"But when?" he asks, and I shrug.

"I have no idea," I say. "Maybe I have been in love with her forever." I start to pace. "But it came crashing to me when she finally moved to Dallas." I glance at him to see if he looks at me with disgust, but he doesn't. "I don't know. It's like one day I'm sitting there and all these things are going through my head. I don't want to even be in my house anymore. I feel like my skin is going to crawl off me and then she calls and it's just in front of my face. I'm not happy because she's so far away from me. I'm not happy because she's starting her life, and I'm afraid she's going to find someone who she is going to grow old with and …" I stop pacing and look at him. "And the thought of her being with someone else shattered everything in me." I put my hands on my hips.

"Dylan," he says, looking at me, and I know he's trying to tell me how crazy this idea is.

"Dad, everything that I think of has Alex attached to it. Every single memory I have is of her in it, and when I think of a wife or mother for my kids, there is only one person who I see by my side." I swallow. "If I can't have her, I don't want anyone else." I put my hand to my chest. "Just the thought of her not being with me … I can't breathe."

"If you really, truly love her, then follow your heart," he says, looking down, folding his hands together. "But, and this is a huge but, be fucking sure." He shakes his head. "It's not just you and her." He lets out a huge deep breath. "It's the whole family that is going to be involved in this, so you have to be one hundred percent certain."

"Do you think I would do this without being one hundred percent certain, Dad?" I ask. "This has been eating at me." The tears come to me. "What do you think they will say?"

"I have no idea." He gets up, coming to me and taking me in his arms. "But we will find out together."

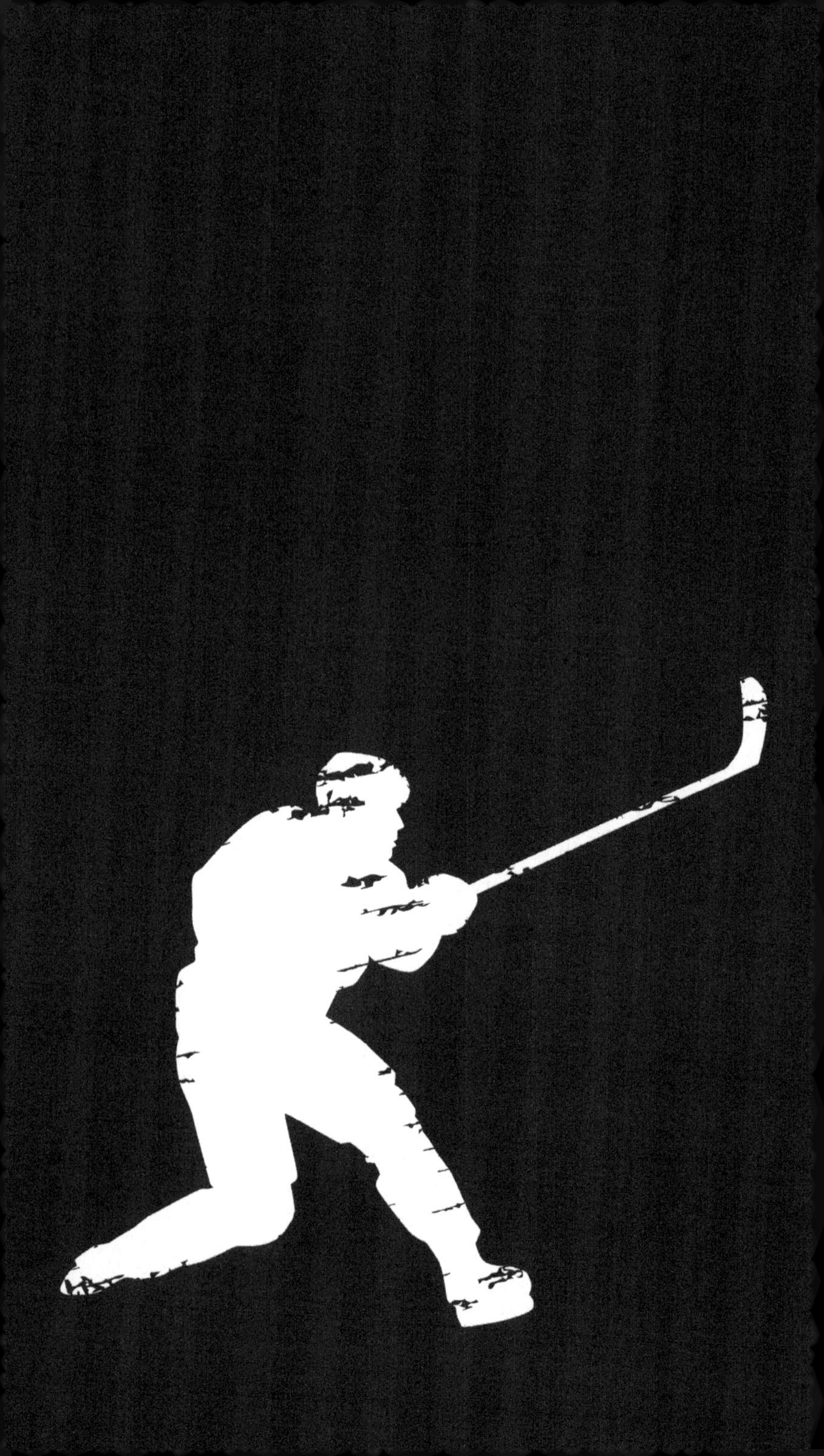

SEVENTEEN

Alex

THE SOUND OF a baby crying fills the cabin as the air pressure starts to change. I look out the window at the darkness outside. I left in the dark, I arrive in the dark. Closing my eyes again until I hear the captain's voice come on. "Ladies and gentlemen, welcome to Dallas/Fort Worth Airport." My eyes flicker open. "The local time is eight twenty p.m." I look out the window as he tells us all to remain seated until the seat belt sign goes off.

I get up when I hear the ping, grabbing my carry-on and walking out of the aircraft. My whole body feels numb and I'm even afraid to look at myself in the mirror. I walk down the carpeted walkway following the signs to baggage claim.

Keeping my head down as the hustle and bustle of the airport just floats around me, I keep my sunglasses on so no one will see my puffy, red, bloodshot eyes. I spot the carousel number on the screen and make my way over, standing right beside it. Walking to it like I'm a robot. My body is numb as I go through the steps to get out of the airport. This whole day has been one motion after another, yet the pain in my chest grows stronger and stronger.

The burning in my eyes each time I blink hurts more and more. That and the fact that I've been up for over thirty-six hours.

When I ran away from Dylan on the beach, I rushed into Michael's villa. The tears came nonstop and all I could do was pray he wouldn't follow me. Jillian and Julia were both lying on the couch watching television when I barged in. Jillian looked over, unsure as to what was happening, while Julia immediately took one look at me and sat up. "I told him" were the only words I said before I had to put my hand to my mouth. To stop the sob that had been creeping up the whole time I told him everything. It took Julia one second before she took over, that is when everything flew into motion. She ordered Jillian to take me into her room and then she rushed out of the villa and she returned five minutes later with all my stuff packed.

Jillian watched me sit in the middle of the bed not saying anything because I was on my phone the whole time. I had booked myself onto the next flight out of there. She also had no idea what was going on nor did she get a chance to ask me any questions because Michael came in and we had to keep him out of Julia's room. "Tell him I'm sick."

She nodded and then looked at me. "Later you are going to fill me in." I just nodded my head knowing that as soon as she went to bed, I was getting the fuck out of there. I stayed in Julia's room, knowing that Dylan would give me the night to calm down before coming to find me. At 3:00 a.m., Julia and I snuck out of the room to the waiting car that got me to the airport for the 6:00 a.m. flight out to Las Vegas and then to Dallas. I've been flying for the past ten hours, and I can't wait to get home.

The buzz of the carousel makes me look around as it starts moving and the bags start to come out. I look around and see that I'm not the only one with sunglasses but I just did come off the flight from Vegas, so ... My bags come out one after another, and when I walk out, the humid air hits me right away as I grab a cab. Only when I walk into my house do I take the phone out of my pocket and send Julia a text.

Me: I'm home.

The phone rings right away, and I know that she was probably on pins and needles all day. "Hello." I wheel my bags to the staircase, and I think about carrying them upstairs, but I know I don't have the energy for any of that. Instead, I walk to the kitchen and grab a water bottle.

"Jesus," Julia says. "That was the longest day of my life."

"How is everything?" I ask, but what I'm really asking is how is Dylan. Every time I close my eyes, all I see is his shocked face as I poured out my whole heart to him. I was so selfish to do that to him, and for the rest of my life, I have to live with it. He was probably disgusted with the thought of me being in love with him. I swallow down the lump that forms again and take a sip of the cool water as my lower lip trembles.

"Well, shit hit the fan this morning when Dylan found out you left," she shares, whispering and then I hear a door close. "Alex, I think you should hear him out."

"Fuck no," I say, walking up the stairs. The whole house feels stale from being closed up. "What did you tell my parents?"

"I told them you got an emergency call about the arena and had to rush back and take care of it or the camp wouldn't be able to start." I nod my head at the excuse that we came up with as we sat in her bed waiting for the time for me to leave. "Wilson knows I'm bullshitting and came to privately tell me that I was bullshitting and that we were going to have words. He said that if there was an emergency, he would have been called." I close my eyes and press the bridge of my nose. "Then he just wanted to know you were okay."

"I'm so sorry." My voice is almost in a whisper, feeling horrible that she had to clean up my mess. "I'll call him tomorrow. I'm going to shower and slide into bed."

"We leave tomorrow," she says, and I know that, eventually, I'll have to face Dylan. I'm just hoping that it's in a long time from now, like at Christmas or even next year.

"Do you know where he's going?" I ask, holding my breath.

"He's flying back to Dallas," Julia says. "My guess is

he'll stay with his parents since they are there for another week."

"Okay," I say softly. "Thank you, Julia. I owe you."

"You bet your ass you owe me," she confirms. "And trust me, I collect my shit."

I laugh and hang up the phone. It rings again in my hand, and I look down to see it's Dylan. I send it to voice mail. The phone is lighting up in my hand as I look down, seeing that I have over ninety-nine-plus text messages. I power down the phone, putting it on the side table and walking to my bathroom. I don't bother turning on the lights as I undress and let the hot water cascade all around me. Every time I close my eyes, all I can picture is Dylan and the shock on his face. The way he just looked at me, the pain is almost too much to bear. When I get out of the shower, I slide into bed and am thankful that sleep comes before I have a chance to think about it.

The next day when my eyes open, they feel over a hundred pounds. My body feels like it's been run over by a Mack truck. I slide out of bed and head to the bathroom, where I get ready and try to put on makeup to make my eyes look normal. I slide on my tight blue jeans and grab my white sleeveless shirt with ruffles down the side of it. I opt for suede wedges instead of heels, knowing I'm probably going to be running around all day long.

When I finally drive up to the rink, a smile fills my face as I grab my iced coffee and walk up the steps and into the arena. "What are you doing here?" Veronica asks. When I started getting busier than even I expected, I hired Veronica to help me with registration for the summer camp.

"I couldn't miss day one," I say with a smile, hoping she doesn't see through me. "How is everything going?" I ask as we walk toward my office. I look up and see that it's just ten minutes past seven, fifty minutes until the kids start to arrive. I'm about to walk into the office when I hear someone behind me.

"Excuse me," the woman says, and I turn seeing her dressed in cutoffs and a top that's seen better days. Her hair even looks matted, and when I look in her eyes, something puts my guard up. The flip-flops on her feet look gray instead of yellow. "Is this the hockey thing?" she asks, looking around, and I look over at the little boy standing beside her. His clothes look like they have seen better days as well. His eyes look tired, and all he does is look around. "We got one of those summer things."

"That starts at eight," Veronica says, and I can see the mother getting pissed at hearing that.

"Well, I don't know what to tell you all," she says, her hand coming up, and I see that her fingernails are dirty as well as the little red dots between her fingers. "I'm here, and I'm leaving."

"That's fine," I say, looking at her and smiling. "We can take him." I look at the little boy who looks up at the woman. I squat down. "Hi," I greet him, smiling. "I'm Alex."

I hear the mother huff out. "I don't have time for this," she says. "His name is Maddox. I'm leaving." She turns and walks out of the arena, and I share a look with Veronica, who just looks at me with her eyes wide.

I look back at the kid, who watches his mother leave. She didn't even kiss him goodbye. "Are you hungry?" I ask, and he nods his head at me. "Why don't we go upstairs and see if I can make you something." I stand, and I hold out my hand to him. He looks at me confused as if he doesn't know what to do with it.

I drop my hand and smile at him. "This way," I say, and he follows me. "So are you excited about hockey?"

He doesn't say anything. He just nods his head. When we get to the cafeteria, the cook is already there and smiles at me when I walk in. "Hi, Gisele," I say. "We have a hungry boy here and were wondering if you had something he could eat." She looks over at the little boy and smiles.

"I just finished making these," she says, walking over to the bagel egg sandwiches. She puts one on a plate, and I walk with him over to the fridge.

"What do you drink in the morning?" I ask, and he just looks at me, his brown eyes just staring at the sandwich on the plate.

"Nothing," he says, and I just swallow as he looks around, and I have to wonder if he's scared.

"Well, how about we start with some apple juice?" I suggest, grabbing the juice box and walking over to the table with him.

I put the plate on the table, and he sits down, almost afraid to touch the plate. "You can eat it," I assure him, and his hand comes out, and I see that they need to be washed. But the way he takes a bite of the sandwich, I know he needs to eat before he needs to wash his hands.

I put the straw in the apple juice for him and offer it to him. He looks at me and then at the juice box. "It's apple juice."

"Is it sour?" he asks me, and I look at him confused. "Last time, it was yellow, and it burned going down," he says, and I look around to see who else would have heard him.

I hide the shock and just smile. "No, this one is sweet," I say, and he takes it, but he just looks at me, not sure if he can trust me. "I promise you, Maddox, it's sweet."

He leans over and takes a little sip, and then when he sees that it's sweet, he smiles and drinks more. He finishes his sandwich, and when he's done, he picks up the plate to lick the crumbs. My heart speeds up as I spend more and more time with him. I wash his hands with him, and when I hold out my hand to hold, just like I do with my nieces and nephew, all he does is look at my hand. We walk back downstairs, and I see Veronica setting up the tables at the door to greet everyone.

"Do you have a bag for Maddox?" I ask, and she grabs the bag that is on the table in front of her.

"I was going to come and give it to him," she says, smiling at him. "Here you go, buddy," she tells him, and he just stands beside me.

"It's your new stuff," I say, and he just looks at me. I grab the bag and squat in front of him. "These are your new shorts and shirts," I say. "It's so everyone looks the same. Do you want to go change?" I ask, and he looks around as David, one of the trainers, comes out of the changing room.

"I can take him," he tells me. "Hi, I'm David." Maddox just looks at him and he follows him into the changing room. He looks over one last time before he walks in as he waves at me.

I hold up my hand as the tears sting my eyes. "Do you have everything under control?" I ask Veronica, and she nods at me as I walk to my office and grab the files in the corner. I grab his file and am ready to open it when my phone buzzes, and I look down, seeing the breaking news.

Dylan Stone is going to Dallas. All the details on his record-breaking contract.

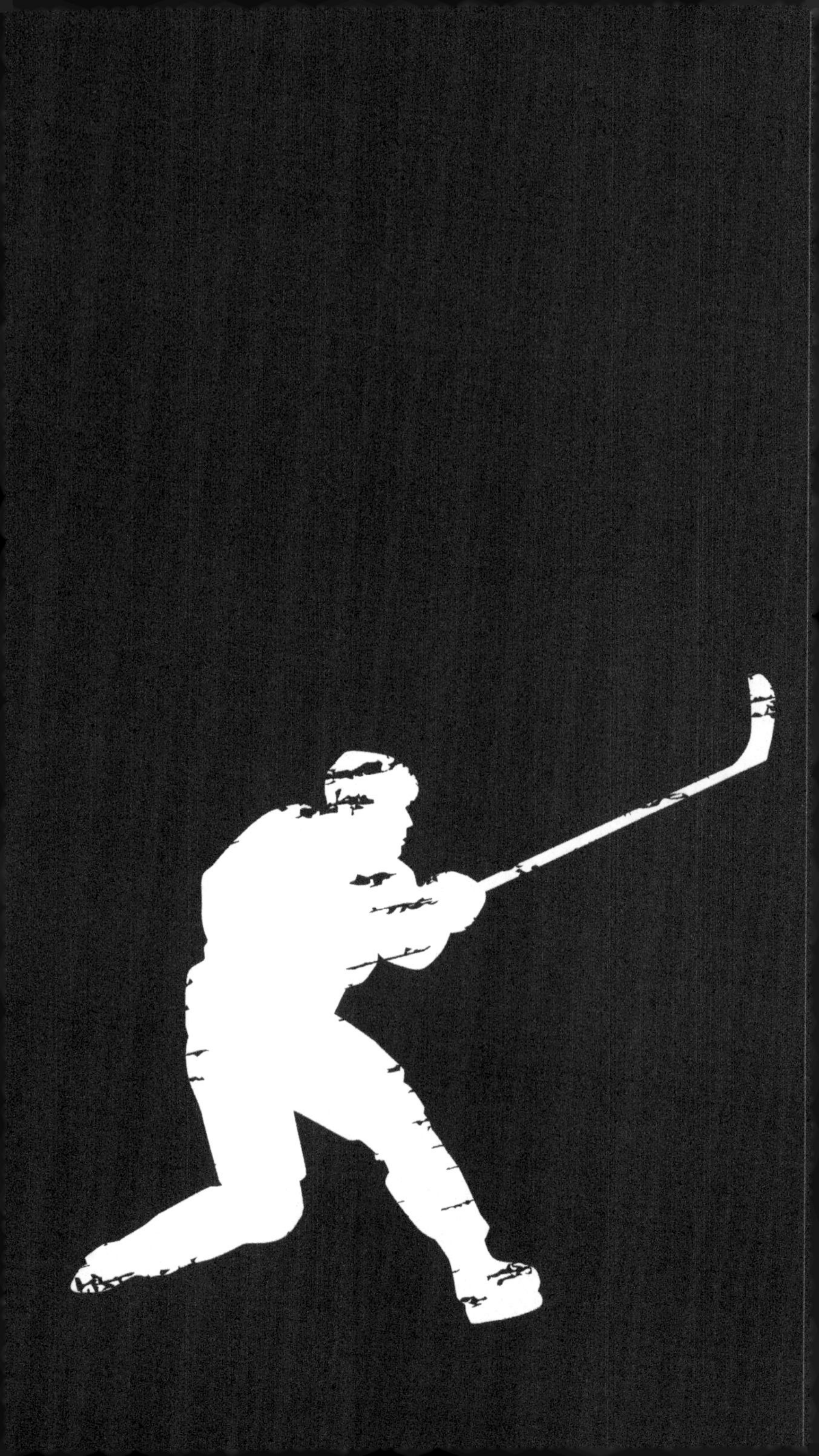

EIGHTEEN

DYLAN

"WELL, ANOTHER FAMILY vacation in the books," my uncle Matthew says as he climbs the steps to the plane. "I already miss you pains in the ass." He looks back down at me.

"I didn't even get drunk!" I shriek. "Why aren't you talking to Chase, who fell asleep naked on a paddleboard?"

"That was the highlight of my trip," Julia announces. "In fact, next year, he should just come naked." She looks behind her at Chase, who just smiles and laughs.

"One with the earth," he says, holding out his arms.

"I almost became one with the earth when I saw my brother's dick," Vivienne retorts. "I think I will have PTSD." She looks at him. "Is that what you did with your Doctors Without Borders? Just showed up with your shlong hanging all over the place?"

"I think I'm going to be sick." I put my hand to my

mouth and look over at Chase. "You're lucky nothing bit you." I walk into the plane and take the first seat that is empty, which is right in front of Wilson and Franny, who are joking with each other. He leans over and whispers something in her ear, and she blushes. "Seriously, you two," I huff out. "Enough with all that shit." I motion with my hand.

I'm buckling my seat belt when someone sits next to me, and I look up to see it's Erika. "How is everything going? Did the news hit?" she says, and I nod my head. Yesterday, after I told my father that I was in love with Alex and he didn't kick me out on my ass, I made the decision I knew I was going to make anyway. I called Erika, and we sat down with Nico via Zoom. "I honestly didn't care how much he was going to pay me because the minute I said yes to him, my whole body just let out this whole rush. Almost like you took the air out of a balloon. "It's the biggest contract out there," she says in a hush. "People are going to think you left for the money."

I swallow now. No one but my father, and maybe Julia, will know why I signed with Dallas. I know that I'm going to have to tell them, but I just don't think it's the time. Especially since I haven't told anyone. "I don't care what people say. I never did," I say, looking around. "The only ones I care about are my father and my grandfather." I look over to see my grandfather with Bianca on his chest while my grandmother holds Bailey.

"Well, get ready for the media storm when we land," she tells me, getting up and making her way back to Cooper. I look out the window as everyone finally loads the plane. My finger taps on the armrest as the door closes. I take out my phone and send Alex another text.

Me: *Alex, please call me.*

I know it will go unanswered, and I know she is going to fight with me when I finally see her, but just the thought of seeing her and finally being able to tell her how I feel will be like the weight of the world is off my shoulders.

The plane is filled with the usual chitchat, and when I look up and see that Franny has left her seat, I turn and look over at Wilson. "Come here." I motion with my head, and he gets up and comes to sit in the chair beside me.

"What's up?" he asks.

"I was wondering if I could volunteer at your hockey camp this summer," I say, and he just looks at me with his eyebrows pinched together.

"Why are you even asking me that?" he says. "I don't take care of that. Alex does." With a smirk, he leans back in his seat and crosses his arms over his chest. He looks at me for a moment and then looks around to make sure no one is paying attention. He leans into me. "I don't know what is going on," he says. "But I know that she left, and it wasn't for any fucking emergency." He looks around again, and I clench my fist. He looks down and sees it, making him smirk and then smile. "Maybe no one else has caught on …" He looks around. "But I have, and if you hurt her …"

"Let's just get one thing clear," I say. "What's between Alex and me is between the two of us."

He throws his head back and laughs. "Fair enough.

You can come by anytime you want." He shrugs. "As long as she approves it." He gets up now. "By the way, welcome to Dallas."

He goes to sit in his seat. When I see my father looking at me, he just motions with his chin, and I shake my head. Ever since I told him about Alex, he's been almost like my shadow. I know that he's doing it to show me his support, and to be honest, knowing that I have it makes whatever hurdles I have to jump over just a touch easier.

The plane touches down, and I'm itching to get to her. I get up, and Julia stands behind me. "You going to go to her?" she asks.

"Nope," I tell her. "I'm not going to go see her at her job." I shake my head. "Besides, being there when she gets home is better." I look at her. "Are you going to give her a heads-up?"

"Nah." She shakes her head. "But if she calls me and needs me to help bury your body, you bet your ass I'll be there."

I walk down the stairs and to the side, waiting for my luggage. I hug everyone goodbye, and my father holds me a touch longer. I walk to the waiting SUV, giving him the address to Alex's house. When I get there, I call the dog watcher and tell her I'm home. She tells me she will be over within an hour. I walk into the house, surprised she didn't change the code. I am even more shocked when I see her luggage all by the stairs. She hates not unpacking when she comes back. I walk upstairs, taking her suitcases to her room, and find her bed unmade.

I sit on her bed and do the creepiest thing I've done

ever. I grab her pillow and bring it to my nose. My heart speeds up even more when the doorbell rings, and I walk down and open the door. Mac barks at me and comes into the house, jumping on me. I get down, and she jumps again as she licks my face. "How was she?"

"Perfect," she says, handing me the leash.

"Did you miss me?" I ask her as she runs into the house and smells around, no doubt looking for Alex. "She isn't here," I say as she looks over at me and runs upstairs to her bedroom. I wait down by the staircase, and four seconds later, she runs back downstairs. "Let's go wait in the living room for her," I say, walking into the kitchen and grabbing a water bottle from the fridge, and when I close the fridge, I see the picture we took at the aquarium. The both of us with our hands in the water with the stingrays.

Turning, I walk to the living room and sit down, looking around. I see the picture of the both of us on the side table, and then I look over at the fireplace and see that there is a picture of us last Christmas, dressed up in the same onesie pjs. I sit forward and put my water on the coffee table.

I'm about to get up when I hear a car in the driveway. Mac sticks her head up, looking at the front door and barking. "Stay," I say as the front door opens, but she doesn't listen to me. She totally ignores me and jumps off the couch and goes straight where she isn't supposed to. I follow her and watch Alex as she looks down at Mac and smiles. The pain I felt in my chest for the past two days is suddenly lifted. She takes my breath away like no one else. Her hair falls into her face when Mac jumps up on her.

"What are you doing here?" she asks, and then her eyes suddenly lift and meet mine.

"Hi," I say softly, picking up my hand, feeling so fucking awkward.

"Dylan." She says my name, and my stomach sinks when she looks down. She takes a deep breath. "You shouldn't be here."

I wait for her to look up before I say the next thing. Once her eyes look up, I can see some tears in her eyes. My mouth goes dry all of a sudden, and my tongue feels like it's fifty pounds. The back of my neck starts to heat as the nerves in my stomach take on an all-time high. I wasn't this nervous throughout my whole hockey career, but now that I am ready to lay everything out to her, everything I thought I would say is gone. Except for the words, "We need to set the record straight."

"There is nothing to say," she says. "Well, that isn't right." She places her purse down on the first step toward the kitchen.

I watch her walk to the kitchen, her hands shaking when she reaches for the water bottle. "Alex, we need to talk."

"We really don't," she replies calmly, and she turns around, looking at me. "I'm sorry." Her voice stays monotone.

"Wait, what?" I asked, confused now.

"I burdened you with how I felt." She walks over to the island and sets the water bottle down in front of her, holding the bottle with both hands. "I should have never told you." The tears come to her eyes, but she blinks them away, and her lower lip trembles. "If I could take it back, I would."

I put my hands on my hips, my nerves turning to anger. "Well, you did, and there is no way in fuck you are taking it back."

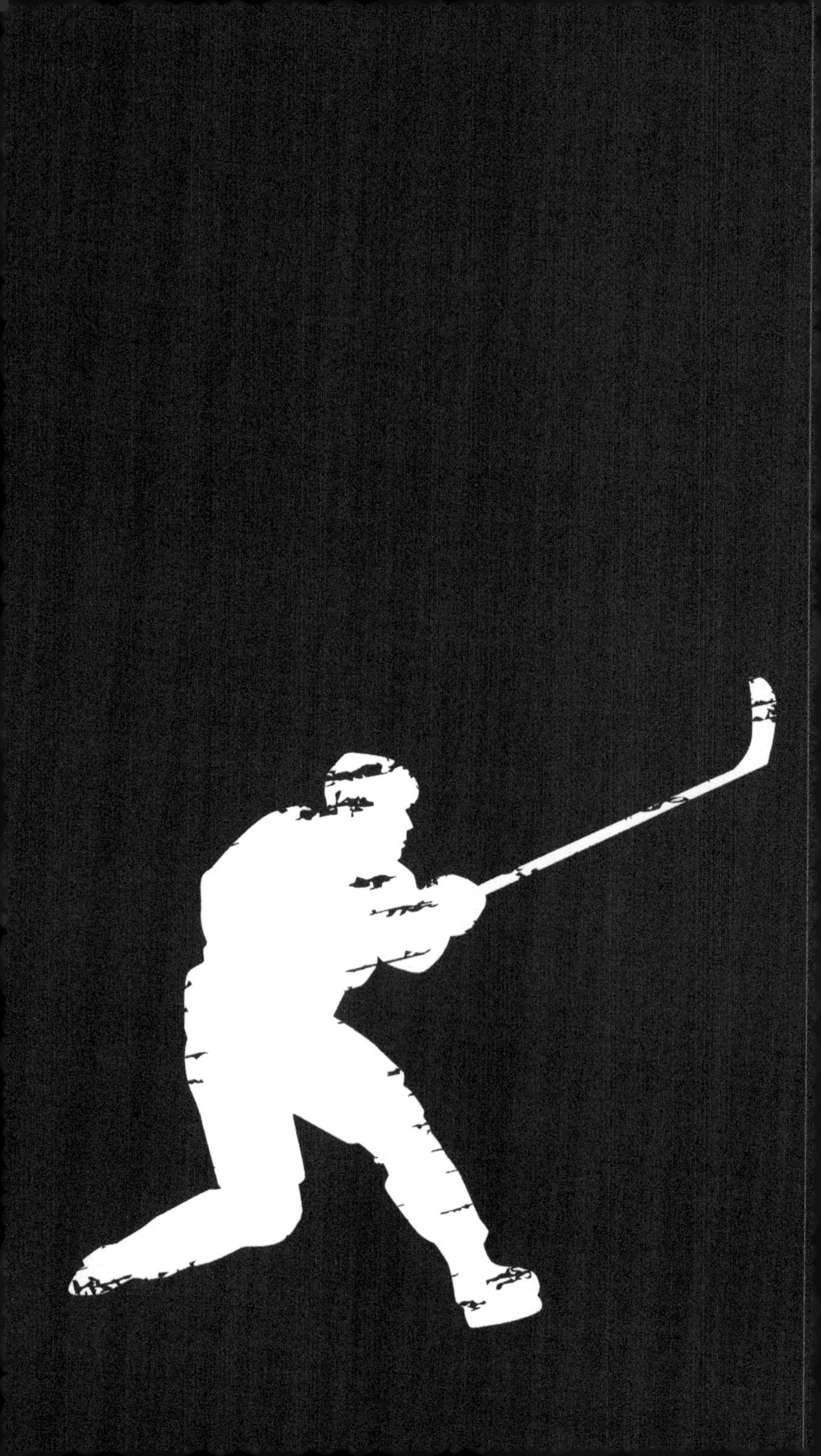

NINETEEN

Alex

I WATCH HIM put his hands on his hips, and my whole chest feels tight. "Well, you did, and there is no way in fuck you are taking it back." His voice is tight, and I put my hands on my hips. "Alex, you have to talk to me." The lump in my throat fills up when his tone goes even softer. "It's me." His hands fall from his hips. "You can tell me anything."

The beat of my heart starts to slow down when Mac knocks my hand. I look down at her, and tears suddenly fill my eyes. When I walked into the house and Mac came to greet me, I knew in my bones he was here. I should have known that he would have come straight here. I should have known, and maybe deep down, I was hoping he would. But seeing him standing here in front of me is more than I think I can bear. "Dylan, there really isn't much more to say." I say his name, and I can't even look up at him. The embarrassment of my words two days ago rings in my ears. I blink away all the tears and finally move my eyes up to look at him, his own tears in his eyes. "I just need a couple of months," I say. "And then we can go back to what it was before."

"What if I don't want that?" he says, and I swear I feel my knees buckle at his words. I just look at him. He stands there in jeans and a T-shirt, and my body aches for him. To touch his hand or even hug him, knowing his hugs pretty much always make things better. "What if I feel the same way?" I swallow, and the beating of my heart echoes so loud in my ears I'm not sure I heard him correctly. I don't have a chance to ask him what he means because he just keeps talking. "What if I feel the same way?" One of my hands goes to my stomach as it sinks and then rises. "What if I'm in love with you, too?"

All I can do is shake my head, the tears escaping my eyes no matter how much I try to forbid it. No matter how much I try to fight it, they are stronger than me. "You don't have to say that," I say, not sure I can even look at him without falling apart in front of him. "You don't have to say that just because I'm crying."

"Alex." His voice is tight, and I look up as he takes a step toward me. "You think I would declare my love for you just because you said it?" He shakes his head. "The past couple of weeks have been torture for me." His own tears run down his face. "I was so fucking confused." His voice trembles. "I didn't know what was going on, and then I came here. When I was with you, it's like all the pieces of all the puzzles finally clicked into place." He takes a step forward. "I …" He chokes on his words now, and all I can do is shake my head, my heart not sure it can handle this.

My hand goes to my mouth as the tears pour down my face. "Dylan, I beg you," I say, my voice giving out on me as the sob comes out. "Please."

He takes a step toward me now, closing the distance. My head goes down as I try not to crumple onto the floor. "Alex," he says in a whisper, and I can see his feet right in front of me. I can feel his heat over me. "My beautiful girl," he says, and I finally look up at him, and his hands come up to grab my face. His thumbs rub the tears away from my cheeks, and I shiver. "On the beach, you told me to choose New York," he says, trying to smile, but the tears just run down his face. "And just the thought of not being able to be with you caused me to collapse on the beach. I couldn't even run after you if I wanted to because my legs felt like there was concrete in them." He smirks. "Also, I knew you wouldn't listen to me."

I laugh, the speed of my heart calming down. "You are probably right." I don't even try to lie to him as I laugh.

"I chose Dallas," he tells me, and I nod my head.

"I heard," I say softly, his hands trembling softly.

"I chose it for you," he says, and I gasp. "And for me. Because I wouldn't have been where my heart was if I chose anyplace else." He moves even closer to me, and Mac just lies by our feet as if nothing is going on. "I want to kiss you." My eyes go big as he says the words. "I wanted to kiss you at the aquarium, but I thought that you would freak out and think I was a freak." He swallows now. "The whole vacation was my private hell. I would sit out on the balcony and just look up, waiting for someone to tell me what to do. Every night, I would say if you came to join me, it was a sign." He shrugs now. "You never did."

"I was too afraid," I say the truth. "Afraid you would see what I was thinking. Afraid that with one word, it would ruin everything." My hands come up as I place them on his. "Afraid I would lose you, and I don't know if I could survive that, but that walk on the beach." I smile. "I knew that I had to let you go."

"No," he says, shaking his head. "You aren't letting me go." He dips his head down as his forehead rests against mine. "I'm not letting you go that easily."

"Dylan," I say so softly, just the two of us can hear it. "Kiss me." I look into his eyes as he lowers his lips to mine. We both keep our eyes open, his hands pulling my face to his, my heart hammering so much in my chest I'm surprised I'm not having a panic attack.

The only thing going through my mind a million miles a minute is that he's going to kiss me. The kiss I've been waiting for since I fell in love with him when I was seventeen and he took me to prom because my date took someone else instead. I knew then that I felt differently for him, but I pushed it away because it felt wrong. I pushed it away, and it was like a bomb, and it ticked inside me until it finally exploded. "Alex." He says my name right before my breath hitches and his lips touch mine, and if my eyes weren't open, I wouldn't have felt it. It takes one second before his tongue slides into my mouth, and my eyes close. We swallow each other's moans as my hands fall from his, and I step into him even more. My arms go around his neck as his hands move from my cheeks, and he buries them in my hair.

My stomach flutters while he rolls his tongue with mine, his head tilting to the left to deepen the kiss. My chest presses into his and I swear this is what heaven feels like. Here in his arms, it's heaven. Everything that I thought a kiss should be is right here. Every dream I've had about this moment is nothing like it.

I'm lost in him, so lost in him I don't hear the phone ring until Mac barks. I let go of his lips, and my eyes slowly open. I'm afraid to look into his for fear that he might regret it. But my eyes don't listen to my head or my heart. His eyes have a glimmer to them, and the smile on his face is so full that his cheeks have moved up. "That was …" He looks down, suddenly shy.

I tilt my head to the side, not moving from in front of him. "It was," I confirm, and he looks at me, and my smile mimics his.

"I have never …" He starts to say and then stops talking, not sure if he should continue. My hand comes up to touch his lower lip.

"I have never had a kiss like that," I start, and he looks at me. "In all my life." My hand cups his cheek. "I've never been kissed like that."

"Um, thanks," he says, not sure, and then smirks. "It was."

"You did good." I lean in and kiss his lips softly, and the ringing starts again. "I should get that," I say to him as he kisses my lips again, and he makes me forget it all until the ringing stops for one second and then starts again.

He looks at me worried as I grab the phone out of my back pocket. Looking down, I find Veronica's number on the display. "Hello," I say, putting the phone to my ear.

"Um, hi," she says, her voice going almost to a whisper, and I can tell something is wrong. "Thank God you answered."

"What's wrong?" I ask right away, my heart speeding up when I think that one of the kids got hurt. Because that is me. I think of the worst-case scenario, so when she comes at me with something less, it won't be as bad.

"Maddox is still here," she says, and I turn my arm to see that it's six thirty. "We waited twenty minutes in case there was traffic." The camp has opening hours of eight to six, so no one is rushing to get there by five, especially for the parents who have a longer route to go.

"Did you call the emergency numbers?" I look at Dylan, whose eyebrows are pinched together as he hears the worry in my voice.

"We did," she confirms. "They are all disconnected."

I close my eyes now. "Okay, I'm on my way." I take a deep breath. "I'll be there in ten minutes." I disconnect the phone and look at Dylan.

"I have to go," I say, and his arms loosen around me. "One of the kids, his parents didn't get him." I look at the phone. "She dropped him off this morning, and she was on something."

"What do you mean she was on something?" he asks,

putting his hands on his hips.

"She was weird, and her eyes were all dilated." I shrug. "Dumped him there and took off. And she hasn't picked him up, and the phones are disconnected."

"Oh my God," he says, shaking his head. "She sounds like a great parent."

"We don't judge," I remind him. "Everyone has problems."

"Oh, trust me," he says. "I'm the last person who judges anyone. I went one week eating peanut butter on toast because we had no money." My heart sinks when he says that, and I can't even imagine what he went through. He never really shares that part of his life with anyone. He'll drop some comments here and there but never anything in depth. "Let's go." He grabs my hand and pulls me out of the house.

"You can stay here," I say, and he stops walking.

"If you get there and the mother isn't there, what are you going to do?" he asks.

"I'm going to drive him home," I say. "Maybe she couldn't get to the arena on time."

"Or maybe she's sleeping through her bender. Either way, you aren't going alone."

"Wow," I say, opening the passenger door when he walks toward the driver's side. "You can get more annoying."

He looks at me and winks. "This is just the beginning."

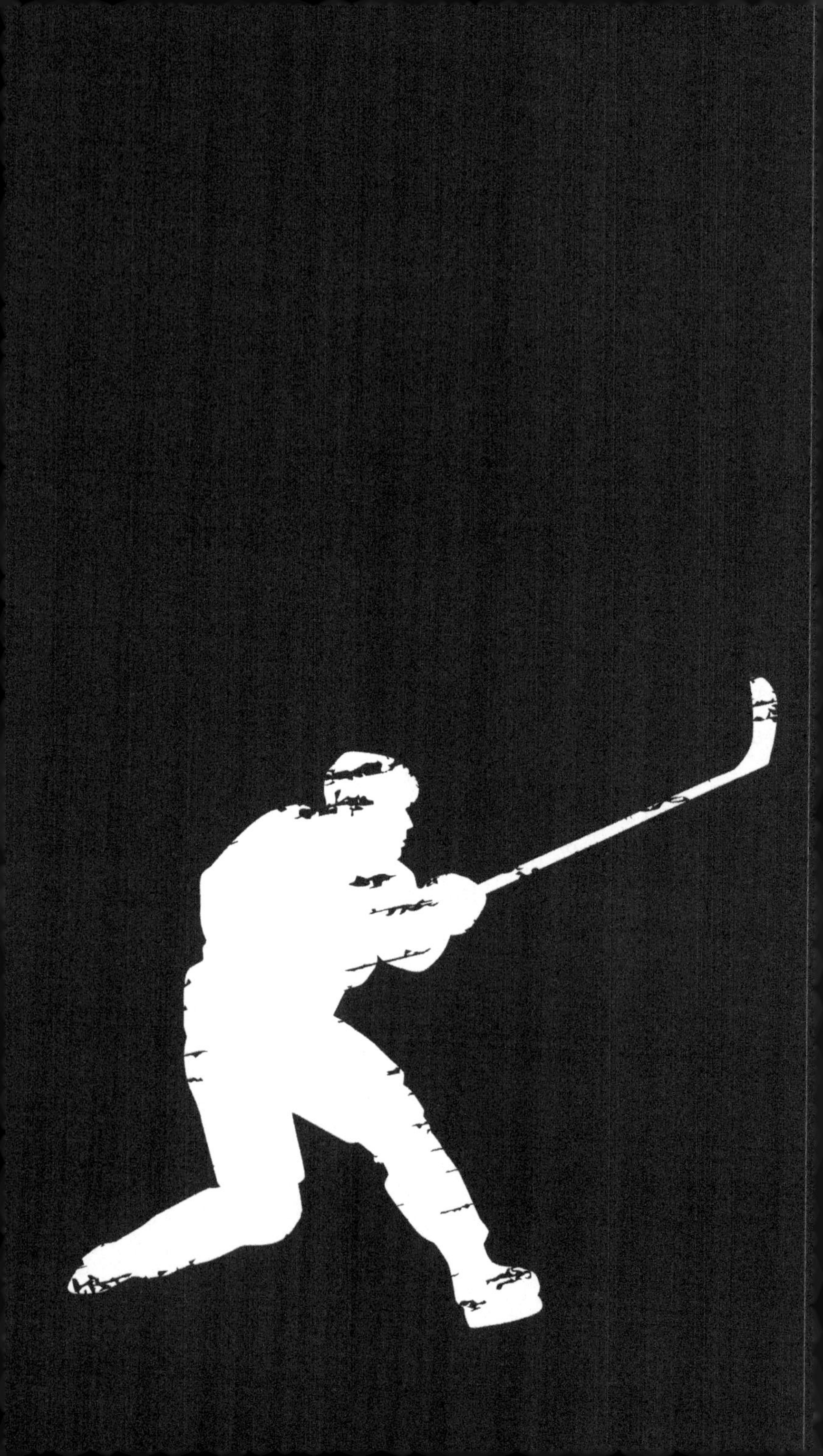

TWENTY

Dylan

"Park there." She points at the parking spot closest to the door that has a No Parking sign on it.

"Will you get towed?" I look over at her, but she is already out of the car and rushing to walk into the arena.

I get out and follow her, walking in and looking around. I spot the kid right away. He is sitting on the bench in front of the door with his head down. His brown hair shines, and I know it's because he took a shower. His shoulders are slumped forward like he's used to being left places and not being picked up, and my feet stop in my tracks when he looks up at me. His brown eyes meet mine, and the look brings me back to when I was seven years old.

"What do you mean they are all disconnected?" I hear Alex talking to a woman, but I just walk past her toward the little boy. He must be scared or, better yet, just numb, and that feeling is even worse than being scared.

"Hey." I squat down in front of the kid. "I'm Dylan." He just looks at me, and his arms and legs are skinnier than they should be. "What's your name?" The look he gives me is a look I've seen before. It's a look that was in my own eyes. *Despair.*

"Maddox." His voice is monotone, and I know that he's been in this situation before. People looking at you and feeling sorry for you.

"Are you hungry?" I ask, my stomach burning as I think about when his last meal was.

He just shrugs his shoulders, and I know that's rule number one for anyone who is ever in our shoes. *Never let anyone in* was my motto. My mother busted her ass for my father and us. Sorry, that is the wrong name for him; the sperm donor who would drag us down the black hole with him. No matter how much I tried to crawl out of that hole. "I can get you something to eat," I say. "It might just be something small, but …"

His eyes come to mine, and they look as if there is no life left in them. There is no lightness to them like the kids in my life. "Hey," Alex says. "Maddox, we are going to take you home." She looks at me with a smile, pretending that everything is hunky-dory, and I know that it's a fucking cycle. "I think your mom got held up."

He doesn't say anything because what can you say. "You have the address?" I ask her, and she nods. She stands up and holds out her hand for his, but Maddox just stands up beside her.

"You must be tired, buddy." I smile at him, wrapping my arm around him and putting it on his shoulder. "I remember when I was in hockey camp, and I would fall asleep on the bus." I look at him as we get beside the car. "Why don't we get something to eat before we drop you off?" He just looks at me, and I know what he's thinking. Nothing that I'm going to do will change tomorrow. Alex just looks at me, and I shake my head, telling her that it's not going to change him. She gets the booster seat from her trunk and puts Maddox in and belts him in. She closes the door and looks over at me. "Are you sure you know what you're doing?" The pit of burning in my stomach creeps in.

"I have no idea what the fuck to do," she says, holding up her hands and looking into the car window. "But I know that if I can take him home, I will."

"Okay." I look around and pull her to me. "Whatever you say."

She smiles up at me, and I bend to kiss her lips. "Let's get him home and then we can get back home and do some more of that kissing."

My whole chest fills. "Oh, is that so?"

"Well, you're very good at it, and I want to make sure that it's as good as it was before," she says, walking to her side of the car. I get in and look back at Maddox, who just looks out at the window. I stop at McDonald's and order him one of everything. He is so tired that he takes just a couple of bites of his burger before he says he isn't hungry.

I put the address in the GPS and look over at Alex when it shows me that it's an hour away. "How the hell did she get to the arena?" Alex mutters under her breath.

"One year, we took four buses." I look over at Alex. "We had to get up at five a.m."

"That's crazy," she says, reaching for my hand, and I slip my fingers through hers as I just look forward at the road. Following the direction of the GPS, I can feel the shift in status as soon as I turn down the block. The houses are older, the buildings have less and less luxury to them. Most of the windows are open as the GPS tells us we have reached our destination. "Oh, boy," Alex says, and I look in the rearview mirror and see that Maddox had fallen asleep, but he opens his eyes and rubs them awake.

I look over at the brown apartment buildings all clustered together. I push away the memories that start coming back, locking them away just as I did all those years before. I look over at Alex. "You stay right next to me," I say as I see little gangs of people forming in the dark corners of the building. "Alex," I warn, looking at her. "I'm not playing right now."

"Relax," she tells me, and I don't have time to tell her anything before she opens the car door. I jump out of the car, meeting her. I look around as she opens the door to grab Maddox.

"What apartment number?" I ask her as we walk toward the front door.

"Three forty-seven," she says as I walk with her and Maddox in the middle of us. When I pull open the door, the humid air comes to you right away. As you walk up the concrete stairs, you get the smell of spices along with sweat and desperation. The sound of people yelling fills the air, as well as babies crying.

We walk up the three flights of stairs. My skin starts to tingle, and the memories come one after another. I look down at my sneakers that I paid over four hundred dollars for. These sneakers might be as much as some people pay for their rent. I look at the door seeing that the doors are stainless steel, most of them dented in. When we come to his door, we both see the yellow notice on the door.

EVICTION. In big, bold black letters.

We both look at each other, neither of us saying a word, and I reach for the handle of the door, expecting it to be locked, but it opens. Alex's arm flies out to stop me from stepping forward, but it's too late because the door opens. Maddox takes a step in like he's getting home. Alex follows him, and I follow her. My eyes scan the room, ignoring Alex's gasp. There is no bedroom; it's one big room. The back wall has two windows that are closed. The main light in the room is on, showing us the dirty rug. The whole place has one piece of furniture, and that is a mattress in the middle of the room, right on the floor. Not even sheets are on the bed, just the yellow stains, and my stomach rises. My head spins around and around, and I think I'm going to be sick when Maddox walks over to the bed and sits down. "No!" Alex yells, frightening him, and I look over at her and see the tears in her eyes.

"It's fine." I smile, trying not to make him feel like he did something wrong and then looking at her. "This is his home," I remind her as I turn to see the fridge, walking over to it I open it and see it's empty. I walk over to the sink seeing it empty, and when I try to turn on the water, nothing comes out. Opening the cupboard over the sink, I see that it's empty. Every single cabinet is empty. "Maddox." I turn, looking at him. "Where do you keep your cups?" He looks at me, getting up and walking to the bathroom and comes back with a red Solo cup. He hands it to me, and I smile at him. "And where are your clothes?" He looks around the room.

"We keep a bag in that corner." He points at the empty corner of the room. I look over at Alex, who has to turn around to wipe away the tears. I look around the room, and it finally dawns on me that no one lives here. Even if you are dirt poor and have nothing, you at least have some sort of belongings. But there is nothing here

"What else is missing?" I ask, looking around at the four walls with the small bathroom in the corner.

"I had a chair," he says. "And there was a cover for the bed."

I hear someone in the hallway, and I take a step out, seeing one of the neighbors. She looks up at me, surprised I'm here. "Hey, sorry to bother you, but do you know the people who live here?"

She takes her keys out and starts to open her door. "No one lives there." She huffs and puffs. "Ducked out of here early this morning. She tried to be quiet, but she was yelling at her child to hurry the fuck up while she carried one box." I nod at her, and if I didn't feel like barfing before, I definitely feel the bile crawling up my throat.

When I walk in, I see that Alex is wiping away a tear. "You need to call Julia," I say, and her eyes go big. I look over to see Maddox lying on the bed in a fetal position, my voice going low. "She moved out of here this morning."

"But." She starts to say. "Where did she go?"

"I don't think she left a forwarding address." My voice stays low as not to wake Maddox. "Either way, we have to call someone."

She pulls her phone out and calls Julia on speakerphone, lowering the volume of her phone. I look over at Maddox, but he doesn't stir. "Hello," Julia answers.

"Hey, it's me," Alex says softly. "I have a situation."

"Oh, good God," she huffs out. "How many situations can you get into in three days?"

"I'm not kidding." Her voice goes tight, and she doesn't give Julia time to talk. "There is a kid from the hockey school."

"Oh, shit," Julia says now.

"Mother dropped him off this morning," Alex explains. "I got a call at six thirty. She never showed up."

"Fuck," Julia curses. "Are you at the rink now?"

"No," Alex says. "We decided that we would drive him home."

"What?" she shrieks. "What the hell is wrong with you? You can never, and I mean never leave with the child. You need to call the authorities."

Alex looks at me. "How the hell was I supposed to know? I was helping. I thought the mother was stuck and couldn't come get him."

"I need you to send me the address right now," she says, and I can hear her moving around. "I also need you to send me his full name and his date of birth." The sound of a door slams. "This is very important," she says. "If his mother or father gets there, you need to call 9-1-1."

I run my hands through my hair. "If he doesn't have a file, he needs to have a file now." Alex hangs up the phone and sends Julia the address.

My eyes go back to Maddox. "What the hell just happened?" Alex says, and I look over at Maddox.

I swallow down the massive lump forming in my throat. The back of my neck gets so hot it tingles all the way to the top of my head. "His life just went from hell to an even bigger hell."

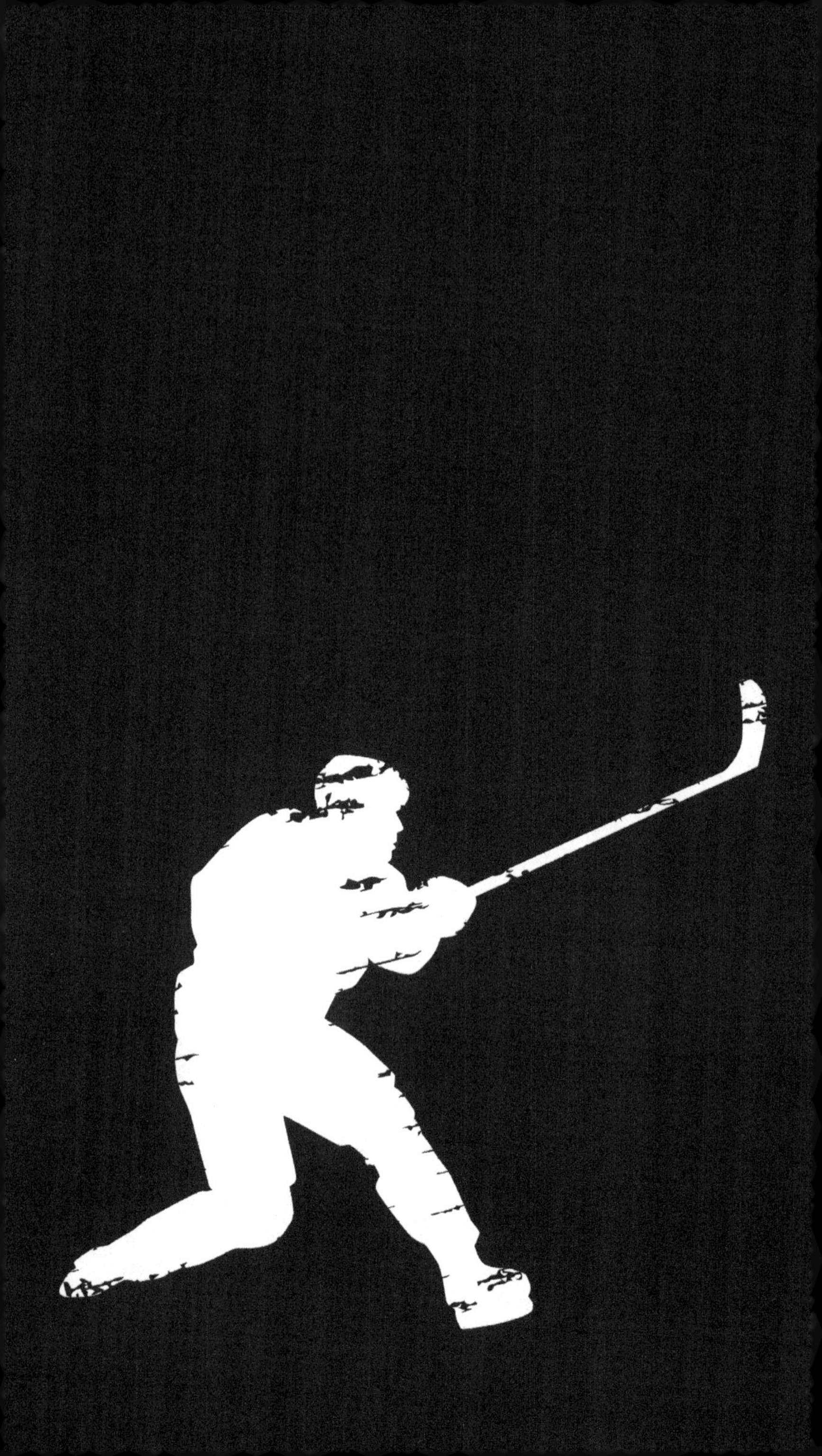

TWENTY-ONE

Dylan

My whole body is tight while we wait for Julia to arrive. The noises in the other apartments get louder as it gets darker outside. I stand by the window, looking outside and see the danger that lurks there. More people are forming in the little group of guys we saw when we walked in. There is a bang in the distance, and I wonder if it's a gunshot. Every single time I hear voices that sound like they are coming closer and closer, I get ready to defend us. The day started off like shit as I finally was able to kiss my girl, and then this happened. This fucking hellhole just brings back all of the memories I've tried so hard to forget.

The soft knock on the door makes me jump up, and I look over at Alex. "If it's not Julia," I tell her, "I want you to take Maddox and hide in the bathroom."

"Dylan," she says, and I can hear the fear a bit.

"This is not up for discussion," I say, walking to the

door. "Hello."

"Open the door," Julia hisses out, and I open the door, and she stands there dressed in jeans and a T-shirt. Two men walk in behind her, and I see that they are police officers. I look over at the bed, seeing that Maddox has opened his eyes for a second and then has fallen back to sleep. "Guys, this is Officer Jordon and Perez." I nod at the men as they walk in and look around.

"Why did you call the police?" Alex looks at her.

"We have to make a report," Julia says.

"What, why?" Alex asks, confused, and I put my arm around her. My stomach that was burning before feels like someone kicked me in it.

"Alex," Julia says, her voice going soft. "You have to make a report so he can go into emergency foster care." The stomach that felt sick before rises up.

"No." Alex shakes her head. "I can take him for a couple of days. Until we locate his mom." The tears come to her, and I look over at the police officers who share a look.

"That isn't how things work, Alex," Julia says, looking at her, and I pull her close to me. "You can't just keep him."

"But he was left in my care." Alex starts to argue. "So technically."

"The contract that the mother signed finishes at six. After that, you aren't responsible for him."

"What's going to happen to him?" I finally ask, and Julia looks at me, and I can already tell that it's nothing good. This kid isn't going to go from here to a perfect life.

"I already called the emergency foster home," Julia says. "They are nice people." She tries to reassure Alex. "He stays there until I can try to locate his mother." She looks down, hiding something, and I can just fucking imagine. "He's already got a file." My heart squeezes. "He was left alone once for four days. Neighbors called the cops, but Mom showed up and said they were lying and she was home the whole time."

"And you guys just believed her?" I ask, shocked, and my voice goes up just a touch.

"From what I read, they came in, did a welfare check, and he had food and water in the fridge, so there really isn't much we can do."

"Food and water?" I shriek. "Did anyone talk to him?"

"He was six," Julia says. "We did two more pop-ins. Everything met code."

"That was two years ago." Alex shakes her head. "He's eight years old now."

"I need to have his whole file," Julia says. The officers nod to her as they look around, and then one walks to the bathroom.

"Can't we take him for the night?" Alex looks at Julia, who tilts her head to the side. She looks at me, and I just nod at her.

"Alex, if it was up to me, I would say sure, but it's not." She walks to her, and she rubs her bare arm with her hand. "There are steps to go through. You have to attend an informational meeting, complete an application, undergo background checks and clearances, attend training and classes."

"Well, wherever you take him," Alex says, wiping away a tear. "Will he still be able to get to the hockey school?"

"I'll make sure of it," she assures us. "Even if I have to pick him up and drive him myself."

"I can help," I tell her. "Whatever he needs."

"Am I leaving?" Maddox says, getting up and sitting on the paper-thin mattress.

"Hey," Julia says, walking over to him and sitting on the floor in front of him. "I'm Julia." She holds out her hand. "I'm a friend of Alex and Dylan." She smiles at him, folding her legs, not giving zero fucks that two days ago she was staying in a five-star resort, and now she's in the ghetto.

"Are you going to take me?" he asks, his eyes motionless.

"Just for a bit." She lies to him, and I want to speak up, but I bite my tongue. "Just until we find your mom, and she can come get you."

"She said she's never coming back," Maddox says, and if I thought I was going to throw up before, it's nothing like listening to him say the words.

"We will see," Julia says. "Do you know where your dad is?" He shakes his head and shrugs. "Do you have an auntie that you guys go and visit?" And he just shakes his head. "A grandma?" Maddox just shakes his head, not saying anything, and I can just imagine the turmoil going through his head. The thought that he is alone with no one that he can go to is unbearable to me.

"Okay, well, I'm going to take you to my friend's house," Julia says to him.

"Is there a bed there?" he asks, and Alex trembles beside me. I turn her and pull her in my arms. "And a blanket."

"There is a bed and a blanket," Julia says. "And tomorrow, you get to go back to the hockey camp."

"Okay," he says, getting up and not saying a word.

My feet move before I can even understand what is going on. "Hey." I squat down in front of him. "Tomorrow, I'll be waiting for you at the rink," I say, and his eyes just look at me like he's heard that before. Empty promises. "Pinky swear." I hold out my pinky. "You know what that means?" I ask, and all he does is look at me. "Means that I have no choice but to show up." Julia gets up and walks over to the officers with Alex beside her. "I know how it feels," I tell him, my own tears starting to burn at the corner of my eyes. "I had a dad who didn't want me either." I look down. "But I didn't have Julia or Alex, and I can tell you they are going to make sure you're okay."

"Okay, report is done," Julia says. "Now off to Paula and Roberto," she tells him. "Do you like cats?" He shrugs. "They have one cat called Stuart Little." She smiles at him, and he just looks at me once before turning, and we walk out of the house.

I stand beside Alex while they load him up in Julia's car. She closes the door and looks at us. "I'll call you when I get everything settled." I nod my head at her as we watch her get into the car. Maddox puts his head to the side, resting it on the door, not looking at us. And

I don't know why I'm happy he didn't because I don't know if I would have survived it.

"Let's get out of here," I say, looking around to see that eyes are on us. I push Alex toward the car and put her in, walking around the car and getting in. Neither of us says anything as we make our way back home.

When we walk in, Mac comes to us, and my body feels like it's numb. "Are you hungry?" I hear Alex talking to Mac, and all I can do is walk over to the couch and sit down. My head goes back, and I close my eyes, and all I see is that fucking mattress in the middle of the room. A mattress with so many stains it turned orange. "Hey," I hear Alex say softly as she comes over to me, and I don't even notice that tears are running down my face. She stops in front of me, getting on her knees between my legs. "Julia is going to make sure he's okay," she says, reassuring myself and her also.

She puts her elbows on my knees. "That could have been me," I say, the words coming out of my mouth. "If I didn't have my mother, that could have been me."

"Dylan," she says softly, and for the first time in my whole life, I tell her things I've never told anyone.

"When I was four, five guys showed up at our front door," I tell her, the memory was buried so deep I only remembered it when I walked into the apartment. "Slammed my mother into a wall." She puts one of her hands to her mouth. "They were looking for my sperm donor," I say, refusing to call that man my father. "I can hear the yelling in my head. My mother was pleading with them to leave me alone. She was going to sacrifice herself for me. One of the guys came over, grabbed the television that we had, and walked out of the door." I rub my hands over my face. The numbness starts to leave me, and a new feeling starts to show up. "And that was just one story." My whole body shakes from the anger, the anger of living through the memories. The anger of being fucking helpless. "That apartment wasn't even that bad," I tell her. "We stayed in rat-infested places. I went to bed with my stomach empty, no matter how much my mother tried. Do you think if we hadn't gotten out of there, I would be where I am today?"

"I do," Alex says. "Your talent isn't something that is taught."

I laugh at her, and my hand comes up to touch her face, her innocent face. Her face is what angels are made of. "I would be just a product of my environment," I tell her. "Sadly, it's a vicious cycle, and unless you get lucky like we did, it's just going to go around in circles. I would probably be one of those guys at the corner trying to make a quick buck to put food on the table. Or who knows." I shake my head. "What if I ended up like my father. A drug addict who would sell the shit he stole from his son." I shout the words, not able to hold it back in. I'm so fucking pissed at having to relive it over and over again.

"Stop," she says, her voice tight. "Stop thinking of the what-ifs." She leans up and grabs my face in her hands. "If we do this whole what-if scenario, that means we would have never met, and I don't ever want to think of that."

I know she's right. I also know that if I keep going down memory lane, nothing good will come of it. "Okay," I say softly, pulling her to me and kissing her lips. "I'm going to go and get in the shower."

She gets up. "I'm going to feed Mac and make sure she's okay."

I nod at her, walking upstairs and going to the shower I used the last time I was here. When I get out and slip into boxers, I walk into the room and see her in the middle of the bed. Her hair is wet and piled on her head. "How long was I in the shower?" I ask her, and she just smiles.

"I figured that I had to rush in case Julia called," she says, and I get into the bed next to her. "She didn't."

"Yeah, I figure it'll take her a bit before she has Maddox settled and stuff," I tell her. "I don't know how she does it."

"I was just thinking the same thing," she says, looking at me. "I don't know how I would be able to just close myself off."

"You can't save everyone," I tell her. "But you can help change at least one person's life." I lie down on my side. "That person is going to be Maddox," I state, not sure what I'm even going to have to do to help him, but I know that I'll do whatever it is, and I'm not going to ask questions.

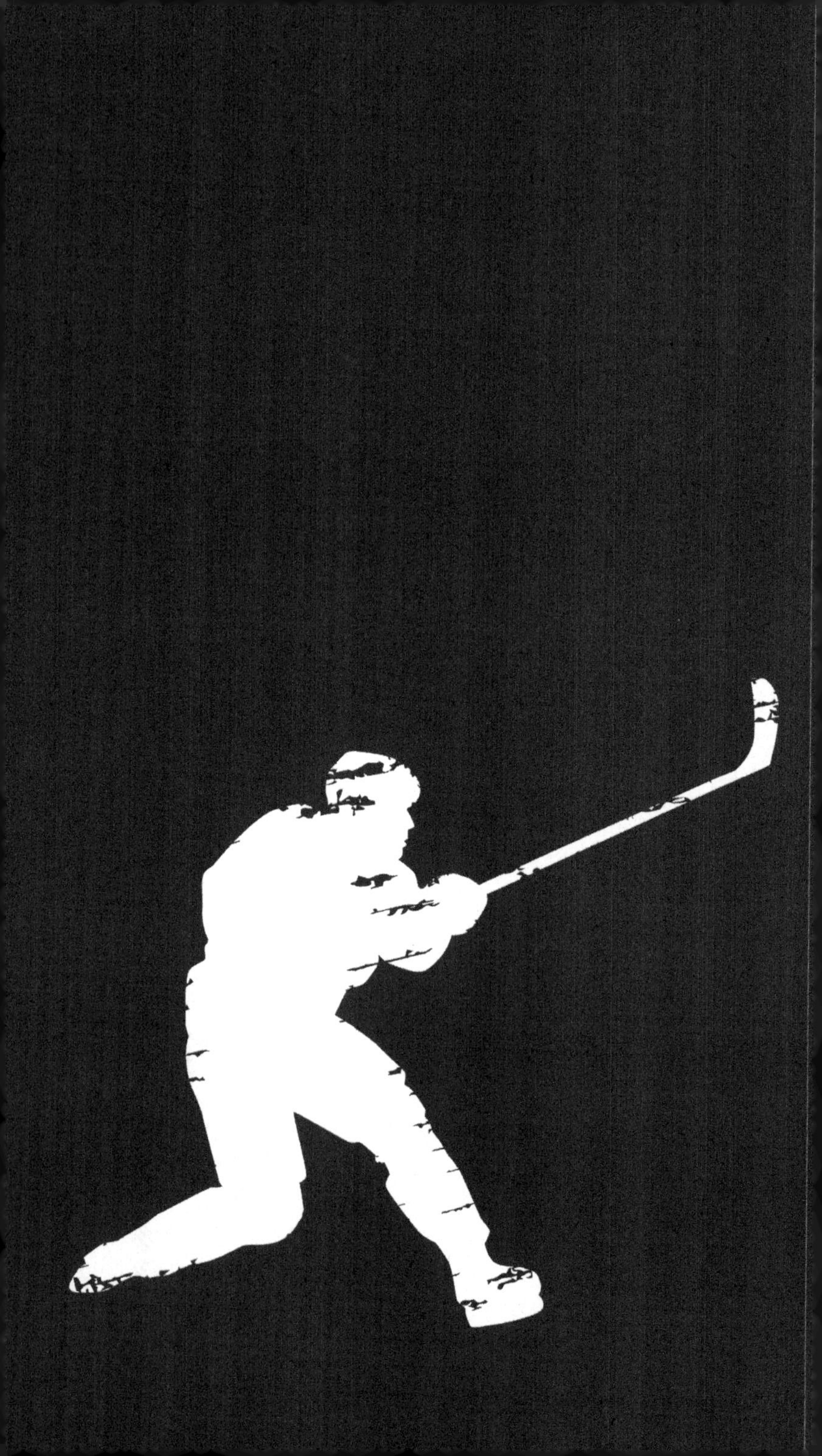

TWENTY-TWO

Alex

THE SOFT ALARM makes me open my eyes, and then I feel weight on me as Dylan leans over me to turn it off. "Morning," he mumbles, and he gets off me, but I reach for him and pull him back to me. I turn in his arms, and he wraps his arms around me, burying my face in his neck. All night long, I would wake and look over at him, but he was always close by. "Um," he says softly as I push myself into his chest. "Alex," he says when I wiggle my covered chest against his bare chest. I kiss under his chin, lifting my leg over his hip. "This is not going to end well." I lean back to see him with his eyes closed as he starts counting. I throw my head back and laugh at him, and then he flips me on my back.

My legs open for him as he settles between them, my legs hitched on his hips and locked behind him. "Oh, this is a lot better," I say, and I can feel his covered cock lining up with my covered core.

"Alex," he hisses with his teeth clenched together as his mouth comes down and crashes onto mine. His tongue slides into my mouth, and my hips lift, making him groan into my mouth. My back arches, making my nipples tingle when they push against the cotton of my tank top. I'm about to rip my tank top off when Dylan moves his mouth and body away from me. He gets off the bed, his chest rising and falling as he looks at me lying in the middle of the bed with my legs spread open. My nipples are pointing through the white fabric, leaving nothing to the imagination. "You." He points at me, and I look at him, his cock outlined in his white boxers. "There is no time for this."

"Umm, I beg to differ," I reply, smiling and turning on my side.

"We have to get to the rink," he says, and I glare at him. "The last thing Maddox needs is to show up and me not be there. I made a pinky promise."

"Well, can you pinky promise me that tonight we can make out?" I hold out my hand for him. "Like a hot and heavy make-out session."

He laughs, coming over and wrapping his pinky with mine. "Fine, twist my arm." He kisses me, and Mac sticks her head up from the floor. Seeing us up, she jumps on the bed and comes to my side, her tail wagging back and forth.

"I'll let her out," Dylan says. "You get dressed."

"She likes when you throw a couple of ice cubes in her water," I say to him as Mac follows him slowly.

"You spoil her!" he shouts, and I don't answer him

because I totally spoil her. I even got someone to come over twice during the day to take her out for walks.

Getting out of bed, I go to the closet and grab a pair of blue jeans that are torn in the front and an oversized white shirt that is short-sleeved and falls off the shoulder a bit. Slipping on a pair of white sneakers, I walk into the bathroom and brush my hair and my teeth. Walking out of my bedroom, I spot him walking out of the spare bedroom, wearing blue shorts and a polo shirt. "You look pretty." He kisses my lips, and it feels like we've been doing this our whole lives.

When we get to the rink, I'm surprised to see Wilson is there at the same time. "Hey," I greet him, getting out of the car. "You're here early."

He nods at me and then looks over at Dylan and glares. "Figured I would get in so you can bring me up to speed." Last night after Julia called me, I sent him a message asking for him to drop by this morning. "I see she allowed you to come in." He looks over at Dylan.

"What can I say?" Dylan shrugs. "I won her over with my charm."

Wilson laughs as we walk in and come face-to-face with Julia, who is sitting on the bench with Maddox. He looks like he's exhausted and he didn't sleep, but his eyes sort of light up when he looks up and sees us. "Good morning," I say, squatting down in front of him. "How was your night?"

"Okay, they had food," he answers as if he won the lottery, and my heart sinks when I look up at Dylan.

"You ready to get dressed?" Dylan tries to push down

the hurt he is feeling, but I can tell in his eyes that it's a difficult thing for him. When he told me the story yesterday, it was the first time he's ever spoken about the hell he lived in. I heard stories through the grapevine, and I remember a bit from when I was younger, but to hear him relive it was torture for both of us. Especially since I couldn't do anything to help him. "Can we get on the ice early?" Dylan looks at me, and I smile.

"It's breakfast first and then ice time," I tell them both. "You can head up and have something to eat before getting on the ice."

Dylan huffs out and then looks at Maddox. "Let's grab some grub," he suggests, holding out his hand, and just like all the other times before, he ignores it and gets up. We all watch them walk up the stairs. I let go of the huge breath I was holding while I watched them.

I wait for them to be out of sight before turning and looking at Julia. "Holy shit, I don't know how you do this every day," I say, sitting on the bench next to her.

"It gets easier," she replies. "Or you become numb. I'm not sure which one."

"Okay, yin and yang," Wilson says. "What the fuck was that?"

"That was Maddox Smith," Julia says. "Eight years old, born to Melissa Smith, father unknown. She was in foster care her whole life and had him the day after she turned eighteen." I close my eyes and fight away the burning that starts in my eyes. "That's all I can tell you." I open my eyes and see Wilson with his mouth open. "I'm going to need his whole file."

"You have it," I told her. "It was a two-page application. We got it from Wayne." I look at her. "He's with the after-school program. I don't know if he has more information, but you can call him."

Julia just nods and gets up. "I have a whole desk full that I need to get to." Julia looks at me. "I'll call you later. I'm working on a couple of things."

Wilson shakes his head when she walks out, and I fill him in about Maddox. "Whatever you need from me." He puts his hands on his hips. "You just name it."

Commotion makes us turn our heads toward the door, and I see most of the men in my family coming in. Uncle Matthew leads the way with Cooper beside him, all of them with their hockey bags over their shoulders. "We have arrived," Uncle Matthew announces.

"Yes," my father says from behind him. "Because no one can see us coming." He smiles at me, and I see my grandfather looking around.

"This reminds me of when I met your grandmother." He smiles, and I see his eyes light up. "She told me to get the fuck out of her rink on the first day." He laughs. "I knew then that she was mine."

"Nothing says you're mine like fuck off," Chase says from beside him. "Where do we change?" he asks, and I look at him with his hair tied up on his head, pointing at the hallway.

"This is fantastic," my grandfather says and looks at Wilson. "You did good."

He walks to the back, and I look at Wilson. "Are you going to be okay?" I ask him, and he just looks at me.

"I'm," he says, standing. "Every time he talks, I'm in awe." I roll my lips, trying not to laugh at him. "Fuck off," he tells me, storming away from me, and I get up, walking to my office.

I set up the ice schedule for the month and get the forms ready for the preseason tryout training. Something that I came up with the week before I left, where the elite hockey players can come and get ready for tryout season. The interest was there, and the form will be going live tomorrow.

"Knock, knock, knock." I hear my mother's voice and look up, shocked.

"Mom," I say, surprised, getting up and going to her and giving her a hug. "What are you doing here?"

"Your father forgot his socks," she says, shaking her head. "He forgets at least one thing every time he repacks that hockey bag." I look over at my desk, seeing all the files piled high. I am going through them, making sure all the contact information is inputted properly. "You look busy. I can see why you took off on an emergency."

"Yeah, just a couple of things," I respond, and then I know she's looking at me. I avoid her eyes; afraid she'll see that this isn't the real reason.

"So you're really going to lie," she prods, and I look at her with my eyes wide now. "Oh, come on. You think I didn't know that there were other reasons you left." She shakes her head. "You aren't as good an actress as you think you are. I saw you the whole week, you were guarded and you had one foot off the island even before we got there."

I look at her and then look out of the office and see that people are coming in and walking around. Walking to the door, I close it and turn to look at my mother. "You're right," I admit, and she tilts her head to the side. "I didn't leave because there was an emergency here." I don't even know how she is going to react to the next news. My heart hammers in my chest. "I left because …" My voice trembles with nerves, and she reaches out her hand and holds mine.

"Let's sit down," she suggests, bringing me over to the couch. "You're shaking like a leaf."

"Yeah," I say, rubbing my hands on my jeans now. "I'm in love with Dylan." I turn to look at her. "There, I said it."

"Oh," she says.

"I know that it may be a shock to you, and I know that this might be a lot to take in." My mouth just has diarrhea. "And I know that it might even tear the family apart. I get it, but …"

"Well, one." My mouth starts to open, but my mother interrupts me. "I kind of figured out that you had feelings for him," she shares, and it's my turn to be shocked. She looks at my face and laughs. "Oh, honey, I hate to tell you this, but I'm pretty sure everyone suspects it." I gasp. "Well, all the women at least." She laughs. "The men can be a bit. Well, slow to see things that are right in front of their noses."

"Wait, how do the women know?" I ask, confused now.

"Alex," she says, sitting back now. "Every time he's

upset, he calls you, and you drop whatever it is you are doing to rush to him. You even know when he's going to call. When we were together, you guys were attached at the hip. It's like a magnet with you two. No matter where you are you find each other."

"I didn't think it was that evident," I murmur, my voice low, almost whisper-like.

"Alex." My mother says my name, and I look at her. She has her own tears in her eyes now. "This isn't something that you just do lightly." She wrings her hands together nervously. "And I know that you have these feelings for him, but it's not just something that you can just declare." I watch her as she struggles with coming up with the words. "What I'm trying to say is that this can't be erased." I listen to her and the words. "Once you go down this road, it can go either one of two ways." I don't say anything because the lump in my throat blocks me from saying anything. "Good or bad, there is no middle ground here."

"Mom," I finally interject. "I tried not to love him." The one tear escapes, and I catch it with my thumb. "I tried everything, and I mean everything, but at the end of the day ... Not talking to him, talking to him. Ignoring him, not ignoring him. Everything."

"The heart wants what the heart wants," she says. I want to laugh at the stupidness of the words, but it's so fucking true.

"I told him." Her mouth opens again. "And he loves me back."

"Well, then," she responds, smiling. "Now here is

another question. Who is going to be the one who tells the boys?"

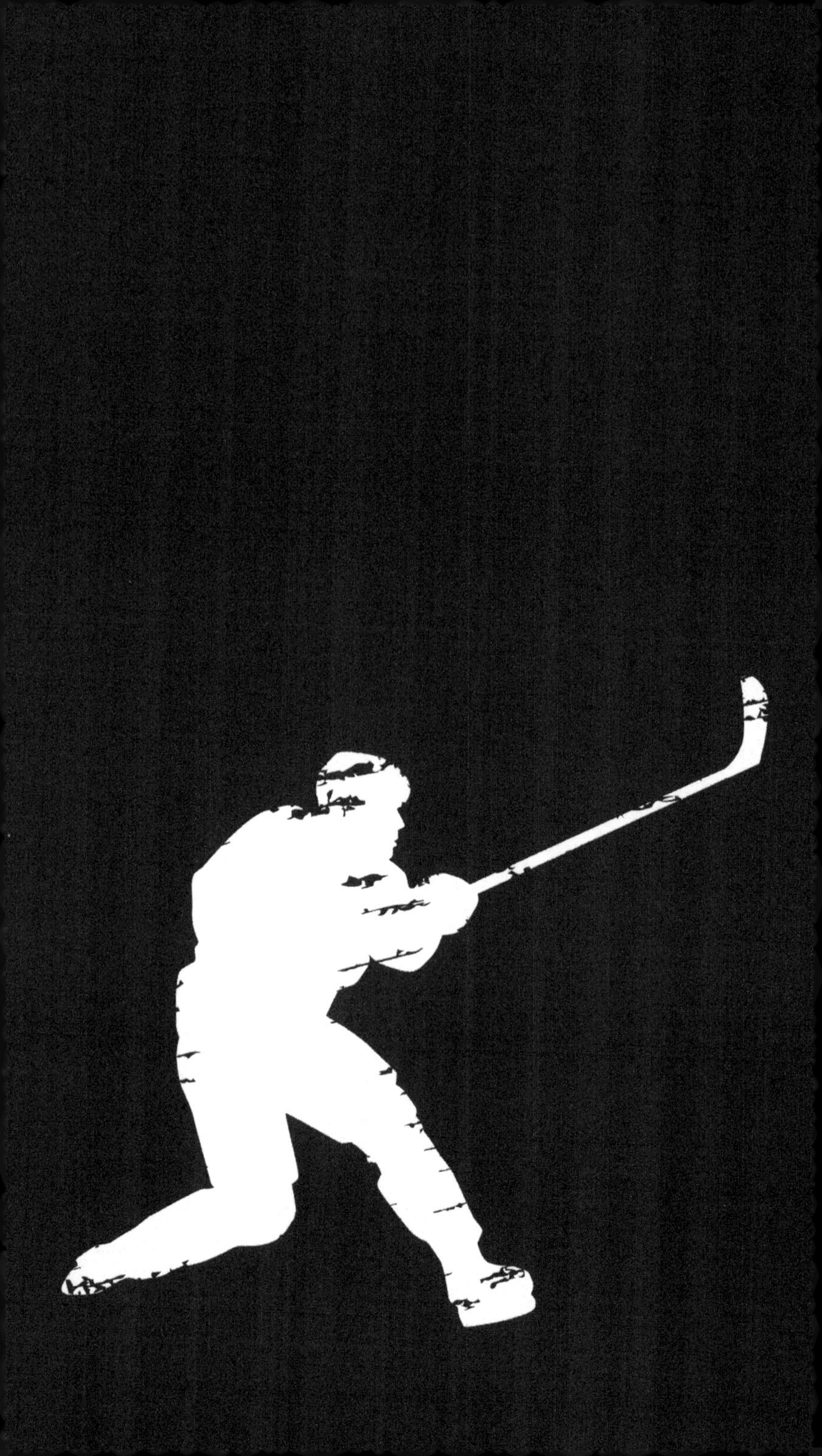

TWENTY-THREE

Dylan

"When you go around the cones," I tell Maddox, "you need to keep your stick in front so you can get the puck if they send it to you. Also, it actually makes you go faster when you move your hands." He looks at me and nods, his head taking everything in like a sponge. The only time his eyes come alive is when he's on the ice. And fuck do I know that feeling. It was the only time in my life that I felt I controlled something. I've been on the ice with him for three days, and unlike the other eight-year-olds who lose focus halfway, Maddox just pushes through. He's scrappy also, his eyes following the puck like a hawk.

"He's a good one," my father says, standing beside me. "Reminds me of you." He laughs as he blows the whistle as the kids come to the middle of the ice. We've been on the ice together, teaching the kids all day. He has experience from when he used to do it for his own hockey school. Luckily, the Edmonton team took it over from him when he left the city to go play in New York.

The kids skate off the ice, and I watch Maddox take off his helmet and grab the bottle of water. He doesn't mingle with the other kids and stays mostly by himself, and fuck if it doesn't make me go back to the same time when I was younger. But hockey came into my life, and everything changed. "Are you guys staying on the ice?" Wilson asks as he skates on the ice. "You guys want to play a game? Matthew and Max are busy picking teams like we're in high school." And I laugh, shaking my head.

"I swear if they aren't fighting or picking on each other," Michael says, skating on the ice while tying his helmet. "It's like they get hives and itch."

We all laugh. "Where were you this morning?" I ask him, leaning on the board, waiting for everyone to come on the ice.

"Do you know what it's like to have twins?" he asks me, and I look at him.

"Yeah, my sisters are twins," I remind him. "You've met them, right?"

"Fuck off," he snarks. "I swear, if one cries, the other has to cry even louder. It's always a fun time."

"That's the worst." I laugh. "I remember I moved in with you guys for six months until they stopped doing that."

"I forgot about that," Michael says, shaking his head.

Max comes out on the ice and tosses Michael and me a shirt. "You two are on my team."

"Oh, goodie," Michael says, grabbing the shirt and

tucking it in his pants as I do the same.

"Why can't you guys just put the jersey on?" Max looks at us, and we both look down at our outfit. We both are in black hockey pants, and the shirt is tucked in the back hanging out.

Michael looks at his father. "The real question is, who did you pick first?"

"Of course I picked you," Max says, looking at Michael, and even I know he's lying, as he tries to avoid looking at us in our eyes.

"Bullshit." I laugh, and he holds his stick up at me. "I had better stats than he did this year."

"I'm his son!" Michael shrieks. "You chose him over me."

"Oh, stop whining," Chase huffs out as he skates on the ice. "How did I go last? And to my own father." I roll my lips, laughing at him. "I played hockey all through college!" he yells.

"Why do you even care?" Cooper asks him. "It's not like you like hockey."

"I like hockey; I just don't love it," Chase replies. "I save lives, not pucks." He winks at us, and we gag.

"This morning," Cooper says, "one of the kids asked if you keep a hammer in your bag."

"It's the blond in my hair," Chase gloats, skating in a circle. "It's the highlights from the sun." If you thought he was big before, with his hockey equipment on, he looks like a beast now.

"Okay, are we playing or not?" Wilson says. "I have shit to do."

Cooper looks at him, laughing. "No, you don't." He points his stick at him. "You need to work off that holiday weight."

"Fuck you," he says, holding up his finger, and all I can do is laugh. "Let's drop this puck."

For the next three hours, we play three on three. We push each other until I swear my legs feel like jelly. I sit on the bench with my father watching as I take a drink of water. "I'm going to tell Uncle Max," I say the words stuck in my mouth when my father looks over at me. "I don't want to sneak around and lie to him."

He just looks at me. "If you're sure," he says, squeezing water into his mouth. "Then I agree with you. The longer you keep it from him, the worse it'll be."

I nod as they skate off the ice, and I look at my dad. "It's now or never." He gets up, and all I can do is follow him into the locker room.

I sit on the bench, looking around the room. I sit between my father and my grandfather. Uncle Matthew sits with of Cooper and Chase beside him. Uncle Max and Michael are talking about something or other. I don't even know. Wilson sits by himself as he leans back against the wall and drinks his drink. I get up and head to the shower, and when I come back out and get dressed, everyone is at the same spot they were before. I look down at the phone and see a text from Alex telling me she's going home to have lunch with Julia.

The voices start to sound like echoes in my ears. My pounding heart drowns out even the voices. "Um," I say softly and I can feel my father beside me put his back up and stop moving. "Uncle Max." I call his name, and he looks up at me, and my whole head is yelling at me to shut up. "I need to ask you something," I say, and Michael just looks at me.

"Dude, you look like you're going to be sick," Michael says, and I don't know why, but Wilson stands up, coming closer to me as if he knows shit is going to go down.

I stand, my legs shaking and so are my hands. My father stands beside me. "Why don't we do this privately?"

"Privately?" Uncle Matthew says, almost laughing. "What the fuck are you talking about? It's family."

He must sense that I'm not laughing or joking, and he just looks at us and then at my dad, who shares a look with him. "I guess there is no good way to say this." My father moves next to me but more in front of me, always protecting me. "I'm in love with Alex," I say the words before I can stop them from coming out of my mouth.

I watch my uncle Max take in my words, and I also feel my grandfather get up from beside me and stand right where my father is just on the other side. "I'm sorry, what?"

"Oh, fuck," my uncle Matthew finally says, getting up. He's pretty much saying what everyone is thinking in the room.

I don't pay attention to anything else going on around me. I know that everyone is standing now, except Chase, who just sits there with his back to the wall. "I love Alex," I say again, and every single time I say it, the pressure in my chest gets lighter and lighter.

"We all love Alex," my uncle Matthew says, laughing awkwardly.

"I don't mean like that." My eyes go to Michael, who is sitting with his mouth open. "I mean, I am in love with her." I wait for the words to sink in with everyone. "I want to be with her." I look into his eyes. "And only her."

Max takes a step forward, making everyone spring into action. Matthew stands in front of me, putting a hand on his chest. "Relax," he says.

"Relax?" he roars, pushing Matthew's hand away from him. "Are you fucking kidding me right now?"

"I am not." I don't even wait for anyone else to speak. "I love her with everything."

"Don't you fucking say it." Max points at me. "Don't you fucking say that."

"Max," my grandfather says, walking in the middle of us and moving Matthew to the side. "We need to take a step back for a second and listen to him."

"My sister," Michael says, and Chase is the only one who laughs. "My sister."

"I know this is a shock to all of you." I start now. "And I can't even explain or tell you when it happened."

"She's your cousin," Cooper states. "I mean, not blood-wise."

"You are not going to even think of doing anything with what you just said," Max says. "I forbid it."

"Dad," Michael says.

"No, are you crazy?" Max yells, his whole body shaking, and I think that maybe I should have told him this when it was just the two of us. "Are all of you insane to even entertain this?"

"Max," my father says. "This is not easy for anyone to hear." He shakes his head.

"Do you know how ridiculous you all sound?" Max says as he runs his hands through his hair. "What do you think the press is going to say?" He shakes his head. "They are going to destroy her. They are going to spin this as sinister as they can and guess what? They are not wrong." He grabs his phone and his keys. "This shit doesn't leave this room," he hisses out. "You." He points at me. "You don't go near her, do you hear me?" He doesn't wait for me to say anything before he storms out of the room.

"Well, that went a lot better than I thought it was going to go," Matthew says, shaking his head and slapping my shoulder. "I hate to be on Max's side, but have you thought about any of this?"

"It's the only thing I've thought about," I confess, the tears starting to burn my eyes. "You think it was easy to say any of this? You all took me into your family. You gave me a family, and …" I shake my head.

"We are your family," my grandfather says, and Matthew looks at him. "Unconventional."

"Is that what we are calling ourselves?" Cooper looks at me. "But can I just ask a question?" He lifts his hand. "Alex Alex." He sits now that everything seems to calm down. "The same Alex who was going to pierce your belly button two summers ago while you slept?"

I laugh at him and close my eyes. "Seriously," Michael says. "Like my sister?"

"I know," I reply, running my hands through my hair. "And I can't even explain it, but when she moved here, it's like a light went off in my head."

"Was it a flashing white light?" Chase asks me. "Because that could mean a stroke."

"You're such an idiot," Cooper says. We all laugh, and just like that, we move on to something else.

"I'm not a professional in all this," Matthew says when he comes close to me, and his voice goes low. "But I'd give Alex a heads-up because if it was me and that was my daughter." He looks at Wilson, who just shakes his head. "I'd be putting her over my shoulder like Donkey Kong."

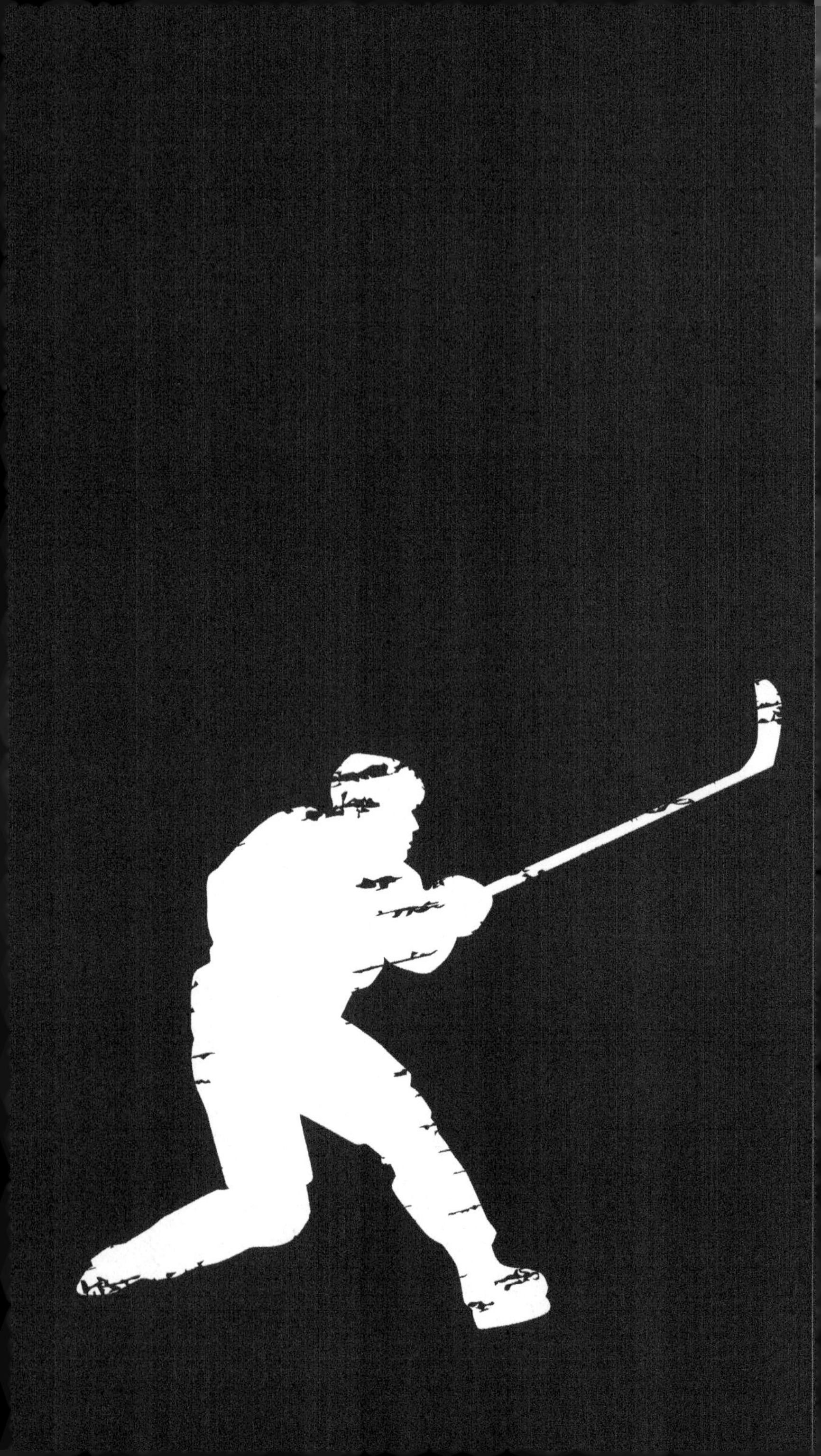

TWENTY-FOUR

ALEX

"ARE YOU SURE you want to do this?" Julia asks me as she takes a folder out of her purse that she brought over. The stack of white papers is held together with a paper clip. I rushed home when she called me and told me she had time to go over the whole application process. I haven't even had the chance to talk to anyone about it, and I know that I'm going to have to talk to Dylan. I'm just hoping he doesn't try to talk me out of it.

I nod my head. "I'm sure," I confirm, excited and nervous all at the same time. She turns the papers towards me so I can look them over.

"If at any time you change your mind." She smiles at me. "We just pull your application and forget it ever happened."

"No." I shake my head. "This is my chance to make an impact on someone's life," I state. "I mean, I know that I'm just the middle person, but if I can help, why not."

"Being an emergency foster caregiver is something that not everyone can commit to. It's the phone calls at three a.m. in the morning, and you have an hour to get things ready. It's at a drop of a dime you can have up to three kids living with you until we place them in either foster homes or group homes." Julia reminds me of what I would be getting into, the same thing she's been telling me since I asked her about it when she dropped Maddox off and called me.

"I'm okay with that," I say. "I mean, it'll be an adjustment for sure, but I think I can handle it." I wipe the tear coming out of my eye. "If I can help the kids for even a little bit." I shrug. "It's the least I can do."

She smiles at me. "After you fill out the application, there is the background check to go through."

"I think we are good for that." I smirk at her.

"You think?" She laughs.

"I mean, there was that one time in New Orleans that I flashed my boobs," I admit, closing my eyes. "But the cop let me go."

"I want to say I'm surprised"—she shakes her head—"but I thought it would be a lot worse." A smile is on her face. "Let's get this application filled out." She hands me the application, and I grab a pen and start to fill it out. When everything went down with Maddox, it was like a light bulb went off in me. It was like another piece to the puzzle was put in place.

My phone buzzes at the same time the front door opens and slams shut. Julia and I look up at each other, not moving as we look toward the hallway. My father comes into the room, and he looks like he's on a tear. I'm about to get up when he looks at me and then Julia. "Hey, Max," she says, and all he can do is look back at me.

"What the fuck is going on with you and Dylan?" His voice is more of a roar, and in all my life, I've never ever heard him so angry.

"Um …" I get up, not sure what to say. Not sure what was said to him. My hands shake as I push away from the counter. The front door opens again, and I hear the click and clack of flip-flops.

"Oh, good," my mother says, looking like she ran here. "I'm in time."

"I think I'm going to go," Julia says, getting up. "As much as I really, really want to be here for this conversation." She grabs her bag. "Do you want me to call anyone?" she whispers to me, and I just shake my head. I knew that this conversation would have to take place. I just didn't think it would happen so fast and so soon. Julia comes to me and gives me a hug. "I'll call you later," she says softly. "Or call me if you need me."

I nod at her as she escapes the room. I wait until the front door closes before I turn to my father. "Now, are we going to have this conversation calmly?"

"Yes," my mother says.

At the same time, my father says, "Absolutely not."

"Max Horton," my mother says, putting her hands on her hips.

"Not now, Allison," he says, putting his own hands on his hips. "Alexandra." He uses my full name. "I'm waiting for you to tell me that all this shit with Dylan is a joke."

"I can't do that," I reply, taking a deep breath and then letting it out. "It's not a joke. I'm in love with him."

"Can everyone stop saying that fucking word?" He puts his hands on his head. "Stop using that fucking word." He stares at me.

"Okay, well, what would you like me to use?" I fold my arms over my chest. "I like him," I say with a smirk. "A lot, some would say it's love."

"Alex," my mother warns me, and I look up at the ceiling.

"This is never going to happen," my father says. "Never!" he yells.

"I don't care," I finally say. I was never the type of kid who would act out. I mean, I didn't always listen, and I didn't always get caught, but when I did, I would always say what they wanted to hear. Even if half the time I was only sorry I got caught. "I'm not going to change the way I feel." I shrug.

"Yes, you will," my father says definitely. My mother steps toward him and puts her hand on his arm.

"Max," she says his name softly. He turns to look at her, and I see his head shaking side to side. The tears coming to his eyes.

"You can't be okay with this, Allison." She puts her hand up to wipe away his tears. "You can't,"

he repeats. His voice is almost broken, making my heart break.

My stomach lurches up and down. "Dad, he's the best

man I know," I say without moving from my spot, and my own tears come now. "And you helped make him that man."

"You can't do this, Alex," he says, his voice breaking. "You need to forget about him for your own good."

I laugh bitterly. "You don't think I've tried that?" I raise my hands, and my sadness turns to anger. "For the past two years, all I've done is date guys. Guys who I would never even look at because I was like *you won't know until you try*. Guys who treated me like garbage. Guys who literally had sex with the waitress in the bathroom while I waited for them. Guys who called me Ally," I scoff out. "Ally because Alex was too much work for them. Guys who stood me up more than once, but I gave them a chance because all I wanted to do was not love him," I admit as the tears run down my face. "Blind dates, dating apps. You name it, I did it. Fuck, I joined Christian Mingle, hoping that I would meet someone, anyone who would make me feel anything. Anything." I put my hand to my heart. "And all it did was cement the fact that I was in love with someone who would never love me back. All it did was show me what I couldn't have. Every time I would see him, my heart would hurt in my chest. It would get to the point I honestly went to the doctor because I thought I had something wrong with this." I point at my heart. "I went through two years of hell trying to pretend that everything was okay when I would go to my room at night and cry."

"Alex." My mother takes a step toward me, but I hold up my hand.

"I went through all of this, telling myself it was wrong. Telling myself I shouldn't feel this way, and I now know he loves me back."

"I will never be okay with this," my father announces. "Never. I will never accept him in my family."

"Max," my mother says, putting a hand to her mouth to stop the sob. "You can't mean that."

"I do," he declares, standing there looking at me. The man who I put all men against, the man who told me that I'm worth all the candy in all the world. The man who also told me I wasn't allowed to ever get married.

"You can't do that to him," I say, my heart hammering in my chest like a jackhammer. "You can't just cut him out like that."

"I can, and I will," my father says. "I will not sit around while you ruin your whole life for one mistake."

"This family," I say, trying to steady my voice. "This family is everything to him. It's the only family he has." I look at him now, knowing he isn't going to change his mind. I know that I'm going to have to sacrifice everything I want for one person, and that isn't my father. "If you do this, it will rip the family apart," I explain, my voice shaking.

"It will." My father takes a stance.

"Then I'll walk away from him." I say the words at the same time that my chest tightens and my mother gasps out loud. "I'll walk away from him." I say the words again, hoping it doesn't hurt, but instead, it hurts me more. It's like a knife being lit on fire and then sliding into my heart. "But know that I'll do that just so he can stay in the family." I make it clear. "I'll do that for him." I wipe the tear away from my cheek. "And only him." I put my hands to my stomach. "This is the only family he's ever had." I look at my mother, who is silently crying as she looks at me. "The only family who has ever loved him, and I'm not taking that away from him. Not now." I shake my head. "Not ever. Because he deserves to be loved by everyone." I want to break down and cry. My legs start to tremble, and I'm about to fall, but I'll be strong. "I'll walk away." I say the words again. "It's not even an option. So, tell me, Dad." I look at him, his chest rising and falling as if he just ran a marathon. "Is me walking away from him going to make everything okay?" His hands are clenched at his sides in a fist, the same hands that made sure I was always okay. The same hands that used to tickle me until I cried. The same hands that used to hold the bike up when I was learning so I wouldn't fall. The same hands that used to wipe away my tears. The same hands I knew that one hug from him would make everything better.

The front door opens, and the three of us are at a standstill. No one moving from our spots, and when he walks in, I don't look over at him because I can't. Because if I do, I'll never ever have the courage to walk away from him. "What's going on?"

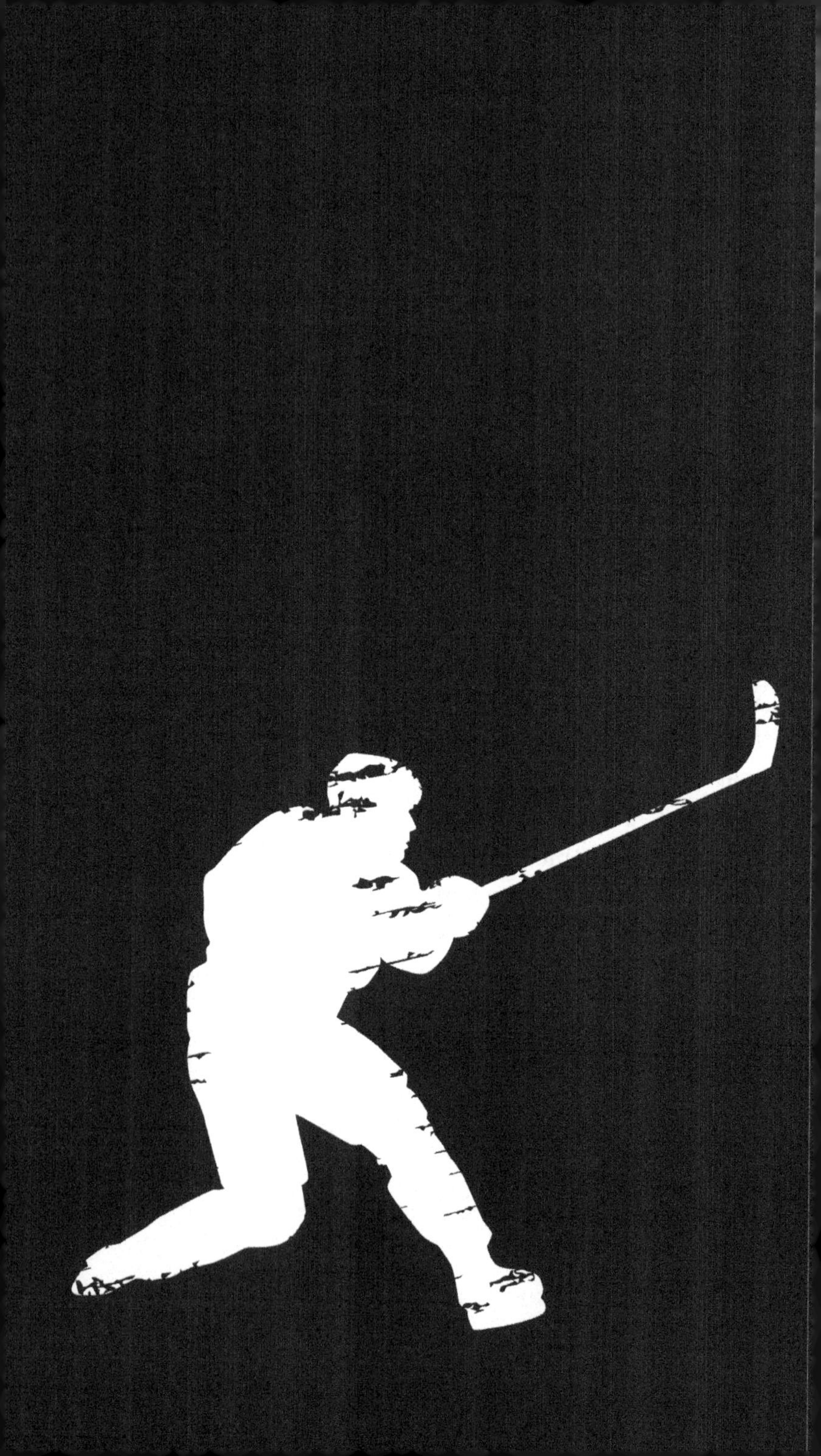

TWENTY-FIVE

DYLAN

I DON'T MOVE from the entranceway as I look at the showdown going on. Allison and Max facing off with Alex, who has tears streaming down her face. "What's going on?" I ask as politely as I can right now. The minute I called her and there was no answer, I knew I had to go to her. I was being asked all these questions, but the only thing I could focus on was getting to her. I was already in the car when Julia called with a warning, and I got here as fast as I could. "Is anyone going to answer me?"

I look at each of them, and for the first time ever, Max doesn't look me in the eye, but I only have eyes for Alex. "I'm waiting for my father to answer my question," Alex says with her shoulders back. Even though she has tears running down her face, she is refusing to fall apart.

"And what question is that?" I ask, the burning in my stomach feeling like my insides are on fire.

"If I walk away from you, will they still treat you like

family," she says, and my legs are about to give out on me. The gasp escapes me before I can stop it, and it just makes her cry even more. My blood is boiling because this isn't how it was ever supposed to be. Loving someone is never supposed to hurt. You aren't supposed to hurt the ones you love, and all I've done is hurt them.

"Do you want me to leave?" I look at her as my heart contracts into my chest. I want to roar out, and the buzzing is starting in my ears as the heat starts to rise in my neck.

My eyes search hers, and she puts her hand in front of her mouth to stop the sob from escaping her. I don't care who is around right now. I run to her, grabbing her face in my hands. "It's going to be okay," I whisper to her. "I promise it's going to be okay." I pull her to me, and she sobs out in my arms. I bring her into my arms as her tears soak into my shirt. "It's okay," I whisper and kiss her head. She trembles in my arms, and I can feel eyes on me. I can feel them both watching me. She wraps her arms around my waist, and I look over at Max now. I'm about to spill my soul to him when the front door opens, and we hear heavy breathing.

"Good God," Matthew says, panting, and looking around, seeing Allison in tears and Alex in my arms. "What the fuck is going on?"

"I was about to stake my claim," I say the word he taught me when I was twenty. You find a woman, and you know she's the one, you stake your claim. He puts his hands on his hips now. I swallow down and kiss Alex's head again as she looks up from in my arms. I push the hair away from her face. "No more tears," I comfort, trying to smile, but the whole time, all I can do is listen to the beating of my heart. I look up and see that Matthew is standing there looking at me, but my eyes go to Max. His eyes look at me holding Alex. "You helped raise me," I say to him now, my voice trembling, but I don't stop because this can be my one and only shot. "Side by side with my father, you showed me what it was to be a man." I feel Alex hug my waist tighter. "My father, you, Grandpa, Matthew." My eyes go to Matthew as he stands there looking at me with a smirk and his arms crossed over his chest. "You made me the man I am." Max's eyes fill with tears. "Showed me what it was to love. Showed me how to love. Showed me what it felt like to be accepted." I look down at Alex, who stands beside me now with one hand wrapped around me as she wipes the tears from the corner of her eyes. "If I'm not good enough for her." I look straight into her eyes, and everything feels settled inside me. "Then no one else is."

"He's got a point there," Matthew says, wiping his own tears, and he looks over at Max. "Who else is going to love her like him?"

"It's not that fucking easy!" Max roars.

"Why can't it be?" Allison asks. She looks at me the same way she did before all of this came out, giving me a smile. Something I was worried about was that she would never be able to look at me like she did. "Why can't it just be easy like that? Listen to them." She walks to Max, putting her hands on his hips. "Your daughter is in love with a man who you helped raise," she says, looking at me. "Who we all helped raise. A man who will treat her with respect. A man who is going to be kind to her. A man who will put her before himself."

"I mean, he better, or else," Matthew says, making me and Alex laugh, "I'm going to kick your ass."

"What about what the press is going to do to her?" Max looks at Allison. "They are going to be vile and mean and drag her through the mud."

"But what if they don't?" Alex asks. "What if they don't care just like we don't care?"

"Alex." Max says. "It's my job to worry and protect you."

"That's my job now," I respond, knowing that there is no way I will ever stop protecting her. "It's always been my job." My thumb rubs up and down her arm. "That will be my job always."

"Dylan, it's not going to be easy," Max says now, his voice going low, and he sits down on the couch behind him. "The whole family will be thrown under the bus."

I don't have a chance to say anything because Matthew laughs now. "Are you kidding me? I was arrested for rape." He points at his chest. "Justin was arrested for assault." He points at Max. "You were arrested for the same thing."

"That's not the point," Max says, shaking his head.

"Then what is the point?" Allison asks. "Because I'm a bit confused." She folds her arms over her chest. "Did I expect them to fall in love?" She looks at us. "No, I didn't. But what are we going to do, not support our daughter and the man she loves?" She tilts her head to the side. "Max Horton, you helped make him who he is. You raised him just as much as Justin did. He learned all of this from you." She turns and points at Matthew. "And you with all this claim stuff. Who talks like that?"

"It's a Stone thing." Matthew smirks at us.

"I changed my mind," Alex says, stepping out of my touch. My arm that was around her shoulder falls to my side, and her hand grabs mine. "Before, I said that I would walk away from him." She looks at me, her eyes filling with tears. "If he could have the family, but I take it back." The lump in my throat fills, and I have trouble swallowing. "I'm not letting him go. I'll go with him and walk away from the family, if that is what we need to do." She smiles through her tears. "I'm sorry, but I won't let you go, and if they don't want us, then we will create our own family." She puts her hands on my hips, looking up at me. "We can be each other's family."

"Like fuck that will ever happen." I look over and see my father standing there with my grandfather. Behind them is Cooper and Michael with Chase. "You are my son," my father says. "No matter what."

"Sorry we're late," Michael says, coming into the room and looking at his mother standing alone. He walks to her and puts his arm around her shoulders. "Fabio over there was chatting with Julia instead of filling us in."

"We're here, aren't we?" Chase says, looking around the room. "And no one is dead."

"Can everyone just for one second be quiet," Max says, getting up now.

"Not if you're going to spew shit at my son," my

father says, putting his hands on his hips.

"Yeah," Allison says, turning on him. "This isn't you," she points out to him. "Your heart is filled with all this love." She puts her hand on his chest, and he looks down at it.

"I'm going to throw up." Matthew puts his fist to his mouth, faking vomiting.

"Shut up," my father says to Matthew. "He's about to apologize for being a dickhead."

"I wouldn't say dickhead," my grandfather says, smiling at Max, trying to ease everyone's nerves. He is always the calm one in the family, always the one to make sure that everyone settles down before things go beyond the part where it can't come back. "He was just looking out for the ones he loves. Isn't that right, son?"

"Yeah, isn't that right?" Matthew repeats. "You know when you stole my sister away from us, and you married her like a barbarian without her family."

"Oh, dear God," Alex says, and for the first time since I stepped in this room, I know that everything will be okay. I know we will have more hurdles, but it'll be okay with her by my side.

Max looks at me. "What you said before." He looks down. "You were right. I helped raise you." He swallows back the tears. "The man you are is the man I had hoped that Alex would find." He looks at her. "He is the kind of man I always wished for."

"I won't ever let you down," I declare. "I won't ever let any of you down." I look around the room at the men who helped raise me, and the men who help hold me up when I don't think I can hold myself up.

"Can you imagine the therapy that this family needs?" Chase talks, and we all shake our heads. "Like we are all certifiable."

"Speak for yourself," Michael says. "There is nothing wrong with me."

"Didn't you knock up Jillian and then not talk to her for five months?" Cooper asks Michael.

"Didn't you get divorced?" Michael throws it back into Cooper's face. The two of them start to throw insults at each other.

"Do you think it's too early to tell them to get the fuck out so we can go and have a makeup make-out session?" I lean down and ask Alex in her ear.

"My father just approved of our relationship. I don't think it would be a good time to tell him we are living together yet."

"Wait?" I say, shocked, and my voice gets louder. "If I'm living here, I have to pay for the house."

"Oh, here we go," Allison says. "I'm leaving." She looks at Max. "I'm also not talking to you," she tells him and turns to walk to us. She gives me a big hug. "So proud of you," she whispers and then hugs Alex. "Dad, can you drive me home?"

"What?" Max shouts at her as she walks out. "Where are you going?"

"Away from you," she hisses. "That was not okay. What you said to our nephew-slash-daughter's boyfriend was uncalled for."

"Forget therapy," Chase says, "we need Jerry Springer."

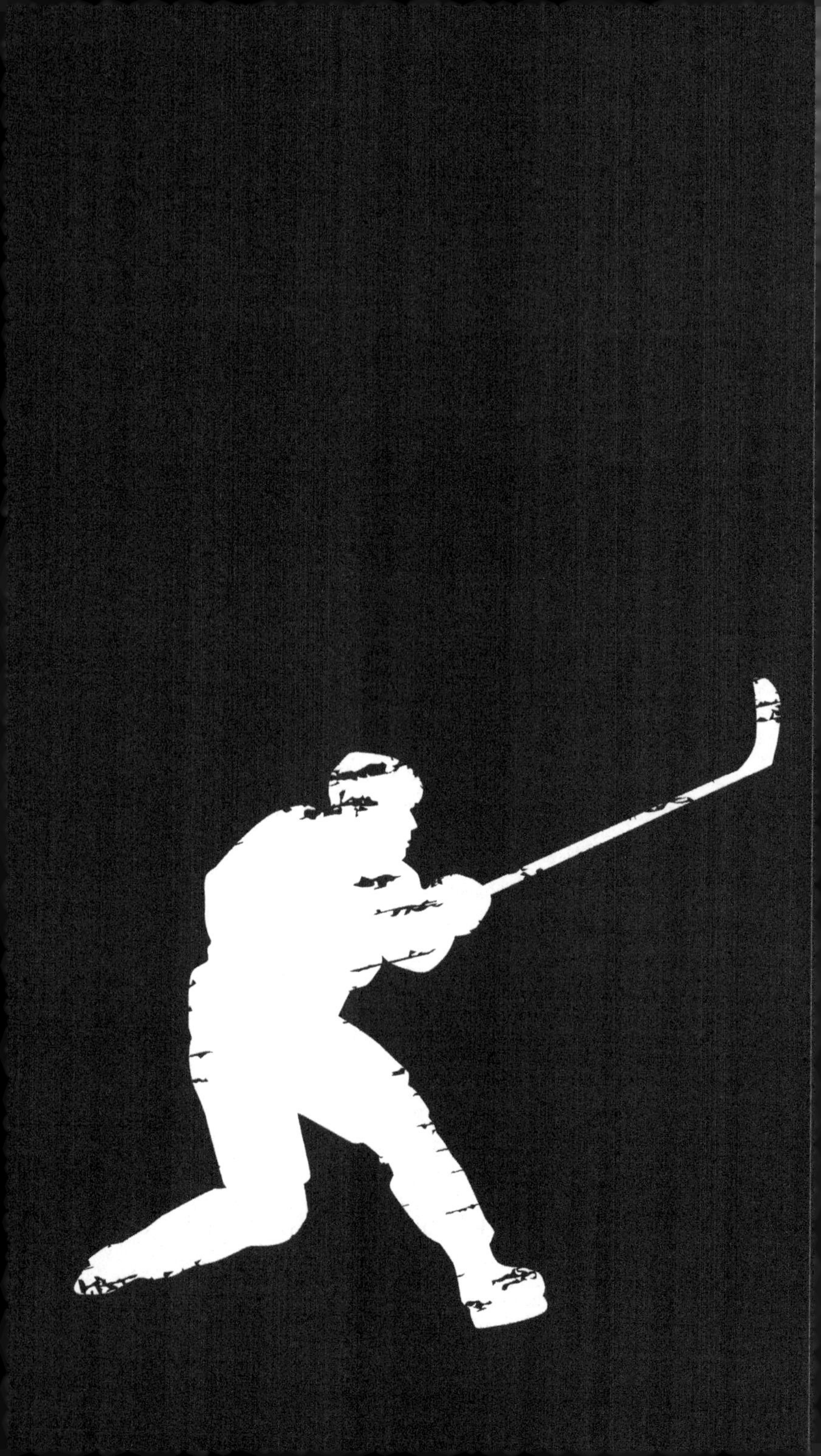

TWENTY-SIX

Alex

ONLY WHEN I look over and see my father shake his head and laugh at Chase's comment do I let the tension leave my body. Dylan notices it right away, and he slips his hand in mine, and my eyes go down to see the small intimate touch. I look up at him and smile. "I'm leaving," my mother says while she walks to me. "I'll call you later." She hugs me and then smiles at Dylan. "Um, your mother," she says. "She needs you to call her after. I'll fill her in, but I know she is going to want to hear from your mouth that you are okay."

"I will." Dylan nods at her.

"Okay, this was fun," Chase says, "but I have an appointment I need to get to."

"What appointment can you possibly have in Dallas?" my uncle Matthew asks, and he avoids answering him.

"Is it for those crabs you caught in Hawaii?" Cooper asks, slapping his shoulder, and they both leave.

"This was fun, but I have to get home to the kids," Michael says, then looks over at our mom. "You coming over?"

"I am," she confirms, walking to him, giving my father the side-eye. "Your father is not coming with us."

"I'm standing right here," my father says, and she turns to him, giving him a glare and then turning to walk out of the door.

"I don't know how all this marriage stuff works," Michael says. "But that look means you're in the doghouse."

"Smart man," my grandfather says and comes over to us now. "You call me later." He kisses my cheek and then goes to hug Dylan. Every single day he calls every single one of us, even if it's for a five-second chat. He sits down and goes through the list. He walks over and looks at Justin as they share a look and then glance over at us, nodding. Turning to walk out of the room, he leaves just my father.

"We are going to talk about this more," he says. "If this is what you guys really decide to do." He shakes his head. "We are going to have to sit down and go over a game plan."

"A game plan?" Matthew asks, laughing. "My daughter's sex tape being leaked needed a game plan." He puts his hands on his hips. "This doesn't need a game plan. It needs one statement, and then you tell them to fuck off."

"It's not that simple," my father defends, shaking his head.

"It's that simple if we make it that simple," Dylan says from beside me. "We've never been ones to talk about our public life," he says of the family. "And we aren't starting now. What's between the family stays in the family."

"Let's go," Matthew urges, slapping my father on the shoulder. "I saw that look Allison gave you. You need all the time in the world to make it up to her."

My father looks over at us and just nods before turning and walking out. The door opens, and we look at each other, wondering who else is coming back when Mac runs into the room back from his afternoon walk. The dog walker leaves his leash at the front and then leaves, slamming the door.

My head hangs forward for just a second, and I close my eyes. The tension finally leaves my body, and I'm not the only one. "I need a drink." I open my eyes and watch Dylan walk into the kitchen and go get the bottle of scotch I keep right over the fridge. He unscrews the top of the bottle and takes a shot straight out of the bottle. He hisses and then looks at me and holds up his hand, offering me the bottle.

I shake my head and walk over to the couch. Sitting down, I put my face in my hands. Mac comes over and sits down beside me, putting her head in my lap. I rub her ears and then look up at Dylan. "Did that just happen?" I turn and look back in the kitchen as he takes another shot and then puts the bottle back.

"That did just happen," he confirms, walking to the living room and sitting on the couch, dropping his head back.

"But how?" I ask him, confused.

"I told your father after practice," Dylan says, and my mouth just hangs open.

"What the hell?" I get up, and he grabs my hand, pulling me back down beside him. "Why would you do that without telling me or at least warning me?"

"It was a spur-of-the-moment type of thing," he says to me. "I hated it being a secret, and I just thought the longer we didn't tell anyone, the worse it would be." I know he's right, and with that, I sink into the couch beside him. I turn toward him, putting my arm on the back of the couch, and he reaches out and grabs my feet, putting them in his lap. "We need to discuss a couple of things." Mac gets up and walks over to her pillow in the corner, spinning in a circle before falling down.

I lay my head down on the back of the couch. "I think there are a lot of things we need to discuss." My stomach fills with all the flutters, but this time, it's not because I'm afraid. This time, it's because the things we need to discuss have to do with us being together.

"Well, the first thing we should discuss is where we are going to live," he decides, rubbing my feet as he looks at me. "I just signed a contract for the next seven years."

"So we have to live in Dallas," I conclude, not upset by this because it has slowly become my home. "I'm okay with this." I smile at him as he smiles back at me. "Check number one off the list. Next."

"What do you think about this house?" he asks, and I look at him confused and then look around the room.

"I love this house," I say to him, seeing the pictures of the both of us scattered all over the place. "Do you not like it here?"

"No, I do," he says, smiling. "To be honest, wherever you are is home."

"If I didn't love you as much as I do and someone else said that around me, I would roll my eyes and fake vomit." I lean in to kiss his lips. "But that was a good one." I kiss him one more time before going back to my previous position. "Now, what were you saying about the house?"

"Well, how many kids are we going to have?" he asks me, and I laugh.

"We haven't had sex yet, and you are already trying to knock me up?" I laugh, and all he does is shake his head and smirk.

"I'm just asking because if you plan to have five kids, we need a bigger place," he explains as if we are deciding if we are eating pizza or burgers instead of getting a bigger house and having five children.

"I never thought about how many kids I would have," I answer him honestly. "I was just going to go with one and see."

"We are having more than one," he tells me matter-of-fact.

"Noted," I say, not bothering to argue because there is no way I could have just one child. "I called Julia today and started the process of becoming an emergency foster parent," I relay, my nerves filling my stomach because if he doesn't agree, I'm going to have to make a decision that I'm not ready to make. "I know we should have spoken about it," I continue, my voice cracking as I think about not being able to help whoever it is. "But"—I shrug—"I couldn't not help."

"I'll call Julia tomorrow," he says softly, pulling me to him, and I straddle his lap. My hands fall flat down on his chest, and the heat seeps through my hands as I feel his heart beating under it. "And start the application process so we can do it as a couple."

I lean down and kiss his lips softly. "I don't want you to do anything you don't want to do," I say softly. "I know it's a sensitive subject, and I would never want you to be uncomfortable." His hands come up to cup my face as he brings my mouth close to his. I smile at him now. "Hi," I say awkwardly, not sure what to say to him.

His thumbs rub my cheeks as his smile fills his face. "I was not going to let you go," he admits, and I hold my breath, my eyes searching his. "I don't care what you promised your father."

"Dylan," I whisper.

"No," he says sharply. "Don't Dylan me. Listen to me. You could have promised him that you would never look at me again." He shakes his head, the thought too much for him to bear.

"Losing the family would have killed you." I smile through the tears.

"Losing you would have killed me." His hand comes down, his fingertips moving along my jaw. "He could have taken you away to a remote island with fire-breathing dragons, and I would find you." He mentions one of my favorite movies ever.

"Aw, just like Shrek saved Fiona." I move my head in to kiss his lips softly.

"Just like Shrek saved Fiona." He smiles, kissing my lips slowly, and then his tongue slides into my mouth. My stomach flutters as his tongue turns around with mine. His hands get lost in my hair as I push myself into his chest. My arms go around his neck as the kiss deepens. His cock gets hard as my hips move up. Both of us stop to moan as my pussy rubs over his hardened cock. My hands go to his neck as my fingers slide into the back of his hair. His hands on my hips slide to my ass, squeezing me and pulling me to him.

My hands go to his shoulders as our mouths stay fused. The kiss that started off so sweet is slowly getting more and more desperate. My hands go down his arms, his arms showing little goose bumps as my hand slowly moves in toward his stomach, my fingertips rubbing over the cotton of his shirt. I can feel his stomach sink in as I slowly lift his shirt. My fingers go to his lower stomach. His heat meeting fingertips, his hands squeezing my ass harder. "Can we take this off?" I pant out as I let go of his lips to rip the shirt off him. I take a second to look at the chest I've seen over a thousand times. It's also the same chest I dreamed about being over me. My head feels dizzy with all that is going on. His hands move from my ass up my shirt now. My body shivers when his hands touch my lower back. I close my eyes as he slowly rubs up and then stops. I open my eyes, seeing him watching me, and I lean in, my hands going back to his bare chest.

"We need to talk about sex." He pants as I start to kiss my way down his jaw.

"That is what I'm trying to do." My tongue comes out, and I lick down to his neck, where I give him little kisses one after another.

"Alex." He moans out my name, and I suck his neck. "Do we want to do this?"

I stop moving and sit up straight. "What exactly are you asking me?"

"We don't have to do this if you don't want to," he says, and I throw my head back and laugh.

"I've done this before," I relay, and he just glares at me, making me laugh even harder. "Oh, come on, don't even try to act like you were sitting at home waiting."

"No," he says between clenched teeth. "I just don't want you to think that we have to rush into this."

I put my hands on his face now. "Trust me, you aren't rushing me into anything." I kiss his lips. "I want to be with you," I say softly, "in every sense of the word."

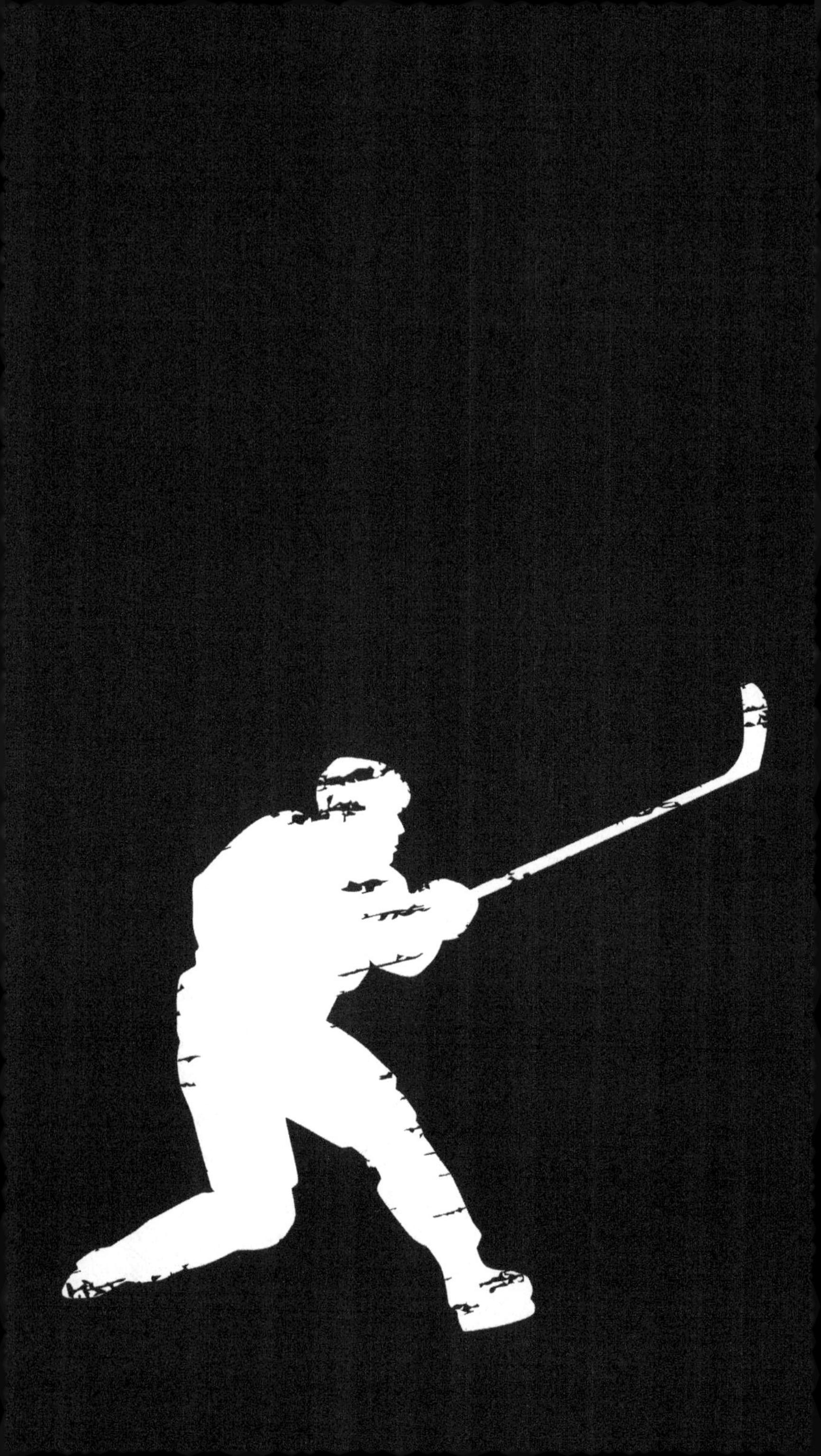

TWENTY-SEVEN

DYLAN

"TRUST ME, YOU aren't rushing me into anything." She leans forward to kiss my lips. "I want to be with you." My whole body wakes up, my cock getting even harder than it was before, and let me tell you, I felt like it was turned to stone. The minute she sat and straddled me, the heat from her pussy came through my jeans right onto my cock, and all I wanted to do was slide into her. Except this was Alex, and I wasn't rushing anything with her. "In every sense of the word."

My hands go to her neck, bringing her close to me, causing her lacy bra to rub against my naked chest. Her tongue slips into my mouth as my hands get lost in her hair. "Alex," I whisper when I let go of her lips. Trailing soft kisses to her cheek, I then move down to her jaw. "I keep thinking this is all a dream." I kiss her neck, and she moves her head back to give me access. Both of her hands are on my chest. I'm sure she can feel the speeding of my heart. "I love you." I say the three words I've been saying in my head for the longest time, secretly hoping that one day I would wake up and she would love me back.

"I love you," she pants out, and my hands leave her hair and roam down to her tits. I cup her tits in my hands, and it's like she was made especially for me. "Yes," she says when my fingertips trail over the top of her bra. "Touch me," she invites, opening her eyes. The need and want are written all over her face. Her hands leave my chest as she leans back to put them on my knees, giving me access to her chest. My eyes go back to her breasts as they rise and fall with each breath she takes. My finger slowly traces the white bra she is wearing, the top of her nipple coming out just a bit when she leans back. One of her hands comes off my leg and goes to her back, and with a flick, her bra slips forward. The straps on her arms fall forward, and my breathing stops when I see her tits for the first time. Plump, round, and fucking perfect. Her pink nipples pebble with the cold air that is in the room. She tosses her bra with our shirts at the side. "Now touch me."

My hands move without me even thinking twice. My thumb and forefinger roll her nipples at the same time. Her head falls back as she pants out, "Yes." Her hips rotate forward, and my cock is being suffocated by my jeans. My mouth waters as I lean in and finally take her nipple in my mouth. Her hips move a touch faster as I switch from one nipple to the next. "More," she says, and when I look at her, her cheeks are pink. Her eyes are a deep blue, and I want to lay her out on the bed and kiss every single inch of her.

I move my hand around her waist and get up. "Wrap up," I urge, and her legs lock around my waist. "I need you spread out for me." She wraps her arms around my neck, her naked chest crushed against mine. "Fuck, I'm going to taste every single part of you," I say when I walk up the steps two at a time. My mouth fuses with hers when I walk into her room, and her hand runs through the hair at the back near my neck. My knees hit the bed, and she lets go of me, putting her knees on the bed.

I push the hair away from her face, looking down at her, my finger touching her cheek softly. "You're beautiful," I say, kissing her cheek right where my fingers just touched. "So fucking beautiful." I can't help but repeat the words as she looks up at me, and she always takes my breath away. "There is no turning back," I warn, my heartbeat filling my ears, my fingers shaking as I touch her. "I'm so fucking nervous," I admit with a smile, and she smiles even bigger.

"I won't bite." She winks at me. "Unless you want me to." She gets up straight now, her hands going to the button on my jeans. I move out of her touch, knowing that the minute she touches my dick, all bets are going to be off. "Is it not okay for me to touch you?" she asks me, her face going white as she sits down on the back of her legs.

"It's not that at all," I reassure her. "It's the fact that if you touch me, I'm going to go off like a firework on the Fourth of July, and it'll be embarrassing for us both," I admit, and her face goes into a sly smile.

"You aren't going to have all the fun here." She gets up now. "What if we touched each other at the same time?" I listen to her now.

"Go on," I say, waiting for her to talk.

"Well, we could both get naked." She gets off the bed now.

"Tell me more," I encourage as she undoes the button to her jeans and the sound of her zipper being pushed down is almost like it's in stereo.

"We get naked and then use our hands to explore each other." She pushes the jeans over her hips. I've seen her in a bikini before, but I've never seen her in a lace string thong.

"Just our hands?" I ask her with a smirk, and she gives me a smirk right back.

"We can use our mouths if we choose," she says, and I hold up my hand.

"Yes, please. There is nothing I want more than to have my mouth on you." I step to her, and she holds out her hand to stop me.

"Don't move another foot unless you come at me with fewer clothes." Her fingers go to my pants, and my eyes never leave hers as I unbutton the top of my jeans. Her eyes move from mine to my fingers as she watches me with all the concentration in her. I slide my pants down my legs and kick them away, leaving just my white boxers on. "Very nice," she says, licking her lips.

"I feel like a piece of meat," I joke with her.

"Oh, I see a piece of meat I want." She comes to me

and throws herself at me. My arm wraps around her waist as she wraps her legs around me, and her mouth falls on mine. The kiss isn't soft and delicate like it was before. No, this one is all tongue and full of need. I carry her to the bed, and my knee sinks into the bed. I lay her on her back, her legs untangling themselves from my waist. Our lips never leave each other as I hold myself up over her. I turn her on the side as her front smashes against mine. The kiss deepens as one of my hands comes up and cups her breast. The nipple pebbles under my touch as I pinch it lightly, swallowing her moan. Rolling it between my fingers, she lets go of my mouth to moan. Her leg hitches over my hip, and then I feel her fingers rub down my chest. She leans in to kiss my neck when I feel her hand move lower and lower. I close my eyes the second her hand rubs over my cock. I can feel the heat through my boxers. I turn her on her back, and she groans. "We said we would be able to touch each other," she mutters while I get on my knees in the middle of her legs.

"You'll get to touch me," I say, bending and kissing her stomach. "I just wanted to kiss you here." I lean back down and kiss her hip bone, trailing kisses and licking her all the way up to her nipple, then taking it into my mouth.

"Not fair." Alex turns her nipple away from me as it pops out of my mouth. "I want to use my mouth, too." She pushes up, taking my nipple into her mouth, and then kisses my chest right in the middle. "I especially want to use my mouth on …" She doesn't say anything else because her hands fly to my hips, and in one motion, my boxers are lowered over my cock, and her mouth has swallowed the head.

"Oh, fuck," I curse, taking in the heat of her mouth.

"I could say the same." She looks at me, smirking. "I don't think I can get this to the back of my throat." She twirls her tongue around the head of my cock. "But I'm going to have fun trying."

She takes most of me into her mouth. "Jesus," I say, looking down at her as she tries her best to get me all the way in. She fists my cock in her hand and slowly moves it at the same time as her mouth. I give her a minute, and then I pull away from her, lying on my back. "Sit on my face." She just looks at me, her lips swollen from my kisses and glistening from sucking my cock. I lie on my back on the bed. "Let's go." I lick my lips and wait for her to come to me. "Let me taste what heaven is." She throws her leg over my head, and I don't even wait for her to come down to me. Instead, I raise myself, my hands going to her hips as I snap the thong away from her. She gasps out when my tongue slides into her as my mouth devours her. I was wrong. This is even better than heaven. My tongue slides out of her, moving toward her clit. I hold her ass in my hands as I eat her pussy, and when I slide my tongue back inside her, I feel her fall forward, and her mouth swallows my cock. I close my eyes for a second as she takes me into her mouth and then works me with her hand. I eat her pussy as if it's my last meal, sliding a finger in her and then another one. She wiggles her ass from side to side, and all I can do is slap her ass, and my cock vibrates when she moans. I lick her up and down, my tongue sliding with my fingers, and then finally, I feel her pussy getting tighter. "Not yet," I tell her. "I want you to come on my cock."

She groans when I push her off me, and she lands on her back, her legs staying open. I can see her pussy glistening, and she moves her hand between them. "Oh, no, you don't." I move her hand away from her as I get between her legs. Holding my cock in my hand, I rub it up and down her slit and then slap it on her clit, and she closes her eyes.

I do it again, using my cock to rub up and down her slit, teasing her clit. "Dylan," she pants, "put it in."

My cock is so hard at this point it feels like steel as I place it at her entrance, and we both watch as her pussy accepts me. I slide into her, and all I can do is hold my breath. She is so tight when I'm balls deep inside her, causing us both to let out a soft moan. "Made for me." Looking down, I pull out a touch before slamming back into her. "You were fucking made for me."

"Yes," she says as her hand slides between her legs and her two middle fingers rub her clit from side to side. "More," she pants out, and I'm not going to let her ask me again when I pull out halfway this time and then slam into her. "Harder." She squirms under me. "More," she pleads. "Dylan." She raises her hips, and the little bit of control I had is out the window as she moves her hips back, opening her legs wider. I lean forward on my hand next to her side. My face is right on top of her as she pants out. I bend my head to kiss her as I fuck her, slowly pulling out to the tip of my cock and then slamming into her. She lets go of my lips to throw her head back and moan. I pump into her over and over again. Our lips hover over each other until I can't even pull out of her anymore because she's squeezing me so tight. "I'm right there."

"Alex," I huff out as she comes on my cock so much her juices leak down to my balls. It's just what I need before I slam into her and I come with her. Finally collapsing on top of her, I bury my face in her neck as our chests press together. "Alex." I kiss her. "Fuck, Alex."

Her chest moves as she laughs. "I think it's the other way around. You just fucked me." She wraps her arm around my shoulder.

"I didn't wear a condom," I say finally. "I'm sorry. I didn't even think." I prop myself up on my arms. "I've never been without one."

"Me either," she says, and I lift up to see her face. "I'm on the pill."

"I know," I tell her. "You have the birth control alarm set in your phone every night at seven."

She laughs, and I kiss her lips. "I love you," I say, and her hands come to my face.

"I love you more." She kisses my lips softly. "Now let's go take a shower and get some food."

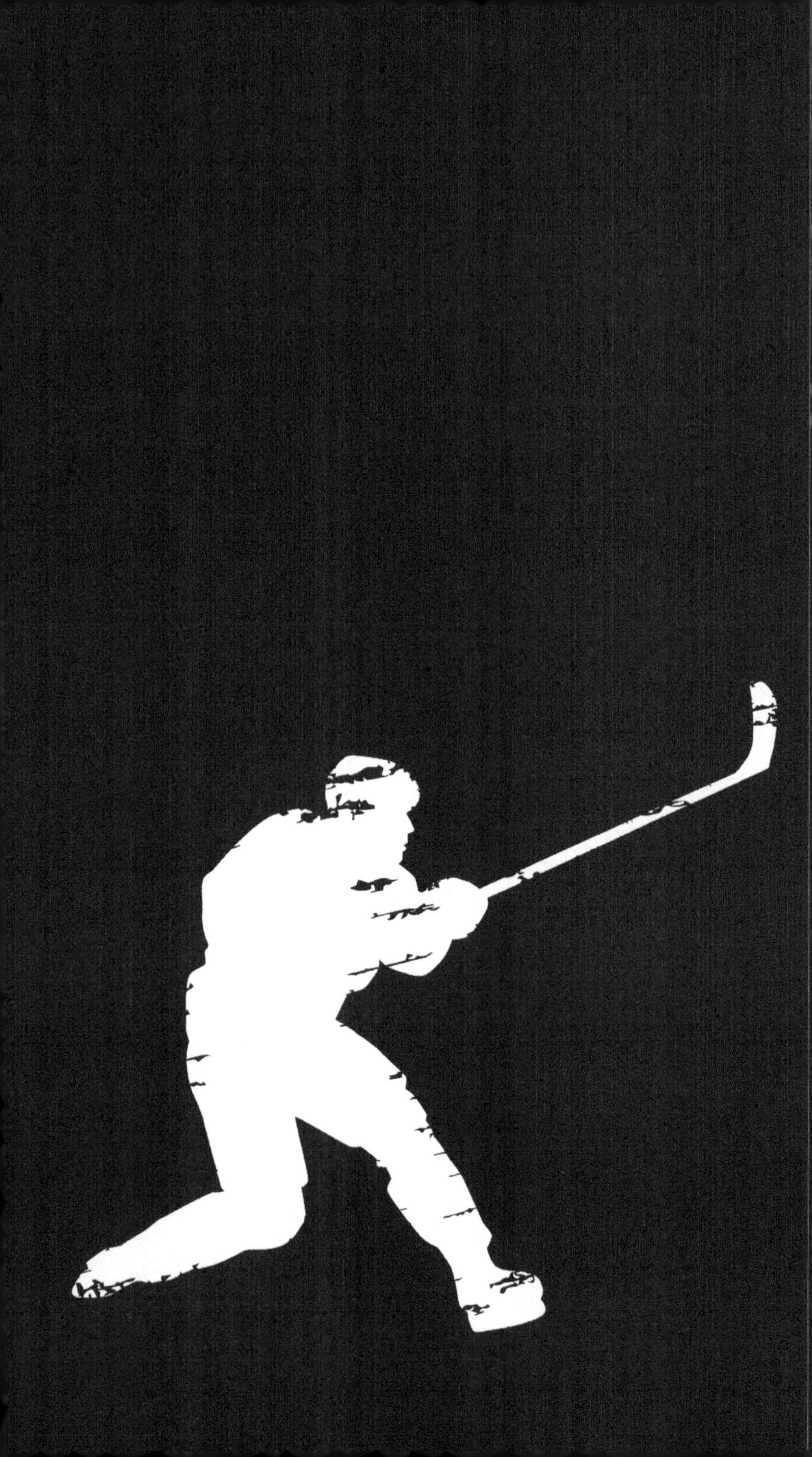

TWENTY-EIGHT

Dylan

"Oh, god," Alex says as I hold her in my arms, and she rides my cock. I'm sitting up in the bed with my back to the headboard, and she is on top of me. My arms are wrapped around her as I help her move up and down on me. When the alarm rang, I reached over to turn it off while she leaned over to grab my cock in her hand. "So good," she says as she picks up speed, and I know she's almost there. "I'm right there."

"Me, too," I say as my balls start to get tight, and when she pulses over my cock, I let go with her. She collapses in my arms now. "Good morning." I kiss her bare shoulder.

"A very good morning indeed." She buries her face into my neck, making me laugh. I'm about to kiss her again when I hear Mac crying by the door, and both of us laugh. We had to kick her out of the room last night when she thought we were playing and wanted to join in. "I bet you she's pissed about you."

"She's a traitor," I say, getting off the bed. "I'm her master."

She tries not to laugh but fails. "You were her master." She kisses my neck and gets off the bed. "Past tense." She winks at me and walks over to the door, and I take full advantage of the view.

I slide my hand into hers as we walk into the arena the next day, bringing her hand to my lips. I can't help but smile. The whole night, being with her over and over again, was a dream come true. From the bed to the shower to the kitchen, I buried myself inside her every single chance I got. I hold open the door as she walks in, and she winks at me. Maddox is waiting for us with Julia, who just eyes us.

"You two did the deed." She points at me, and I look at her, shocked. Then I look over at Maddox to see if he's listening, but instead, he sits there looking down at his legs.

"How did you know?" I ask.

"You're walking with a pep in your step, which means your baggage has been emptied." She talks in code at the same time as Alex holds up her hand for a high five.

"The eagle has landed," Alex says, looking at me. "And planted in the nest."

"I don't even know what we're talking about anymore," I state and then shake my head as the two of them giggle. "Hey there," I say to Maddox, who just looks at me, his eyes not giving away anything. "How did you sleep?" I ask him, and he just shrugs his shoulders, not saying anything.

"I think someone is hungry," Alex observes, squatting down next to me. "Do you want to go upstairs and get something to eat?"

"Why don't you go with Alex?" Julia suggests. "You didn't eat much last night."

Maddox looks at Julia and then hops off the bench. Alex looks at me and then Julia. "Let's go. I think there is a cookie with your name on it," she says and walks with him toward the stairs. He walks a bit behind her, but Alex takes her time.

"What's going on?" I ask Julia, who looks at me.

"It's normal," she explains. "The first couple of days are always new, but it's sinking in that his mother is probably never coming back." I have to sit on the bench because it feels like someone kicked me in the balls. "It usually comes after they are switched from foster home to group home." She sits next to me. "But he was quiet all night, and then this morning I asked if he was okay."

"And?" I quiz, looking over my shoulder to see if he is coming back.

"He asked me if I was going to take him to another house," Julia says. "I told him that we were still looking for his mom." She is quiet and looks down at her hands and then up. "He said she didn't want him, so she wouldn't be coming back."

"I was wrong," I say, looking forward. "I thought it was bad. It's worse than that." I look at her. "Can you imagine how many times she must have told him that?"

"I can tell you from experience," she says. "He was

told that every single day, morning and night." She gets up. "The only thing that is a blessing is that hopefully he finds someone who gives him all the love so he doesn't remember this."

I look at her. "Speaking from experience." I get up. "He's going to remember this forever."

She nods at me. "Well, good news is that there has been no news of his mother," she says. "She was due to get her check and food stamps and never showed up." I shake my head. "So either one, she isn't around, or two, she has money. I'm going with number one."

"How long before he's placed in a home full-time?"

"The average is between nine to twelve months," she says. "It all depends if we find her or not." She takes a deep breath. "Well, I have to get to the office."

"I don't know how you do it," I say, and she laughs at me.

"I stick to no-strings relationships," she tells me. "I'm a hollow soul."

"You lie," I tell her.

"Maybe," she replies. "I'll see you later," and she turns, walking out backward. "Tell Alex I'll call her later for the debrief."

"Debrief?" I ask, confused.

"How long you took?" She holds up a finger. "How many times she had the big O?" She holds up another finger. "Are you a grower or a shower, or are you both?" She holds up her third finger and then looks down at my junk, and I literally shield myself with my hands, making her laugh. "Have a great day." She turns and walks out of the arena at the same time as my father walks in with Matthew.

We walk to the room together, and I'm so lost in my thoughts that I don't hear my name being called. "Hey." My father hits my leg, and I look at him. "Someone is looking for you." He points at Maddox standing in the doorway. He is fully dressed in his hockey gear with his hockey stick in one hand.

"Hi," I greet, "what's up?" I ask Alex and then look down at Maddox.

"He wanted to know if you were going to be at his practice," Alex says, looking at me and then down at Maddox.

"Yeah," I confirm, nodding. "I'm going to be there. Do you want to wait in here while I get dressed?" I ask him, and he shakes his head when he looks over and sees Matthew and my dad.

"That's my dad," I say, pointing at my dad, who comes over and puts his hand out to shake Maddox's hand, but Maddox just holds his stick in his hand. My father looks at me and then holds his fist out for a bump, but all Maddox does is look at it.

"Tough crowd," he says, smiling and squatting down in front of Maddox. "So do you like hockey?" Maddox nods his head. "Okay, I'm going to be watching you out there."

"Okay," Maddox says and turns around, walking back to the room he probably changed in.

"I'm going to go and make sure he's okay," Alex says, and I nod at her.

"What was that all about?" Matthew asks when I turn to walk back and put on my skates.

"He was abandoned here by his mother," I say, and I look at both of them, who just look at me with their mouths hanging open. "We took him home, and all there was in the apartment was a ratted stained mattress in the middle of the room. He's been in foster care ever since."

"The fuck?" Matthew says, and I don't even have the energy to answer him. Instead, I grab my helmet and head out toward the ice where the kids are all skating and falling down. Maddox is the only kid skating by himself. He is teaching himself at this point. Where all the other kids just fall down, he gets up and continues. He keeps to himself, and when Matthew blows the whistle, all the kids go over to him, including Maddox.

I watch the kids while Matthew explains what is going to happen, the only one focusing is Maddox, who chews on his mouth guard. He skates over to me on the side when Matthew blows the whistle. "You know what to do?" I ask, and he nods his head as I pass him the puck. He takes the puck on his blade and skates around the circle, never once letting it leave the blue line. His eyes follow the puck the whole time, and his concentration is clear on his face. He moves the puck with ease, unlike the two other boys who follow him.

He doesn't fuck around like the rest of the boys while he's on the ice. Instead, all he wants to do is skate and puck handle. When the buzzer sounds, he's one of the last boys off the ice. "You did good," I praise, tapping his helmet.

"It was fun," he says. "Are we doing it again?"

"If you want to stay on the ice with me, you can," I say, and for the first time since I've met him, he smiles at me. The simple notion puts another puzzle piece into place inside me, and I can't say anything to him because the lump in my throat is the size of a golf ball.

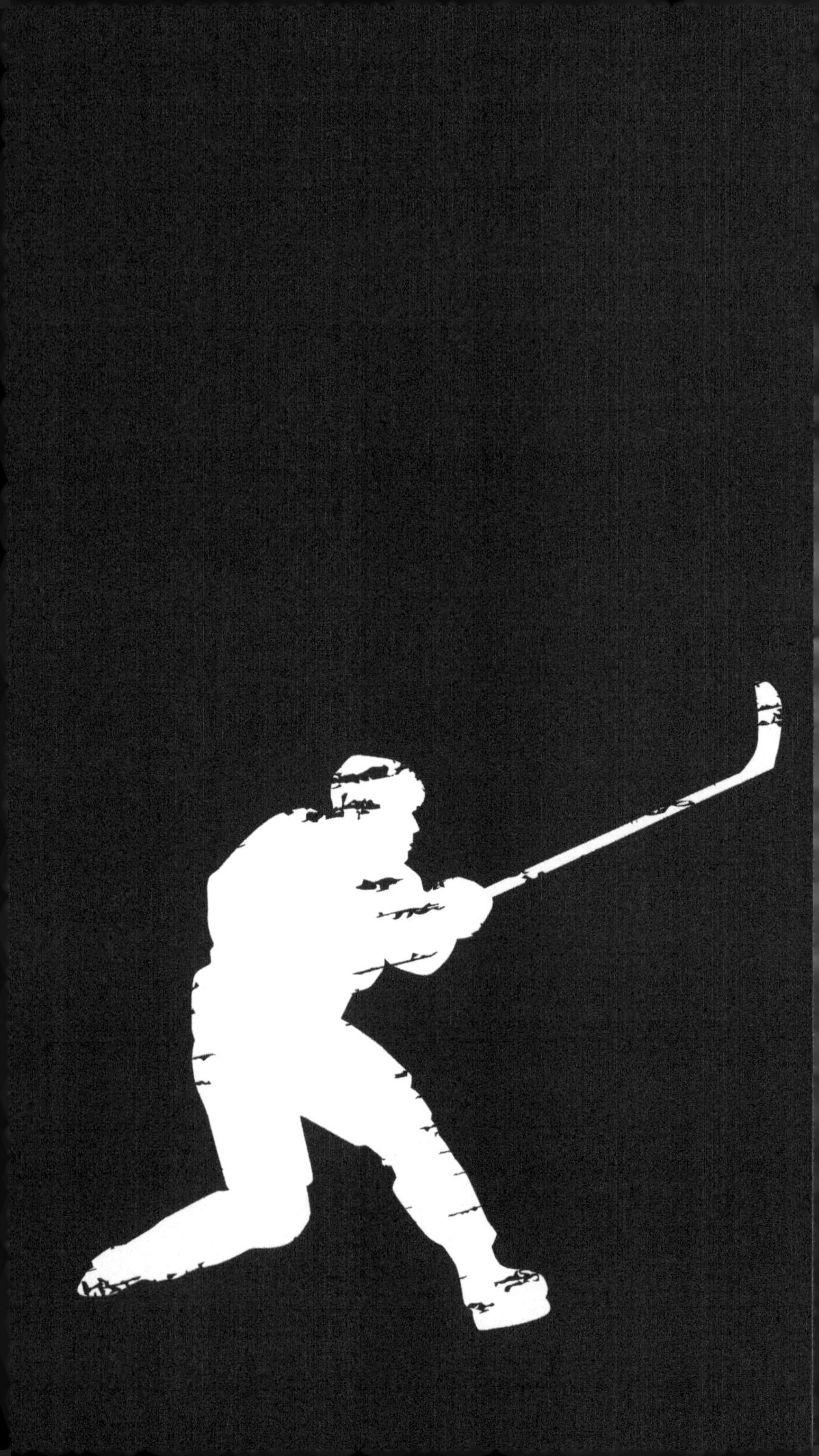

TWENTY-NINE

ALEX

"HEY." DYLAN STICKS his head into my office, and I can't help but smile when I look up at him. "I'm going to take Maddox over to the park to do some off-ice training." He walks into my office, and I see him wearing gym shorts and a T-shirt. A baseball hat is on his head backward, and his blue eyes shine so bright.

I push off from my desk and stand. "Hello," I greet, trying not to smile, but I can't help it. I smile so much my cheeks hurt. "It's almost lunchtime."

Walking around my desk toward him, I stop in front of him. "Hi," he says, leaning his head in and kissing my lips softly. "I'll have him back before lunch is over."

"Or." I wrap my hands around his neck and get up on my tippy-toes. "I can pack a lunch, and we can have a picnic in the park." He puts his hands on my hips and pulls me toward him.

"I like that idea so much better than mine." He rubs

his nose against mine. "I'm going to go and get Maddox, and you can meet us there."

"Fine," I agree. "If you twist my arm." I kiss him one more time before he turns and walks out of my office. I watch him walk toward Maddox, who stands there waiting for him. He's dressed almost the same as Dylan, except his hat is forward and not backward. Dylan bends down in front of him and says something to him, and he looks up, and I wave at him. Dylan puts his hand on his head as they walk out of the arena.

I watch them for as long as I can, and when the phone rings I see it's the groomers.

"Hello," I say, answering right away.

"Hi there, just letting you know that Mac is ready to be picked up," she says, and I look down at my clock and see that if I go and pick up Mac, I'll still be able to meet them at the park for lunch.

I grab my purse and walk out of my office. "I'll be out for lunch," I announce to Veronica sitting down at the desk. "I have to go get Mac, and then I'm joining Dylan at the park. I'll have my phone if you need anything."

"We'll be fine." She smiles at me as I turn and walk upstairs. Grabbing two bags, I fill them with food and snacks, along with water and Gatorade. The heat hits me as soon as I walk out of the arena and get into the car.

Mac is so excited when she sees me walking in. She has a pink bandana wrapped around her neck, and when I squat down in front of her, she licks my face. "Come on. I'm going to take you to meet a friend," I tell her while I put her in the back seat of the car and make sure I tie her in.

When I pull up to the park, I can see Dylan and Maddox off to the side doing lunges side by side. Dylan's telling him a story. "Now you be a good girl," I tell her when I look in the back at her. She finds Dylan right away and starts to bark and cry in excitement. I open the door for the back seat, grabbing her leash, and then go to the trunk to get the lunch I picked up.

There are other kids in the park since it's summer vacation. A group of teenagers are on the soccer field playing. Another group of kids are chasing around a kite as it flies in the air. There are five or six moms sitting in a circle as they watch their kids in the distance playing with each other. The playground structure to the side is full of kids. I make my way over to them. "Hey," I say when I get close enough, and Dylan smiles. "I brought food." I hold up the bags and then look over at Maddox, who doesn't move toward me until Dylan does. "And I brought Mac," I say, letting go of the leash because I know she is going straight to Dylan.

"Hey there, princess," Dylan says softly and then looks over at Maddox. "This is our dog," he tells him, and Maddox just looks over at him. Mac makes her way over to Maddox and starts to sniff him. "Do you like dogs?" Dylan asks Maddox, who just shrugs. "She's gentle." Dylan rubs Mac's head. "But don't let her fool you. She will eat your toast if you go to the bathroom and leave it on the counter."

"Does she get in trouble?" Maddox asks Dylan, who just shakes his head.

"Nah," he says, rubbing Mac. "She's a good girl. I got her when I was all alone and I was lonely." Mac nudges his hand. "She kept me company."

"I thought we could have a picnic." I smile down at Maddox. "Have you ever had a picnic?" I ask him, sitting on the grass in the shade.

He shakes his head and looks at me as Dylan sits down, and he slowly follows. "Well, a picnic …" Dylan starts to talk, grabbing a bag and taking the stuff out. "Is when people sit on the grass and eat their lunch or supper."

Maddox sits down, and Mac follows him and sits right beside me. He looks over at Dylan, who just smiles at him, and then hands him a sandwich. "Thank you," Maddox says softly, taking the sandwich from him.

He grabs half the sandwich and eats it, and I watch him eat. "You are hungry," I say when he finishes his sandwich faster than I think he should and I offer him another.

"So how do you like the house you are staying in?" Dylan asks, lying on his side and looking at Maddox. Mac sits beside him now as if she's in protection mode, and I can't help but smile at her.

"It's okay. I get to eat food when I want," he says, and the sandwich bite that I just took wants to come up. "The bed has two blankets," he adds, shocked, and I just want to grab him and give him a hug.

"That's cool," Dylan says like it's not a big deal.

"Yeah, and they don't get mad at me if I wet the bed by accident." He opens up to us. "They don't make me sleep in it."

I blink away the tears and look down at the sandwich in my hand, but I can't see through the tears. My hands shake a little bit when I hear Dylan. "After we finish eating, we can kick around the soccer ball."

"Okay," Maddox says. When he finishes his second sandwich, I offer him an apple, and he takes it. Only after he finishes the apple and drinks a bottle of water does he stand. "Are you going to play with us, too?" he asks me, and I just smile at him.

"If you want me to," I reply, cleaning up the mess and putting it in the bag. "But I'm better at tag."

"What's that?" he asks, and I clap my hands together in glee.

"Tag is when one person is it, and they have to catch the other person," I explain to him. "When you touch the other person, they are it."

"Can we play?" he asks me, and I just look over at Dylan.

"I'll be it," Dylan says, getting up after cleaning up his garbage. "But just because you're little doesn't mean that I'm not going to catch you."

"Okay." The way he says it, I can hear a lightness in his voice. His brown eyes are lighting up just a touch, I can't help but smile at him

Once I have all the stuff out of the way, I stand. "You ready?" I ask Maddox, who nods his head.

"Okay, I'm going to count to three," Dylan says, grabbing the leash from me, and stands there with Mac beside him, and my eyes open as I look down at Maddox.

"Run," I say as we run in opposite directions. Dylan counts to three and then comes running to me with Mac by his side, barking the whole time, no doubt to show Maddox how to play. I run away from him, and then he follows me in a circle. Mac runs to me, jumping on me at the same time Dylan touches my back shoulder. I can't help but laugh.

"You're it," Dylan huffs out. I squeal when his hand touches my shoulder, and I turn around to chase him back, but he ducks and runs to the side.

I stop and look at both of them. Mac stands beside me, waiting for me to move. Maddox looks at me, and then he runs toward Dylan. Mac takes off before me, running back to Dylan barking and jumping. "I'm going to get you," I say to him, and he runs behind Dylan and then takes off. I chase him in a circle, and I wish I was saying that I was giving him a break, but I wasn't. The kid is really fast. I reach out my hand to touch him, and he escapes by ducking to the right. "Dammit!" I yell, and there in the middle of the park, something happens that neither Dylan nor I could have ever expected. Maddox throws his head back and full-on belly laughs, the sound making my feet stop. My eyes fixate on his smile that lights up his whole face. "I'm going to catch you," I warn, and he just runs faster. It's so carefree that anyone looking at him would think he's just another little boy, but what they don't know is the hell that this child is living. Mac runs alongside Maddox, never leaving his side, not even coming to Dylan or me.

"Don't let her catch you," Dylan says as he runs past

me, and I stick out my hand, touching him.

"You're it," I say, running away from him as fast as I can, but he grabs me around the waist, and Maddox isn't the only one laughing. Mac jumps up and licks Maddox's face, making him laugh even harder.

"Not so fast," he says into my neck as he kisses me. All I can do is laugh as his hand tightens around me.

"You're it again," Maddox says, running past us with Mac jumping and trying to lick him again.

"I'm going to get you," I threaten, escaping from Dylan's grasp. I chase him for a good minute and finally touch him. He smiles when I tell him he's it and then turns around and heads for Dylan.

I don't know how long we play tag for, but when we stop, Maddox's face is flushed pink, and he finishes off a whole bottle of water. His chest is heaving when he stops drinking, and he wipes his mouth with the back of his hand. I'm busy making sure Mac is drinking when he says the words that make me want to do this every single day. "That was fun," he says, drinking again.

"If you want, you can go and play on the playground before we head back to the rink," Dylan says, drinking his own bottle of water.

I see Maddox look over at the playground. "I never played in the park," he says. "We went a couple of times, but it was to sleep."

My heart stops in my chest, and my eyes fly to Dylan, who just motions with his head not to make a big deal out of it. "But then the police came and kicked us out."

"Well, we can go play now," I say, making it a

point to change the memories he has of being in the park to something happier. He follows me toward the playground. "Do you want to try the monkey bars?" I point at the bars that no one is on. "It's fun."

"I can show you," Dylan says, walking toward the monkey bars. I sit down with Mac sitting right beside me at the edge of the park on the grass, watching Dylan teach him how to get across. He tries his hardest with his little arms to go across, and every single time, he makes more and more progress. Kids play around them, but Maddox is focused on the task at hand.

Nothing can prepare me for when he finally makes it across. I get up from the grass when he goes halfway, my body tense as he moves from one bar to the next. You can see the pain in his eyes as he almost slips, but his other hand finds the steel bar again. "Come on," I mumble under my breath as he makes it through to another bar.

Finally, he gets to the last one, and when he reaches for it, I throw my hands in the air in celebration for him, then I put my hands on my head when I see him struggle with the other arm. I can hear Dylan's voice softly encouraging him as he puts his hand behind him to help in case he falls. "You can do it," he says to him. "Just focus." When he reaches forward, his hand grabs the last bar, and his mouth goes into the biggest fucking smile I have ever seen on him. When his feet touch the bar, Dylan grabs him and hugs him so big. Maddox's arms just fall to his sides, not sure what to do, and I have to sit down at the thought that no one has ever hugged him. Dylan must sense this and puts him down as he runs over to me.

"I did it," he says with a smile. "All by myself." Mac nudges Maddox's hand with her head, making Maddox pet her.

I hold up my hand to high-five him, and he slaps my hand. "You did it, buddy," I say, my chest so full and so proud of him. I blink away the tears that are stinging my eyes and sniffle. "It's time to head back." I get up, dusting off the sand from my jeans and waiting for Dylan to walk to us. He slips his hand in mine as we walk back to the bags and load up the car. Mac gets in beside Maddox and sits next to him, watching out the window.

Neither of us says anything as we get back to the arena. Julia is there waiting for us with a smile. "Sorry we're late, we got hung up at the monkey bars," I apologize, looking down at Maddox to see if he is going to smile, but his shield is back in place.

"We'll see you tomorrow," Dylan says to him, and all Maddox does is nod at him. Julia leads him back out toward her car, and when I look at Dylan, all he does is shake his head. "Are you done for the day?"

"Yeah." I look around, and everything appears to be in order. If it's not, they will call me.

We get back in the car and I look out my window as we make our way home. When we get into the house, Mac gets out of the car and walks right toward the back door. I watch her walk outside and finally turn around. "My stomach hurts." I put my hand on my stomach. "Like it hurts knowing that he isn't here with us."

"I know," Dylan says softly, sitting down. "I was

thinking the same thing." He runs his hands through his hair.

"It's crazy, right?" I ask him. "Everything that is happening. The need to protect him. The need to make sure he goes to bed happy. The need to make sure he eats properly. The need to make sure that he feels loved." I shake my head. "I …" I start to say, but I'm at a loss for words.

"I know," Dylan agrees. "I know."

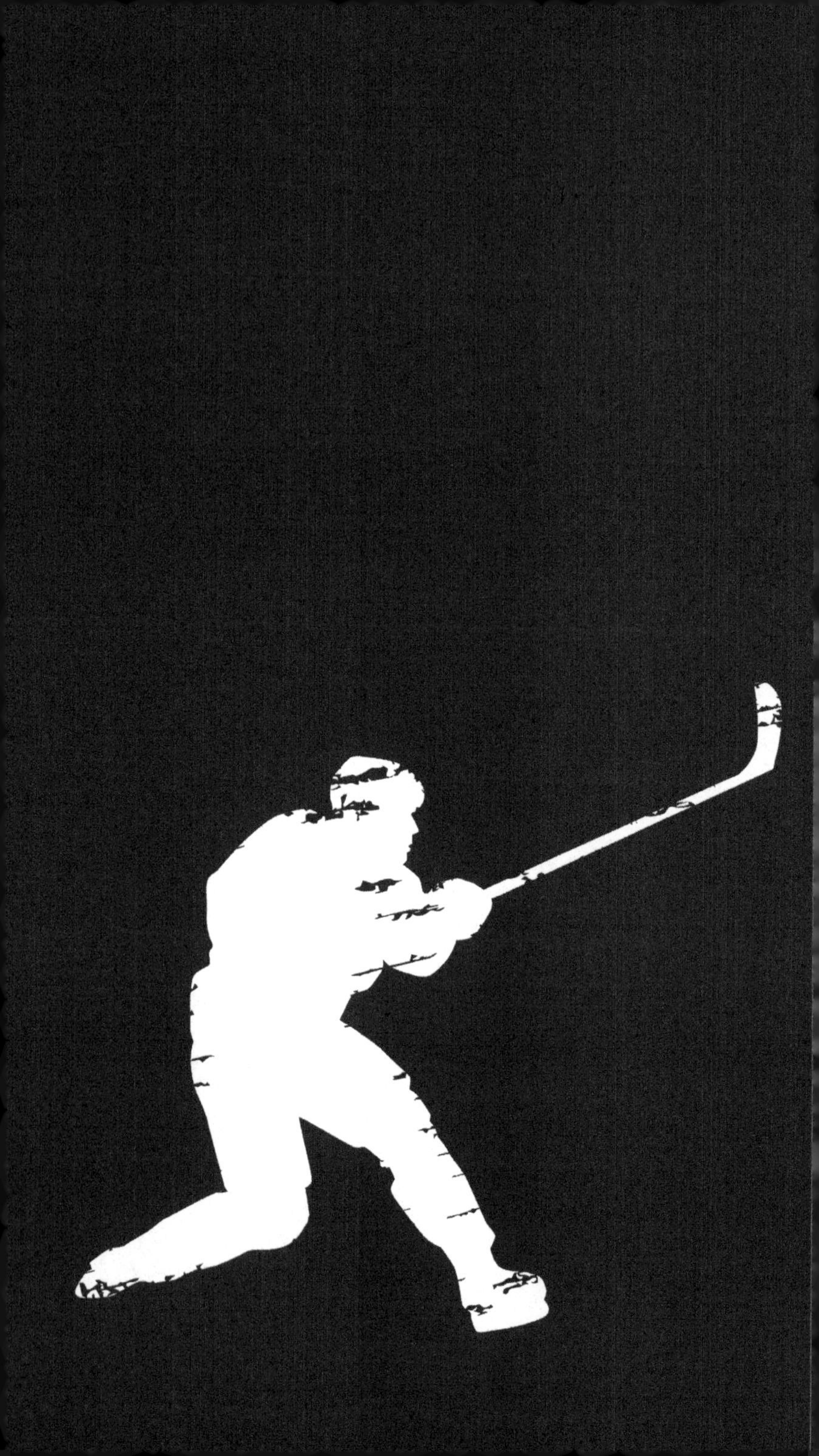

THIRTY

Dylan

"Hey," I greet when I see Julia the next day. All night, I tried not to think of what Maddox was doing, but as soon as I closed my eyes, all I saw was his face. Then his words would echo in my ears. I can't even imagine what he went through. I thought I went through shit when I was growing up, but at least I had my mother to protect me and show me love. He had no one, and the thought alone cuts me off at the knees.

"Hi," she says, looking down at Maddox. "Someone was excited about getting here today. He woke up extra early."

I smile and squat down. "You ready to hit the ice?" I ask him, and for the first time, I can see a little light in his brown eyes as he nods. "Why don't you go say hi to Alex, and we can go upstairs and have breakfast? I'm starving."

"Okay," he says, walking away from us. I watch him

until he walks into the office before I get up and turn back to Julia.

"I have a question," I say, my heart hammering in my chest.

"Hopefully, I'll have an answer for you," she says, smiling.

"What are the chances we can get Maddox for the weekend?" I ask her, not sure if it's even possible.

"You can't just take him for the weekend, Dylan. He's not a library book that you sign him in and out." She just looks at me.

"I know that," I huff out. "But what if you brought him here to the rink on the weekends? What if we offer weekend hours?"

"Do you offer weekend hours?" She tilts her head to the side.

"No," I admit. "But I would come in on the weekend, and we can skate. I'll talk to Wilson about it, and if I have to rent out the ice myself, I will."

"I can ask his foster parents. I'm not sure if they will be okay with that. It will throw off their routine."

"I want to adopt him," I say the five words I've wanted to tell Alex all night but was scared to admit it. Julia looks at me, shocked as well. "I don't know the first thing about being a parent."

"Okay, one, that isn't true," Julia says. "You come from a family that pretty much runs itself." I smile when I think about it. "And, Dylan, I really think you need to think about this."

"I have," I tell her, taking a deep breath. "It's the only

thing I have been thinking about. When I was eight, I got into my father's hockey camp. I want to think he was made to be my father, and I feel the same way about Maddox. This whole thing, me leaving Montreal, admitting that I was in love with Alex, moving here. Coming here to help out, it was all for a bigger purpose, and that was Maddox." I'm pretty sure I'm rambling now. "I know we are young but there is nothing that we won't do for him."

"Dylan, you have to be one hundred percent sure," she says softly. "Before I start the paperwork or do anything like that, I have to be sure you are going to be in one hundred percent." She looks over at the office and sees Maddox coming out with Alex. "Have you spoken to Alex about it?"

"Not in so many words," I admit. "But I don't think she is going to have an issue with it."

"I'll see what I can do, and we can talk about it," she says, and I just nod at her.

The day flies by, and when he leaves with Julia again, a void is right back where it was yesterday. When I watch him walk out of the arena beside Julia and then feel Alex's hand slip into mine, I swallow down the lump. As the hours ticked by, he got quieter and quieter. While he got changed out of his hockey gear, I sat with him, and everything inside me was yelling not to show him how sad I was. So I kept a smile on my face, and we made plans on what we were going to do on Monday. Well, I made plans, and he just listened. I am going to have to gain his trust. He probably had so many empty promises in his life he knew better than to trust anyone. "He'll be back on Monday." Julia lets us know that the family already made plans, and they didn't want to change them as they wanted to gain his trust.

"Then what?" I look at her, my chest feeling like it's being crushed. "Then we don't see him until Monday." Alex doesn't say anything to me. All she does is lean into me and kisses my arm.

"You have the gala tomorrow for the foundation," she reminds me. "First time Dylan Stone is going to be making his debut as a Dallas Oiler." She smiles at me, and her smile makes the pressure on my chest lighten up just a touch.

"Did you get a dress?" I ask. Her eyes go big, but I don't know why she's surprised by this question.

"I didn't know I was going." She laughs. "It's the first time on the red carpet. The press will be all over you."

"It'll be the best time to bite the bullet and make our grand entrance." I put my arm around her and lean in to kiss her lips. "I'm sure you have something you can wear."

"Of course." She rolls her eyes at me. "Because everyone has a dress to wear to a gala hanging in their closet."

I laugh. When we get home, she goes into her closet while I grab my iPad and start to make a plan of my own. The next day, I slip out of the house when the girls come over to glam her up. I grab Mac and her leash because I'm leaving her at my parents' house for the night.

Two hours later, I'm walking back into the house,

my hands shaking. "Hello!" I yell up the stairs, and she comes out of the bedroom, wearing a white robe. I can't help when my stomach flips over at the sight of her. Her hair is loose and in soft curls, and her makeup is just perfect. I walk up the steps and pull her to me, kissing her lips.

"You get one kiss," she says, taking a step back. "Or else you'll mess my whole face." She comes back in for one more kiss. "Besides, you have like thirty minutes to get ready."

"All I need to do is shower," I say, walking back into the room and seeing the lavender dress that she is wearing lying on the bed. "Pretty," I say, "And it's loose, so I can slip my hands under it easily."

She throws her head back and laughs. "Yes, that is exactly why I chose it." She shakes her head. "Go shower."

I shower and then slip on my blue dress pants with a white button-down shirt. When I walk out of the shower, I see her slipping into the dress. She smiles and comes to me. "Can you zip me?" She turns around so I can zip her. Once it's zipped, I lean in and kiss her neck. "How does this look?" she asks me, and I can see her hands are shaking from the nerves. She stands there in a long-sleeved lavender dress. It crisscrosses over the chest, and the shoulders have silver beading. The waist is tight and then lets loose again. She ties the bottom of the sleeves, and then you see the sleeves puff out just a touch.

"You look so beautiful," I say. She walks over to the bed, and I see the slit in the dress showing off her long, lean leg. She sits on the bed, putting on her silver high heels, when I walk back into the closet and finish getting dressed. I slip on the matching jacket and then slip the black velvet box into my pocket. "I have something for you," I say, walking out with a square box in my hand. She's still sitting on the bed.

"I'm nervous," she admits, getting up and coming to me. "It's stupid, though. We've attended these things before."

"It's different," I tell her. "This time, I can hold your hand and lean over and kiss you."

She smiles at me. "That you can." She looks at the box in my hand. "What do you have there?"

"Well, since it's our first date," I say, smirking at her. "I was going to get you flowers."

"That box doesn't look like flowers." She laughs as I hand her the box. Her hands come up to grab the box, and she turns it to her and opens it, a gasp leaving her when she sees the diamond earrings I bought for her. "Oh my gosh." She touches one of the earrings with her finger. "They are so pretty." She looks at me, blinking away the tears in her eyes. "I'm going to wear them tonight," she says, turning toward the mirror so she can put them on. My heart hammers in my chest when she turns around and sees me on bended knee. "Dylan," she says, not sure, and she puts one of her hands to her mouth.

"Your dress is missing one more thing." I joke with her, and my palms get all sweaty. "God, I thought this would be easier." I laugh nervously. "Alexandra, every single memory I have in my life is with you beside me."

I reach up and grab her hand in mine. "From as far back as I can remember, the only person who I wanted there for anything was you." I smile at her as one of the tears escapes her eyes. "There are so many more memories to make. So many more memories that I want to make." I grab the box from my jacket. "The only thing I know about these memories is that I want to do them with you beside me." She sobs quietly. "As my wife."

She laughs and cries at the same time, her smile so big that I can't help but get up to kiss her and then go back down on my knee. "Do you want to make memories with me?" I ask her. "Do you want to be my wife?"

"There is no one in this world I want to do life with besides you," she says. "When you came to Dallas and I asked you what your future looked like." She wipes away the tears. "And you said married and a family, it was the first time in my life that I didn't see me beside you." My heart sinks. "I went to bed that night and cried."

"Baby," I say, getting up now, wiping her tears away. "It was always you," I whisper. "It's always going to be you. My heart doesn't beat without you. All the future memories are blank unless you are in them. Marry me," I say, bending my forehead to hers. "Please be my wife." I hold my breath, not even shy to admit that I would beg her on my knees to make her say yes.

She looks at me, her hand coming up to hold my face. "Forever," she says. "I'll love you forever." I swallow now. "You're my forever."

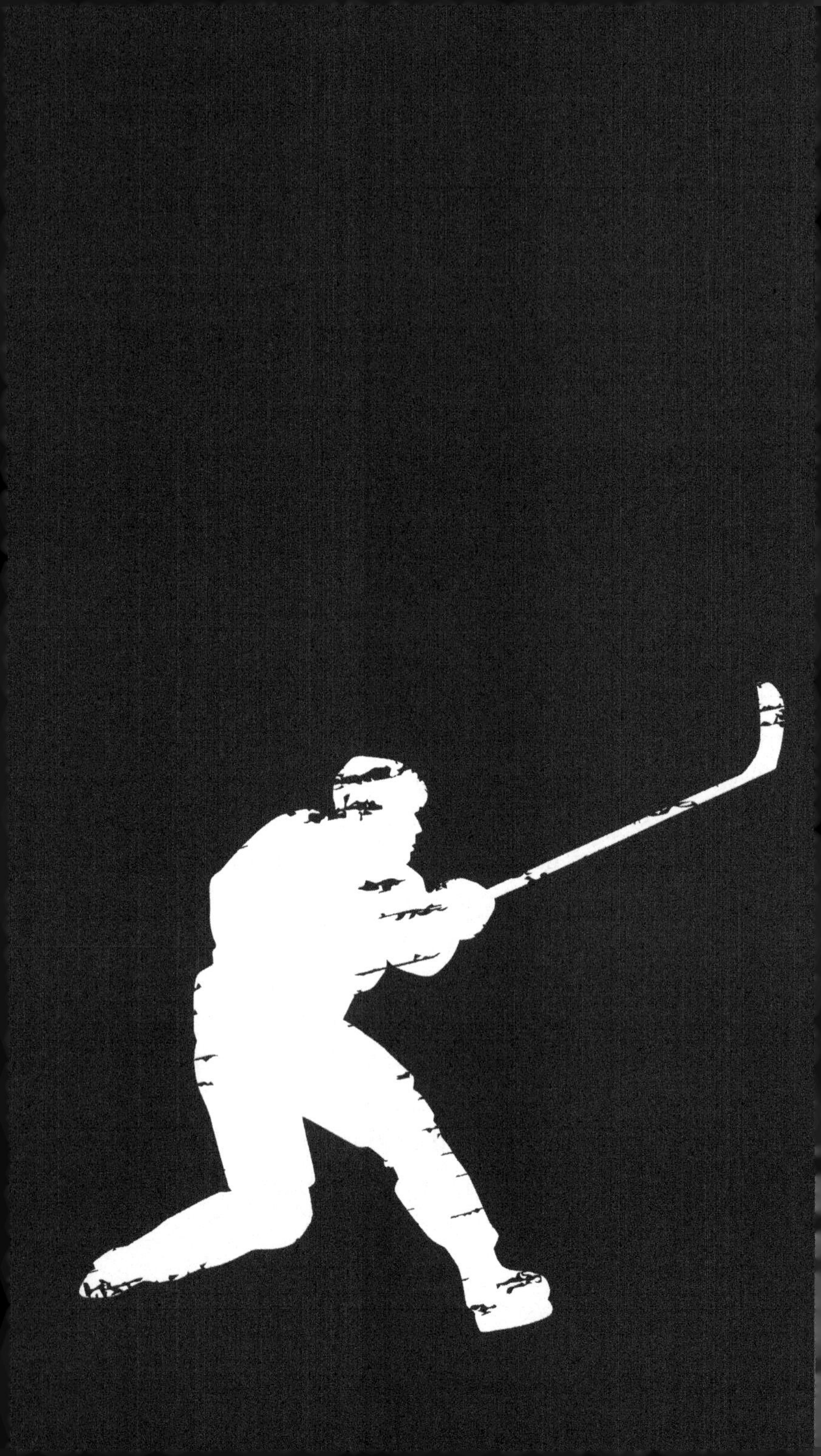

THIRTY-ONE

Alex

I LOOK INTO his blue eyes, and the only thing I can think of is I don't think I can ever be this happy. His lips crash onto mine as he pulls me to him, and the taste of tears fills our kiss. He lifts me up and buries his face in my neck. My hand goes to the back of his head. "I love you." I place my cheek on his head.

The doorbell rings. "That's the car." Neither of us lets go of the other one. "We should get going," I urge, but we still don't move. He puts me down slowly after a minute and then looks at me. "What?" I ask him, watching his face, and then his eyes find mine.

"It's time to slip on the ring," he says with a shy smile as he takes the ring out of the box, and I hold out my left hand. I gasp when I see that the ring looks like my mother's engagement ring.

"Oh my God," I gasp when I finally look at it. "You remembered," I say of the conversation we had when I was sixteen, and I said I wanted the same ring as my mother but oval. I look down, seeing the rose gold ring with the oval-shaped diamond in the middle. Little white diamonds fill the band. "Oh my goodness." I want to say more, but the doorbell rings again.

"We should get going," Dylan says, grabbing my hand.

"This sucks," I say, slipping my hand in his. "Aren't we supposed to have sex after getting engaged?" I walk down the steps with the dress flowing around my legs. "I'm thinking that is like rule number one. You know, to cement the contract."

He laughs at me as we walk out the front door, and the driver is waiting beside the car. He opens the back door, and I get in before Dylan. "Engaged," I say when Dylan sits beside me, and the driver closes the door. I hold up my hand, looking at it. "Like from boyfriend to fiancé in a week." I smile at him as he leans in and kisses my neck with his arm around my back, pulling me to him. "Is that where you went?" I ask him, wanting to know all the details.

He shakes his head. "I went to Uncle Matthew's," he tells me. "The guys were all waiting there."

"What guys?" I ask, shocked.

"My dad, your dad, Grandpa." He names the only three guys who really matter in all of this.

"My father?" I say, shocked by this news.

"Well, I asked your mom yesterday, and then today, I asked your father." His words shock me, and I have to put a hand to my chest. This time, it's not from the crushing pain but instead from the fullness of it. "I was planning on doing this next week." He grabs my left hand, kissing my finger with the ring on it. He looks down at it, and his whole face lights up. "But seeing you all dressed up and knowing that we are going to be coming out as a couple, I want everyone to know that you're mine forever."

He releases my hand, and I look down at my own hand, so blissfully happy I can't help the tear that escapes me. "Married." I look up at him, and all he can do is lean over and kiss my lips so softly. His hand comes up to hold my chin, and he rubs his thumb back and forth. "Can one be happy and then suddenly so nervous that they are going to throw up?" I ask him, looking out of the window once the car stops.

I put my hands to my stomach as I see the whole scene in front of me. We have three cars in front of us. The barricade where the fans are all lined up with their phones out, taking pictures and yelling at the players who are getting out of their cars. The car moves up one more spot and I can see the blue and green carpet now, matching the team colors. The press is all lined up facing the white backdrop that has the foundation's name and the team name stamped across it. A couple of reporters are there, interviewing some of the players. The car moves one more spot, and my hand goes to my stomach. "Do you want to just go as we always do?" I hear him ask me and look over at him. "We can just walk the carpet as we always do." His eyes meet mine. We've been on the red carpet before, always together laughing and joking.

"No," I say, shaking my head. "As nervous as I am

about coming out." I smile and pick up my hand. "This ring says otherwise."

"That it does." He smiles as the car moves forward and then stops. "You sure?" he asks me one last time before the car door opens beside him.

"More than sure," I assure him, pushing down all the nerves I have. He steps out of the car and fixes his jacket before holding out his hand for me. I slip my hand in his, and all my nerves are gone. I don't know how the press will spin this, and to be honest, I don't care. The only people whose opinions matter to me are our families. Other than that, it's icing on the cake.

I hear his name being called as soon as he climbs out, and he smiles and turns to the crowd. "Go and sign some stuff, Mr. Stone." I point at the little kids jumping up and down when they see him. He lets go of my hand, and I step to the side, not wanting to be in anyone's way.

The car stops, and I look up, seeing Michael get out of the car with Jillian beside him. He comes over and smiles at me, kissing my cheek as the press yells his name. "You ready?" he asks me, and I take a deep breath and put my hand to my stomach, not even aware of the gasp that comes out of Jillian.

"Oh my God," she says. Her hand comes to touch my hand, and then she drops it when she looks around. "Is that what I think it is?"

"Well, if you think it's a friendship ring." I look at her. "You're wrong."

"He said he was waiting." Michael shakes his head and then walks over to the crowd with Dylan.

The two of them pose for a picture together and then apart. More and more players arrive, and when Cooper gets there, the roar of the crowd is deafening. He comes over to hug us at the same time Dylan comes back to stand beside me. "Nice of you to show up," I say, smiling at him and then looking at Erika, who is just smirking. I look over at Cooper now. "I don't even want to shake your hand," I say. He laughs, and I put my hand on my forehead.

"What the fuck?" he says to me. "He did it already." He looks at Dylan, who puts his hand in mine. "My cousin and my cousin are getting married," he jokes, making Michael groan.

"It's much better than my cousin and my sister," Michael says, putting his hand in Jillian's.

"Okay, let's do this," Dylan says now, looking at me. "Ready?"

"No," I answer him honestly. "But YOLO."

Cooper walks in front of us as he starts down the carpet. "You didn't go see the fans," Erika reminds him.

"We'll do this with the family, and then I'll go over," he says, looking at us. "Here goes nothing."

He walks down the carpet in front of us, and Michael follows us. "Look here!" they all shout, and we stop walking, posing together.

"Wait," Franny says, walking down the carpet with Wilson's hand in hers. "Now you can take the picture," she says, and we all laugh.

"What took you so long?" Jillian asks her.

"Have you seen my husband?" She side-eyes Wilson

with a wicked smile. "If you think he looks hot in a suit, you can imagine how hot he is out of the suit."

"I've seen him out of the suit," Cooper says. "He's not that hot."

I laugh as Wilson shakes his head. "The car had a flat tire." He tries to make up the excuse.

"You have a hickey," I say, pointing at his neck that is being covered a bit by his jacket collar.

Franny looks at him and smiles. "That's not a hickey," she gloats. "Those are teeth marks."

"I'm going to barf," Michael says as a reporter calls Dylan's name.

"Here we go," he says, looking at me as he walks over to the reporter who is waiting for him.

"Dylan Stone," he says, smiling at him. "A Dallas Oiler."

I look over at Dylan, my chest beaming with pride for him. My hand squeezes his just a touch, and his thumb moves over mine. "It's a weird thing." He smirks. "Going to take some getting used to."

"Was it a difficult decision to make?" he asks him, and Dylan just nods his head.

"It was one of the most difficult I had to make." His voice goes soft, and he looks over at me. "But I had to do it for my family."

"It's going to be some good hockey watching the three of you on the ice." He smiles at us.

"I can't wait," Dylan says. "We usually train with each other every summer, so it's going to be interesting to see the dynamic on the ice."

"It's going to be good seeing the family cheering for the same team." He laughs.

"Only person I care about cheering for me has been cheering me on since I was twelve," he says, picking up our hands and kissing my fingers.

"Oh my God," Franny gasps out. "You're engaged."

"Um," I say, my eyes going big, but the smile on my face is so big my cheeks hurt.

"I guess you got the scoop." Dylan looks at the reporter and then leans in and kisses me.

"So I guess we need to scratch you off the list of most eligible NHL bachelors," the reporter jokes.

"You can definitely scratch me off that list." Dylan chuckles.

"Wait," the reporter says. "Aren't you Michael Horton's sister?"

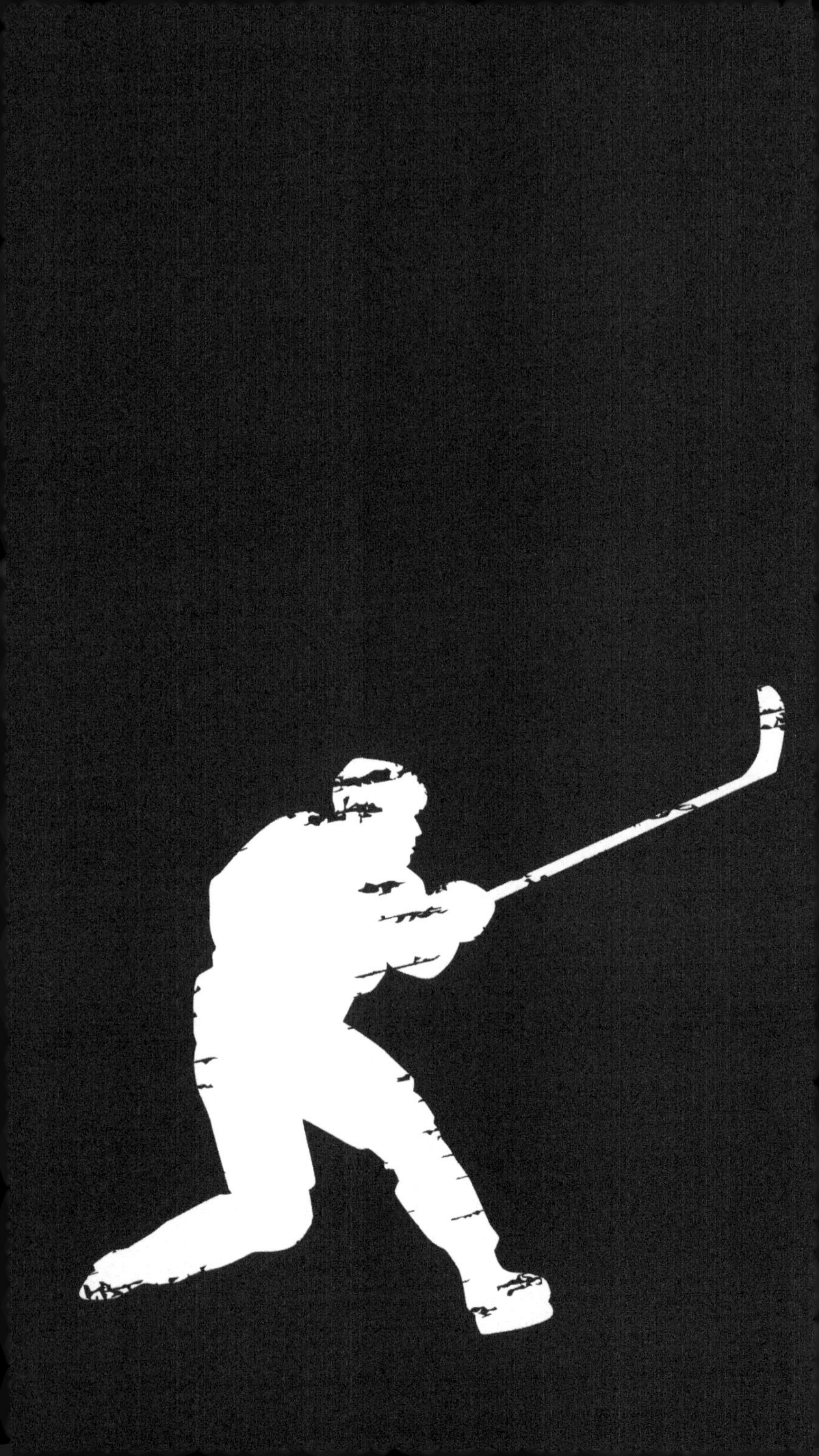

THIRTY-TWO

Dylan

"What time is it?" I mumble when I feel her move away from me, falling to my back. My eyes are still closed when I feel the covers move. I think she's getting up to go to the bathroom, but then I feel her hot mouth on my cock. "Hmm," I moan, opening my eyes and seeing her hair covering her face as she sucks my cock.

I close my eyes for a second to take in the feeling. Every single time she touches me, my body feels like an electric shock is going through it. When her hand grips my shaft, I open my eyes once more, and this time, I move her hair away from her face so I can watch her. She's on her hands and knees in the middle of my legs with her ass in the air, swinging side to side, and I know she's playing with herself. "Swing your ass over here," I say between clenched teeth when she lets go of my cock and licks down the shaft toward my balls. "Alex," I say as she jerks my cock. "Sit on my face," I order, lifting up my head and watching her watch me with a smile.

"I have a better idea," she says, getting up and straddling me. She holds my cock in her hand as she aligns herself over me and slides down. I watch my cock disappear inside her, the only sound is of us both moaning out. Her hands go on my stomach as my hands go to her hips as she lifts herself up with her legs and back down again.

"This is much better," I say. My hands go to her tits, pinching both nipples at the same time and then twisting them, and I feel her pussy pulsate when I do that.

"So much better," she huffs, moving her hands to the middle of my chest. She rotates her hips once and then moves up and down on my cock. Her hair falls to one side, and she looks like a sex goddess. "So close." She doesn't stop moving as I lean up to suck a nipple into my mouth. "Yes," she hisses, her pussy getting tighter and tighter as I do the same thing to the other nipple. "Fuck, I'm going to come," she says, and I watch her eyes close as her pussy gets tight around my cock, and I feel her wetness all over me. I wrap my arm around her waist in the middle of her coming and flip her on her back. My cock never leaves her pussy as she wraps her legs around my waist, and I fuck her as hard as I can. My head goes to her neck as her whole body engulfs me. "Again," she pants, and I fuck her over and over again until we both moan our release.

Her legs and arms just squeeze me tighter when I turn to get away from her. "No," she groans, making me laugh. I'm about to kiss the shit out of her when the doorbell rings. Both of us stop moving as I look over at the clock and see it's a little after ten.

"Are you expecting someone?" I ask, looking at the doorway.

"Yes, of course, I'm expecting someone. That's why I woke up with your cock in my mouth," she sasses me, and her legs and arms fall to the sides. I slide out of her, and she gets up, grabbing a shirt and slipping it on her.

"Where the fuck do you think you're going?" I grab her around her waist when she is about to walk out of the room, and she laughs.

"I was going to answer the door," she says as the doorbell rings again.

"Don't leave this room," I tell her as I grab a pair of shorts. "Unless I call you."

She rolls her eyes at me, and I know she isn't going to listen to me. I walk down the stairs as the bell rings again and open the door, seeing a delivery guy there. "Mr. Stone," he says to me, and I nod my head. "We have a couple of things for you." He turns to walk back to the van and opens it, showing me a whole truckload of fucking flowers.

"Babe!" I yell behind me but see her walking down the steps in a robe now. "Not better," I say, and she laughs.

"Who's at the door?" she asks me the same time her phone rings.

"What the fuck is going on?" I ask her as she walks over to the kitchen. "Doesn't anyone sleep anymore?"

The guy comes back with two vases of flowers. "There are six more."

"From who?" I ask, and he just shrugs his shoulders, and I turn to walk into the kitchen.

"Okay." I hear Alex say, and then her head goes down. "We'll be there in an hour."

She puts down the phone. "Um, that was your dad and your mom, who were both not happy that he had to read about their son's engagement in the papers."

"Papers?" I say, shocked as the guy comes back in and just puts the flowers on the kitchen counter.

"Who are these from?" she asks, and I just shrug.

"What papers?" I ask her, confused as fuck looking at her as she smiles at the guy.

"There are four more," he says to her.

"Is it in the papers?" I ask her, grabbing her phone and opening it and seeing the picture of the both of us from last night. We are side by side, I don't know what she is telling me, but all you can see is me smiling as she looks at me. It's our favorite picture of us together and I'm going to be adding it to our framed pictures. Then I scroll down and read the headline, and I want to vomit.

Kissing Cousins.

I stop even breathing, afraid how she is going to react to this. I scroll the article and then look up at her as she smiles at me. "The flowers are from Nico and Becca." She holds the card. "This one is from Leo and says you're a punk-ass pussy, and he's not talking to you but that he's happy for me." She laughs and then sees my face. "What's wrong?"

"Your father was right." I think about not telling her but knowing she'll find out anyway.

"What are you talking about?" she says, putting the cards down and coming to me now.

"Oh, well," she huffs out. "People are idiots," she says, not even bothered by this whole news.

"This doesn't bother you?" I ask her, trying to read her face.

"Does it bother me?" she repeats my question. "Yes." She shrugs. "Do I care? No." She smiles. "I care more that our friends and family know the truth and stand behind us." She points over at all the flowers. "This is all that matters to me. That our friends and family support us."

I'm about to say something else, but I don't have time to ask her anything because the front door opens, and I hear running.

Julia comes into the room, and her face is filled with tears. She looks at us, and something about her being here makes my heart stop. "We can't find him."

Everyone says that when something traumatic happens, you always feel like you leave your body. It's at this moment that I know what everyone is talking about. The room comes to a standstill, and the beating of my heart echoes so loud in my ears I don't think I understand what she's saying. "What do you mean?" I hear Alex ask her.

"They went to get him this morning in his room, and he wasn't there," she says, frantically looking around. "They called the police and then called me. I came here, thinking maybe he came here."

"How would he come here?" I roar. My hands shake

as the front door opens, and I hear more footsteps.

"We came as soon as Julia called," Wilson says, looking like you just dragged him out of his bed. Franny follows him dressed as if she just picked the first thing out of her closet. The front door opens again, and I hear more people coming into the house, and I see Michael running in with my father and Max. "We called Matthew. He got things rolling."

"He's alone," Alex says, the tears running down her face, all eyes on her. "When was the last time they saw him?" She looks around at everyone and then back to Julia. "I have to go get dressed." She turns and runs up the stairs, and Franny just follows her upstairs.

"Julia." I look at her. "You need to tell me everything," I say, swallowing down the bile coming up my throat. "And I mean everything."

"They put him to bed last night," Julia starts. "He was not himself all day. He was quiet and withdrawn. He kept asking them how long until he was able to go to the rink," she says, wiping the tears away

"Oh my God," my father says. "Have you checked the rink?"

"I'll go over there," Wilson says. "Tell Fran." He runs out.

"He didn't want to eat dinner," Julia says. "Asked how much time was left until he was going. Every single hour, he got quiet, and they went to tuck him in."

"How does an eight-year-old run away from the house in the middle of the night?" Alex asks when she comes down the stairs wearing shorts and one of my T-shirts.

Her hair is piled on her head; her face streaked with tears.

"You guys don't get it. Do you know how many times he's probably done that during his life? Escaping in the middle of the night," she says, and I can't help but put my hand on the counter not to fall. My own memories come back to me. The times we had to leave quickly. The times we had to leave to escape whenever people were coming to find my father but instead would find us. The amount of time we walked around at night not looking at anyone, my mother shielding me with her body the whole time. "This isn't something new to him."

"I'm going to be sick," Alex says, putting her hand to her stomach, and Max goes over to her.

"He's going to be fine," he tells her, taking her in his arms.

Julia's phone rings in her hand, and everyone stops what they're doing to look at her. "Hello." She puts the phone to her ear. Looking at us, she shakes her head and walks out of the room.

"I have to get out there," I say, walking to the stairs and running up them to the bedroom. I slip on a T-shirt and grab my running shoes, then run down the stairs.

"Where are you going to go?" My father waits for me at the bottom of the stairs.

"I have no idea, but sitting here doing nothing isn't going to help him," I reply, putting on my shoes.

"If you're going, I'm going," Alex says, and I walk to her and take her face in my hands. She looks into my eyes, fighting back the tears that want to come out, but it's a losing battle.

"You need to stay here with Julia in case they call," I explain, using my thumb to wipe her tears away.

"But what if you find him and I'm not there?" she says. "What if he thinks I don't love him?" Her head falls forward as I pull her into my arms. Her body shakes with her sobs. "He must be so scared."

I kiss the top of her head. "We are going to find him," I assure her, taking a step back. "I promise you that." I hold her face in my hands again. "I'm going to go and get our boy."

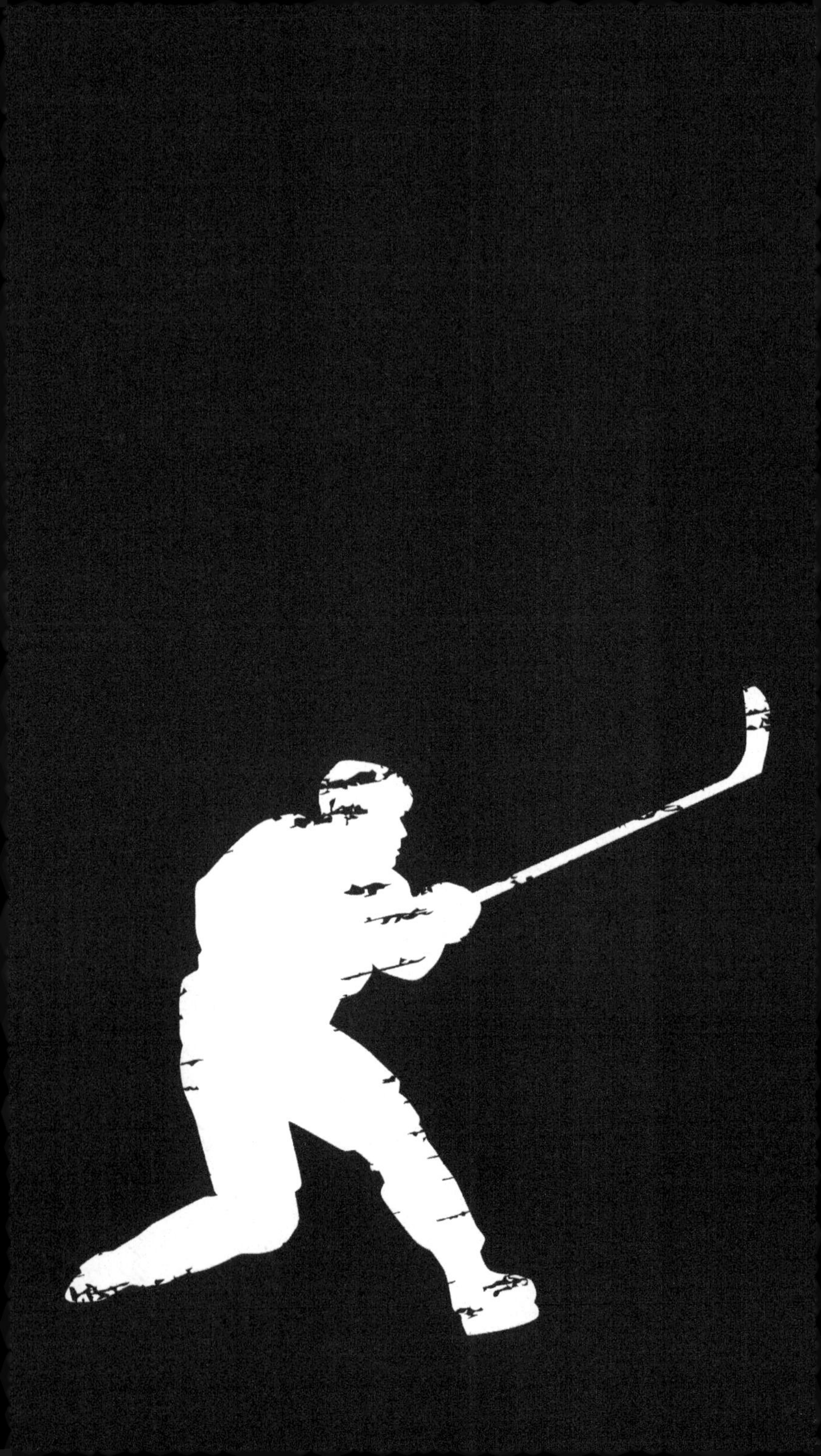

THIRTY-THREE

Alex

He kisses my lips one more time before he turns and runs out of the room with his father and Michael behind him. My father is there when my legs give out to catch me before I hit the floor. The only thing I can see in my head is Maddox the last time I saw him. I can even hear the sound of his laughter if I close my eyes tight enough. "It's going to be okay," my father says. The front door opens, and I watch, praying and hoping that it's Julia telling me they found him.

But instead, my mother and aunt Caroline stand side by side looking at me. Mac runs over to me all excited but must sense something is wrong because she just lies next to me with her chin on my leg. My hand's rubbing her head when Matthew comes in behind them, "What's going on?" Caroline is the first to ask me in almost a whisper, and my mother slides her hand into hers for emotional support, not sure herself what is going on.

"Where is Justin?" she asks and the worry fills her face.

"He's fine," my father reassures her. "He's gone to look for Maddox."

"The little boy?" my mother asks, and I look up at my dad, my head spinning around and around, trying to make all the plans.

"I need a lawyer." I look at my father, whose arms fall away from me. "I need a lawyer, a good one." I walk over to the fridge and grab a bottle of water. "I need to stop crying because that isn't going to help find Maddox." My hand shakes as I unscrew the top of the water bottle and take a small sip. The cold liquid runs down my throat, but it still feels dry. "I'm going to adopt him," I tell everyone in the room. I'm not sure how many are surprised by this news, but none of them says anything. Instead, they give me a chance to continue talking, knowing I'm not finished. "When they find him, I'm going to need a lawyer to help me fight for him."

"Whatever you need," my father says, looking at Matthew.

"We will get whoever we need to get to make this happen," he assures me.

"I need to prepare a bedroom for him." I look over at Franny, who smiles at me, blinking away her own tears.

"I know a couple of people who love to shop and can probably have things delivered today." She grabs her phone from her back pocket and turns around to walk out of the room.

"Where is Julia?" I ask. The front door opens again, and Julia comes into the room.

"We need to talk." I look at her, and she just looks at me. I know how hard her job can be. I didn't before, but now that I've seen firsthand what she must go through every single day, I know it's not pretty. "When they find Maddox," I say, not even going into the worst-case scenarios in my head, "I am going to have a lawyer petition to get him placed here."

"I'm already ahead of you," Julia replies, walking to the fridge and taking out a water bottle. "I was on the phone with a couple of my colleagues who are aware of the case." She takes a sip of the water. "And we've all come to the decision that placing Maddox here would be best for him." She puts her hands on the counter. "But it's not in our hands. We've done everything we need to do. You've applied to be an emergency foster parent. The application was pushed through, and your background check was completed." I swallow, waiting for the other shoe to drop. "I already put in my referral."

"I'm sorry." My aunt Caroline steps forward. "But she needs to know what she's dealing with." She looks at Julia. "We need to know what he's been through if we are going to be able to help him." She wrings her hands together.

"You know I can't tell you guys anything," Julia says. "You think I don't want to?"

"I think that there are things that you should keep confidential," my mother says now. "But if we are going to help him, we need to know what tools we need."

"This is all you need to know." Julia swallows. "He is an eight-year-old boy who hasn't had anyone love him in his whole life." Her words come out, and every single one stabs me in the heart over and over again. The pain is like shards of glass going through me. "He was left at school from the time it opened until the time it closed. He had the same clothes on for two weeks once, before the school gave his mother a bag of secondhand clothes, which she then turned around and sold. A little boy who used to wet the bed occasionally, so you can imagine." I hear a gasp, and I have to sit down. I walk over to the couch as Julia continues, "That little boy has seen more horror than we can even think about. He has walls up so high nothing can knock them down. He has no idea what a hug is or even why you give them. He knows nothing about family. He knows nothing about anything really." I close my eyes. "He's emotionally unavailable." She looks me in the eyes. "I don't know if he'll ever be okay."

"Is there a father in the picture?" Caroline asks.

"No." Julia shakes her head. "There was none listed on the birth certificate, and when she was asked about it, she said she didn't know."

"Are you sure about this?" My mother comes over and sits beside me, followed by Mac, who sits beside me for support as if she knows I need her. "I know you want to help him."

I shake my head, not wanting her to finish what she is going to say. "I knew the minute I saw him," I start to say. "There was a reason I came back early." I look at my mother and father. "I wasn't supposed to be here, but I was, and there was a reason. I was sent back for him."

I wipe away the tears. "He's …" I don't even know if I have the right words to justify what I feel for him. "He's mine." I shrug, smiling through the tears. "I can't explain it any other way."

"Then we will get him all the help he needs," Matthew says now. "We will get him people to talk to and show him what love is."

"What family is," my father says, looking at Matthew, and the two of them share a nod.

"If anyone knows what he's going through," Caroline says, sitting on the couch in front of us, "it's Dylan." She shakes her head, wiping away the tears. "No matter how much I tried to shield him, he knew what we were going through. But at least he had me. He had love from me. This poor boy," she says, leaning over and grabbing a tissue out of the box on the end table when all of a sudden, Julia's phone rings along with my father's and Matthew's.

Everyone jumps up, looking at Julia first, who answers, and then my father and then my uncle. I look at their faces. The whole time, my heart is hammering in my chest. I push back the fear that he's not okay. I watch to see if they will look at me, knowing that if he's hurt or not okay, no one will want to make eye contact.

"He's okay!" Julia shouts, running to the front door as we all follow her. "I'll be there in fifteen minutes." She runs to get into my father's car. My mother is in the front seat, and I sit in the back with Julia.

I don't even know who is following or if the other people are coming with us, but I don't care. "Where is he?" I ask her.

"Dylan found him." She looks at me as she types on her phone. "He was at a park near the house." My hand goes to my mouth. "He was sitting waiting by the monkey bars."

I close my eyes, and all I can see is his face. "He must have thought we didn't care."

"Police are waiting for us to see if we should have him transported to the hospital," Julia says. "I'm trying to get an answer if we can see a judge today, but it's Sunday," she says, and I shake my head.

"You are going to have to pry him out of my arms," I state, looking out the window.

"That's exactly what Dylan said, and it almost got him arrested," Julia shares, and my head whips around to look at her. "Luckily, I know the officer."

"It's good to have friends everywhere," my father says.

"He's not that kind of friend," Julia defends, and my mother laughs. "I mean, we get friendly, but that's about it."

If it was any other time, I would have a comeback, but all I can think about is getting to my guys. When we pull up to the park, my eyes roam the whole place, and I'm out of the car before my father puts it in park. "Dylan!" I shout his name and see him sitting on the bench right off the side in the shade. Maddox sits beside him, drinking a water bottle. Justin stands beside the bench. His face looks white like a ghost, and two police officers stand beside the bench on the other side talking to each other.

I run toward them, only stopping when I get in front of the bench. I reach out and grab Maddox, pulling him to me. Then I let him go and hold his face in my hands. "You scared me," I say, not even sure if I should tread lightly. "I was so scared you were hurt." I rub his cheeks with my thumbs. Looking over at Dylan, who has his own dried tears on his face, no doubt having gone through exactly what I just did, if not worse, thinking he would find him hurt.

He just looks at me. "I'm not hurt." He finally speaks, and it's like music to my ears.

"Are you sure?" I ask him and look at his arms, seeing that they are dirty, and his legs look like a bruise is forming on his shin.

"What's this?" I ask, looking at the bruise.

"I fell when I did the monkey bars," he admits to me. "I almost made it, but I slipped."

"You could have hurt yourself," I scold. "You always need someone to watch you when you do things like that."

"Okay," he replies. I bring him to my chest, looking around seeing all of my family have come to the park. I hear car doors shut and see my grandparents walking into the park. The whole family has come to show their support, and I just can't help the tears that come.

"Oh, my," my grandmother says from behind me. "He looks just like Dylan did."

"He does," Caroline says. "He really does."

"We need to take him to the hospital," Julia says from beside me. "They want to just make sure he is okay and have it documented that nothing is wrong with him." She gets down next to me in front of Maddox. "We need to take you to the doctor," she tells him. "And then we are going to have a little talk."

"Okay," Maddox says, and he jumps off the bench, turning to hand the water bottle back to Dylan. He looks at Dylan then. "Are you going to come with me?"

"I'm not leaving you, buddy," he says to him, getting up and standing beside him. Dylan puts his hand on his shoulder.

Maddox looks at me now. "Are you coming, too?" he asks me, and I just nod my head at him. He just looks at Julia, who smiles at us. I start to walk, following her, when I feel Maddox slip his hand in mine.

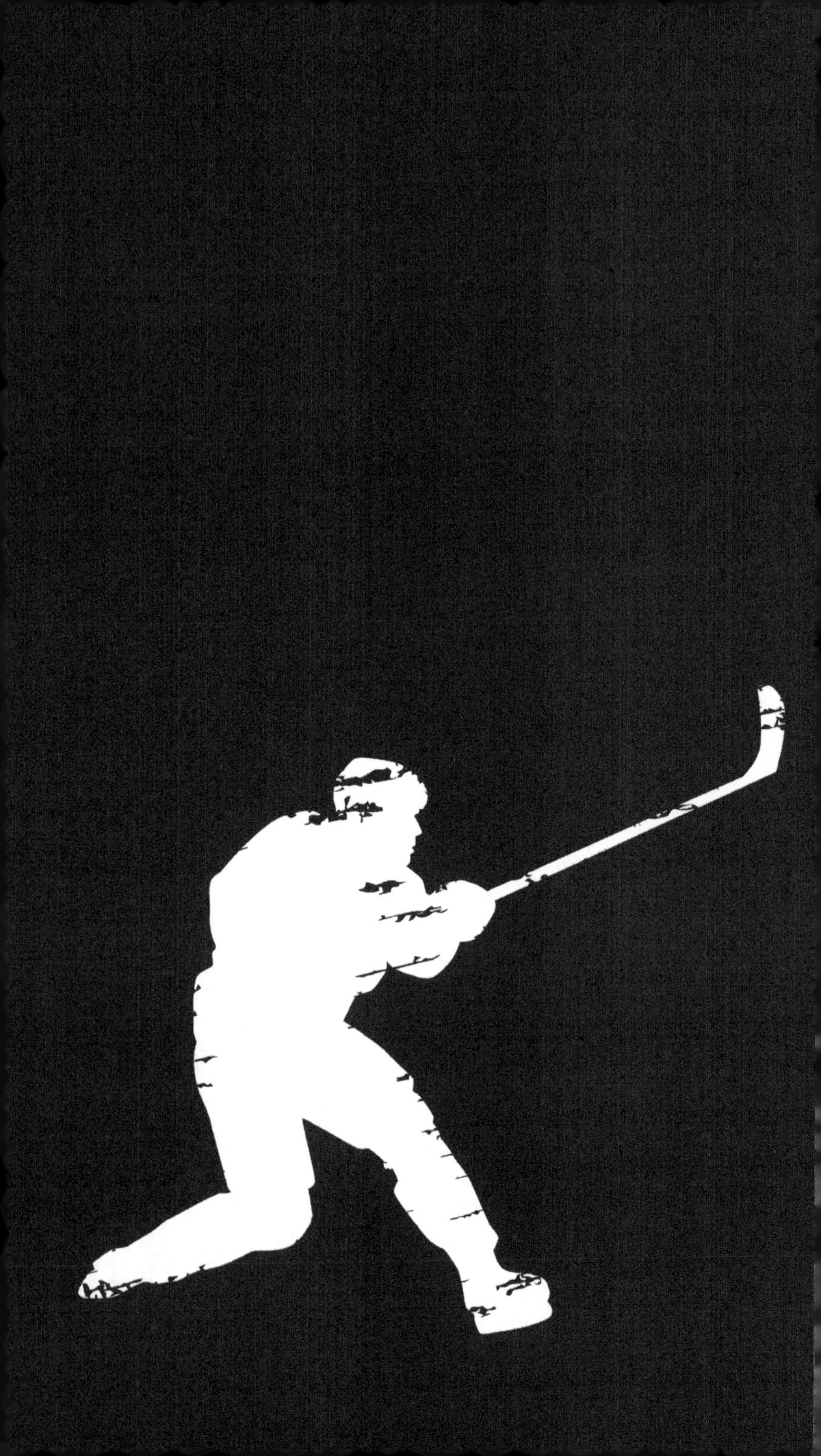

THIRTY-FOUR

DYLAN

"JUST WAIT HERE," the nurse says to us when we walk in the hospital. She looks down at Maddox. "They can come and see you when the doctor is done." He looks over his shoulder as he follows her toward the brown doors that close as soon as he walks into them.

"I'm going to go start filling out the forms and complete the report," Julia says, walking away from us.

I feel Alex slide her hand into mine and turn to bring her to me. The past hour has been the most excruciating of my life. "I can't believe you found him." She wraps her arms around my waist, and all I can do is wrap my arms around her neck and kiss the top of her head.

"I was so fucking scared." I admit the words that I didn't even tell my father as we drove in the car. "I was so scared we would find him hurt or even worse."

"How did you find him?" She lets go of me and looks into my eyes, and one of my hands comes up and touches her face.

"The only thing I could think of was the park. So, we called Julia and asked for the address and then drove from park to park." I won't tell her how I jumped out of the car and scared about fifteen to twenty kids by yelling his name. I also will wait for later to tell her that I almost ended up in handcuffs. I look back at the door, waiting for the nurse to come out. "I'm not leaving him."

"I know," she says softly, putting her hands on my hips. "I said the same thing."

"Okay," Julia says, coming back to us now. "The report is filed with the police. I've spoken to my boss, and she pulled a couple of strings to get a judge to sign off on you getting temporary emergency custody of him."

"Temporary," I repeat the word, and she holds up her hand.

"You have to go from temporary to permanent," she explains. "But it's a good thing." She looks at both of us. "Would be a touch better if you were married and not living in sin, but …" She smirks. "One step at a time."

"So what does this mean?" Alex asks her, and I can feel her beside me almost shaking.

"It means that as soon as the doctor clears him, you can take him home," she sighs, and I feel like I can breathe again. "I will, of course, have to escort him to the house and make sure that everything is in proper order."

"Of course," Alex says. "We have the spare bedroom, but tomorrow I can make sure I go out and get everything that he needs."

She looks at us and laughs, shaking her head. "You

think with the family you guys are in that you're going to get home and it's not going to be done? I can bet you money your mother"—she points at Alex—"has a whole wardrobe for him to wear, and your fathers"—she moves her fingers from both of us—"are assembling a bed as we speak. Throw in Matthew and I'm thinking there may even be a paint job in there."

We can't help but both laugh because she isn't wrong. The nurse comes out and looks at us. "Doctor just signed off." She looks at Julia and then at us. "He's a bit dehydrated, but other than that, no broken bones."

"He has a bruise on his leg," Alex says. "I saw it when we found him. And his arms are dirty, but we are going to have him take a shower." I put my arm around her shoulders and pull her to me, kissing her head while the nurse just smiles at her.

"I'll put that in my notes," she says. I rub Alex's arms as she walks away. "You can go in and see him."

"Well, you two," Julia says. "Go and tell him where he is going."

I take a step toward the door when Alex grabs my hand. "What if he doesn't want to come with us?" she asks, and I can see the worry all over her face. "His whole life, everyone has told him what to do and where to go."

"We can ask him, then." I bring her hand to my lips. "I never thought of it like that, but you're right. It's time for him to decide."

"I hate to be the bad news person. But that kid is going with you." Julia folds her arms. "So you better be damn good at convincing him." She glares at us, and we walk past the two brown doors. Looking into the first room, we see him sitting on the bed with his feet dangling off the side.

"Hey," I greet, walking into the room, and he looks up at me.

"Am I going back to the people?" he comes right out and asks us. "Are they mad?"

"One," I say, walking to sit beside him on the bed. "I don't think they are mad. I think they are worried. They just want you safe." His little legs just swing nervously. "What if I were to tell you that you don't have to go back to Mr. and Mrs. Pinto?" He looks at me, not saying anything. "And if I were to ask you if you wanted to come home with us?" He looks at me and then looks at Alex.

"You don't have to say yes if you don't want to," Alex says. "We were hoping that you would want to, but if you don't, we can look at someplace else."

"Can I still do hockey?" he asks, and we both nod. "Is there a bed at your house?"

"There is a bed," I say.

"With blankets?" I swallow down the lump.

"With blankets and pillows," Alex confirms to him as she blinks tears away. "And we have some food also."

"Is Mac going to be there?" he asks, and I can't help but smile and nod my head. "Okay," he says softly, and if only he knew what that meant to us. If only I could pull him to me and hug him. But I'm afraid to scare him off, afraid that it'll push him away and then he won't want to come with us. "I'm a bit hungry," he shares, looking at us, and we just stare at each other. "But I don't need to eat."

"Oh, honey," Alex says, putting her arm around his shoulder. "We can have whatever you want to eat, and you will get to meet my mom and dad."

"Is your dad coming, too?" He looks at me, and I nod.

The knock on the door makes all of us look up. "Are you ready to go?" Julia smiles, and Maddox jumps off the bed.

"I'm going to their house," he tells Julia, "and I won't leave."

She squats down in front of him. "You promise?" He just nods his head.

"Let's go see their house, then," Julia says to him. He looks over at Alex and me, waiting for us. I get up and hold out my hand for Alex, and she slides her fingers through mine as she gets off the bed.

Maddox walks in front of us with Julia. When we get outside, Julia tosses me the keys to my father's car, and I don't even know how they made this happen, but I don't know why I'm surprised. We get into the car, and we drive home, none of us saying anything.

I park in the driveway and look in the back at Maddox as he stares at the house. "Welcome home, buddy," I say, getting out of the driver's side and opening the door in the back for him.

Alex and Julia wait on their side for us, and when I walk around the car toward them, I feel him slip his hand into mine. I almost stop walking to look down at it, but I don't want him to pull back from me. I open the front door, and I can hear voices; when we walk in, my parents are there with Max and Allison. "Hi," I greet, smiling at them, and they look at us with tears in their eyes. Mac comes to us with her tail wagging even more when she sees Maddox beside me. She comes over and sniffs his feet. She starts to lick his hand, and he lets her.

My mother's eyes and nose are as red as Allison's. "Maddox, you know my dad, Justin, and that's my mom, Caroline." I point at my mom, who comes over and squats down in front of him. Mac sits next to him, not moving from between us.

"Hi there," she says to him with a huge smile and tears. "You remind me of this guy." She points at me. "When he was your age." She gets up and walks over to my father, who takes her in his arms as she cries into his shoulder. The memories of what we went through for sure going through her mind.

"And this," Alex says, walking to Max. "Is my dad, Max, and that's my mom, Allison."

"Hey, buddy," Max says to him, smiling, and Allison just waves nervously.

"This is our home," I say. "This is the kitchen and the living room."

"His room is ready," Allison says. I just look over at her, and she just rolls her eyes, trying not to cry but fails when she turns not to show us.

"Shall we go see your room?" Julia asks, turning to walk up the stairs. "You know I used to sleep here sometimes," she tells Maddox. "I think you're gonna like it here."

"If you start singing," Alex says from behind us, making me laugh.

When we get to the front of the closed door, I'm almost afraid of what my family did. I open the door, and my mouth hangs open. Mac runs into the room ahead of us and goes straight for the bed, lying down on it. The big queen-sized bed is in the middle of the room with the word PLAY over the bed in lights. The white comforter and blue pillows show it's a boy's room. There are four pictures on one wall, one is a soccer ball, one is a basketball net, one is a group of baseballs, and then the last one is a picture of Maddox in hockey gear.

He walks into the room and looks around. "Are we all sleeping in here?" he asks, and I shake my head.

"No, this is all yours," I say, putting my hands on my hips. "This is where you sleep or just come up and play."

"It's so big," he says, and his eyes are wide when he looks over to see a bookshelf with books on them. He reaches out and then holds himself back, looking over at us to make sure it's okay.

"Whatever is in this room is yours," I assure him. "If you want to touch it, you touch it. If you want to play with it, you play with it."

"You just have to clean it up when you're done, and if I'm not mistaken …" Alex says, walking over to the closet and opening it. The closet is full of clothes, all separated by color and styles. "These are all yours also."

She walks over to the chest of drawers and opens them. "You have everything you need right here."

"How many kids live here?" he asks, looking at us.

"Just you," I confirm, smiling at him and then looking at Alex, who comes over to me. She wraps her arms around my waist, and I kiss her forehead. I look back at Maddox, who stands there with us. "It's the three of us." I look back at the bed. "And Mac."

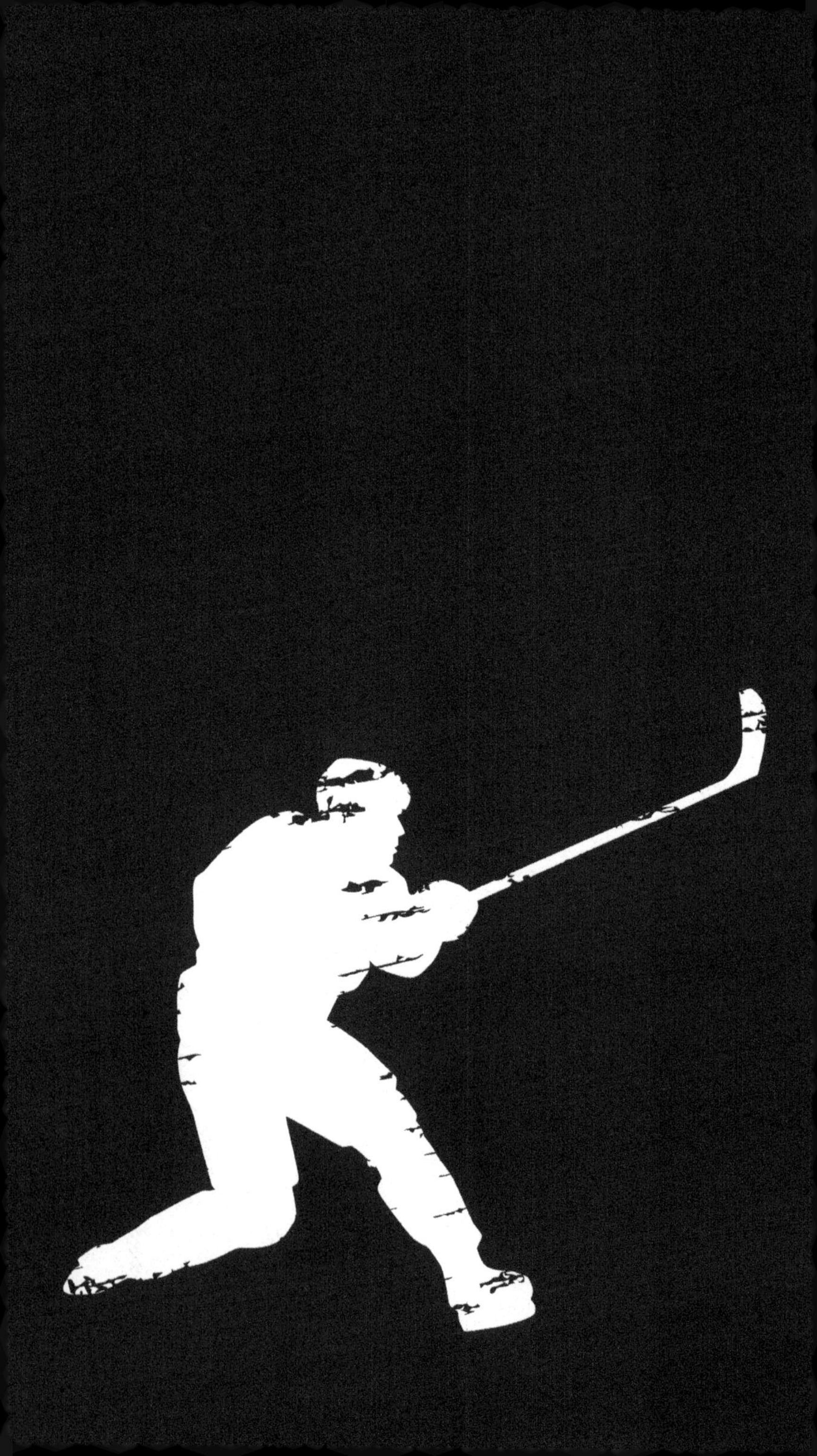

THIRTY-FIVE

DYLAN

As I HEAD to my car after my workout, the phone in my hand buzzes. I look down and see that it's my dad. "Hey," I answer, getting into the car and turning it on. The heat outside is almost unbearable, something that my cousins used to complain about but I never actually believed until now.

"Hey yourself," my father says. I can hear that he is also driving. "What are you doing?"

"Just got done with off-ice training," I say, pulling out of the gym parking lot. "I'm not going to lie, I'm hurting." I laugh.

"I told you not to take two weeks off," he reminds me.

"I wanted to spend time with Maddox." It's been a month since we've had him, and he's the best kid I know.

"How is it going?" he asks, and I take a deep breath. "Oh, boy."

"It's going good," I say, finally. "Great even, except

last night."

"What happened?" my father asks, his voice filled with worry.

"He wet the bed," I say, "and then instead of saying anything, he tucked himself in the corner and slept on the floor." My chest compresses when I say it.

"Fuck," my father says out loud.

"Yeah, that sounds about right," I say. "I found him this morning curled up with Mac beside him." I shake my head. "I was so fucking angry that he was on the floor and I didn't know what to do."

"Welcome to parenting," he says, and I roll my eyes.

"I never understood it." The words start to come out. "That day that …" I start, the memory coming back to me as if it was yesterday, the lump in my throat is so big I don't know if I can say anything. My father just waits for me to gather my thoughts. "That day when he showed up at church." I blink away the tears that are now coming full on. "When you"—I clear my throat—"fought with him."

"I'd do it all over again," my father says softly. "Every single day for the rest of my life, I would fight for you."

"I know," I say, my eyes filling with tears. There has never been one day since we met that I doubted how he felt for me. "It made my stomach burn. It made my whole body shake with this unspeakable anger that I never knew I had in me," I breathe out.

"It's love," he says. "It's a love that is unbreakable."

"I want him to trust me," I say, "and to come to me when he's hurt or happy or just because."

"Son," he says, "do you know how many people he must have tried to trust who just burned him? The number of people who told him one thing and then did something else. Fuck, his mother, the one person supposed to love and protect him dumped him off like he was a fucking library book." His voice gets higher, and I know that everyone in the family feels the same way about the situation. "So even though you love him with everything that you have and you want him to see it, you have to go in it and remember how you felt."

"What do you mean?" I ask.

"You were that age, and your father …" he starts to say.

"He's not my father," I say, my voice tight.

"Relax there, you know what I mean," my father says. "Like I was saying, he did things that are unspeakable and your mom shielded you until she couldn't anymore. He never had that." I listen to my dad. "So now it's like you proving to him that no matter what, you'll be there. And it's going to take a lot more than you saying it for him to believe it."

I pull into the driveway. "One day at a time," I say, repeating the words he has always said to me.

"One day at a time," he says, and I can even see him smiling. "Now go and gain some trust."

"Love you, Dad," I say.

"Love you more," he says. "I'll FaceTime you later." I smile. He calls Maddox every single night, even if it's for just a five-second conversation. It's something that Maddox actually asks for.

"I'm home," I say as soon as I walk into the house. I look up the stairs to see if anyone is upstairs and then hear Alex.

"In the kitchen," she says, and I walk down the hall toward the kitchen and see her washing her hands. I walk to her, putting my hands on her hips. "Hi," I say, bending and burying my face in her neck. "I missed you."

"It's been four hours." She laughs and turns her head to the side to look at me, and I lean in to kiss her lips.

"It's four and a half," I say when I let her go and then lean in to kiss her again. "Where is Maddox?" I ask, looking to the living room and seeing it empty.

"He's outside trying to teach Mac how to do the obstacle course that you guys built together," Alex says, and I look out the window. Seeing him talking to Mac who just looks at him.

"How was today?" I ask her.

"It was interesting. He didn't know why he needed two pairs of shoes for school, and then when I told him that we had to get him more shorts for school, he said he didn't need them."

"I mean." I try not to laugh. "He has enough clothes for seven kids."

She shrieks, "Go outside!" She points toward the back door. "He wants to go into the pool."

"Go change and meet us there." I smack her ass and then walk outside.

"So you are going to roll over," he tells Mac, "and then jump over this." He runs over to the cone. I have to say that with Mac, he lets his guard down. She's his best friend, and Mac doesn't leave his side. She doesn't even care anymore about us. It's all about Maddox.

"Hey," I say. Mac looks at Maddox and then at me before she comes over to me. "Hey, princess." I rub her neck and then look over at Maddox.

"Come here, buddy. I want to talk to you," I tell him, and he puts his head down and comes to me.

"Are you mad?" he asks, and I shake my head.

"No," I say, smiling, "but this morning, I was sad." He looks at me with his eyebrows pinched together.

"Is it because I wet the bed?" he asks. "I'm sorry."

"There is no need for you to be sorry," I tell him. "I felt sad that you slept on the floor."

"It was okay." He tries to pretend that it meant nothing.

"When I was your age, I got into hockey summer camp," I tell him, and he looks at me. "I was so happy because I got a whole bag of new equipment." I smile, thinking back to that day. "I'd never had anything new. My mom would have to buy my stuff secondhand, or the church would give us stuff." I sit on the grass, and he sits in front of me. "Then when I went home, my dad took my stuff away from me." He just looks at me. "All my new stuff was gone."

"Did you cry?" he asks, and I nod.

"When my new dad came to see me, Justin, he took me in his arms and told me that it wasn't my fault." I smile. "Just like when you wet the bed, it's not your fault."

"But," he starts to say, "what if you get mad and then want me to leave?"

My heart stops in my chest. "There is nothing, and I mean nothing that you can do that will make me want you to leave. When you are hurt and you don't come to me, I get sad. You know why?" He shakes his head. "Because it's my job to make you better. It's my job to hold your hand. It's my job to hold you when you fall. It's my job to read you a story at night. It's my job to tuck you in at night." I want to drag him to me and hug him, but I don't want to push him. "So the next time …?"

"Next time," Maddox says, "I'll call you."

"Perfect," I say, getting up when the back door opens and Alex steps out.

"Why are you guys not in the pool?" she asks, looking at me and then Maddox.

"Dylan gets sad when I pee the bed and don't tell him," Maddox fills her in, "so now when I pee, I am going to tell him."

I reach over and pull him to me, kissing his head. "That's my boy," I say and then let him go. "Now." I stand up, taking off my shirt. "Race you to the pool."

The sound of laughing fills the yard when I jump into the pool, and he follows me. Mac is right behind him, and the four of us stay in the pool for the rest of the day.

When I walk up the stairs after dinner, I can hear him talking. "Mac, you have to tell me if you don't want to do the tricks," Maddox says. "I have to take care of you." My heart explodes as he repeats the words I said to him today to Mac. I look into the room and see Mac lying on the bed with her head down. "I won't be mad if you don't want to jump."

"Ready for bed?" I ask, and he just nods at me, getting into bed now. Mac lies on her side. I tuck him in and kiss his head. "Good night, buddy."

"Night, Dylan," he says, and I walk out. "Thank you," he says softly, and I turn to look at him, "for not being mad at me."

"Love you, buddy," I say, and I walk out with the weight lifting off my shoulders. "One day at a time," I mumble to myself. "One day at a time."

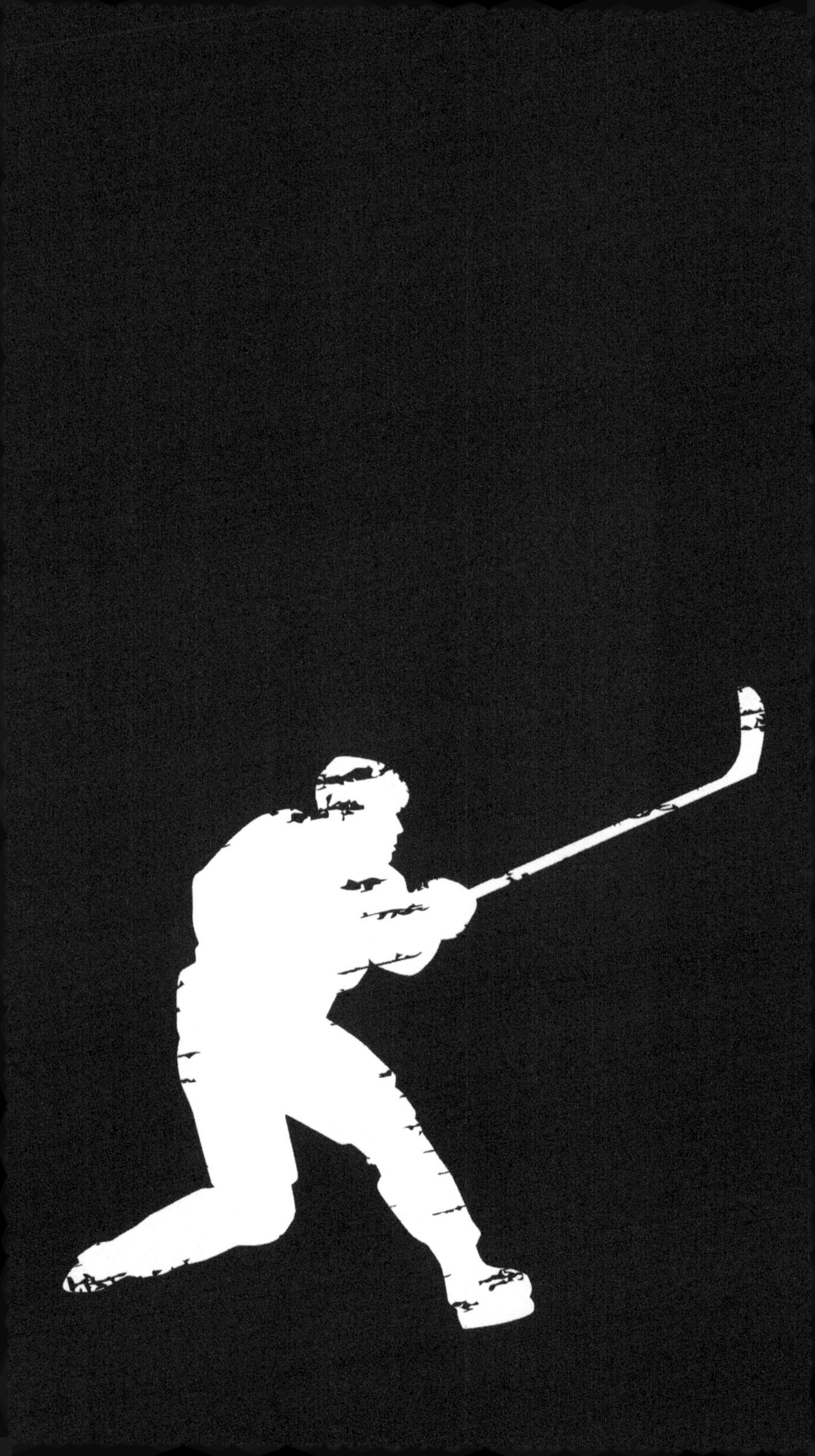

THIRTY-SIX

ALEX

Seven Months Later

"I'M SO NERVOUS." I stick my head out of my closet and look over at Dylan sitting on the bed doing something on his phone.

He looks up at me, and his blue eyes light up as he smirks at me. "Baby," he says softly. He doesn't call me that all the time, but when he does, my heart literally skips a beat, and my stomach does flips. "It's going to be fine."

I shake my head, walking out of the closet. "What if it isn't fine?" I ask, looking over at the door to make sure that Maddox can't hear me. "What if he says no?"

Dylan gets up from the bed and comes over to me, putting his hands on my face. "I promise you, it's going to be okay."

"You haven't been here in two weeks," I say of the

longest road trip that he's been on, and normally, I would have joined him, but having Maddox changed all that. "He's been really quiet."

Ever since we brought him home that day seven months ago, it's been a learning curve for all of us. It wasn't all roses and butterflies; he was still that shy boy, but he was opening up more and more. When I went to wake him one morning and found him trying to hide the soiled clothes that he had an accident in, it broke me in two. He had to learn to trust, and every day was a test for him. The first time he had a fever, he fought it all day long, not complaining, and only when I went to kiss him on the head did I feel he was warm. I guess in his mind, the less of a burden he was, the more I wanted to keep him.

School was going amazing for him. He was excelling and his grades were through the roof, but making friends was very hard for him. Especially when he thought every day with us would be his last. I have to say Dylan handled it a lot better than I did. He would speak with him one-on-one when I would just want to smother him with love and hugs. It was very hard on the family, when all they wanted to do was shower him with all the love that they could but knew that it had to be earned, so they would do what they could for him to know they were there. He has a very special bond with my grandfather, which is why they have been spending so much time here in Dallas. Another bond that he has is with my father, who is here when Dylan isn't. I know it's all going to be worth it in the end when he can finally be the carefree boy we all want him to be.

"You are overthinking this." He kisses my lips. "Just trust me."

"Yeah, yeah," I say to him, shaking my head. "I'm just." I blink away the tears. "I don't want to lose him."

"I'm done," Maddox says, coming into the bedroom, and I turn my head to wipe away the tear that just escaped. "I finished all my math, and I did my reading."

"Good," Dylan says to him, and when I turn back around, I see Maddox staring at me. His eyes are like hawks as he takes me in.

"Are you ready?" I ask him.

"Why are you crying?" he asks me, and I am so mad at myself.

"I'm just happy Dylan is home," I reply, smiling up at Dylan as he wraps his arm around my neck and kisses the side of my face.

"Now are you ready to go and see some animals?" I ask him, walking to him and running my hands through his hair. He smiles up at me and nods his head. "Good, and tomorrow we have family lunch."

Grabbing my purse before we leave, I look over at Dylan, who is talking to Maddox. My stomach is burning with nerves. I don't even pay attention to whatever they are talking about. Instead, I look out the window and replay Julia's conversation with me two weeks ago.

"We found her," Julia said as soon as I picked up the phone. I stopped stirring the pasta and looked over to see Maddox sitting at the counter doing his homework.

"What do you mean you found her?" I whispered into

the phone, looking over my shoulder, hoping he wasn't paying attention to me.

"Maddox's mother," she said, and everything in me turned cold.

"Hey." I smiled at Maddox, ignoring the way my heart was beating. "You can go have iPad time for a bit."

He didn't even question it, just pushed away from the table and went into the living room. My eyes stayed on him the whole time. "What happened?" I asked as quietly as I could, the burning coming to my eyes. "Is she okay?"

"Oh, she's fine," Julia said, and I could tell from her tone that she was pissed. "She was in a homeless shelter in Mississippi. Had the attitude of a..." She stopped herself before she said something she shouldn't. "Bottom line, she doesn't want him. Wants to take herself off his birth certificate, so he doesn't come looking for her money," she hissed out. "Her money while she is in a homeless shelter."

"Oh my God," I said, looking over at Maddox.

"With that said, we have a court date for you to officially adopt him," she explained.

It's why the past two weeks have been a whirlwind. We had people coming into the house to do inspections, and a couple of therapists and social workers came in and spoke with Maddox. My nerves were a mess, and it just made it even worse when he became quiet.

"We're here," Dylan says as he pulls up to the aquarium, and I look over at Maddox, who avoids making eye contact with me.

When we walk in, a guide is there waiting to take us around. Dylan was able to get us in privately after they closed. Ever since he skated on the ice, he's become their city hotshot. Going out with him is almost unbearable, but the team is doing better than they ever have, and I couldn't be happier for him.

We walk with Maddox in the middle of us, looking up at the sharks that are swimming overhead. "So, Maddox." Dylan starts to talk, and I can see that he's nervous now. "We have to talk to you about something."

"I know," Maddox says. His voice goes low as he stands there looking at us. "I kind of figured it out." Dylan and I just look at each other. "I'm going to go live at another house, aren't I?"

"What?" Dylan says, and all I can do is shake my head side to side, the big tears forming in my eyes, not making it easy to see him.

"No!" I shout. "Of course not. Why would you think that?"

He shrugs and wipes away a tear with the back of his hand as he tries to be strong in front of us. "They came to talk to me the other day when I was at school," he says. "Wanted to know if I was happy."

"Well, the reason they did that," Dylan explains now. "Was because they wanted to know if you wanted to stay with us." He just looks at Dylan confused. "Like forever."

"So I wouldn't have to leave?" he asks both of us. "And I can stay with you guys?"

"Yes," I confirm. "But only if that is what you want,"

I say, not even bothering to wipe away my tears. "We want to keep you forever. We want to adopt you." I stop talking because the lump in my throat is a boulder, and I can't get another word out.

"We want to make you ours forever so no one can take you away from us," Dylan says, his hand sliding into mine. "The three of us will be a family."

"If I say yes," he says, "does that mean she can't come back for me?"

I can't help it. I turn my face and bury it in Dylan's shoulder. "It's okay," Dylan says to me softly and then I feel his small arms wrap around my waist.

I stop crying, shocked that he's come to me. He's given me a couple of hugs, but it's always a side hug and never full on. I look down at him and see him looking up at me. "I don't want to go with her," he tells me as I turn and hug him to me.

"You don't ever have to go with her," I say, vowing to never repeat what she told Julia. "I love you." I say that every single time he gets out of the car or he comes home from school or when I tuck him in at night. He has never said it back, and I know it's because he doesn't know what love is.

"I love you, too," he says and then looks at Dylan. "And you, too." Dylan looks like he just won the fucking Stanley Cup. His face breaks into the biggest smile as he takes us both in his arms. "Do I have to tell Julia that I want to stay with you guys forever?"

"No," I tell him. "What will happen is we have to go to the court, and the judge will ask you if you want to live with us," I explain to him a little bit. "And then once he says okay, then you are ours forever."

The smile fills his face so much that his blue eyes become hazel. My hand comes up to cup his face. "So that makes you guys my parents."

"It means that we get to take care of you every single day. It means that when you are sick, we make sure you get better. It means that when you have a problem, we help you solve it. It means that." I swallow now. "We get to love you forever, and we get to watch you become the best person we both know." I cup his cheek.

"Do I have to call you mom?" he asks, and I shake my head.

"You can call me whatever you want to call me. You can call me Alex just like you call me now."

"You do more than my mom did," he says now. "She never made sure I was washed. She never made sure I ate my veggies. She never made sure I did my homework."

"Everyone loves in a different way," I say.

"You never told me you didn't want me." He steps away from me. "You never told me I was a loser." He rubs his cheek with the back of his hand. "You never told me you hated me. Not once." My heart breaks for this little boy who did nothing to deserve what she said to him. "You never told me you wish I would just die."

"Hey," Dylan snaps. "What she said to you doesn't mean anything," he tells him. "My father called me words that I can't repeat, but you know what I did? I made sure that I was never that person." He puts his hands on Maddox's shoulder. "I'm going to be the one who helps you do that. I'm going to make sure that you never become what she said you were. I'm going to be by your side when you become greatness."

"Okay," Maddox says. "Can we go to the judge now?"

Dylan and I just laugh now. "No, we have to go in two days," I say, and then we turn to walk out of the shark tank. "Do you know that we had our first date here?" I state, and he just listens to our story.

Two days later, with the courtroom packed full of our family and some of our friends, we officially become a family of three.

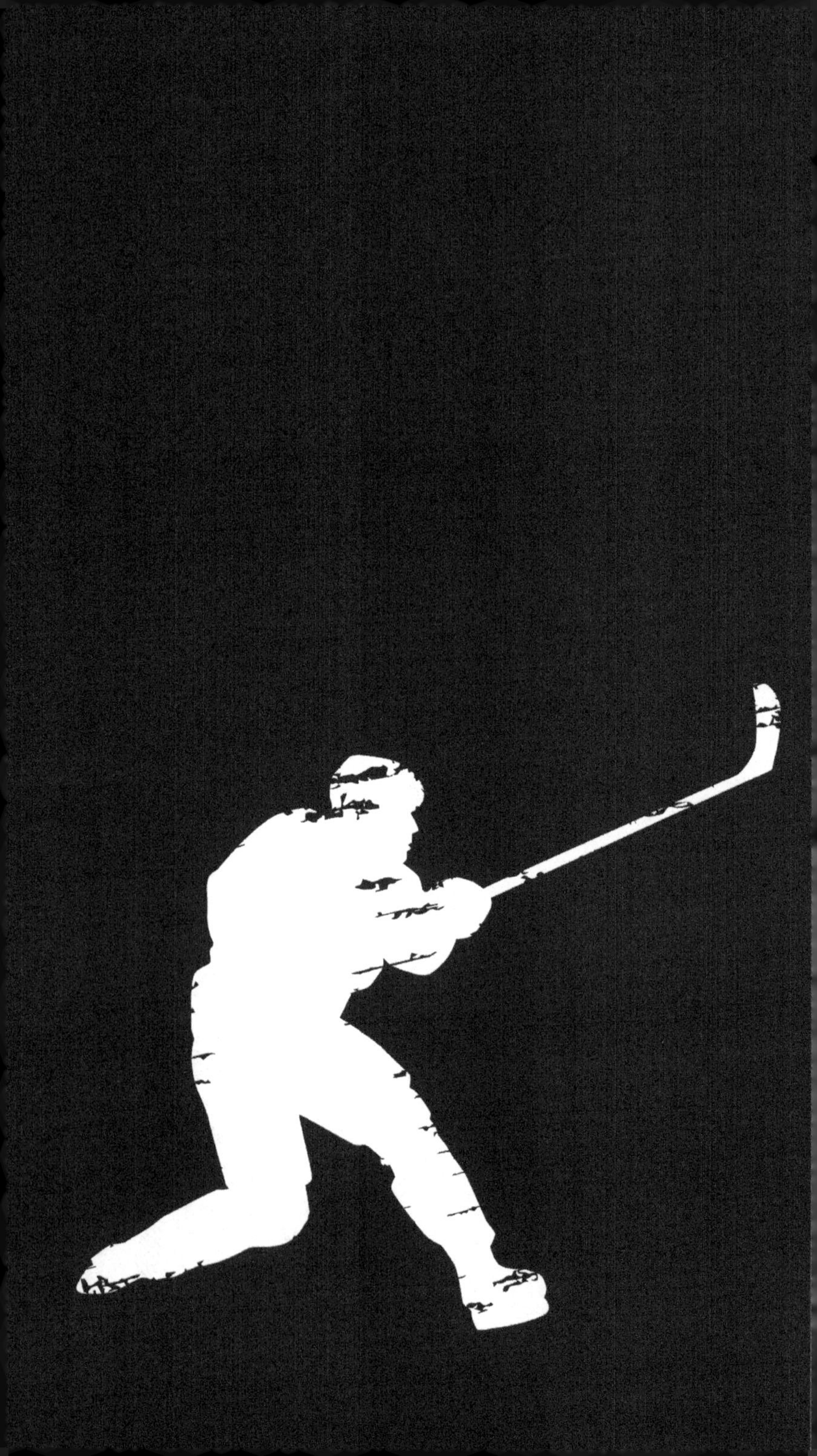

EPILOGUE ONE

DYLAN

Three Months Later

I TRY TO catch my breath as I look up at the Jumbotron and see that there is one minute left in the game. One minute and the score is one nothing for us in game six of the Stanley final. We have one minute to hold the lead before we win the fucking Stanley Cup. The building is electric, and the fans are on their feet, and I have to zone it all out. I have to focus on one thing and one thing only, the game at hand.

My eyes go back to the play in our zone as the guys take their place for the face-off. I watch Vegas win the face-off and start their play in the zone. Ralph tries to poke check it out of the zone but misses as the puck goes back to Vegas, who then passes it to the defenseman as they set up the play. Every single second feels like an hour, and with every single pass, you literally hold your breath. Their goal is empty as the extra attackers on the ice make it even more nail-biting.

"Grant!" The coach yells Cooper's name for his line, and Michael and I get ready to get on the ice. The whistles blow when our goalie covers the puck, and Vegas calls a time-out. I look up at the time and see that we are twenty seconds away.

"We can do this!" the coach shouts. "We got this, but can someone put the fucking puck in that empty net?" He's trying to keep his cool, but even he's starting to look on edge. I smirk and get on the ice, skating over to the play beside the goalie.

"It's just another game," Cooper says to us. "Just another game."

"I think I'm going to throw up," Michael says. He starts to look around, and I block his face with my hand.

"Don't do it," I warn. "Don't look up at the box. Just focus on the game. Twenty seconds and then we get to go on a family vacation."

"Oh, I forgot about that great news, fifteen hours on a plane with you guys," Michael gripes. "Who chose Bora Bora?" he asks, and I can see the nerves are gone from his eyes.

The referee comes back over with the puck in his hand. Cooper holds the stick in both hands as he leans down, getting ready for the face-off. The banging of the crowd starts the minute the puck is dropped. Cooper wins the face-off, and the puck goes to Miller as he passes it to Ben, who passes it to Cooper, and I hustle away from the defenseman. Cooper looks like he's going to pass it to Michael, but then he slides it to me. The defenseman tries to block the puck with his stick but just sends it to me. I can feel him behind me, and I just shoot the puck down the ice, and it feels like everything happens in slow motion. I can hear the crowd going wild. I can hear every single beat of my heart. I can hear my breathing as if it's in stereo.

My eyes watch the puck as Michael skates past me, and then it happens. It slides into the net, and I leave my feet. The roaring of the crowd is almost deafening, and I take my mouth guard out and throw it in the air once the red light behind the net goes off. The horns blow as I turn and jump with Michael. Cooper comes over, and the three of us are all yelling. "Holy fucking shit!"

Two more of the guys jump on us, and only when they let me go do I look up at the box and see my family.

Alex is standing there clapping her hands, and beside her is Maddox, who is wearing an Oilers jersey with my name on it. He throws his hands up to the sky, and it fills my soul. I skate to the bench, high-fiving everyone, and look up to see that five seconds are left in the game. Vegas stands in the middle of the ice, waiting to get it over with.

We skate to the middle of the ice, and the puck drops, but nobody does anything, and when the horn blasts, the gloves and sticks go flying. We skate toward the goalie, and everyone jumps on him. The fans hit the windows, and slowly, everyone starts to skate to the center ice. I look up to see Maddox standing in front of Alex who has her hands around him, my father beside them with his arm around Alex and his other hand on Maddox. The handshake goes quickly. No doubt Vegas just wants to get the fuck off the ice. It is one thing to lose but losing in the home arena is hell.

I skate to the bench where they are handing out the baseball caps with the champions all over the front. I spot Nico, who is hugging the coach, and he comes over to me. "Told you I would try," he says, slapping my shoulder. "Thank you."

"I didn't do it alone," I remind him, and he nods his head as he walks to Cooper and has a few words with him.

I take off my helmet as the Stanley Cup is being set up. I look out of the corner of my eye and see Michael being interviewed, and then he calls me over. Ever since they called Alex and me kissing cousins, I haven't really granted interviews. Max was the only one who went on the record that day and said, "Looks like Dallas needs to do some research before they print stuff."

Other than that, no one commented. Even though we were asked about it, it was off-limits, and finally, after the first month, they just stopped asking the question. But I was still pissed about the headline, and I made sure they knew.

"Hey," the reporter says. "Congratulations."

"Thank you," I say, smiling at him and looking up to see that the interview is on the Jumbotron. I put the hat on my head. "It's surreal," I state, finally taking in the crowd and the moment.

"I have to ask you," he starts, and I wait for it. "You

finished last year, and you surprised everyone with the trade." I nod my head. "I know it wasn't easy, but it got you here, and you're a Stanley Cup champion. Tell me how it feels."

"It's really crazy, to be honest. I never thought I'd play for anyone else, but things just happened, and I signed here. My only goal was to come into the season proving to everyone that Nico made a good choice on taking me."

He laughs and looks over at Nico, who holds his hands over his head and claps. His smile is so big. "Besides that, what motivated you?"

I put my hands on my hips, feeling the tears come. "That's a big question," I admit, looking up at the box and raising my hand to wave at my family. I blink the tears away, but they fall anyway. "I didn't have the easiest start to life. As anyone who does their research knows." I make a jab at him. "It doesn't matter where you come from. It matters what you do with what you have." I look up at Alex, who has a hand to her mouth. "But most importantly, my family," I say, my face filling with a smile. I look at Alex, and I put my hand in front of my mouth and blow her a kiss. No one knows this, but we are surprising everyone by getting married two days after we get to Bora Bora. The only person who knows is the one setting it up for us there. "My best friend and rock. She was the reason I chose Dallas." I smile. "But the one person who motivated me the most has to be my son." I point at Maddox, who jumps up and down and points at himself while he looks over at Max and my father. "The sky is the limit, kiddo."

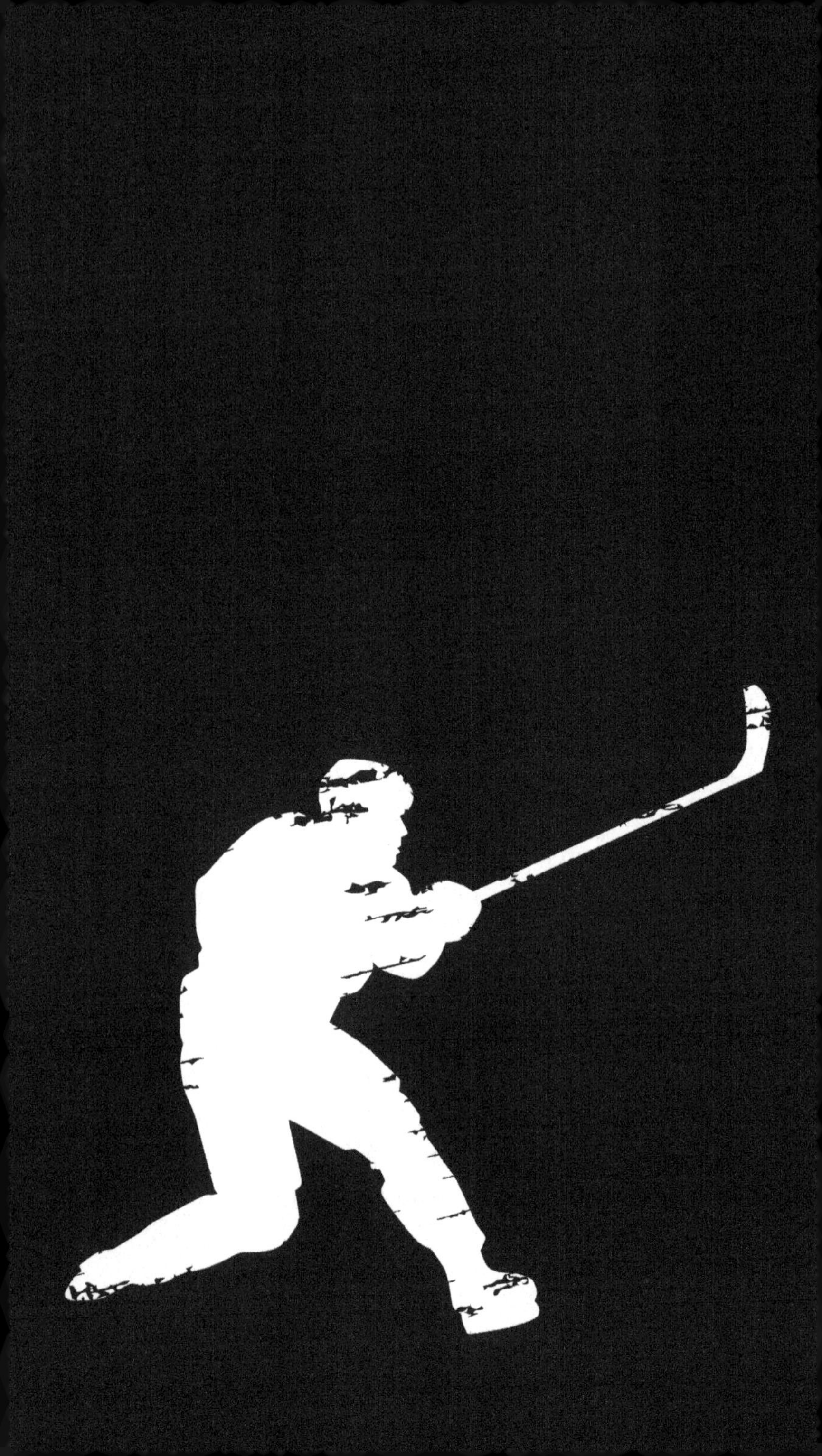

EPILOGUE TWO

ALEX

Five Years Later

"WHAT IS THAT I hear?" I ask, putting my head back down on the pillow. My eyes close, and my body finally relaxes into the bed. "Is that the sound of silence?"

"Hmm," Dylan says and turns to his side to bring me closer to him.

"No." I push away from him. "This is why we have Irish twins," I say. "Every single time I get the all clear, you want to knock me up again."

"You mean twice." He laughs as he buries his face into my neck, kissing me. Six weeks ago, I gave birth to our baby girl, Maya. Twelve months before that, I gave birth to our son, Maverick. "I did it twice, actually," he says. "Technically, I did it only once."

"Well, there isn't going to be a second or a third time," I say, turning on my side and cuddling into him. "I love our babies, but I'm so tired."

"Why don't I take the next feeding?" he whispers, pushing the hair away from my face. "Tomorrow morning, I'll wake up with the kids."

"We have everyone coming over tomorrow," I remind him and close my eyes with his arms around me.

I wake up when I hear our Maya squawking beside me. "Sorry, I just need your boob, and then I'll take her."

"What about the bottle in the fridge?" I ask sleepily, pulling down my nursing bra. Our daughter finds it as soon as I put it next to her mouth.

"She finished both," Dylan replies, squatting down by the side of the bed. "She must be going through a growth spurt." He leans forward and kisses her head. She kicks her feet, thinking he's going to take her away from me. I turn over and switch her to the other boob, and my eyes slowly drift closed. When I wake up a couple of hours later, my breast is still out, leaking a puddle beside her.

"Morning," I say, moving her to me. She happily takes my nipple while Maverick lets out the biggest cry of his life.

I look over to see Dylan getting up out of bed. "There he is." I hear his voice through the baby monitor.

"Da da da da," he says, and I can picture him jumping up and down in his crib. I listen to Dylan talk to him about what he dreamed about, and then I hear him give him kisses until he giggles. "Mama."

"Yeah, yeah, I know. You only tolerate me," Dylan says, and I can hear him walking down the hall with him. "She's feeding Maya." He walks to the door and comes in. "See, let's go get a bottle, and then you can have Mama." He leans down with him so I can kiss him, and when he goes to walk out of the room, Maverick throws his head back and cries, pointing at our bed.

"Go get the bottle and come back." I move Maya off my nipple and sit up, switching her to the other nipple. Propping the pillow beside me. "Come here, baby boy," I say, and he walks over to the bed and grabs the cover in his hands, pulling himself up on the bed. He crawls over with his smile, showing his two bottom teeth. "Gentle," I say when he comes beside me and lies down.

"Baby," he says, pointing at Maya.

"Yeah," I say and look over at Dylan, who smiles and goes to make a bottle. I take Maya off my boob, and she looks around, blinking her eyes as she takes in whatever it is she is seeing. I lay my head back, trying to wake up as she kicks and punches between my legs lying on the bed.

"Here we are," Dylan says, coming in with a tray, and I see a bottle and two cups of coffee. He hands Maverick the bottle, who smiles and grabs it. "For my love," he says, leaning down and kissing me. Even after all this time, he always makes my belly flutter when he kisses me. I keep waiting for the day when it feels old. I keep waiting for the day that I don't get so giddy when he comes home. Every single day with him by my side is better than the last. He walks over to the other side of the bed and lies down on his side.

We hear Maddox's bedroom door open and hear his feet coming down the hall. His brown hair is all over the place, and he wipes the sleep from his eyes. "Morning," he mumbles as he comes into the room.

"Happy gotcha day," I say with a smile and hold out my hand for him. He comes over to my side of the bed and lays his head on my shoulder. He's taller than I am, and from the looks of it, he might even be taller than Dylan. I kiss his shoulder as he walks to the end of the bed and lies down across it.

"Maddy," Maverick says with the nipple of the bottle still in his mouth. He sits up and crawls over to him and lies down beside him. He might love us, but Maddox is his best friend. I didn't know how Maddox would feel about having a baby come into the house, but he embraced the role of big brother with all the maturity I knew was in him. He turns around and lays his head on his arm, and Maverick follows. He wraps his arm around him as they cuddle.

"Happy gotcha day, son," Dylan says, and Maddox opens his eyes and smiles at him.

"Why do we do this every year?" he asks us, and I just smile.

"That is one of the best days of my life," I say, and he just shakes his head. "I became a mom that day." He just shrugs. "Thank you."

"For what?" he asks me.

"For saying yes." I wipe the tear away from my eye. "And for choosing me to be your mom."

"Dad," Maddox says, "time for you to kiss her tears away," making us laugh.

The doorbell rings, and then the front door opens.

"Why would you ring the doorbell if you are going to walk in anyway?" I hear my mother ask my father.

"It's gotcha day," he says. "We have to be here when he wakes up."

"I think you ringing the doorbell will wake them up," my mother argues with him, and we all laugh on the bed.

"Up here," I say, looking at Maya just taking in all the noise around her. We can hear my father running up the stairs, and when he gets to the bedroom door, we all laugh.

"Happy gotcha day," he says, and his shirt has the words:

Gotcha Day. I'm the Grandfather.

"Oh my God," Maddox says, getting up. "What are you wearing?"

"Don't feel left out," my mother says, holding up two bags in her hands. "We got shirts for everyone."

"Great," Maddox says, walking to her. She holds her arms open, and he hugs her. He came out of his shell a year in.

"Your shirt is the best," my father says, taking it out, and we see that it's red. "And it's a different color."

"This is the same color as the balloon in *IT*," Maddox says, making us all laugh as he opens up the shirt. He puts it on, and I read the front.

Gotcha Day.
They got me.

"Turn around," my mother says to him, and then I read the back.

Forever.

"And ever," Dylan says, leaning into me and kissing me.

"And ever." I smile. We started out as two small kids not knowing each other and then slowly grew into friends and then turned into each other's rock. Not knowing that what we felt for each other was a one-of-a-kind love you can't explain. I couldn't explain it even if I tried. The only thing I can say is you get only one forever, and I only want to do it with him.

Made in the USA
Monee, IL
30 April 2022